THE UNCOMMON RIDER

THE UNCOMMON RIDER

EXCEPTIONAL S. BEAUFONT™ BOOK 1

SARAH NOFFKE

MICHAEL ANDERLE

First US Edition, November 2019
Version 1.06, April 2021
eBook ISBN: 978-1-64202-569-9
Print ISBN: 978-1-64202-620-7

THE UNCOMMON RIDER TEAM

Thanks to the Beta Team
Mary Morris, Nicole Emens, John Ashmore, Kelly O'Donnell,
Larry Omans

Thanks to the JIT Readers

Angel LaVey
Dave Hicks
Deb Mader
Dorothy Lloyd
Jackey Hankard-Brodie
Jeff Eaton
Jeff Goode
Larry Omans
Mary Morris
Micky Cocker
Misty Roa
Nicole Emens
Paul Westman
Peter Manis

If I've missed anyone, please let me know!

Editor
The Skyhunter Editing Team

Once again and a thousand times more, for Lydia.

— Sarah

To Family, Friends and
Those Who Love
to Read.
May We All Enjoy Grace
to Live the Life We Are
Called.
— Michael

Nothing in the last eight-hundred years had prepared Adam Rivalry for this. Atop and astride his dragon, Kay-Rye, he'd defeated leagues of armies, taken down lines of trebuchets and sent murderous monsters into extinction, yet, he'd never faced a beast like the one trailing them presently.

Icy winds raced through his long hair and beard, sending them flying over his shoulder as Kay-Rye swerved to avoid the strange projectiles the thunderous monster fired at them. It was a magic that Adam had never seen before. The beast didn't move with the wind like the dragons, but rather cut through it, making a noise like a thousand vibrating drums. The monster also left behind a chemical smell that burned Adam's nose.

Daring to look over his shoulder as they passed through a dense cloud, Adam tried to make out the form of the enemy. As far as he could tell, it was covered in strange armor. Not a dragon, and not a bird. Its wings didn't fold and expand like Kay-Rye's. Instead, they stayed stick-straight.

Its attacks didn't come from its mouth or from its rider, who was locked inside a clear compartment on the top. They shot from under the wings, large metal capsules that had many times whistled by Adam's head or scraped Kay-Rye's wings, injuring him little by little. There was also a weapon on the top of the creature that fired rapid projectiles that were harder to avoid since they were smaller.

The dragon was okay, though. They'd make it to the Barrier of the Gullington soon. Then no matter how close the beast was to them, they'd disappear into the mists, safe once more.

Adam and his dragon would return once they'd rested. He knew the monster was guarding something that it had harmed. The dragonrider might not know much about his new enemy, but he knew it deserved no mercy.

It was Adam's job to protect. He and Kay-Rye had taken an oath to uphold justice. Even if they hadn't been able to do that properly for several hundred years, there was little stopping them from returning to that mission now.

The sun had just set on the other side of the Pond. The night belonged to the black dragon, giving it speed and increased agility. Adam lowered himself, his chin barely grazing the neck of the dragon he'd known for most of his life.

We'll be through the Barrier soon, Adam thought, feeling the dragon slow. Only in battle did they choose the more draining method of telepathy to communicate with one another.

We won't make it in time, Kay-Rye insisted. He nearly halted in mid-air, and the lights from the modest village below began to blur when they started to free-fall as the dragon folded his wings into his body.

Wind whistled past Adam's ears as they plummeted. Pushing against the force of the fall, he peered up to find that the monster had put on a sudden burst of speed. It shot forward, quickly covering the distance to where they had been. The beast turned into a nosedive as soon as it caught the change in their direction.

How did you know that was going to happen? Adam asked.

Instinct, Kay-Rye simply answered, unfolding his wings and regaining height.

More of the cottages on the eastern hills were turning on their lights for the night. Adam watched them with affection, remembering when that area was unsettled. He'd spent most of his life in this area of Scotland, and he wasn't going to allow this monster to ruin it. As a dragonrider, he wouldn't stand for bullies, especially not in what had become his homeland over these centuries.

Kay-Rye's wings flapped furiously in perfect rhythm with the wind. They were again headed back to the Barrier. As fast as Kay-Rye was at night, he couldn't outpace the beast. It made up the space between them in seconds, sending multiple attacks.

Adam tried his best to shield, but the assaults were unrelenting, exploding through his spells and continuing undeterred.

He sent two attacks off-course as Kay-Rye sped through the clouds, spiraling to the side, his massive wings soaring through the darkness, perfectly camouflaged by the night. Although, wherever they flew, no matter how well the dark masked the black dragon, the monster's attacks seemed to find him, almost like it was using a homing spell of sorts.

We must make it to the Barrier, Adam insisted, feeling Kay-Rye's exhaustion like it was his own. This chase had gone on for what seemed like hours, the strange creature behind them never slowing. It wasn't natural. It almost didn't seem to be alive, but rather a machine. Adam had never heard of a contraption the size of a dragon that attacked like this. However, there were many things he didn't know about the modern world, he realized. If granted more time, he'd learn. He'd adapt. He'd figure out how to outmaneuver and overpower the thing gaining on Kay-Rye's tail, flying several yards behind the dragon.

Even with the increased power of the night, Kay-Rye was no match for the many projectiles that whizzed by, one of them tearing straight through his wing, which bent back at a weird angle. Adam held on for dear life as his dragon toppled to the side, his wing dragging uncontrollably in the wind like a flag, knocking into him.

The dragon's screams unleashed a pain inside Adam so deep that he felt his heart might pound out of his chest. They had to land. Kay-Rye was too injured to continue much farther, but the monster would pursue. It was out to kill, and the Barrier was too far to reach.

Adam had only one option left.

Don't, Kay-Rye urged, a soft pain in the single word as he tried to make his broken wing work.

I have to, Adam stated, adrenaline shooting through him as he stood up on the back of his dragon, twisting around to face the strangest enemy he'd ever seen. He pooled his and Kay-Rye's collective energy, not unleashing it until it nearly made his chest explode.

With a guttural scream, Adam shot the attack at the monster barreling through the night sky. The use of that much magic depleted them both severely, leaving them with few options should they need more power. However, Adam's attack hit the front of the beast with a punishing blow, knocking it to the side and tearing off one of its wings.

Adam was about to rejoice, feeling the first bit of hope in hours. Smoke flew up from the center of the creature as it spiraled to the dense mountain range below, crashing in a fiery burst. Thankfully, they were past the village and over the unchartered territory that surrounded the Gullington.

Yes! Adam whipped around, ready to guide his injured dragon home when he froze, his eyes wide as his mouth sucked in what would most assuredly be one of his last breaths. Racing toward them, faster than they could avoid, uninjured or otherwise, was another of those strange weapons the monster shot. This one must have been sent prior to Adam's attack. It sped forward, then turned around and came back in their direction.

Kay-Rye worked to hold his injured wing straight as he glided for the hills below. They might be able to make it. Out-maneuver the attack. Get to the safety of the grass and the caves.

Both held onto this hope, feeling the doom in the other's hearts as they made their final descent. The projectile zoomed at their back, closing in like a hungry dog on a hunt.

Adam gripped the reins tighter. Held closer to the creature that was more a part of him than his own skin and bones. He didn't close his eyes when the blast met its target, hitting Kay-Rye in the backside and exploding fire over Adam as well.

The dragonrider didn't let go of hope even as Kay-Rye stopped flying, spiraling into a free-fall, his wings like broken kites, tangling in the wind.

Adam didn't let go even as they tumbled onto the stony earth, the dragon rolling onto his already broken body, smashing it even more. He did close his eyes when he felt Kay-Rye's breaths slow to almost non-existent quickly after impact.

Whatever the monster was they'd angered that night, it was a force they weren't prepared to defeat or survive. The oldest living dragonrider hoped with everything that he had left that his brothers would be in a better position to fight this enemy if they should ever come in contact with another like it. And he hoped they did, because it was evil, and what it guarded needed their help. He knew that much, without knowing why.

Kay-Rye pulled his head around, awkwardly gazing back at Adam, who was lying half under him. There was no point in moving the dragon. They both knew it was over.

"It's been a good run, my friend," Adam said, coughing up blood. He felt something sharp cutting into his chest.

"It has," Kay-Rye replied, his breaths too far apart, eyes drifting closed.

"Thanks for the ride."

"The pleasure has always been mine, Adam."

And with that, the dragon and his rider took their last breaths together, closing out the end of an era.

CHAPTER TWO

On the edge of a giant's yard in a city that was never quiet, the first dragon's egg in over a century began to hatch.

Sophia Beaufont sucked in a breath as a large crack started at the top of the blue egg and split down the side.

The full moon was the only light in that area of the yard, showing the progress the dragon made as he worked his way out of the shell, making a strange noise that wasn't music and wasn't crying. It was the sound of birth. Of awakening. The echo of the soul of the dragons who lived deep in the consciousness of the creature getting his first glimpse of the moon's ray in this lifetime.

Only a few months ago, Sophia had found herself in a strange magical shop among mortal dwellings. That was when she'd magnetized to the egg before her, sealing her fate.

A dragon hadn't magnetized to a rider in a hundred years. Dragons were actually thought to be extinct, but the truth was, there had simply been little reason for them—until now.

The time of the dragonriders was starting anew. Only a few knew it was being reborn with the gentle cracking of the shimmering blue egg sitting on the soft patch of ground before this young girl now.

Sophia and the egg had both grown at alarming rates since magnetizing to one another. She had always been well ahead of her age mentally, but now her body had caught up with her.

Losing her childhood hadn't mattered. Having her fate chosen on a random trip to a shop hadn't bothered her. It had all made sense from the beginning because Sophia Beaufont always knew she wasn't a normal magician.

Most didn't come into their magic until they were older, at least in their teens. Honing those skills took time. None of that had applied to Sophia. She might have been born to parents who she couldn't remember, who had been taken from the Earth when she was only three years old. She might have spent much of her childhood alone. But she was no victim. From the beginning, Sophia knew her life wouldn't take a predictable course. And at this point, there was absolutely no certainty in her future. But she knew something with true conviction—one day, she wanted to be like her big sister.

Without knowing why, Sophia was positive the dragon quickly breaking out of the egg had chosen that particular night to hatch for a specific reason. Over the last few months, Sophia had spoken telepathically to him. Hearing him in her head felt second nature. Right then, though, all her attention was on the cracking that seemed to echo so loudly she thought everyone nearby could hear it.

However, no one approached as the dragon poked his head through the top of the shell, knocking a large piece out of the way. He swept his neck to the side, breaking out of the bonds that had held him for so many years. Had it been a decade? A century? A millennium? Sophia didn't know. The dragon had simply said he had been waiting for her to be born. To be ready.

She reached out, wanting to help with the arduous process, but pulled back her hand, sensing that wasn't her job. The dragon she knew so well and was meeting for the very first time threw his head covered in small horns down and to the side, smashing the rest of the shell to bits. His tail whipped behind him, knocking the back of the egg to dust. He shook like a dog, shuddering off the rest of the shell. It was then that the moonlight shone on him, properly showing the entirety of the dragon.

She'd never seen a blue like what covered him. His scales were sapphire dipped in crystals, radiating the light.

This girl hadn't known what it felt like to be in love until that moment. She knew, at her core, that she loved the creature before her with her whole heart. He was good and brave, and undeniably connected to her in every way for the rest of their lives.

This dragon would be her life force, and she his. Neither could prosper without the other. His aches would be hers. Hers, he'd feel intimately. A rider and its dragon signed on for more than a long life of sacrifices and challenges. They signed on to experience everything in tandem.

The dragon stood as steady as if it weren't his first time. He took a step with no hesitation as he lowered his green eyes, blinking at the young girl before him. He only came up to Sophia's shoulder, but he was growing by the moment.

She took a step forward, not feeling steady but hiding it.

"And so we meet like it's the first time," the dragon said.

"Isn't it?" Sophia asked, running her eyes over him as he tested his wings with a sticky sound, unfolding them and then pressing them back beside his body.

He shook his head. "Oh, no, we've met many times, Sophia Beaufont. Or so I believe."

She nodded and turned her gaze to the moon. "Why tonight?"

A pleasant expression came over the dragon's face as he followed her gaze. "Each dragon is connected to an aspect of the Earth, whether it be night, day, the ocean, the winds—"

"The moon," Sophia said, realization dawning on her.

"Yes," he affirmed. "For however long we have here, I'll be strongest on the full moon. And so will you."

Sophia took a step forward, then knelt and looked up at the dragon before her. He was more beautiful than she could have ever imagined, full of timeless wisdom. It was impossible to think that the consciousness of the dragons lived in him. And yet, as she stared into his eyes, she could hardly doubt it.

"It's time to name me, Sophia Beaufont. But do it with diligence."

She lifted her hand, not hesitating before running her fingers over the top of his snout. Her hand sank to his scales at their first meeting, the union as natural as a baby's first breath.

Sophia smiled, unafraid as she stared into the eyes of the most ancient type of magical creature in the world, and the one who would live beside her from now until the end of her own life.

"I named you long ago," she began, her pupils contracting from the bright moonlight. "Even before I met you. Before I became a dragonrider, I knew you, and I knew you'd be Lunis."

The blue dragon bowed his head, silent respect in the movement. "Yes, my name has always been Lunis, but only my true rider would know that. Well done, Sophia."

CHAPTER THREE

The fountain pen scratched on the parchment, making one of Hiker Wallace's favorite sounds in the world. He liked simple things: the smell of coffee, the sounds of the morning, and a long ride over the Expanse.

He glanced up, his eyes finding the crackling flames in the fireplace, which slightly mesmerized him as he thought about what else to include in that day's log.

Flipping to the page before, he read yesterday's entry and frowned. It was pretty much identical to the one from this day. He turned back to the week prior, then the month before, and finally last year. Almost all the submissions were the same. The Dragon Elite always did the same thing at the Gullington: ate, trained, studied, cared for the dragons, and got plenty of rest. Still, Hiker always kept the log. Records were important, even if they didn't differ from day to day.

He closed the logbook and sat back in his chair, his gaze drifting out the window to where the Pond stretched for as far as he could see, even with his enhanced vision. Lately, the monotony of each day had made him restless, waking him up with dreams of the life he lived before mortals were blinded to magic. It wasn't so bad, though. Usually, he could put himself back to sleep. He wasn't like Adam, who was consumed with picking back up the dragonriders' mission.

The world wasn't ready yet, though, Hiker thought, pushing up from his desk and striding back and forth in front of the fireplace.

The older dragonrider hungered for the fight again, the chase. He wanted to take back the mantle of the Elite and resume their role as adjudicators for the mortal world.

They weren't ready, Hiker told himself, although it was getting harder to convince himself of that since the mortal world could see magic again.

Long ago, Hiker, Adam, and many more dragonriders had ruled the world, intervening in the affairs of mortals and keeping the peace. And then one day, the dragons were all like ghosts, unseen by mortals.

That simply made the riders of the Dragon Elite appear to be loons, professing that they had dragons. Overnight, mortals had forgotten about magic, and worse, they couldn't see it. What was the point of serving as the judge, jury, and executioner to a world that didn't believe they existed?

And so, the Dragon Elite had disappeared, many of them confining themselves inside the Gullington, the Elite's headquarters. Since the world couldn't see them, they were soon lost.

Not all stayed in the confines of the Gullington. They were too restless to be confined. Some disappeared. Some mysteriously died. And the others, Hiker and Adam, learned how to simply exist.

Centuries passed.

The world outside the Gullington changed, but the Dragon Elite knew nothing of it. They stayed inside the Barrier for the most part, wondering if they'd die without a purpose.

And then, very recently, everything had changed. Hiker wouldn't have even known about it if not for their housekeeper Ainsley. She'd been at the market, buying the food for the week. She ran all the way back, not shifting into her normal appearance when she stormed into Hiker's office. He pulled his sword, wondering what the strange old man was doing there. Ainsley shifted back to her normal appearance, her auburn hair framing her pointy chin.

"Sir, I have news," she stated, curtsying to him in her normal manner.

"Go on, then," Hiker had demanded, sheathing the sword he hadn't used in quite some time.

"Mortals can see magic again," she'd said in a hushed voice.

Those five words should have changed everything for the Elite, but they hadn't.

Presently, Hiker strode back over to the logbook and flipped it open again, reading the entry from that day, when Ainsley brought the news from the village. There had been a celebration among the riders then. They had consumed more mead in a day than they usually did in a year. There had been much talk about the future. About mortals.

He flipped to the next day. It read the same as the day before. And then the day after that...until things went back to how they had been. The Dragon Elite woke, ate, trained, studied, cared for the dragons, and got plenty of rest.

Even after the news that mortals were finally awake again, nothing had changed for the riders, and their leader was responsible for that. It hadn't been an easy call for Hiker to make, but he still stood by it.

Mortals weren't ready.

"Give them a few hundred years to adjust to magic before we startle them with dragons," he'd told Adam.

His oldest friend and fellow rider hadn't been happy about that.

The two had disputed it time and time again, but Adam knew Hiker was right; mortals needed time to adjust. According to Ainsley, just the sight of a fairy flying around the market had sent many mortals running to lock themselves in their cottages. How would they react when a dragon flew down from the sky and a rider slid off it, stating they were there to oversee all disputes among mortals?

They would panic.

And then it would be another few hundred years of solitude for the Elite. Hiker could handle that. He had.

Adam, though. It would kill him, as it had many a rider before.

No, it was better for everyone if the Dragon Elite stayed put, safe inside the Barrier. Then when mortals were ready, the riders would reign once more.

He went to check the log again, thinking there was something he could add. Quiet, the gnome, had caught an extra fish that day. That was worth noting.

Picking up his fountain pen, Hiker had just begun to add to the log when the globe that sat next to the bank of windows displaying the Pond beeped.

He jerked up. Dropped his pen. Eyes widened.

It had been a century since he'd heard that noise.

The pen rolled across the desk and dropped on the oak floor, landing with a clacking sound. Hiker jumped and looked down at the still-rolling pen. He pulled his eyes back to the globe. Five red dots were lit on the huge globe that was inlaid with gold from the giants. Stone mined from the gnomes' caves made up the bulk of the sphere, and the wood was the finest Polynesian teak, given to the Dragon Elite by the elves. The magic that tracked every dragonrider on Earth had been gifted to them by the magicians, specifically, the warriors of the House of Fourteen.

The globe was more than an incredible piece of art made by the major magical races. It was the way Hiker tracked the riders, which hadn't been a problem in…a long, long time. Hiker had little reason to keep track of the riders since they'd stayed inside the Gullington for the most part. But...

He strode over, hoping it was a glitch.

The magicians messed up long ago, and the problem was only now becoming apparent, he told himself.

Or maybe the metals, wood, and stones had made the magic malfunction, and the gnomes, giants, and elves were to blame.

He swiveled the globe around until he found the blinking red dot.

It had been a long time since Hiker had sucked in a gasp like the one that assaulted his chest now.

It wasn't a malfunction.

It *was* one of his.

It was Adam.

He was in trouble.

The lights on the globe tracked the dragonriders, and they blinked when they were in mortal danger. And it appeared that his oldest friend was—

The door to Hiker's office burst open. Evan stood at the threshold, his chest rising and falling with panic.

"Hiker, you need to know—"

"Adam is in danger," he answered, cutting off the youngest dragonrider.

Evan's dark skin wouldn't register his flush, but the shock on his face was apparent when Hiker responded. "How did..." His gaze flew to the globe. "Oh, of course."

"He'll be fine," Hiker stated, wishing he could turn off the constant beeping that signaled a change in a rider. It told when they were in trouble or new riders needed to be picked up. It had been a long time since he'd heard that, although there had been false alarms from Los Angeles in California, United States lately.

"What has he gotten himself into?" Evan asked, pushing his long dreads out of his face as he leaned over to peer at the blinking red dot.

"I'm sure it's just because he's left the Gullington," Hiker stated, taking a breath to loosen the stress in his chest.

"I went to the Cave to check on Coral, and I noticed that Kay-Rye was gone," Evan informed.

"You did the right thing by coming here," Hiker said, placing his hands behind his back as he turned toward the bank of windows that faced the Pond. The sun was setting now, night falling, making for a beautiful display as the full moon rose over the Gullington. Hiker caught his reflection in the window.

He hadn't changed much in five hundred years, still sporting the same long beard and kilt, and the armor that he'd inherited from his father. Even though he didn't need its protection, he still wore it every day. There were some things one never stopped doing. Habit was the strength of a successful man. He was certain it would bring him back when the time came.

"He's gone looking for cases," Evan stated, glancing out the window.

Hiker nodded. "Yes, I expected this. Adam has been growing restless. I don't think this was his first time outside the Barrier lately."

Evan swung his head around, shock covering his face. "Really?"

Hiker shrugged. "He thought he had spelled the Elite Globe to hide his activity, but I've seen him leave a few times."

"But is he okay?" Evan asked, glancing over his shoulder at the globe.

"Yeah, he probably got himself into some trouble we're not used to," Hiker stated.

"Like gawkers on the ground?" Evan asked.

"That or one of the other new technologies Ainsley has told us about."

Evan tapped the larger man's arm. "You don't think she's right, do you? The modern world doesn't really have witchcraft that allows them to spy on us from space or whatever else?"

"I think she calls it technology," Hiker answered. "And no.

Don't worry about it. I'm certain the world hasn't changed that much in the hundred years since you joined us."

Evan let out a breath of relief. "That's good to know. Then I'm sure you're right. Adam is probably—"

The flat-lined beep cut the dragonrider off.

Hiker swung around. Rushed toward the Elite Globe. Pressed his face to the dot that glowed brighter than all the rest.

"No!" Hiker yelled, knowing what that sound meant even though he hadn't heard it in quite some time.

"I-I-It can't mean…" Evan asked, stuttering.

Hiker would have rushed off. Rescued his friend. Crossed the Barrier, but by the time the beeping started, it was over.

He stepped back, shaking his head in disbelief. "He's gone."

"No!" Evan argued. "We can get to him. Kay-Rye. We can save them."

Hiker had lived long enough to know the truth. "We can't."

The leader of the Dragon Elite had lived long enough to know that doubting the Globe only led to insanity. Every leader had tried to change what it said, but once they realized it only spoke the truth did they have any peace.

"So he's gone? How?" Evan asked.

Hiker strode for the door to his office. "That's what we're going to find out."

He'd pulled open the door and was almost through it when a different beep echoed from the globe, pulling his attention back. Hiker would have believed his friend was back and the globe was wrong, but he knew the slightly higher beeping that the globe was emitting. It didn't mean an old dragonrider was back. It meant a new dragon had been born.

Evan backed up, looking at the Elite globe and Hiker. "What is it?"

The leader of the riders couldn't believe it. It had been over a hundred years since he'd heard that sound. He had told himself it might not happen again in his lifetime, but here it was. Not since

Evan had he heard that sound from the Elite globe. It was the echo of birth, of awakening, of something remarkable.

Hiker shook his head, dispelling the strangeness building in his head. "On the very same night one rider has fallen, another has risen."

CHAPTER FOUR

In his lifetime, Hiker had lost many, but no one like the person he was approaching. He and Adam had spent several hundred years together passing time. Waiting to be needed again. Arguing about what needed to be done in the meantime.

There was no one who got under Hiker's skin like the man he was rushing toward. And no one he loved more who still breathed on this Earth, besides his dragon Bell, of course.

At the Barrier, Hiker paused, realizing it had been a long time since he'd left the Gullington. He'd portaled out recently, but only briefly, and that was different from crossing the border.

From his place on the slick grass, he could see Adam and Kay-Rye sprawled out roughly a hundred yards away. They had made it so close to safety, and yet, close was the difference between life and death.

The guys halted at Hiker's back, probably sensing his trepidation. Evan hadn't crossed the Barrier in quite some time. For the others, it had been more than the normal span of a lifetime. There was simply no reason to leave anymore.

He wished he'd taken the time to get his dragon Bell. She couldn't do anything, but it would have made the next part easier.

"Brothers," Hiker began, his gaze falling on Evan, then Mahkah's and Wilder's faces. Like Hiker, they were much older than most magicians, having the longevity of their dragons, but it didn't show. Mahkah and Wilder appeared to be in their early twenties, even though they'd both spent over two centuries on this Earth. Evan was still a baby by dragonrider standards at just over a hundred years old, but he at least appeared mature enough to drink a beer in a pub—not that he'd ever been given the chance to do so.

"We don't know what's out there," Hiker continued. "Whatever took Adam down could still be on the prowl. Stay vigilant, and at the first sign of danger, call your dragon. Otherwise, simply show your respect."

"Is he dead?" Mahkah asked, stepping forward, his long black hair falling out of his ponytail and into his face.

One of the hardest things Hiker had had to do in a long time was nod in response to that question. If the Elite globe had indicated it, then Adam wasn't even holding on by a breath. It was too late for goodbyes. It was too late for anything but the burial of the greatest rider and dragon Hiker had known in many centuries.

Adam should have been the leader of the Elite. He and Hiker both knew it. He was older. More experienced. Magnetized to the larger, more dangerous dragon Kay-Rye. But the thing about Adam was that he'd never wanted the role. He preferred to fight rather than lead. He craved the hunt over determining the strategy. Adam liked detective work without all the responsibility that went with looking after the others. He loved the resolutions that only a dragonrider could bring to any dispute...or he used to.

Hiker was the one who wanted to lead. He had always felt more protective of the others, so he became the one who led them—even when there was nothing to lead them toward except for another day of monotony.

Taking in an unfulfilling breath, Hiker drew his sword and swung around, stalking out past the Barrier. The air on the other side of the invisible wall was different. Colder. Laced with strange smells, reeking of the modern world.

Hiker held his breath as he strode toward the bodies on the other side of the field. The dragon and rider had crashed, the heavy beast landing on top of Adam and crushing him. However, the expression on his dead friend's face wasn't one of anguish. Hiker could tell that Adam had died staring into the eyes of his best friend by the angle of their heads. He also knew something dangerous had attacked them, based on the scorch marks on their flesh.

He breathed through his mouth, not wanting to remember this moment punctuated by the smell of burned skin, hair, and leather.

The guys spread out behind him, their weapons held at the ready as they sidestepped around the dragon and rider.

Damn it, Adam, why couldn't you leave things alone? Hiker wondered, studying the many wounds marking their bodies.

"I don't think there's anything out here," Wilder said, his eyes scanning. "Whatever it was is gone."

Hiker nodded. "They were on their way home when something attacked them, I'm guessing."

"But what?" Mahkah asked.

The leader of the Dragon Elite looked at the darkening mountains. "It's hard to tell. The world out there isn't the same one any of us knew. That's one reason we aren't to return to it yet. We need time. The *world* needs time to adjust."

The men all nodded, having heard this argument from Hiker many times, especially in the evening when Adam challenged him over drinks.

"It could have been an accident," Evan reasoned.

"Maybe," Hiker said, narrowing his eyes at a bright spot in the sky between two ridges far in the distance.

"Simi and I can do a patrol," Wilder offered.

"No," Hiker said at once, swinging around to face his men. "Adam had been looking for trouble lately. It appears that he found it. I won't have any of you risking your lives tonight. This only proves what I've believed since mortals awoke and started seeing magic again. If we are to take back our roles, first we have to understand how the world has changed. We can't simply rush out there, or we will get ourselves killed. Mortals and the magical races who have long believed we were dead or knew nothing about us in the first place will be frightened when we make an appearance. I don't know what attacked Adam and Kay-Rye, but I assure you it was something that felt threatened by them."

"And something of great power," Mahkah observed, his eyes running over the large black dragon, who was at least thirty feet long.

"Rest assured, I will give this matter my full attention, determining exactly what we need to prepare ourselves for when we do finally venture out into the world," Hiker stated with confidence, trying to hold together his tough exterior as the full implications of his friend's death sank in.

"But not yet, right?" Evan asked.

Hiker shook his head. "No, we're not ready. The world isn't."

He waved the men toward the Gullington. "Go back now. Send Quiet to help me. Tomorrow morning, we will hold a memorial for our brother."

The men all nodded, reluctantly turning their backs and heading for the castle, which wasn't visible from that side of the Barrier.

When the riders had disappeared, Hiker returned his attention to Adam and Kay-Rye's bodies. He would only have a few minutes before Quiet, the groundskeeper, showed up to help. He didn't really need the gnome's help, but rather some time alone. Not to grieve, though. That would come later. Hiker needed answers. He needed information.

Waving his hand at the bodies, he muttered a spell he hadn't used in a very long time. Like riding a dragon, the magic came back to him. Both lived in his bones.

The area around Adam and his dragon sparkled with light that rose a few feet off the ground and began to trail in the direction opposite the Gullington. Hiker followed it with his eyes until it disappeared behind the mountain ridges.

He lifted his hand, letting out a low-pitch whistle that only his Bell would hear. Within a minute, the red dragon soared from the Cave, in his direction. Her majestic wings cut through the air, making fast progress as she approached. Just seeing her made Hiker feel better.

She had no issues passing through the Barrier, although it had been a long time for her as well.

Her face turned to the side as she landed and peered at the bodies lying at Hiker's feet. She didn't show any emotion in her green eyes, just blinked, following the track of sparkly dust that trailed in the opposite direction.

"Whatever attacked them is over there, isn't it?" Hiker's dragon asked.

He nodded, pulling himself onto her back without difficulty even though she wasn't tacked up for a ride with a saddle and reins. "Yes, and you know what we have to do with what we find, right?"

The dragon's gaze returned to the bodies lying in the grass, which was quickly growing stiff with frost. "Of course. And tomorrow?"

"Tomorrow we will grieve, Bell," Hiker stated, holding onto the dragon. "Tonight, we will find out what killed our dear friends."

CHAPTER FIVE

The sun would rise over the Gullington in just under an hour. Hiker stared out the dark window that would soon be lit by morning sunshine. He never got tired of seeing the Pond shine with rays of morning light, but on this day, it felt like an insult to the grief in his heart, which craved the dark for a little longer.

The men would be up and ready for the memorial soon. Hiker had one very important thing to do before they were awake.

He looked down at the piece of parchment under his fountain pen, thinking of the person he was sending the note to. Liv Beaufont was a Warrior for the House of Fourteen, but that didn't even begin to explain who she was, based on the information he'd gathered recently.

She had led the House of Fourteen from where it had been—stuck in the dark ages—to where it was now, full of magical races who acted together for the betterment of society. This Warrior was the reason mortals could see magic again. She was therefore the reason that the dragonriders would soon have a role in this world after centuries alone and unseen.

And she had, as he expected, been hiding something…or rather, someone.

Hiker wondered if the new rider who had magnetized to a dragon was his age when it happened to him, forty years old. Or maybe he was older? Or like Evan, he was in his early twenties?

This immediately made him wonder about the new dragon. He knew there were rogues spread across the globe, although past expeditions to find them had been failures. Dragons wouldn't be found if they didn't want to be.

If it were any of the dragons that he'd heard about, then they were quite old. Not as old as Bell or Kay-Rye, but still, they'd be a good addition to the Elite.

He set the fountain pen to the parchment, beginning his note.

Dear Warrior Beaufont,

As I suspected when I paid you a visit recently, you have been harboring a dragonrider. I now have confirmation of this and believe he is in close proximity to you.

Hiker glanced up, thinking. The Elite Globe had given him that information. Before, when he'd confronted the warrior, it had been simply a guess, but now that the rider had magnetized formally to his dragon, it was concrete. He could pinpoint his location exactly, and it showed this person was in close proximity to the warrior for the House of Fourteen.

It made sense. The House was full of experienced Warriors. This filled Hiker with excitement. The guys, Evan, Mahkah, and Wilder, had been so young when they magnetized to their dragons. Hiker'd had to teach them so much, on top of training them on how to ride. It would be nice to have an experienced magician in their midst. Still, he didn't like the timing—right after Adam's death—but that was how things happened sometimes.

He returned to writing the note.

Below I've included coordinates outside our borders for the newest dragonrider to use to find our location. Only a rider will be able to pass through our barriers, so I encourage you not to share the approximate location of our headquarters with anyone. It will cause them nothing but suffering since we are prepared to fight anyone who ventures close to our lands.

Hiker shook his head. He was tempted to say more, but he realized he'd be lying. The Elite's numbers were not what they had been, and now, without Adam, they were at a serious disadvantage.

He hung his head, realizing how sad his predicament had become. Once, the Dragon Elite had been the strongest force on the globe. Presently, he had three riders who had never properly been in battle, and soon, he'd have a brand new one. A man he'd have to train from the ground up.

Hiker sucked in a breath, undeterred as he returned his focus to the page. He'd build the Dragon Elite back to what they once were. Better. He'd make them better. And once mortals were ready, they'd rule over their affairs, as was once their role.

Warrior Beaufont, respond right away to this message with confirmation. I want word about this new rider, and that he is on his way to me. I will respond in kind by letting you know once he's under my authority.

Sincerely,
Hiker Wallace
Leader of the Dragon Elite

CHAPTER SIX

It had been a hard day for Liv Beaufont. She hadn't slept in…
well, the last time hadn't been that day. And maybe the one
before that. She'd lost track as she trudged to her apartment, intent
on curling up in her bed and snoozing for days.

She sighed. Who was she kidding?

She'd get maybe four to five hours before some emergency
awoke her. That was fine. The House of Fourteen was robust, full
of members voting on issues that pertained to the magical world
and made it a better place. Surprisingly, she loved her demanding
job.

Mortals had recently been awoken to the presence of magic,
and seven had joined the council, presiding over important
matters.

Still, Liv wondered, when given the chance for such luxuries,
who took care of the mortal world? The House of Fourteen had
the job of enforcing laws for the magical races, ensuring that no
one abused their powers. Before magic was visible to mortals,
she'd always suspected that the police and firefighters and whatnot

took care of their affairs. But now...well, things were a bit more complex.

She shook her head, both in exhaustion and confusion.

"Things are a lot more complex," she said as she rounded the corner to her apartment.

"You're talking to yourself...yet again," Plato, the small black and white cat beside her, said. Well, he wasn't really a cat. In the magical world, the mysterious and mischievous creature was known as a lynx, and not much was known about them.

"I'm not either," she said, shaking her head again. "I'm simply answering myself."

"That makes it worse," he stated.

"Well, that's what happens when I'm not allowed to sleep." Liv shrugged and pushed the black hood of her cape off her head, looking forward to taking off the garment and getting into some pajamas.

"So, you should know...before you go up..." Plato's voice trailed away, and he stopped at the base of the stairs.

Liv turned, already rolling her eyes at the lynx. "What?"

"Well, you have mail."

She tilted her head to the side. "How do you know that?" Waving off the question, she shook her head, used to his mysterious ways of knowing things. "Never mind. And if I do, it's just spam from some mortal business."

"It isn't, actually," he said coyly.

Liv lowered her chin. "So you're telling me that someone who isn't mortal has put mail in my postbox, even though none of the magical creatures I know use such a method? Why?"

He pretended to watch the traffic on the street behind her. "Beats me."

"Beats you, eh?" she asked. "Are you sure you're not just playing games with me so you can get upstairs first and take the best spot in the bed?"

He gave her an incredulous expression. "Would I really do that?"

She stuck her hands on her hips. "Every chance you get."

"Seriously, you've got mail."

Liv strode toward the post box she hardly ever checked. "Why wouldn't this magical person just send me a message on my phone, or, I don't know, some other way that is way more efficient?"

"You'll find out soon," he said, a hint of teasing in his voice.

"Seriously, Plato, if you know something, you can just tell me."

"I can, but it's better this way."

She shook her head. "For you, maybe."

Liv opened the post box, a bit nervous about what could be residing inside the small compartment. Tentatively, she retrieved a thick envelope sealed with wax and embossed with a seal of a capital E. On the front, in old English cursive, was her name: Warrior Liv Beaufont.

"Who writes letters anymore?" she asked, studying the envelope.

"People," Plato answered, knowing full well he was being less than helpful.

Shaking her head at the lynx, Liv opened the correspondence, unprepared for its contents.

It would change everything. Although she'd known it was coming, she wasn't ready for it.

CHAPTER SEVEN

"How did he send this, by carrier pigeon?" Liv asked, flipping the envelope over to look for a stamp.

"I think you're focusing on the wrong thing," Plato said astutely.

She lifted an eyebrow. "You're right. I think he actually wrote the letter by hand. Do you know how to do that? I'm not sure I can even hold a pen."

Plato rolled his eyes. "Is that your takeaway after receiving and reading correspondence from the leader of the Dragon Elite?"

"Well, he already popped into my kitchen, scaring me half to death while I was in my pajamas making nachos," Liv stated, remembering when she'd first met Hiker Wallace. He'd had a clue that she had a dragonrider, or future rider, around her. Without her permission and apparently breaking through all her wards, he showed up in her kitchen. It wasn't the best first meeting, but she thought it had mostly gone well.

"What did you tell him then?" the lynx asked as if he didn't already know the answer.

"Well," Liv began, drawing out the word, "I would have told him about the dragon egg and Sophia then, but for one, he hadn't hatched yet. Secondly, Hiker kept referring to this new rider as 'him,' so I was thinking maybe he was asking about a different new dragonrider who wasn't my little sister."

"Liv," Plato said, censure in his tone.

She threw up her hands. "What? He said, 'If you learn of the presence of a rider, I want to know about *him*.' And since I hadn't learned about this 'him,' I didn't think Mr. Hiker needed to know anything."

"Liv," Plato said again, a challenging quality to his voice.

Liv sighed. She knew Sophia was the first female dragonrider in history. Hiker wasn't prepared for this. It probably wasn't even an option in his head, but that shouldn't be the reason Liv stopped this amazing thing from happening for her sister. "Fine. Fine. Sophia's egg has hatched. I knew this was coming, but before, I was trying to delay it. She's already lost her childhood, and now she's going to have to go off to this strange place where I can't even accompany her. Sue me for trying to delay the inevitable for as long as possible."

"You do know that I was a lawyer in a past life," Plato remarked casually.

"Of course, you were," she said, not doubting this. The lynx also did day-trading and wrote novels while she slept, apparently.

"And I get that you don't want her to leave, but—"

"I can't hold onto her forever," Liv interrupted. "I get that. But now this Viking from another century demands that my little sister and Beauregard come to his headquarters permanently."

"I think she named her dragon Lunis," Plato corrected, hiding a smile.

Liv laughed, remembering when she'd met the dragon earlier that day. He was no doubt the most beautiful creature she'd ever seen. Lunis had had an opportunity to get to know Liv during his long stint living in his shell in her house, where he could hear all the jokes she made. Then, he didn't like being called random names. Out of the shell, he was even more opposed to the idea. Sophia had told her she should be glad that he didn't have fire yet.

"So, what are you going to do?" Plato asked, eyeing the letter in her hand.

"Well, I don't have a pen, so I guess I'm screwed," she stated with defeat. "There's no way I can return his message. I guess I'll just have to quit my job as a Warrior for the House of Fourteen, sell all my possessions, and move Sophia and Burt to a remote island, where I'll use the full extent of my magical powers to shield them from the Dragon Elite."

"Or…"

Liv gave the feline an annoyed expression. "Or, I guess I can write back Mr. Penmanship and tell my lovely baby sister that she has to go to a secret boarding school I know zero about and can't visit. Then I'll promptly take up drinking. How early is too early to start shots of whiskey in the morning?"

"Or…" Plato challenged again.

Although she was pretending, this hurt. Liv had lost so much. Her parents. Her older sister and brother. Her combat instructor. Many friends. And now, even though she wasn't losing Sophia, it felt like it. "Or…I'll do the right thing, but only because you're making me."

"That's what I'm here for," he said matter-of-factly.

Liv twirled her finger, magically making a new piece of parchment appear, filled with flowery writing. She read over it once before nodding. "Okay, that will do."

"Are you sure about that?" Plato challenged.

Liv cut her eyes at him. "Yes, it will do, cat. Shush your face."

"But you—"

"I believe I said, shush it!" Liv snapped her fingers and the letter disappeared, using the directions Hiker had given her.

"You realize you're complicating things," Plato said, lowering his chin.

Liv shrugged. "Am I? Or am I giving my little sister the chance she needs? First impressions are everything, after all."

CHAPTER EIGHT

Clark Beaufont kept fussing with his tie.

Liv swung around to face her older brother, who was a Councilor for the House of Fourteen. "Would you stop fidgeting?"

He froze. Gave her a slight expression of offense. "I just want to look my best."

She shook her head. "You're not the one going off to join a group who ride dragons and does... Wait, we have no idea what they do. Just like we don't know where Sophia is headed, or if there are masked murderers stalking the perimeter. Or if she'll be cold at night."

Because everyone Liv knew enjoyed rolling their eyes at her at least once during every conversation, that was exactly what Clark did as they waited for Sophia on the other side of the yard. Rory Laurens was the giant who had agreed to transform his yard so the dragon egg would be content during incubation. The modest yard, which used to have a small vegetable garden and fruit trees, was now filled with a lava pit, a dense tropical forest, and the many strange magical animals that had arrived due to the presence of the dragon egg. They'd leave when the dragon did, which would be very, very soon.

"First off," Clark said, rummaging in his messenger bag, which was slung across his shoulder. He retrieved a large book known as the *Forgotten History*. When Liv had awoken mortals from the spell that had made it so they couldn't see magic, the real history they'd forgotten had been unearthed. It had been her brother's job to read up on everything they didn't understand. He flipped through the large volume, stopping on a page. "According to this, the role of the dragonriders is to be adjudicators over mortal affairs. They are considered more powerful than countries. Their decisions are law, and when they take sides due to resistance, wars are inevitable."

Liv blew out a breath, blowing a rogue piece of hair out of her face. "Great, I feel so much better about Sophia skipping off to this place. And here I was worried she'd be in danger."

As if he didn't hear her, Clark licked his finger and turned the page. "The Dragon Elite live in a place known as the Gullington. Since no one except for dragonriders or those who serve them, can know the exact location or enter what they call 'the Barrier,' it is probably one of the safest places on Earth. So I don't think we have to worry about masked murderers."

Liv crossed her arms over her chest, fully aware that she was being unreasonable. "'Those who serve them,' eh? Think I can get a job as a barmaid or a chef for the Elite? Maybe I could be their IT gal."

Clark snapped the book shut. "There aren't many details about the riders in the archives or in Bermuda Lauren's book, *Mysterious Creatures*. However, what I have learned is that they are pretty old-school, although no one knows much about them since they've been in hiding since mortals couldn't see magic."

Liv sighed, nodding. She'd read the entire section in Bermuda's book about the Dragon Elite too. It was the primary source about all magical creatures, written by none other than the mother of the giant whose yard they were currently in, waiting for their little sister and her dragon.

"Besides, I've had your cooking, and I don't think you'd last long among a bunch of hungry riders," Clark stated, putting the book away.

"Not everyone can be Julia Childs like you, Clarky," Liv said, sticking her tongue out at her brother.

As if they weren't full-grown adults with two of the most prestigious magical positions in the world, he stuck out his tongue at her too.

Liv slapped him, then caught sight of Sophia and Lunis approaching from the other side of the yard. "Would you act right? They are coming."

He slapped her back. "That's it, we're sparring later."

"Because you want a black eye to go with that morose suit you're wearing?" Liv asked.

He glanced down at his starched appearance. "What's wrong with this suit?"

"Besides that I wore it to a funeral once?" Liv remarked.

"You did not," he countered. "And you're one to talk, Ms. Goth." He gestured at her.

She was wearing her usual black pants, top, and cape and had her sword Bellator strapped at her hip. But today, there was something new to her outfit.

Soon she'd be giving that away, though, and feel quite naked, but mostly because the person she was giving it to would be leaving for a long time. Liv had gotten used to having her sister around. At the end of a long day, there was nothing better than looking into her sister's sweet face. There was something about Sophia Beaufont that gave Liv hope that the world was going to be okay, even if evil ran rampant every single day despite her constant efforts to police magic.

"My outfit isn't goth," Liv argued as Sophia strode gracefully around the lava pit, the majestic dragon perfectly in time with her steps. "This uniform is meant to keep me inconspicuous. What's your excuse, Mr. Councilor of the House of Fourteen? Are you applying for a butler position with the Dragon Elite?"

Clark fluttered his eyelashes at her with annoyance. "I don't look like a... You know what? Today, I'm not arguing with you."

"Really? What if I tell you that the Beef Wellington you served for dinner last night was chewy?" Liv asked.

Clark's mouth popped open, offense heavy in his eyes. "You said it melted in your mouth!"

Liv cocked a half-smile. "It did. Melted like a car tire."

"You know, if you're going to be that way then—"

Liv never found out what threat her brother was going to volley at her because a second later, Sophia and Lunis crossed the space between them, arriving faster than she had ever seen them move. It was a strange, fluid speed as if they were walking and then transported forward all at once. Liv hadn't taken her eyes off them as they approached, and yet, they'd skipped over the space, arriving in record time across the yard.

"Are you two arguing?" Sophia asked with an authoritative tone to her voice, although there was a slight smile on her face.

Liv pointed at her brother. "He started it."

Clark shook his head, elbowing Liv in the side. "We all know that she always starts it. She said I look like I'm dressed for a funeral."

Sophia snickered. "Well, you both have on pretty somber outfits."

In contrast to her siblings, and as usual, Sophia Beaufont appeared as old as time, yet with a strangely modern flair. She'd always seemed to be able to assemble an outfit with the same careful consideration as a rocket scientist creating a space-worthy device.

Currently, she was wearing black leather pants that were braided at the hip. Her top was a practical piece of blue and silver armor that made her appear both fierce and edgy. The magnificent sparkling blue dragon beside her and she looked both ready to fight a battle or walk down a runway…if dragons actually did such things.

"In my absence, do you think you two can get along?" Sophia asked, her blue eyes sparkling.

Liv ran her eyes over her sister's blonde hair and perfect features. Each day, she looked more like their mother, Guinevere Beaufont. Sophia hadn't been old enough to remember them when their parents died. Regardless, she'd inherited their goodness. Their bravery. Their loyalty to that which was good and right in the world. That was why, although Liv didn't want her little sister to leave, she knew she'd inevitably be okay.

She *was* a Beaufont, after all.

"We'll be fine," Clark stated. "Don't worry about us, Soph."

"If you promise not to worry about me," Sophia said, chancing a glance at Lunis, who didn't seem to care about the whole exchange much. He appeared ready to charge off, although Liv wasn't sure he could fly yet. She'd only seen him lumber around the backyard and eat the steaks Rory threw out for him.

"I know you're going to be fine," Liv said, stepping forward.

Lunis' tail swished suddenly, giving her pause. She leveled her gaze at the dragon, and there seemed to be an unspoken arrangement between them. Not only did she suddenly feel better about her sister's safety, she only wanted her to go if she was with the magical creature before her.

If Liv was honest, she'd been a bit resentful that Lunis was taking her sister away. But now, seeing them together, it told her what she'd known in her heart all along.

Dragons and their riders were more than a team; they were one. What happened to one happened to the other. Their lives were longer because of their bond, and neither would tolerate the abuse of the other.

Sophia wasn't being taken from her. She, by virtue of being

who she was, an incredible magician since birth, had been given the highest honor in the mortal or magical world.

Liv's little sister was the youngest dragonrider in history, and she was the first female. No matter how sad Liv was to see her go, she was damn proud that Sophia Beaufont was someone she knew. Someone she loved. Someone who loved her.

CHAPTER NINE

The three siblings were nervously quiet for a long moment, no one seeming to want to say goodbye.

"Well…" Sophia began, trailing away and staring at a garden fairy who was harvesting Rory's vegetable patch on the far side of the yard. Autumn was coming.

"Yeah, well…" Liv said, remembering when she'd abandoned family, thinking they were better off without her. Now they were all she had. Well, besides the strange magical community who wouldn't lose her number, no matter how many spells she'd tried.

"Ummm, well…" Clark said, knitting his hands together.

"I'm sure I can still contact you," Sophia blurted.

"But if you can't, we won't fret," Liv stated at once, not wanting her sister to worry when she had this new life to conform to.

"But if you had an extra second and access to a barn owl…" Clark's voice trailed off.

Liv slapped him on the chest. "She's not going to Hogwarts, and remind me later that you get two black eyes."

Sophia laughed on cue. That was typical Soph. She giggled when it was funny and when it wasn't and when she was about to kick ass. It was just who she was. She didn't laugh to cover nervousness. It was because she found most things in life to be strangely awesome and absurd at the same time.

"I'm sure they have ways to stay in contact," Sophia remarked. "If not, I've got the magical tech Liv gave me."

"It will work on the moon," Liv explained. "You don't have to add any settings. Just turn it on, and it will work. If it doesn't, you just have to leave. And never go back."

Sophia tilted her head to the side. "Seriously, guys."

"Yeah, seriously, guys," Lunis said, still not amused.

"Seriously, Gerald," Liv said, tilting her head at the dragon. "Haven't you ever said goodbye to your favorite person?"

"Hey," Clark said, turning to Liv, offended. "We are born so close together that we are pretty much twins."

"So?" Liv asked him, shrugging.

"So, why am I not your favorite person?" he asked.

"Have you looked in the mirror lately?" Liv asked.

Sophia giggled. Liv stored that sound in her mind, telling herself she'd hear it again. These men who rode dragons, and thought so highly of themselves that the magical world believed them to be the best ever wouldn't take that magic from her. She wanted to hold onto that, anyway. But when you love someone, you set them free.

Liv shook her head. "In all seriousness, I want to say something."

Sophia straightened, now nearly as tall as her sister. She shouldn't be, but dragon magic made people change rapidly, apparently.

"Yes?" Sophia asked expectantly.

Liv shook her head. "It's not your turn yet, Soph. I want a word with Drago."

Everyone, including the dragon, shook their heads. Liv stepped forward, looking down at the dragon, who was growing fast, just like Sophia. She would reach her full height of just under five feet in a matter of days. As to the dragon, it was still unclear, but he was still sizable, currently bigger than a mastiff.

"Hey, there, Lunis," Liv whispered.

"You used my real name," the dragon said, not appearing amused.

"Well, I *do* know it," she said with a smile. "I just want to say—"

"Protect her. I'm aware," Lunis replied.

Liv shook her head. "You already know the important stuff. Protect her. Love her. Watch out for her. But you don't know what I'll say next."

The dragon just peered into Liv's eyes, unblinking. She'd never regarded a beast like the one before her. He was timeless. Wise. Beautiful. And utterly perfect, just like Sophia Beaufont.

"I want to tell you a family secret you don't know," Liv stated, leaning forward. She whispered into the dragon's ear, hoping he understood every one of her words.

His green eyes showed he'd registered her seriousness when he pulled away. "Every night?"

Liv nodded, hiding her smile. "Every night."

Sophia stepped between them. "What did you tell him?"

Liv let the laughter unfurl. "It was nothing, Soph. I just told him about your bedtime routine."

Sophia looked at the dragon and her older sister. "No, that wasn't it. She told you...wait. What happened? Someone tell me."

Liv shook her head. "It was nothing. I just told him that I love you more than life itself, and never to allow anything to happen to you."

Sophia rejected that at first, but shook her head, forcing a smile. "Okay, thank you."

Liv backed away, realizing that one day, Sophia would know this was a lie and that she'd told Lunis more. That was fine.

Clark took Liv's place, pulling a closed container from his bag. "I made you some brownies for the journey, which I realize isn't long, but still. I thought that when you got there, if you were hungry, and the food…"

"Thank you," Sophia said, taking the container from her brother and hugging him. "That was very thoughtful of you."

Liv knew Sophia and Clark had more time together. She should have expected they'd be closer. It was just so hard to let go of the one thing in her life that was purely good.

Sophia pulled away, her knowing eyes sliding to Liv's. "I don't want to go yet…"

Liv didn't give herself the luxury of believing that meant her sister didn't want to go for a century or two. Still, she held her breath.

Sophia stepped up even with her sister. "I don't want to go until I thank the person here who is responsible for giving me the courage to do this." Sophia wiped tears from her eyes that hadn't been there seconds ago. "You see, I wouldn't have had the strength to do this if I hadn't watched you, Liv, conquer evil."

Liv shook her head. "No, Soph. You've got it all wrong."

As she always did, Sophia disagreed with a single look. "I remember how weird it was for you to go out into the world and fight when you hadn't known anything but a tame life. And yet, you just did it. Every day that you came back was an inspiration. I remember looking at you and thinking, I just want to be like my big sister."

Liv sucked in a breath. If she had a time machine, she'd change everything. Past Liv would not fight evil. She'd just stay at home and play Yahtzee with her little sister. Being brave had come at a cost. She'd set an example she couldn't undo now. She'd set a ball in motion.

Sophia grabbed her hands with impressive strength. "You, Liv, gave me the courage to do this. I want to be exactly like you. I want to fight evil. I want to make this world a better place. Because of you, and because of Clark, I know how to do that."

Liv was a strong person. She'd changed the world that year,

making it how it was supposed to be, yet she wanted to crumble right then. Instead, she drew an elven-made sword from her hip, offering it on her hands to her little sister.

"If you are to fight evil, as the Beaufonts have always done, you'll need the best sword." Liv bowed her head and offered the blade to her sister. "Please take Inexorabilis. As you know, this was our mother's sword, and now it belongs to you. It will guard you in ways no other sword can."

Sophia looked up with exasperation at her sister. "How?"

Liv shook her head. "The secrets of every sword and its master are unique." She glanced at Lunis. "Just as I'm sure the secrets of every rider and dragon are."

Sophia took the curved blade, feeling the weight as she stepped backward. "I don't remember it being so beautiful."

Clark smiled. "I'm thinking the same about you right now, Soph."

Liv smiled at her brother, not wanting to fight with him anymore. "We should let her go. I'll open the portal." She glanced at Sophia before opening a bright circle that shimmered blue and green, creating a hole to the other side of the world. "The Gullington will be straight ahead, although you'll have to step forward to find it. Lunis will know."

The dragon bowed his head. "Thank you, Warrior Beaufont. I'll ensure that Cynthia gets there safely."

"Her name is…" Liv stopped, narrowing her eyes at the dragon. "Well-played, dragon. Well-played."

He nodded.

Clark stepped up and hugged his littlest sister. Liv joined, wrapping her arms around the pair. There were tears. There were unspoken words. There were things said that no one but a Beaufont got to hear. But when they stepped apart, the tears were visible for all to see.

These were three who didn't want to let a single one go.

Liv held out her hand between them. "No matter where you are, we'll be together."

Clark placed his hand on top of Liv's. "Together, we'll always get through."

Sophia covered theirs with her small hand. *"Familia est sempiternum."*

That was the Beaufont family motto, and those words were magic.

They closed their hands together, holding each other tight.

When it was time, Sophia stepped back, signaling to the others to let go.

All wiped away tears.

Liv shook her head.

Clark smiled.

And Sophia backed toward the portal shimmering behind her.

"One last thing, my love," Liv called, coming forward again.

Sophia turned her head to the side, listening. "Yes?"

"They, the Dragon Elite, don't know you're a girl," Liv admitted with a cowardly smile before pushing her sister though the portal. Lunis shook his head and followed, a half-smile on his face.

CHAPTER TEN

"Are you kidding me?" Sophia exclaimed, falling through the portal and landing with a thud that knocked the breath out of her.

Unlike any other time she had portaled, it closed almost on her, as if it were trying to spit her out or cut her in half. Lunis didn't appear to have the same issue; he stood casually on the other side and regarded her with mild interest.

Sophia gave the portal, which was closing fast, a look of offense.

"It's the wards on this land. They don't allow portals to stay open for long," Lunis offered, letting out a long huff through his nose. That was the first time that Sophia had seen him do that, and she noticed a bit of smoke flowing through his nostrils. He had said he wasn't sure when he'd get his fire power, but didn't think it would take long once he was around other dragons. Apparently, that sped up the developmental process.

Sophia gazed around, taking in the strange land where she stood. Instinctively, she knew it was Scotland by the enchanting green hills and rolling mist. It was vibrantly green as far as she could see, and there was a smell in the air that reminded her of memories she didn't remember having.

"They are mine," Lunis told her, sensing her thoughts.

Used to losing the privacy in her head, she gave him a look, encouraging him to keep talking.

"Well, not really mine," the dragon corrected. "They are the memories of my ancestors, who have resided here through the ages. The Gullington, the riders' headquarters, has always been the home of the dragons. My memories are strong here."

"Where are we to go?" Sophia asked, turning in a complete circle but not seeing anything but grass and trees.

The dragon nodded toward the north. "That way."

Sophia summoned a traveling cloak, the chill in the air going straight through her. She was used to sunny Southern California. Trekking across the hills of dewy Scotland would take some getting used to. She held her head up, enjoying the brisk air on her face, holding her chin high as she strode forward.

She pulled the cloak tighter around her neck as they hiked through the grass. Sophia hadn't brought anything with her besides her mother's sword since she didn't want to show up with a large trunk, appearing like a kid going to summer camp. She figured the Dragon Elite would have most things she needed, and she'd summon the rest. It was a skill she'd been good at from an early age, as well as disguises.

In actuality, Sophia had been skilled with complex spells since she was extremely young. She'd already mastered magic that mature magicians still couldn't perform. She had never known why, but had also learned not to question such a gift.

"Why do you think Liv didn't tell the Dragon Elite I'm a girl?" Sophia asked Lunis, whose green eyes were searching the hills. He had a strange expression on his face. She hadn't had much time to study his features since he'd hatched, but she already knew them well, seeing them perfectly in her mind's eye when he wasn't around.

"Besides that, she loves to play games?" Lunis answered.

Sophia laughed, her usual reaction to almost anything. Apparently, according to her mother, she had been born innately happy. For some, it was a choice. For Sophia, it was who she was at her core.

"Yes, besides that," she stated.

"Well, you're aware that you're the first female dragonrider in history," Lunis stated, moving with methodical grace.

"Yes, but shouldn't that be the very reason she told the leader about me?" Sophia asked.

He shook his head as they headed farther toward the rolling hills. "The dragons and riders are many things, but progressive isn't one of them."

Sophia paused and faced Lunis. "But what about you? You're not a stick-in-the-mud, right?"

He huffed. "I'm not a typical dragon. I was incubated away from my kin and exposed to many modern things, thanks to you and Liv and the others."

"We did get you a lava pit like you asked and moved you out of Liv's place when you complained about the air conditioning and the television blaring," Sophia argued as they continued walking forward.

"Yes, and I appreciate that," Lunis stated. "But still. You'll soon learn I'm not like other dragons, and that is absolutely as it should be, because you, Sophia Beaufont, aren't like any dragonrider before you."

"Because I'm a girl?"

He shook his head. "You're a woman, and you need to start thinking of yourself that way. I know you grew up fast, speeding past many years of normal development, but this should be second nature for you at this point. Mentally and emotionally, you are no different than any other eighteen-year-old magician."

Sophia nodded. When one didn't progress at the same rate as others, one didn't really know any better. It's not like Sophia knew what she was missing, just as she didn't know what it was like to struggle with complex spells. Something told her the challenges in her life were about to start, and with full force.

"But you're not a unique rider just because you're a female," Lunis continued. "There is that, but you were chosen because inside you is a quality that hasn't often been found in other riders through the centuries."

"Are you going to share what that is, or should I guess?" Sophia asked.

"It's better if I don't," he stated, turning his attention to the hills ahead.

"Fabulous," Sophia snarked. "I totally won't be consumed by thinking about this."

"You should know," Lunis began, "that the riders won't take to your sarcasm like those you are used to."

"You mean, like the giants I hang around all the time, who have little sense of humor?" Sophia questioned. "Or maybe you're referring to Father Time, who tolerates zero sarcasm."

"Although I know you're used to less comedic magical races, I was referring to your sister, who is always joking about one thing or another," Lunis stated.

Sophia stuck her hands on her hips. "So, I have to be all rigid and serious?"

Lunis shook his head. "No, I'm simply telling you what to expect. I wouldn't want you to make a joke and expect anyone to laugh. When there's dead silence after a quip, you'll know why."

"You're not saying I can't make a joke?" Sophia asked.

"I wouldn't dare tell you how to act in that regard," Lunis answered. "Actually, I encourage you to be exactly who you are. That's why you're my rider. If you hold back, it will mean you're not your true self, and it will take us longer to progress."

"Progress?" Sophia asked.

"Well, there will be a lot of training," Lunis stated. "Combat, strength, flying—"

"Yeah, when do we start that flying business?" Sophia asked, looking at the gray sky, almost expecting to see dragons cutting through the roaming clouds.

"I do have to fly first," he answered.

"Right," Sophia stated. "So you think that will come to you like the fire when you're around other dragons?"

"I can't see the future."

Sophia sighed. "I really hope that's the last time you use that reply since it's mostly worthless."

"I knew you were going to say that," he retorted.

"And here I thought you couldn't see the future."

The two walked in silence for a long minute, Sophia enjoying a quiet like she'd never heard before. She didn't realize until that moment that her life had always had background noise in it. At Liv's, there was the noise of the traffic on the street outside, and in the House of Fourteen, there were all sorts of strange noises from the other residents or the oddities of the magical structure.

The mist ahead cleared all at once, as if a wind blew it away in one swift motion, revealing a castle unlike anything that Sophia had seen in books, movies, or her mind. It was like many Scottish castles, with weathered, mossy stone, rising high and mountains framing it. However, there was something different about the four-story castle that stood only a hundred yards away. That didn't seem far to Sophia, but she knew crossing that space would change everything forever, and therefore it felt too short. Maybe she could back up and take the hike again?

"Wow, it's beautiful," Sophia exclaimed, feeling a strange vibration in her chest.

"Oh, good, you can finally see it," Lunis stated with relief.

"You've been able to see the castle the entire time?" she asked. "Why didn't you tell me?"

"What did you want me to do?" Lunis asked. "Sketch you a picture? There is no point telling anyone anything until they can see it for themselves."

She shook her head. "I'm almost certain that statement will come back to bite me in the ass later."

"Then maybe you ought to keep your eyes open," he warned.

The castle wasn't large, but that was relatively speaking. It had to have at least a hundred rooms. Still, nestled on the banks of a lake with tall mountains surrounding it, the structure appeared small when she knew it was really gigantic.

The lake around the castle shimmered, reflecting the clouds overhead and the mountains all around. In the distance were stony caves that drew Sophia's attention.

"That's where the dragons reside," Lunis informed her, sensing her thoughts.

"Oh, do you want to go there?" she asked, realizing she was out of breath.

"And miss the excitement of what's to come?" he asked.

Sophia regarded her dragon with an expression that probably only she could get away with, and still, she felt internally scorned afterward for some reason.

"Did you just do that?" she asked Lunis, feeling something scrape her insides.

He gave her a knowing smile. "Maybe."

"You're naughty."

"Just wait," he stated, promise in his voice.

"So, we go to the castle, then?" Sophia asked.

"If you're ready."

Sophia drew a breath, strangely finding it easier to breathe suddenly. She drank in the fresh air, feeling like her lungs were full for the first time ever.

Nodding, with a determination she'd never experienced, she said, "Yes, I'm ready. Let's meet the Elite."

CHAPTER ELEVEN

The entryway to the Castle hadn't been this clean in a century. Not since Evan joined the Dragon Elite and they all waited in front of the grand staircase, just like now.

Hiker Wallace was wearing the same uniform he had for the last few centuries. He didn't change for new arrivals. What he did do was ensure his men were prepared.

"Who will train him for combat?" he grilled them for the third time.

"I will," Wilder answered, his heels together and chest high, although his brown hair was flopping over one eye as usual.

Hiker nodded with approval, deciding not to say anything about Wilder's unkempt hair. What did it matter? The new dragonrider wouldn't care how they looked.

"Who is in charge of dragon maintenance and riding?" Hiker asked.

"I am," Mahkah stated proudly, wearing traditional Native American clothing for the special occasion.

Hiker strode back and forth, eyeing Ainsley, who was in the form of a British maid in an upper-class area, wearing a black uniform with a lacy apron. He halted in front of her, giving the elf-shapeshifter a rude stare.

"Is it too much, sir?" she said, curtsying slightly.

"Just a bit," Hiker answered.

"I just thought that it would make things come across a bit more polished if you had a—"

"Polished? This is a dragonrider we're welcoming," Hiker interrupted. "He's not concerned with what the housekeeper is wearing or how the groundskeeper looks." Hiker waved his arm at the gnome beside Ainsley whom they called "Quiet." He, in contrast to Ainsley, was wearing jeans and a flannel sweater, with a cap covering his mostly bald head.

"What he cares about is finding his home for him and his dragon," Hiker continued. "A place where he can train and become one of us. That has nothing to do with the stateliness of this place or the food you will serve tonight. We are riders. We can go without luxuries. We were made for the cold, the battering winds, and the fight."

"But what happens when this dragonrider learns there is no fight?" Evan dared to ask, his shirt untucked and his face covered in dirt from one of his earlier adventures.

Hiker let out a long breath. That was apparently the newest dragonrider's job. He was to ask the questions no one else wanted to ask nor answer. He was forever to be a pain in Hiker's ass. Maybe the new rider would change this, though, making Evan behave to set an example. One could only hope, Hiker thought.

The leader of the Dragon Elite swung around, his sword nearly hitting the grandfather clock in the entryway. "This man, whoever he is, and no matter his skill level, won't be ready for a fight for quite a few years. It shouldn't matter to him that there is no fight. As dragonriders, we have to be ready for anything."

"What did you say his name was?" Ainsley asked, having shifted to her normal appearance. She was willowy, with high cheekbones and auburn hair, and appeared to be in her early twenties, although she was centuries old. Beautiful wasn't a word anyone would use to describe the redhead, although "interesting" was often used. Strange. Unearthly. Maybe that was why she used her unique skill so often to change the way she looked to something more common.

"I didn't mention what his name is," Hiker answered, continuing to stride back and forth. There were few thrills in this life currently, but this new dragonrider was definitely one of them. However, he was still recovering from the death of his dearest friend, so the excitement felt wrong. Hiker pushed back anything that felt like emotions. "I was told he goes by S. Beaufont."

"What kind of name is S?" Evan asked, looking at the others.

"It's not a name," Mahkah answered. "It's an initial."

"But what does it stand for?" Evan questioned.

"Maybe Steven?" Wilder offered.

"Or Sean?" Mahkah suggested.

"It could be Sam," Evan remarked.

Hiker blew out a breath. "It will do us no good to ponder such things. It doesn't matter what this rider's name is. The point is that we have a new dragonrider. We have a new dragon, the first in a hundred years. I want to make something very clear to all of you."

He looked around, making eye contact with every one of his men, then Ainsley and Quiet. "It doesn't matter what this man looks like. It doesn't matter what strange things he wears, based on the modern time he's come from. No matter what he knows or doesn't, we're going to accept him! Is that clear?"

Everyone looked around as if waiting for the other to answer. When no one said anything, Hiker stomped, making the floorboards shake. "Is that *clear*?"

"Yes, sir," they said in unison.

A chime filled the air, marking the arrival of the new dragonrider.

CHAPTER TWELVE

All the men stood frozen, simply listening to the low chimes of the doorbell that seemed to go on for longer than Hiker had expected. It had been ages since anyone rang those bells.

A hundred years was a long time to go since welcoming a new rider. It was the longest stint for Hiker. There had been others between when Evan and Wilder came. And then others between Wilder and Mahkah. But those riders didn't last for one reason or another. Either they'd buried them in the cemetery in the Expanse, or they'd left of their own accord.

Hiker liked to think the riders belonged at the Gullington, but it wasn't true. There were no laws that stated that riders had to be together. Hiker knew he had to let them go, and when he did, their mark on the Elite globe disappeared, making the world inside the Gullington feel smaller. But now, there would be a new rider to join them. And that gave him hope.

Hope for the future. Hope that the dragonriders could rebuild their numbers. Maybe this was just the beginning, and many more would be joining them. That was inevitably what they needed if they were ever going to show themselves to the mortals.

"Well," Hiker scolded Ainsley, holding out an arm to the door. "Are you going to get it?"

The redhead scowled right back at him. "And here I thought appearances didn't matter. So what if the housekeeper opens the door?"

"Ainsley," Hiker said, a warning in his voice.

She shifted back into the old English maid with an apron and lace cap. "Yes, Master. Of course, Master." The elf bowed and made for the door.

"Ainsley," he repeated.

She shot him a mischievous glare over her shoulder. Her face had returned to its normal appearance, but her clothes were still those of an upper-class maid.

"I'm just teasing you," she said, shaking her head. Her auburn hair cascaded down her back as her clothes melted into how they had been before, a plain dress and boots.

Hiker shook his head. He would have fired Ainsley if she hadn't been with him since the beginning. He was certain he wouldn't be able to find a thing without her, but admitting that to the elf was never going to happen.

The door to the Castle was roughly fifteen feet tall. When it was opened, it brought a draft through the foyer that usually drifted all the way up to Hiker's office. Just like in other important areas of the Castle, there was a large stained-glass window of an angel set into the door. Glass wasn't the most practical material to have at the front of a castle unless what was set into it protected the place better than any barricade could. Ainsley peered through one of the clear pieces of glass and made an inaudible noise.

"Are you ready?" she asked, peering back at the men, who were standing in a row.

"Go on, then," Hiker answered. He just caught a sly smile on her face, but he didn't have a moment to wonder why because she promptly swung the door open, bringing with it a gust of icy wind.

Sophia gave Lunis a tentative expression. He was like a Great Dane standing next to her, although she could have sworn he'd grown an inch in the twenty minutes since they'd crossed the hills outside this castle.

The door swung back and an elven woman with a freckled face and long red hair greeted her, an impish expression bouncing around in her green eyes. She bowed slightly. "Welcome to the Gullington," she said with an Irish accent.

Sophia was about to open her mouth to reply, but found her throat dry. Instead, she simply nodded in gratitude.

"I hope your journey was satisfactory," the woman continued, holding her hip close to the door, which was only partially open.

Again, Sophia opened her mouth to reply, but the woman's eyes darted to Lunis. She gasped.

"Wow, what an absolutely beautiful dragon," the elf exclaimed. "Simply breath-taking."

"Ainsley!" a man boomed from behind her. "Would you let him in?"

The woman looked over her shoulder. "Him? Do you mean the dragon?" she asked in an innocent tone.

"Of course, I mean the dragon, and the rider too!" the voice yelled.

"Okay," Ainsley said in a teasing voice. "But you might think about choosing your pronouns better."

With that, the woman pulled the door all the way back. Standing squarely in front of a giant wooden staircase with intricate molding were five rough-and-tumble-looking men. At the sight of Sophia, their eyes widened with shock, and their mouths fell open.

CHAPTER THIRTEEN

No one said anything for a long minute. Sophia found she enjoyed watching the disbelief build in the men as they studied her and then Lunis, confusion covering their faces.

In front of the other four men was the tallest and biggest. His blond hair fell to his shoulders, and he wore traditional Viking clothing. He appeared to have just stepped out of the pages of a history book. His beard twitched, and hesitation roamed in his blue eyes.

The man cleared his throat. "You're S. Beaufont?"

Sophia grunted inside. *S. Beaufont? Really, Liv? That's the name she gave to the Dragon Elite for me?*

She stepped forward, daring to cross the threshold of the giant castle. It was even more exquisite inside, with a large wooden chandelier hanging overhead, and strange artifacts lining the walls. "I prefer to go by Sophia, actually. But yes, I'm S. Beaufont."

"Sophia?" the guy on the far left said with a laugh in his voice. His black dreadlocks hung over his dark skin as he flashed a grin at her.

"Yes, Sophia," she repeated, drawing out her name. "Or you can call me Soph, or S. And what should I call you all?"

The Viking in the front took a step back, appearing to be about ready to tip over. He tilted his head to the side, shaking it slightly. "Y-y-you're a girl."

Sophia's nose flared with annoyance. "Woman, actually."

"I'm one too," the elf said, closing the door after Lunis entered and took the spot next to Sophia. The woman curtsied on Sophia's other side. "However, they don't see it. I might as well be a hermaphrodite for all they know. Pleasure to meet you, S. Beaufont. I'm Ainsley, the housekeeper."

Sophia smiled at her, about to extend a hand to the only welcoming face in the castle.

"You're-you're-you're a female?" the Viking said again as if he was having trouble assimilating the brand-new information.

Sophia halted, turning to him. "Yes, we've already been over that. I have been a female all my life."

"Which is exactly how long?" the Viking asked, apparently not thinking that introductions were necessary. He shook his head. "I mean, how old *are* you?"

She tilted her head back and forth. "That's a bit tricky. I was nine years old when I magnetized to Lunis." She indicated the dragon beside her. "But I'm eighteen now, for all intents and purposes."

If learning that she was a woman was a lot to deal with, this new information was a mighty blow to the Viking. He pressed his hand to his forehead and looked down on the floor like he'd lost a contact lens, although Sophia was certain he didn't wear them. Riders wouldn't need such things since the magic of the dragon healed them of such imperfections.

"Eighteen…" he said, continuing to shake his head.

The guy in the middle elbowed the one with dreadlocks. "That's even younger than you, mate."

The Viking turned to face the men, and Sophia got the impression that he'd given them a dirty look by the way they all straightened up, holding their chests high. "And you say you magnetized to your dragon when you were just nine years old?" the man asked, turning back to face Sophia.

She sighed. "Well, yes. Again, my name is Sophia. And you all are?"

"Very confused," Ainsley whispered at her shoulder, seeming to enjoy the tension. "You see, a rider has never magnetized to a dragon at such an early age."

"Oh, he wasn't hatched at that point," Sophia corrected.

A *crack* echoed through the hall when the Viking slapped the side of his leg. "Say what?"

Sophia glanced at Lunis. "He was still in the egg. Unhatched, you know?"

"You've had your dragon since it hatched?" the guy on the right said. He wore his black hair in a braid down his back and was wearing Native American clothing, Sophia guessed.

"Is that peculiar?" Sophia asked.

"It's a first," the man said, shaking his head and appearing impressed.

"That we know of," the Viking corrected, his voice suddenly booming.

"Well, he is a little guy, isn't he?" the guy with the dreads said in a mocking voice. "Bit of runt, if you ask me, for being almost ten years old."

Sophia flashed Lunis a look, but he didn't appear insulted. "He hatched only a day or two ago."

If the Viking was thrown off before, he was absolutely floored by this information. He threw his hands up, whispering as if praying to the gods.

Ainsley laughed, clapping her hands with delight. "Oh, I love it. He'll be bigger than Coral in a week."

"He will not," the guy with dreads shot back.

"He will," the man with the ponytail argued. "He'll be bigger than all our dragons at this rate. And growing beside his rider, well, it will make him quite impressive."

Sophia let out a breath. "I get that you all know exactly what's going on here, but I'm still a bit confused."

"Hiker…" Ainsley said, a commanding tone in her voice.

The Viking had started to pace, muttering to himself as he stroked his beard.

"*Hiker!*" she repeated.

He halted as if suddenly waking from a daze. His eyes landed on the housekeeper.

Ainsley pointed at Sophia. "Would you be so kind, as the leader of this merry little bunch, to introduce yourself?" She said each word with great precision.

His eyes slid to Sophia and then down to the floor again, apparently having a hard time looking at her. "Yes, of course. I must apologize. We weren't expecting such a young rider."

"The youngest in history, actually," the guy beside the one with dreads said. His brown hair had flopped over one eye, and he had a mysterious boyish charm about him.

"Right," the man apparently called Hiker said. "And ummm, well, a new dragon. That is not something we were prepared for."

"Or the fact that I'm a woman," Sophia added.

"Woman. Yes, woman," he said, waving her off. "I hadn't even noticed."

Sophia internally rolled her eyes.

"His name is Hiker," Ainsley cut in when the Viking went silent again, staring with bewilderment at the floorboards. "Hiker Wall—"

"I can introduce myself," he scolded.

She shot him a defiant expression. "That's funny because it didn't look like it."

The Viking looked at Sophia and flinched as if staring straight into her eyes somehow pained him. His lips pressed together, and his face went white. Finally he extended a hand to her. "I'm Hiker Wallace, the leader of the Dragon Elite."

Sophia wrung his hand, wondering if he was gripping hers extra lightly for her benefit. It didn't seem like the kind of handshake a man of his stature would offer. She gave him the same handshake she'd give anyone, which was strong and firm.

He pulled his hand from hers quickly, pivoting to face the men at his back. Gesturing to them, he said, "We are the Dragon Elite."

"I think she's gathered that much," Ainsley stated.

Hiker appeared to restrain himself as he shot the housekeeper a simmering expression.

"As I was saying," he continued, "over here we have our youngest dragonrider, Evan McIntosh."

The guy with dreadlocks stepped forward and bowed to Sophia. "At your service, my lady."

This seemed to test Hiker's patience. "We will not treat her like a damsel in distress, is that clear?"

"I simply thought that as the new rider, she—"

"At least he thought for once," the guy beside him said.

Hiker shook his head. "And this is Wilder Thomason." He indicated the man beside Evan, who had his hair covering his face. He pushed it out of the way to show both of his blue eyes, which were instantly captivating. "He is our expert on combat and weapons. You'll train with him…when the time is right."

"I'm ready to start immediately," Sophia offered enthusiastically.

"When you're ready," Hiker argued, stepping forward and indicating the rider dressed in Native American clothing with the long braid. "And finally, this is Mahkah Tomahawk. He is our dragon-care expert. When you're ready, he'll teach you how to care for… what did you say his name was?"

"Lunis," Sophia announced.

Hiker's chin snapped down. "So, the moon is his element?"

"Yes, he was born on the night of a full moon," Sophia answered.

"Two nights ago," Hiker said, combing his hand over his chin.

"Yes, it was really amazing," she added.

Hiker's eyes fell shut for a moment, as if disbelief was overwhelming him. "Are you telling me you were there when your dragon hatched?"

Sophia glanced at Lunis and back at Hiker. "Well, yes. Why wouldn't I have been there? And when he hatched, I knew his name was Lunis."

"Wow." Mahkah stepped forward, kneeling to look at the dragon with awe written on his face. "You two are unlike anything I've ever read about. The stuff of legends."

"I think," Hiker cut in, waving Mahkah to take back his spot in formation, "that it is simply different than the legends we've been exposed to. I'm sure that in some realms, this is not unique."

"I thought this was the home of the dragonriders," Sophia stated.

"It is," he answered. "But not all history is known. Some has been forgotten. Lost. Or stolen."

Mahkah shook his head. "Simply amazing, no matter how you look at it."

Hiker let out a long sigh. "I think that pretty much does it. Ainsley will show you to your room, and—"

"Actually, there's someone you didn't introduce me to yet." Sophia pointed to a gnome who stood on the other side of Mahkah. He had his face down, which was partially obstructed by a cap.

"Oh, he's not a rider," Hiker stated.

Sophia's head snapped up to look at him. "So? He's a person, and I'd like to know his name."

The gnome glanced up at her. His eyes filled with amazement.

Hiker huffed. "Well, go on then. Introduce yourself, Quiet."

The gnome opened his mouth, and something at a volume below a whisper fell from his lips.

"Sorry," Sophia said, turning her head to the side. "I missed that."

Again the gnome muttered something so low under his breath that Sophia leaned in to hear it. Giving him an apologetic smile, she shook her head. "I'm sorry. The travel must have stopped up my ears. What did you say your name is?"

"We call him Quiet," Hiker stated, appearing close to losing his patience. "He's our groundskeeper."

"But what is his name?" Sophia urged.

"We call him Quiet," Hiker repeated. "He doesn't say much, and when he does, we can't hear it most of the time. He's soft-spoken, to say the least. I wished I could say that about some of the others." Hiker cast a glance at Evan, who looked over his shoulder as if thinking the leader was referring to someone behind him. After briefly glancing at the wall, he shrugged.

"Anyway, as I was saying," Hiker continued, "Ainsley will show you up to your room, and Mahkah will show Lunis to the Cave where the other dragons are."

"Okay, thank you," Sophia said, giving Lunis a tentative expression. She didn't want to leave him, and she instinctively knew he felt the same about her.

Ainsley set off up the stairs. "Follow me, S. Beaufont. We'll get you settled before dinner."

Sophia started after the housekeeper, climbing the large staircase.

"And Lunis, you'll—"

The dragon ignored Mahkah and followed Sophia up the stairs.

"Actually, Lunis," Hiker cut in.

Sophia turned at the first landing, as did her dragon, who was a few steps behind her. She felt a strange heat coming from Lunis as he lowered his head and swished his spike-covered tail, careful not to strike her.

Hiker swallowed. Nodded. "Right. Just for tonight, I don't see any reason you can't stay in So…S…Mistress Beaufont's room."

At the conclusion of his words, Lunis swung back around, giving Sophia a look of satisfaction.

"All righty, then," Ainsley said, her voice teasing once more. "I guess I'll upgrade you to the master suite. This way, Sooo… I mean, S… I mean Miss." She cast a delighted grin over her shoulder at Sophia as she continued up the stairs.

Sophia couldn't help but giggle at the strangeness of this all. She had thought she was the one who would go through a major adjustment, but she had been dead wrong. These men had no idea what was going on or how to deal with her.

CHAPTER FOURTEEN

After the new rider and her dragon had disappeared, Hiker turned to face his men. Evan and Wilder appeared to be hiding their amusement. Mahkah was doing a horrible job of hiding his astonishment. And Quiet, well, his eyes were wide as he looked up the stairs where the new rider had disappeared as if expecting her to come back at any moment.

"Okay," Hiker said in a low voice. "So we delay training for a few years. Maybe we simply give h-h-h..."

"Her," Wilder supplied.

"I know that," Hiker spat. "I was just thinking."

"But sir," Mahkah interrupted. "Why would we delay training?"

"Well, because she's young, and her dragon is—"

"In the prime position to learn," Mahkah cut in again. "Most dragons are rogue before magnetizing to a rider. Lunis is domesticated. We don't have to worry about his behavior. He seems to be very cooperative, unlike most dragons, who have to be tamed first."

Hiker rejected this at once. "No. She's not ready."

"But, sir." Wilder stepped forward. "Didn't you say that we were to accept this new dragonrider no matter what? No matter their skill or their—"

"Wild," Hiker said, a strong warning in his voice.

The younger rider held up his hands. "I'm simply saying, sir, that you seem to be discounting her because she's...well..."

"A she," Evan supplied.

"That's not it," Hiker argued. "Her dragon isn't full-grown yet."

"Which seems like a great opportunity for her to learn combat and master it," Wilder offered.

"And also a good time to teach her dragon care," Mahkah added.

Hiker growled low, his eyes teeming with frustration as he stared at his riders.

"Don't worry, sir," Evan stated proudly. "I get your hesitation. You don't think she can cut it because—"

"Enough," Hiker stated, cutting off the young rider before he could say something too close to the truth. "If Evan thinks he knows what's going on, then we've all got problems."

"Hey, I'm no longer the newbie," Evan offered. "Give me a little credit."

Hiker shook his head and made for the stairs. He needed some time to think. To process. To figure out what he was going to do with the...girl.

He pivoted at the landing. "I expect you all at dinner tonight."

"When have I ever missed a meal, sir?" Wilder asked.

"Or I?" Evan added.

"Finally, you're being cooperative." Hiker turned again but spun back around at once. "And before dinner, tuck in your shirt, Evan. Wilder, comb your hair. Actually, all of you, take a bath before dinner."

CHAPTER FIFTEEN

Sophia was distracted by the many oddities she came across as Ainsley led Lunis and her through the halls on the second floor of the Castle. She stopped several times, blinking at statues that seemed to blur in front of her, morphing into a centaur and then into a Pegasus. It was more of a trick of the mind than anything.

"Keep up, or I swear you'll get lost," Ainsley warned, striding in front of them. "This is unlike any place you've ever been.

Sophia pulled her gaze off her current distraction. "Oh, I'm sorry. I was just preoccupied with the decorations in the Castle."

"These aren't decorations, and this isn't any normal castle," Ainsley warned, stopping to pull a large ring of keys from her pocket.

"They aren't?" Sophia asked.

"The decorations are enchantments," the elf explained. "They either protect us or they guard us, or they do both. There are also all sorts of other things I still don't understand about this place after five hundred years."

"You've been here for five hundred years?" Sophia asked, catching up with her.

Ainsley thumbed through the keys, discarding some after a single glance, although they all looked the same. "Well, at least five hundred years, but I lose track, especially in the last century."

"Wow," Sophia said, giving Lunis a sideways look. He was taking it all in, studying every single detail as he intently listened to the elf. "You leave the Castle, though, right?"

Ainsley nodded as she tried a key in the door. "Of course. I go to the village to purchase our supplies."

"Oh, so I'm guessing Amazon doesn't deliver out here," Sophia joked.

"Amazon?" Ainsley's brow lifted. "You mean the river? No, it doesn't deliver here. Why would it?"

Sophia waved her off. "Sorry, it's a reference to modern culture."

The housekeeper tried another key in the lock. "Oh, well, you'll have to explain those to the lot of us, I'm afraid. None of us has been out of the Gullington in quite some time. Not really. Maybe for a field trip to Tanzania or something, but those are rare, especially these days. I go to the village, but the others stay around here. Adam might have caught your references, but well…"

Sophia tilted her head to the side. "Adam? I didn't meet him."

The door opened, and Ainsley's face broke with relief. "Bloody hell, it only took a few dozen tries." She coughed when she entered the room, waving her hand in front of her face. "This is a larger suite, which should be big enough for you and dear Lunis. I'm sorry it's not very clean. The housekeeper for the Castle is utterly useless. Just ask Hiker; he's always going off about how incompetent she is."

Sophia laughed, her eyes drinking in the space. It was, in fact, incredibly dusty, as if it hadn't been cleaned in a few hundred years, but the ancient architecture and uniqueness of the furnishings still came through.

When Ainsley pulled the thick drapes back from the floor-to-ceiling windows, the light illuminated each detail in the space. The colors of the room were muted, maybe from age or dust, but the craftsmanship of the furniture was incredible.

A four-poster bed with curtains tied around each post sat against a stone wall on the far end of the room. Beside it was a sitting area with tufted leather chairs and a tray with a tea service sat on the table between them, as if the person who had once stayed here had just popped out after the refreshments.

Overhead hung a round iron chandelier studded with a dozen candles, and along the far wall was a large fireplace and a door.

Ainsley swiped her hand through the air, and flames burst to life in the hearth and on the candles, cascading even more light over the large room.

Sophia could now see that large oil paintings hung on the wall, most of men proudly dressed for battle.

"Now, we don't have electricity in the Gullington since it disturbs the dragons, so I'll be in each morning to light your fire and candles," Ainsley explained.

"Oh, I can do that on my own, I'm sure," Sophia replied. "Since Lunis has hatched, I've gotten fire magic as well as many other skills I didn't have before."

The elf shot her a skeptical expression. "You should tell the others that. They can't pick up their dirty socks to save their lives. They can ride majestic dragons and spar for hours, but the second their candles need replacing, their legs are all of a sudden broken."

Sophia smiled, studying a tapestry of a unicorn on the wall. "Well, I guess I can understand a tiny bit since they do have to attend battles regularly."

A laugh popped out of Ainsley's mouth. "Battles? Oh, none of these blokes have seen a battle in ages."

"What?" Sophia exclaimed, watching as Ainsley swiped her hand around the room, magically cleaning it.

The elf glanced sideways at her. "It really isn't my place to say anything about the matter. Not that that ever stops me, but I told Hiker I'd be on my best behavior with you. At least, for the first decade or so."

Sophia opened her mouth to ask more questions, but the elf disappeared into the adjoining room. Lunis was already curled up in front of the fireplace like a dog deciding to take a quick nap.

She turned her attention to the windows, where the evening light was coming through. The room had a brilliant view of the hills and mountains in the distance, which were partially covered in clouds and mist. It appeared to be raining ever so slightly.

"The bathroom is in pretty good condition, considering," a man's voice said from behind Sophia.

Spinning around, she drew back at the sight of the old man who was hobbling on a cane, his gray hair pulled into a low ponytail. "Hi!" she squeaked. "What happened to Ainsley? Who are you?"

A wicked smile curled up the edges of the man's mouth, and before her eyes, the figure morphed until the housekeeper was standing before her once more.

"Sorry for startling you," Ainsley stated. "I shift when I'm excited, most of the time not even realizing that I've done it. I have to admit, having another woman here, especially a new dragonrider, is thrilling."

Sophia shook her head as if trying to dispel her confusion. "You're a shapeshifter, then?" She'd only read about them. They were incredibly rare, harnessing magic that most couldn't fathom. This was immediately intriguing to Sophia since one of the skills she'd mastered early was disguises. She'd changed Liv's appearance many different ways for secret missions, but it required a great deal of magic and wore off quickly. The idea that someone could do it at will was fascinating.

"Yes, so if you see a stray cat or a loose dog running around, that's me," Ainsley explained. "Those are two of my favorite forms to take. Makes it bloody easy to negotiate the passageways in the

Castle, as well. They can become quite narrow, especially when the Castle is feeling extra gloomy."

Sophia swallowed, nodding. "So, the bathroom is through there? Do I need to get water from you for the bath, and what do I do with—"

"The waste?" she interrupted. "You flush it."

"What?" Sophia questioned.

"We live in the dark ages when it comes to knowledge of popular culture and electricity, but we wouldn't dare go without plumbing," she stated. "It was an upgrade we made a few centuries ago. We even have hot showers, although the men still don't seem to think they need to take one regularly."

"But..." Sophia scratched her head. "I'm a bit confused about how you've all lived in this place for so long, cut off from the world, yet..."

"We are magical creatures," Ainsley explained. "You'll find there are things we know nothing about, and other things we're quite caught up on. It sort of depends."

"But if you don't leave the area, then how?" Sophia questioned.

Ainsley shrugged. "One of the many mysteries of the Gullington." She strode toward the door, turning around to gauge the room. "Yes, I think this should do for now. I hope it's to your liking."

Sophia thought the room was beautiful. Not really her taste, but enchanting all the same. "It's wonderful. Thank you."

"Very well, S. Beaufont, I'll fetch you for dinner, or you won't find it," Ainsley stated.

"But it's downstairs, right?" Sophia asked. "In the dining hall? Just off the entryway? I can find that."

Ainsley snickered. "You'd think. But the Castle of the Gullington likes to play with newcomers."

"So even if I know the way, I won't be able to find it?" Sophia asked.

"Especially if you do, actually," Ainsley answered. "The Castle doesn't like know-it-alls. You're a new arrival. It wants you to be lost. You should pretend to be that way, at least for a little while." She lowered her voice, leaning close to Sophia. "Do it for the Castle's benefit."

"You're acting like it has feelings," Sophia stated. This was a weird statement for her to make, having been raised in the House of Fourteen, which was very much alive. However, it didn't have feelings. It did change depending on who was in the House, and the library was definitely a place where one could get lost, but it wasn't like the Castle of the Gullington because she never remembered it having hopes or desires that she was aware of.

"Oh, it does have feelings," Ainsley stated. "If you can believe it, this place gets offended if I don't compliment every corner of it on a regular basis. That's half my job as the housekeeper, to be honest. Now you know, so when you see me giving the atrium lavish praises, you'll understand why."

Sophia's eyes ran over the room with a new curiosity. "Okay, well, then, is there anything else I need to be aware of? Should I compliment the walls?"

"Only if you mean it wholeheartedly," Ainsley said with a smile. "The Castle can tell of insincerities, which is probably why it keeps dumping Evan out of his bed on a regular basis."

"I'll keep that in mind." Tentatively, Sophia eyed the tall bed, which was on a raised platform with steps leading up to it. She definitely didn't want to be thrown from it.

"All right, I will see you in about an hour," Ainsley stated, lingering in the doorway for a moment. "Oh, and S. Beaufont?"

"Yes?" she answered.

"Don't worry about Hiker." She winked. "He'll warm up to you. Just give him a century or two."

Sophia gulped, wondering how her life had changed so dramatically in one hour. "Right..."

CHAPTER SIXTEEN

"I don't think we're in Kansas anymore," Sophia said, turning to continue to take in the room.

Lunis cracked an eye. "Scotland. We're in Scotland."

She sighed. "I know that."

"But it isn't the Scotland most have seen," he added. "The Gullington isn't on any map."

Sophia stared out the window. "What exactly is the Gullington? Is it the Castle, or does it include the grounds?"

"You'll get a tour tomorrow."

"How do you know that?" Sophia asked.

"I just do," he replied coyly.

"Hey, what Ainsley said about electricity. Is that why you didn't like living at Liv's place?" Sophia questioned.

He shook his head. "Mostly, I didn't like that Clark's cooking filled the apartment with strange smells and Liv's cat watched me sleep."

"I watch you sleep," Sophia teased.

"And I you," he countered. "As we've discussed before, I'm not an average dragon. I've been raised in the modern world. I'm not sure how it will affect me, but electricity has never bothered me." He lifted his head, looking around the old room. "Actually, you think you can get us a television in here?"

"How am I going to power it?" Sophia asked.

He lowered his chin, regarding her through hooded eyes. "Your sister is an expert with magical tech. I'm sure she can help."

"Oh, right." She huffed. "Can you just imagine what Hiker would do if I outfitted my room with a bunch of magical tech?"

"Hiker is going to have a fit regardless of what you do."

Sophia thought for a moment. "Yeah, he's not very fond of the idea of me being...well, *me*. Or you being just hatched."

"That is part of your role for the dragonriders."

Sophia spun away from the window, her hands on her hips. "What do you know, Lunis?"

He closed his eyes. "Things."

"Like?"

"Like that you have a pivotal role which will revolutionize," he answered.

"The Dragon Elite?" she asked.

He opened his eyes, the piercing green always startling her. "The world. But sure, let's start with the Dragon Elite. First, I'm going to take a nap."

Pulling her phone from her pocket, she glanced at it. As she had expected, there was no reception. Liv had actually updated her phone right before she left. "Well, even magical tech doesn't work here."

"It will," Lunis stated. "It just needs to be updated based on the current wards."

Sophia held the device up. "And unsurprisingly, there's no WiFi here."

"We can fix that too," he stated.

"Why is it that you seem antsier than me to have technology?" Sophia asked him.

"Because the new season of *Stranger Things* is coming out," he answered. "I need to find out what happens. Life without Netflix is meaningless."

A laugh popped out of her mouth. "You have to be the strangest dragon in the world."

"I am yours." He yawned loudly, a growl echoing through the room. "You should change for dinner. Wear that blue dress I like."

"Which one?" Sophia asked. "You haven't seen me in any blue dresses."

"No, I haven't, but pick one I'll like."

"You're going to dinner?" Sophia asked.

"Of course. I'm starving," he said, sounding insulted at the idea he wouldn't attend.

"But Hiker wanted you in the Cave with the other dragons," Sophia argued. "How much longer do you think you can stay here?"

"Depends on how much I eat tonight," he stated.

"Ha-ha. But seriously."

"I'm growing, but I'd prefer to stay here for the time being."

"Until you can't fit through the door anymore?"

"Dragons have a mysterious power that allows us to fit through places that we shouldn't."

"Like a cat in a box? There are the videos on YouTube—"

"That is the last time you will liken me to a feline," Lunis interrupted.

She shrugged. "I'm not sure a dress is the right attire for tonight. Those guys are already having an aneurysm trying to deal with me being a girl. I'm not sure I should throw it in their faces right now."

"Do something with your hair as well," Lunis stated as if he hadn't heard her. "Maybe do your makeup, too."

"Lun, I really think downplaying my femininity is for the—"

"Scratch that," he cut in. "Definitely do your makeup."

"I want them to take me seriously," she argued.

He lifted his head again, blinking at her with annoyance. "This coming from the girl who said, and I quote, 'We aren't allowed to show our feminine side in battle as if that's a mark of weakness. But what if it's just the opposite? Shouldn't we display both?'"

Her jaw dropped. "You weren't there when I said that to Liv." She remembered the conversation because that was when she was still expected to become a Warrior when Liv stepped down. Then she became a dragonrider, and everything changed.

"I know things," he simply stated in reply.

She shook her head at the dragon. "Okay, so you want me to put on a dress, do my hair and makeup, and get you a television. Anything else?"

"Read the book on the desk," he stated.

Sophia glanced around. "There isn't a desk."

In the corner next to the fireplace, a small writing desk suddenly appeared. She shot a gaze at her dragon. "Where did that come from?"

"It was there all along, but you didn't know to look for it," he answered.

Sophia sighed. "How is this place even stranger than the House of Fourteen?"

"A different brand of magic."

She strode over to the desk and picked up a thick volume sitting on its surface. "*The Incomplete History of Dragonriders.*" Flipping the book open, she squinted to read the Old English text. "No wonder this thing is incomplete. The dude who wrote it probably got a hand-cramp."

When there was no answer from Lunis, Sophia shot him a look. "This is the book you want me to read before dinner? You do know I can't speed-read, right?"

Again no answer.

She was about to say something else, but the loud fake snore that reverberated from the dragon made her stop. Sophia shook her head, taking a seat in one of the armchairs in front of the fireplace and curling up with the strange book.

CHAPTER SEVENTEEN

"I think it's a bit much," Sophia said, eyeing herself in the mirror. There hadn't been a full-length mirror beside the bed until she'd needed it. Apparently, that was another of the mysteries of the Castle. She made a mental note to need frozen yogurt later and wait for the dispenser to magically appear.

"I think it's perfect," Lunis countered.

Sophia had magicked a pale blue dress that was tight, sophisticated, and conservative. The collar went all the way up her neck and the hem to her knee. The sleeves were quarter-length, and the lacy material gave it an air of softness. She'd exchanged her riding boots for nude heels, and as Lunis had requested, piled her long blonde hair on top of her head in an elegant twist. Her makeup was the final touch, being understated and also accentuating her best features.

"Are you sure about this?" Sophia asked, facing the dragon.

"So," he began, standing and taking up a great deal of the space in front of the fire, "you can go down there in armor, making them think you're one of them. But the fact is, you're not. Don't try to conform to their standards. Make them uncomfortable. Make them see you as you are. You aren't a dragonrider who happens to be a girl. You are a woman who happens to be a dragonrider. Never let them make you feel bad for that."

She stared at her dragon for a long moment, slightly confounded by his words, which strangely made sense. When she could form no direct reply to his message, she said, "What are you going to wear?"

"Ha-ha," he stated, running his tongue over his sharp teeth. "I could use a bath soon, though. Do you think you can upgrade the bathtub in there to make room for me?"

"I can, but I'm not taking baths after you anymore." She shook her head. "You never clean up after yourself."

"We haven't even spent that much time together, and you're already using absolutes." Lunis shook his head. "I'm not sure if I should be impressed by how you've employed language or offended by how you've abused it."

A knock at the door made Sophia start unnaturally. She wasn't used to being on edge, but she was a thousand miles away from her comfort zone—literally and figuratively.

***

"I approve of the dress choice," Ainsley said over her shoulder as they sped through a wide corridor. She had taken an identical appearance to Sophia, wearing the same dress. "It's just a bit awkward that we chose the same outfit tonight. What are the odds?"

Sophia laughed and looked at Lunis beside her, glad he was going down to dinner too. Ainsley had been in her normal form when Sophia had opened the door. After they'd gone a few yards down the corridor, she'd shifted to match the dragonrider's appearance. Sophia didn't mind since she thought it would take the pressure off her. Or maybe make the guys laugh. Or blow up in her face entirely. Still, she trusted Lunis, so if he wanted her to wear a dress, that was what she'd do.

"I hope you're hungry," Ainsley said, leading them down the grand staircase.

"Oh, I hope you didn't go all out for us," Sophia said, holding onto the railing since she found the floor slippery under heels. Landing on her butt as she descended wasn't the way she wanted to make her entrance.

"I didn't," Ainsley stated. "I only mean, I hope you're hungry because otherwise, you'll probably find the food inedible. It seems that usually the guys only like my food if they are starving. I have never mastered cooking all these years, probably because I serve as a shrink to a crazy, self-absorbed castle."

"She's lying," Wilder called as he slid down the banister on the other side of the staircase, landing in the entryway with a giant grin and his arms wide like he just completed a show number on a stage. "Ainsley is a brilliant chef. She only downplays her skills because Hiker complains for one reason or another."

"Maybe he should cook, then," Sophia stated dryly.

Wilder tilted his chin to the side, a wolfish expression on his face. "I like her already," he told Ainsley.

Because they were identical, Sophia didn't know how Wilder knew which of them was the housekeeper and which was her. She assumed it was because Lunis was at her side and Ainsley had been talking about cooking earlier.

"Oh, you'll simply love her after a brief conversation," Ainsley replied, turning to smile at Sophia. "And she bathed, which might be a first for any rider before dinner."

Wilder lifted his arm, smelling. "I bathed. I even brushed my hair."

The dragonrider did appear a bit more polished than before, his button-up shirt pressed and tucked into his pants and his hair neatly parted on the side and brushed back.

"See?" Ainsley said, looking over her shoulder as she led the way to the dining hall. "You're already having a positive influence, S. Beaufont."

All the other men were seated in the dining hall when they entered. It was a large room with a table that could easily seat twenty or more. It seemed strange that everyone was nestled at the far end by the fireside.

Hiker looked up from the head of the table, his eyes wide as if Sophia had decided to wear a Halloween costume to the meal. Mahkah and Quiet both stood at once at the sight of her. Evan simply picked his teeth with his thumbnail. However, all the men appeared much more refined than earlier. The dirt had been washed from Evan's face, and Hiker's beard was much less gruff in appearance.

"Sit down, men," the Viking commanded, then his eyes fell to Lunis, and he scowled. "We don't usually have our dragons at the table or in the Castle."

"He's just a pup, though," Wilder protested, striding around them and taking a seat next to Evan.

"We all know *he* knows where he belongs," Hiker said through clenched teeth, his eyes narrowed.

Lunis strode around the dining room table, swishing his spiked tail and knocking into furniture lined up along the wall, instantly and casually smashing it to bits. He appeared unflustered by his wake of destruction as he crossed the space, taking the spot he'd easily made for himself by clearing that side of the room.

Wilder glanced over his shoulder at where Lunis had settled and saw a heated expression in the dragon's ancient eyes. "I don't know about you people, but I think we should let him stay."

"Yes, most definitely," Evan stated, shaking his napkin out and tucking it into the collar of his shirt.

Quiet muttered something inaudible as well.

"When he's ready to move to the Cave, he will," Mahkah stated with gentle wisdom.

Hiker looked at the debris that Lunis had left in his path.

"Hopefully, there will be something remaining of the Castle after that."

"Well, again, this is new territory," Mahkah reminded. "None of our dragons could even enter the Castle when they first magnetized to us and came to the Gullington. They were much older and larger. And of course, not domesticated."

Hiker dismissed this at once and pointed at Sophia. "Go ahead and take a seat." His eyes then darted to Ainsley beside her, identical in appearance. "Fetch dinner, would you?"

The housekeeper curtsied. "Yes, Master. Just like a good dog, I'll go fetch." She shifted into the form of a collie and sprinted for the kitchen.

Wilder laughed. "I always love it when she does that."

Sophia approached the table carefully, taking the seat next to Quiet. "How did you know which one was me?"

Wilder pointed to his temple. "The scar."

Sophia brushed her hand over the side of her face. "I don't have a scar there."

"No, but Ainsley does," Evan explained, removing the metal lid from a tray and peering at its contents. "When she shifts, no matter what form she takes, it's always there."

Having shifted back to her normal appearance, Ainsley entered through the kitchen, holding a large covered tray. "I guess you men couldn't keep my secret for even a single day."

"Oh, you'll still fool her a time or two," Wilder stated, his nose in the air, sniffing. He grimaced. "That isn't…"

Ainsley nodded proudly, laying the tray down in front of Sophia. "It is. In honor of our new member." She lifted the lid to show a round meat thing. It didn't smell enticing, but it definitely smelled.

Evan pushed away from the table. "Yeah, on second thought, I'm not as hungry as I was."

"Sit," Hiker commanded.

Evan did as he was told, his eyes reluctantly on the tray of meat.

"Haggis?" Sophia asked. "Meat cooked in a sheep's stomach?"

Ainsley smiled. "And she's cultured as well as beautiful. Now I'll just go and *fetch* Lunis' supper."

Hiker rolled his eyes at the use of the verb. "There's a whole pasture of sheep for him to fetch on his own."

"I'm not sure if he's ready for that yet, sir," Mahkah offered thoughtfully.

Wilder leaned forward and whispered to Sophia, "The haggis doesn't taste as good as it looks."

She eyed it. The mound of grayish substance didn't look appetizing.

"Thankfully, there are potatoes and vegetables," Evan stated, disappointment in his voice. He reached for a piece of bread at the same time as Quiet, taking the top piece before the gnome got to it.

Ainsley returned with a large slab of meat that she laid in front of the dragon. She proudly stood peering down at him, her hands on her hips. Sophia gave Lunis a tentative glance.

"He would prefer it if you didn't stay right there," she said to the housekeeper, sensing Lunis' thoughts.

"Oh!" Ainsley stated. "Of course! I'll just go over here, Lunis. I'm not watching you."

Hiker appeared to be fed up with this display. He yanked the lid off the mashed potatoes and began slopping them onto his plate, his eyes on the others as he splattered the table with flecks of food.

"Shall I serve you first, S. Beaufont?" Ainsley asked.

Sophia offered her a weak smile. "Thanks."

"What I don't get," Evan began, chewing on the bread, "is how did you change? You didn't bring any luggage that I saw."

"You wouldn't notice if she swung a suitcase in your face," Wilder spat.

Beside Sophia, Quiet mumbled something inaudible.

Ainsley laughed, sliding a thick slice of gray meat onto Sophia's plate. "Quiet, I absolutely agree with that. You've got Evan pegged."

The young rider scowled. "What did he say about me?"

"You would have heard it if you were listening," Ainsley stated, sliding a thick slice onto the gnome's plate.

In reply, he said something else that once again, Sophia couldn't make out, even though her ear wasn't far from his mouth.

"Right you are again," Ainsley said to the gnome, serving the others, who all eyed the meat with disgust.

"Who wants the potatoes?" Hiker asked, holding the tray up.

The whole table clambered for the side dish. Hiker handed it to Mahkah. "And back to Evan's question. Sophia, how did you change? I was wondering why you hadn't brought anything with you."

She glanced down at her dress. "Well, I didn't need to. I'm fairly good at magicking clothes and other things that I need for myself."

"You transported those clothes from…" Evan looked around. "Where's she from?"

They exchanged confused expressions. Hiker, Sophia knew, was aware of the answer, but he didn't appear to be about to admit it as he chewed.

"Yes, I transported them from my home in North America," she answered, pushing the haggis around with her fork.

"Wow," Wilder stated, grabbing the roasted vegetables and piling them on his plate. "Evan can't even transport a pair of shorts from upstairs."

"The Castle makes it impossible, I tell you," Evan retorted.

"Where in North America?" Mahkah asked.

Sophia realized that this would have also been his home once. "Oh, Southern California. I was actually raised at the House of Fourteen, but you might all know it as the House of Seven."

Evan fanned himself. "Oh, she was around the hoity-toity types. Those Councilors and Warriors run the magical show, don't they?" He glanced at Hiker, who remained stone-faced.

Sophia was certain the leader of Dragon Elite knew her backstory. How could he not? And yet he was just sitting there, waiting for her to disclose it. "Actually, I was in line to be a Warrior for the House of Fourteen. My sister Liv—"

"She's the one who freed mortals from the curse so they could see magic once more," Wilder interrupted, leaning forward.

"Oh, yeah," Ainsley said, having finished serving everyone and taking a seat on the other side of Sophia. "She's a real hero."

Quiet muttered something Sophia thought might be a swear word.

"She's the reason we might have a job to do soon," Evan stated. Catching a heated glance from Hiker, he sat back. "I mean, when the time is right. Which isn't now."

"What do you mean?" she asked. "What do the dragonriders do? No one seems to be able to tell me, and Ains—"

"Didn't get you enough haggis," the housekeeper said at once, grabbing a spoonful of the meat and piling it on top of Sophia's potatoes, the only thing she had planned on eating. "There you go, love. My apologies. Eat up."

"Thank you," Sophia said with zero enthusiasm.

"So, your dragon hasn't mentioned anything?" Mahkah asked.

"Only small bits," Sophia stated. "And I had limited time to read the book in my room."

"Book?" Hiker questioned.

"Yes, *The Incomplete History of*—"

"How did you get that out of my office?" Hiker interrupted, making Lunis' head snap up from the mess of meat he'd made on the floor. The Viking took a long breath, calming. "Right, the Castle. It appears it's already responding to you."

"Funny, because I've been here a lot longer, and it doesn't do a damn thing I want," Evan sulked.

"That's because you're an imbecile," Wilder stated matter-of-factly.

Quiet muttered.

Ainsley smiled in reply.

"Anyway, the riders," Sophia stated. "I'd like to know our purpose and what mortals have to do with it."

"So your sister—" Hiker began.

"She's the one who has changed everything for all of us," Wilder stated. "I don't get out much, but I hear her name."

"From who?" Ainsley asked.

"From people," he countered smugly.

"So, a potential Warrior from the House of Fourteen," Evan asked, sitting back in his chair. "A bit of royalty right at our table."

"Well, I gave that all up," Sophia stated. "Once I magnetized to Lunis' egg, I knew I'd never become a Warrior. I didn't want to, and Liv is better at it anyway. She's built to maintain justice."

Wilder snickered. "What do you think we all do?"

"Well, I wish someone would tell me," Sophia shot back, her temper flaring.

Hiker cut his eyes at Wilder. "I think that conversation is best left for tomorrow. That's when I'll give you a formal tour of the Gullington, although you probably shouldn't wear a dress for it."

Sophia glanced over her shoulder at Lunis, who had finished his meal and looked much happier about it than she did about hers. He had known that tomorrow she'd get a tour. She guessed it wasn't that big a prediction, considering the circumstances.

"And then I'll start training, right?" Sophia asked excitedly.

"Well," Hiker said, pushing up from the table and patting his stomach, although he'd also not eaten much. "I think we'll get to that when the time is right. There's no reason to rush."

"But I was really hoping—"

"To get a good night's rest," Hiker cut in. "Yes, I think that's in order as well. I'll see you all tomorrow." With that, the leader of the Dragon Elite left.

When he was gone, Ainsley leaned forward. "I didn't figure you would be hungry for dessert, having filled up on the main entrée."

"Why is my heart breaking in my chest already?" Wilder asked.

"Oh, I don't know," Ainsley said with a shrug. "But I didn't make the chocolate cake I was going to. Didn't want it to go to waste since you'd all be stuffed on haggis."

Evan looked at Sophia directly. "I'm so glad you're here," he said dryly. "Can you summon me some chocolate cake from North America?"

"Sometimes I can bring food," she stated. "But it's not always safe. The time zone will probably spoil it."

"Still, it's impressive that you can change your appearance," Wilder said, turning to her. "Can you make Evan appear less horrible?"

Sophia laughed. "My skills on others don't last very long. Nothing like Ainsley's."

"Speaking of which," Wilder said, looking around, "where has the sneak gone?"

Sophia turned around to find that the shapeshifter had disappeared. A moment later, she heard a squeak and saw a small mouse scurrying up the stairs.

Wilder pushed up from the table. "Great, she's gone. Let's go raid the kitchen for real food." He glared down at Sophia as if daring her to join him.

She didn't need much encouragement. She was up, following him to the kitchen, with Evan on their heels. Sophia didn't want to get into trouble, but she was starving and excited to explore more of the Castle, even if it was with a pair of strange, bumbling guys.

CHAPTER EIGHTEEN

The portrait of Adam Rivalry had moved to the top of the center of the grand staircase. It had also doubled in size. Now Adam was as tall as Hiker as he looked out of the oil painting, Kay-Rye beside him on a hillside.

Hiker sucked in a breath as he regarded the large painting. The Castle missed the dragonrider, that much was clear. The leader of the Dragon Elite didn't know how long the ancient building would display the rider in the most central spot. Maybe days or months, or if it was like the last time, it would be a quarter of a century.

He felt someone approaching from behind him. He turned without making noise, scanning the stairs. There didn't appear to be anyone there, but that didn't mean anything.

Sighing, Hiker said in a gruff voice, "Go on then, Ainsley. Show yourself."

The housekeeper scampered over the top stair in the form of a field mouse, her nose twitching. A smile graced the rodent's face before she shifted into her full form as an elf. "I was simply cleaning the stairs, sir," she said, curtsying.

"Oh?" he asked.

"Yes, there are some stubborn crumbs and bits I couldn't get up in human form, so I thought—"

"You must really think me an idiot," he stated.

"No. I'd never think that about you, sir," she replied sheepishly. "Bullheaded, certainly. Closed-minded most of the time. Difficult—"

"I get the point," he said, turning to face the corridor that led to his study. There wasn't any work to do, but sleep wasn't in his future. Not anytime soon, if at all that night.

She lifted her chin, regarding the large painting of Adam and Kay-Rye in front of them. "Oh, I see the Castle has done some rearranging. I was wondering when that would happen."

"Yes," Hiker said, not having anything else to add.

"You miss him, don't you?" she asked.

He gave her a look of annoyance.

She waved off his expression of offense. "Of course, you do. I know. It's more of a rhetorical question."

"Adam and I hadn't gotten along recently," Hiker said, surprised by the remorse in his voice.

"You mean in the last several centuries?" She laughed. "You two were at each other's throats regularly. I got tired of having to serve his meals in his room, but I understood. He was trying to keep the other men out of your disputes."

Hiker shook his head, regret billowing out of him.

"You know, when I was a child, my brother and I used to fight insanely," Ainsley began. "We were always tearing into each other about one thing or another. I'd say the sky was blue, and he'd argue that it was gray—"

"It probably *was* gray," Hiker countered.

She rolled her eyes. "My point is, of all the people in my life, I loved few more than him. That was why we argued. Because at the end of the day, I knew no matter what we had said to each other, it didn't matter. We still loved one another fiercely."

Hiker yawned. "Thanks. That was the story I needed to get me tired. I think I'm finally ready to retire for the night."

She smiled, used to Hiker's guarded nature. It was slightly endearing when she had the patience for it. "I know you and Adam didn't see eye to eye about things regarding the riders, but you loved each other fiercely, which was why he opposed you. Well, and also, you're stubborn as hell and refused to see his point of view."

Hiker huffed. "That's not true. He was simply wrong."

"I'm not going to weigh in on that age-old argument of yours," Ainsley stated. "I know you're conflicted about it even more now that he's gone."

"I am not," he argued.

"Then why haven't you been sleeping lately?"

He scowled at her. "You really should spend less time spying and more of your efforts removing the spiderwebs from the rafters."

She waved her hand over her head, muttering a spell. "There. That's done. Anyway, I know you're trying to be careful, not wanting to rush into things after the mortals have awoken from their curse. You do what you think is right, but my point is that you need to *actually* do what you think is right."

"Once again, you've made no sense." He pressed his hand to his temple. "Thanks for the headache."

She pursed her lips, undeterred. "Fine, I won't belabor this point. That was not the reason I followed you."

"Oh, and here I thought you were actually cleaning the stairs," he countered snidely.

Ainsley stuck her hands on her hips. "You know you're going to have to train her."

Now Hiker was angry. Ainsley never respected boundaries, but this was too far. "She will be trained."

"When?" she argued. "In a decade? In two? When you can't ignore that she actually exists anymore?"

"She just got here!" he boomed. "What do you want of me, woman?"

A smile crossed the elf's lips. "Acknowledge her as just that. As a woman. And train her. I get that she's not what you expected, but—"

"Not what I expected?" he interrupted. "That's the understatement of the century."

"And I'm sure it scares you that if she's the newest dragonrider in all this time, what does that say about how the world has changed outside the Gullington?" Ainsley observed.

"That's not it," he seethed.

She admired the painting, fondness welling up her eyes. "Adam knew how the world outside the Gullington had changed. He got out. He learned about the world. Taught the other men. Delivered us information. That was one of the reasons you two argued so much."

"You're fired," he snarled.

She nodded. "I'll be out in the morning, but one more thing before I go. I think that many of the things that challenged you about Adam are what you're dealing with with S. Beaufont."

This statement brought a grimace to his face. "They aren't remotely close, and can't be compared. Adam was the oldest living rider of the Elite. He was my best friend, even though he loved to take risks—"

"Or maybe that was exactly *why* he was your best friend," she cut in.

He swung his gaze around. "No, I think it's because I'm limited on options at present. It's not like the Castle is bursting with riders like it once was."

"And yet, you and Adam were close when there were dozens of riders here," Ainsley dared to say.

Hiker's jaw flexed. "You think you know everything, don't you?"

"Well, I have the benefit of having known you for most of our lifetime, so I won't apologize for not allowing you to lie to yourself or me."

The leader of the Dragon Elite let out a low growl. "I'm going to bed. You can let yourself out. It's been nice knowing you."

Ainsley smiled and turned for the stairs. "Absolutely. Have a lovely night. See you tomorrow, sir."

He rolled his eyes as he headed toward his quarters, realizing he was never going to be rid of the nosy elf and unsure of how he felt about that.

CHAPTER NINETEEN

Stuffed from raiding the pantry, Sophia held her stomach as she laid in bed, listening to all the strange sounds in the Castle. Lunis was already snoring, having gone up to bed an hour before she did.

It surprised her how easy it was for her to hang out with Evan and Wilder, laughing with them while she spooned peanut butter into her mouth straight from the jar. It was peculiar because they were strangers who had lived in a castle and ridden dragons for a hundred years. But that wasn't the reason it was strange to hang out with them. The truth was, Sophia hadn't ever really had friends. Not her own age or any other age.

From early on, she'd been different from her peers, even though she'd been taught in the House of Fourteen with other talented children from magical families. Most didn't have their magic until they were in their teens. Sophia had come into her magic when she was four years old.

She remembered the day vividly. She'd been playing with her doll, wanting it to interact with her, and it had come to life and done just that. It stood, walking over to the china set and poured them both cups of pretend tea. After that, Sophia stayed away from the other children, not wanting anyone but her siblings to know she had her magic so early.

Lying in bed, looking up at the canopy overhead, illuminated by the dying fire, Sophia tried to wrap her brain around her new life. She was a dragonrider. She could digest that without issue, strangely.

She had a dragon lying at the foot of her bed. That also wasn't weird. It felt as though she and Lunis had always been together.

She was about to fall asleep in an ancient castle that was alive and had emotions and desires and expectations. That also wasn't too hard to accept, since most of her life, the things around her didn't act as anticipated by most.

But the idea that there were strange magicians in this castle who were like her, unique and advanced in their own ways, who she could laugh with—that was hard to digest. It would take this dragonrider a long while to fathom the possibilities of friends. She closed her eyes, hoping that the reality felt as good as the idea.

CHAPTER TWENTY

It took Sophia several seconds to figure out where she was when the morning light streamed across her bed, nearly blinding her.

"Oh, did I wake you?" Ainsley asked in a high-pitched voice. "My apologies, Miss. Someone broke into my pantry, and that had me up early. Guess I forgot the hour."

Sophia sat up, bleary-eyed, seeing spots around the room. "Morning."

"You have peanut butter on your face," the elf said, snapping her fingers at the fire and making the flames jump to life. The ones in the chandelier overhead did the same thing, bringing warmth and light into the cold room.

Sophia blinked until her vision cleared, seeing Lunis' head lying on her bed, his gaze on her. He appeared ready, even if he was still—like something was brewing inside him. She wiped her hand over her mouth, finding that she in fact did have something sticky on her cheek.

"What time is it?" Sophia asked, yawning.

"Early," Ainsley answered. "We don't really pay much attention to time around here because...well, what's the point? We eat when we're hungry and sleep when we're tired. The men train every day, and that's pretty much it. Welcome to monotony."

Sophia's brow scrunched up, picking up on a new bitterness in the housekeeper's voice. "Are you okay, Ains?"

The housekeeper looked over her shoulder, Sophia's dress from the night before in her arms like she was going to launder it. "What did you say?"

"I asked if you were all right?" Sophia repeated.

"No, the second part," the shapeshifter insisted.

"Oh, I guess I called you Ains. My apologies. We tend to shorten names in my family. My sister Olivia became Liv, and I'm Sophia, but they usually call me Soph. And Clark. Well, he's just Clark, but if we could shorten his name, he'd have a fit. He's a bit rigid like that."

"My brother used to call me Ains," the elf said fondly. "I haven't been called that in quite some time. Usually I'm just called 'Would-you.'"

Sophia laughed. "Would-you is a horrible name."

"I agree, S. Beaufont, but if I tell them that, they'll just call me it more. 'Would-you get me more tea?' 'Would-you' clean my boots? 'Would-you stop prancing through the corridor as a bear?" the housekeeper said, doing an impression of the men.

"Why do you call me that?" Sophia asked.

"S. Beaufont?" Ainsley replied. "Well, it is your name, isn't it?"

"Sort of," Sophia stated.

"Well, I just think it suits you. You're the first female dragonrider. I remember when you walked into the Castle. They were all expecting a Steven or a Sam, but little Sophia Beaufont strode over the threshold. It was a beautiful moment." She clapped her hands to her chest, looking up with great fondness.

"That was yesterday," Sophia stated.

Ainsley glanced at her in confusion. Blinked. "Yes, I guess it was. Felt like ages, though. Anyway, you better get up and get ready. Breakfast is going on downstairs. It's always the same spread, the same conversation, and the same humdrum nonsense."

"Sounds fun," Sophia said in a sarcastic tone.

"It isn't," Ainsley said, making for the door. Once there, she turned, offering her a cunning smile. "That's why I can't wait to have you show up and shake things up a bit."

Once Sophia was dressed, she and Lunis found Ainsley in the corridor in the form of a sparrow. The bird chirped at her, and strangely, she knew that meant to follow the housekeeper down to breakfast.

Ainsley flew quickly down the long hallway, making Sophia nearly run to keep up with her. Lunis moved with unique grace, not fast, but making incredible progress.

At the landing of the grand staircase, Sophia paused, admiring a large painting of a man with a huge black dragon. She read the placard beside it: Adam Rivalry and Kay-Rye.

Lunis halted beside her, also immensely intrigued by the painting.

"This wasn't here yesterday, was it?" she asked him.

He simply shook his head.

"Oh, S. Beaufont," Ainsley said from behind her, having turned back into her normal form. "You're not very good at following me or rules, it seems."

Sophia turned, embarrassment covering her face. "I'm sorry. I just—"

The housekeeper burst out laughing. "Don't apologize. I mean, after this, you're on your own as far as getting around the Castle. You'll get lost, but I have every confidence that you and the Castle will get along just fine. I think it likes you."

"You do? Why?" Sophia asked.

Ainsley shook her head. "And as far as rules go, well, they are stuffy devices that Hiker likes to put too much weight on, so break them all you like. Just clean up the pantry the next time you decide to raid it, would you?"

Sophia nodded. "Yes, of course." She pointed over her shoulder. "This painting. It wasn't there yesterday. Why is it here now?"

Fondly, Ainsley glanced at the large portrait of the man and the dragon. "Oh, the Castle is grieving for Adam. It misses him terribly, as do we all. But he was the best amongst us, so it's no surprise."

Sophia hurried down the stairs. "Adam? Did something happen to him recently? Can you tell me about him?"

Ainsley glanced over her shoulder at the dining hall, from which the clanking of dishes and the smell of coffee were wafting through the air. "I best not, S. Hiker hasn't said much, but I don't think he'd like me to indulge you in such things."

"But I thought you just said I should disregard rules?" Sophia challenged. "What about you?"

Ainsley winked at her. "I've already broken a dozen rules this morning. I'm well on my way to reaching my quota. The thing about rule-breaking is that you have to know when to do it and when to not." With that, she pivoted on her heel and hurried down the stairs.

Sophia rushed to keep up with her. "Why did you say the Castle likes me?"

"Because it told me so," Ainsley stated matter-of-factly.

"It can talk?" Sophia asked, wondering why that would be strange, considering everything else she'd learned so far.

"In many ways," Ainsley stated. "The Castle communicates in its own ways, but you have to be willing to see it. I wake up every morning saying, 'I can see the unseen,' and that keeps my eyes open to things the others miss."

It wasn't a spell, but it was absolutely brilliant, Sophia thought. "'I can see the unseen.'"

The shapeshifter nodded. "Keep a lookout and you'll hear the words of the Castle, which will make you wiser than most, not that you aren't already."

"Like the painting of Adam?" Sophia asked. "That's one way it's communicating."

Ainsley peered up the stairs to where the portrait stood. "Yes, that's one way. His room has also been locked, and no spell I can cast opens it. I'm guessing it will stay that way for a long time. A pity, too. He had many important things in there."

"Like what?" Sophia asked, feeling Lunis beside her, his interest also piqued by this news.

"I've said too much already, Miss." Ainsley turned toward the dining room.

Sophia and Lunis exchanged curious expressions. She was so locked in communicating with him silently that she didn't realize everyone had paused as soon as she'd entered the dining hall.

Sensing the new tension, she pulled her gaze from the dragon's. Hiker's teacup was hovering just in front of his face. Evan appeared to be in mid-chew. Wilder's mouth was simply hanging open, and Mahkah's pastry was pinched in his hand, unmoving.

Sophia looked over her shoulder to see if there was a large bear lurking behind her. There wasn't.

"What?" she asked, turning back to them and peering down at her outfit, wondering if she'd put on her armored top backward.

Ainsley, who had disappeared into the kitchen, strode back in carrying a large tray of meat. "Oh, they just aren't used to seeing something so pretty. Oh, and you're wearing that strange thing we're not used to."

Sophia's brow scrunched as she studied her outfit, trying to figure out what Ainsley meant.

Wilder snapped his fingers repeatedly. "Yeah, what's that thing called?"

Evan shook his head. "It's been too long. I can't remember."

Ainsley set the tray down in front of Lunis and hurried back toward the kitchen. "Color. She's wearing color. It is nearly burning my eyes."

It suddenly made sense to Sophia. Her top was blue mixed with silver. She studied the men, who were all wearing grays or browns. She shook her head. "Well, I can help you all diversify your wardrobes. I'm pretty good with style."

"Fashion should never be a concern of a rider," Hiker pronounced bitterly.

Evan turned to the Viking. "Oh, I don't know. I think you'd look stunning in mossy green. I bet it would make Bell fly faster, too."

Sophia wanted to respond to Hiker's blatant attack on her personality and interests, but she held her tongue. She wanted him to warm up to her, not hate her guts, although he wasn't endearing himself to her either.

"Now, Lunis, my lovely," Ainsley began, carrying in another tray and placing it in front of the dragon, who had already polished off the first course. "I have a rack of ribs and some other sizable parts of a cow I slaughtered for you this morning."

"Dragons should be doing their own slaughtering," Hiker snapped, finishing his tea.

Ainsley turned to face him, her hand on her hips. "Were you hunting your own food when you were less than a week old? No, I believe you were sucking your mum's—"

"It smells like something is burning," Hiker interrupted, his nostrils flaring. "Would you go check on it?"

Ainsley's eyes skipped to Sophia, a slight smile in her eyes. "Of course, sir. Would-you, at your service."

"Lunis is perfectly on track as far as development goes," Mahkah offered, his tone calm. "Of course, I'd like to do an assessment soon, if that's all right with you, Sophia."

She looked at Lunis before nodding. "Yes, we're fine with that."

Hiker's eyes slid between the dragon and Sophia. She was going to ask why he had such a strange expression on his face, but

Wilder took her opportunity, tapping on the table in front of Mahkah. "Well, they've already mastered telepathy, so I'd say he's on track. I think Coral is still trying to achieve that with Evan, but since the bloke has no thoughts in his head, it's difficult."

Mahkah didn't laugh, although he appeared slightly amused.

"Ha-ha," Evan stated, cleaning his plate and looking around the table for something else to eat.

"You better pull up a seat, or there won't be anything left," Ainsley said, coming back from the kitchen carrying a tray of fresh fruits and cheeses.

A loud burp fell out of Evan's mouth as he stuck his fork in a piece of ham. He jumped, and his gaze snapped to Hiker. "What did you do that for?"

He simply shrugged. "Oh, did I? No reason, you mannerless twit."

Evan rubbed his leg under the table. "Since when were manners a thing around here?" His chin slid to the side until he saw Sophia taking the seat next to Mahkah. "Oh, right. Guess we have to be on our best behavior now that we dine with royalty."

Hiker sighed. "It wouldn't kill you to show a little decorum."

Evan grimaced. "It might, actually."

Sophia almost started when Quiet took the seat next to her soundlessly. She smiled at the gnome. "Good morning."

He looked as though he'd just come in from the cold, his nose red and his clothing damp.

He simply nodded, looking around the table at the spread that was quickly dwindling. There was less than a spoonful of eggs left, and only the burned bacon remained. However, no one had touched the fruit, so she decided to load up on that.

"Who wants the last pastry?" Evan asked, pointing to the lone muffin lying on the tray of crumbs.

Quiet held up his short arm and mumbled something inaudible.

"Anyone?" Evan glanced around, his gaze avoiding the gnome. "Just speak up if you want it."

The others kept their focus on their own food, most of them shoveling bites into their mouths.

Again, Quiet waved his hand, muttering something.

"Well, if no one wants it, I'll just help myself to a third," Evan stated, grabbing the pastry and taking a bite.

"What the…" Sophia's eyes filled with rage.

Lunis rose at Evan's back, making both him and Wilder, who were sitting together on that side of the table, tense.

"Quiet wanted that pastry," Sophia fired at him.

Evan swallowed without chewing, looking over his shoulder at the dragon, who was close to towering over him. "He didn't say anything."

Sophia spied Hiker sitting back in his chair, watching this exchange. "You know as well as everyone else at the table that he asked for it by holding up his hand and saying something."

"Well, he should have spoken up," Evan declared, taking another bite of the pastry. He was trying to act casual, although his eyes kept drifting to Lunis, who hadn't stood down.

Wilder edged his chair over slightly, trying to put distance between him and his friend.

"I heard him, and that was quite rude," Sophia stated.

Evan smiled, then laughed, looking at Lunis. "It was a joke. It's a game Quiet and I play."

"No, it was mean-spirited," Sophia said, demanding Evan's attention. "No one likes to be mistreated."

She leaned forward, thinking she had to have a more intimidating appearance than even her dragon.

Evan hid a shiver as he put the half-eaten pastry on his plate and pushed it away. "Well, Hiker, look at the new rider," he said, smiling at their leader. "She likes to stick up for the little guys."

"Do you really allow him to act like such a fool?" Sophia asked Hiker.

The Viking simply shook his head, standing from the table. He leveled his gaze at Lunis, who still appeared ready to attack either Evan or Hiker, depending on Sophia's command. Hiker stepped to the right as if trying to get around the dragon, but he simply copied the movements. He then took a step back, but Lunis took a pace forward.

Finally, Hiker turned to face Sophia. "In a hundred years, I've had zero success with trying to get Evan to act like anything but a buffoon. Now, when you're done, you and your dragon will join me out front."

Sophia blinked up at him. "For what?" she asked with anticipation, hoping her training would start.

"For a tour, of course," he said, striding around the other side of the table to avoid Lunis as he took his leave.

Sophia didn't take a single bite of her food. Instead, she rose and followed Hiker out. Lunis breathed hard, sending hot air over Evan before taking off after Sophia.

It was early, and both rider and dragon were eager to learn more about the Gullington.

CHAPTER TWENTY-ONE

Cold like Sophia had never felt before whacked her in the face when she left the Castle. She pulled her cloak tighter around her neck, but it did little good. The wind seemed to find its way through tiny crevices, piercing her skin and settling in her bones.

"This place is no joke," she said to Lunis. He had his face up to the sky and a pleasant expression on it as if the icy winds were a thoughtful greeting from the heavens.

"It was once thought that the weather here would harden our riders, preparing them for flight," Lunis informed her, once again pulling from the collective consciousness of the dragons. Sophia had wondered lately why he didn't fill her in on the history or the purpose of the riders, but he seemed to have a need to keep some things to himself. Many in the magical world were this way, so Sophia didn't push things.

Although the sky was covered in clouds, obscuring the sun, the light hurt Sophia's eyes when she tried looking out at the grounds spreading around the Castle. She reasoned that it was because of the reflection off the sea of green that went on for miles and miles.

Standing with his back to the Castle and staring off at the mountains was Hiker Wallace. He wasn't wrapped in a traveling cloak or shivering like Sophia. When she strode up next to him, he was sweating as if he'd just run a race.

"I'm here," she said, trying to hide the chatter of her teeth.

"What spell did you just use?" Hiker asked, continuing to stare out at the rolling green hills.

Sophia pursed her lips, thinking. "What do you mean? I didn't use a spell."

He narrowed his eyes as if she wasn't telling him the truth. "How come you didn't make any noise when you approached just now?"

Sophia was going to answer, but Lunis cut her off. "Because she isn't a clumsy orangutan."

This seemed to anger Hiker more. "Your dragon makes jokes."

Smiling fondly at Lunis, she nodded. "Sometimes he even plays practical jokes. There was this one time—"

"Oh, Angels above," Hiker said, staring up to the heavens with a pleading expression on his face.

"I don't understand. Are dragons not allowed to have personalities?" Sophia asked.

"Why do giraffes eat the leaves on the tops of trees?" Hiker returned as if this was the answer to her question.

She shrugged. "Because they are so tall. That makes the most sense."

"If your dragon were a giraffe, he would eat from the bottom of the trees."

Now it was Sophia's turn to narrow her eyes at the Viking. "So there's only one way to do things here, is it? Either we act like you, or we are wrong? In the world I come from, there's more than one way to skin a cat."

Hiker was undeterred. "I'm not sure of this world of yours if they skin cats. Apparently, the modern world isn't that civilized after all."

"It's an expression," Sophia said, laughing. She couldn't stop herself. "And you can turn your nose up at Lunis for being different. Judge me for whatever reason you like. But we'd like a tour of the Gullington, regardless."

Hiker seemed to be wrestling internally with something. "Fine, but it's an arduous trek to the Cave. You'll have to keep up."

Sophia set off beside the large man. Even though his long strides were double hers, she had no trouble staying beside him, even when they began to climb up a steep hill. Easily she asked, "What is this land?"

"We call it the Expanse," Hiker said, and she caught a hint of breathiness in his voice. "It's the grounds Quiet takes care of."

"And the Expanse and the Castle are all inside the Barrier?" Sophia asked, watching as Lunis lifted off the ground slightly, his wings carrying him over the stony path, although he wasn't technically flying. More like gliding.

"Yes, and that is all part of what we call the Gullington," Hiker said with pride. "It has been the home of the Dragon Elite for as long as we've existed."

Sophia sucked in a breath when they reached the top of the incline. The sharp inhale wasn't because she was winded from the steep ascent. It was because of the unbounded beauty she saw from the top.

Hills so round they looked too perfect to be real spread out in all directions, cascading one on top of the other like a child's drawing. They continued for miles until plunging into a lake of placid water. Much like the hills at their back, the water seemed to go on forever, similar to the ocean, not even ending at the horizon.

Straight in front of them was the largest of the hills, which rose sharply. At its top were large boulders and an opening.

"That's the Cave?" Sophia asked.

Hiker nodded, pausing as they looked out. Maybe he was appreciating the view, as was Sophia. Or maybe he was catching his breath, based on the heavy rise and fall of his chest.

"How will we get up there?" Sophia asked, looking for a path up the steep hill similar to the one they just climbed.

"We don't," he answered. "No rider has ever been up to the Cave. It is not our home. Just as dragons don't go into the Castle, we do not go into their dwelling."

Sophia turned to Lunis, who, she was relieved to see, wasn't deterred by the leader's sullen nature. "Maybe we should get an Airbnb since you're breaking so many rules by being in the Castle."

She was certain he'd make a joke about how they would lose their deposit on that rental, but Hiker cut in before the dragon could respond.

"I'm not sure what this air-thing is that you speak of," he said. "But I've decided to allow Lunis to stay in the Castle until he is strong enough to fly up to the Caves, even if I do believe he could climb up there."

Sophia kept her sarcastic retort locked inside her mouth. "And when does a dragon start flying?" She'd asked Lunis already, but he hadn't given her an answer, whether because he didn't know or didn't want her to know, she wasn't sure.

Hiker cut his eyes at Lunis, who had his head up high and his nostrils flared as he smelled the fresh air. "I don't know. All of our dragons had matured in this way when they magnetized to us."

"If we aren't allowed in the Cave, how do we meet the other dragons?" Sophia asked.

One of his eyebrows raised sharply. "Meet the other dragons? You won't. They have little interest in a brand-new rider and an inexperienced dragon who can't even fly." Hiker pointed toward the large body of water. "It's three miles to that bluff. That's where we are headed next. Watch your feet. The stones here are unforgiving for those who don't know how to handle the uneven terrain."

Sophia, having grown up locked inside the House of Fourteen most of her life, hadn't been hiking...well, ever. Her siblings had been protective of her, not allowing her out on field trips. It wasn't until Liv came back into her life that she was taken out of the House on adventures, but that was usually only down to West Hollywood or around Santa Monica. Still, as Sophia crossed the Expanse, she felt born for such treks.

The demanding wind sped past her face, whipping her hair and barreling into her shoulders. And yet, she loved the feeling like it was reminiscent of a home she'd never known.

At one point, she found herself passing Hiker on the path. She slowed to ensure she didn't get too far ahead of him.

"So, you're quiet on your feet and hike with an agile grace," he observed. It didn't sound like a compliment, the way he said it.

"She was born a dragonrider," Lunis stated when they came to the bottom of the steep hill.

"We were all born that way," Hiker argued.

Lunis swung his head around to face the man. "No, you became that and were chosen. Sophia Beaufont was born with the traits it took you fifty years to hone."

Hiker pressed his lips together. "I'm not sure I'd count that as a compliment. She was born with talents instead of achieving them."

"I think I would," Lunis argued, smoke billowing from his nostrils. "If any others had been born the same as her, they would have been ruined by this point. From an early age, she could have anything that magic could bring her. What would most children do with that power? Hiker, what would you have done with that?"

The Viking lowered his chin, letting out a very long breath. His eyes shifted back and forth before he swung around and strode over the slick earth. "We will walk in silence for the rest of the way to the Pond, so as to not disturb the flock."

Sophia didn't know what he meant until a herd of sheep grazed over the rolling hill where they stood. The sea of white, puffy sheep was such a beautiful contrast to the bright green hills that Sophia halted, taking in the pristine sight. The animals were peaceful and moved as if they were one, although there had to be hundreds. Maybe even a thousand.

Once she'd collected herself from the sight, she caught up to Hiker, who took a detour around the herd, allowing them to pass in front as he took the path to the left, veering toward the Pond.

As if on autopilot, Sophia's boots carried her easily beside Hiker as she eagerly watched the animals trotting beside one another, fluffy and mild. She'd never seen a sheep in real life, having been sheltered. Not only was hiking something new to her, but farm animals, exotic cities, and pretty much anything that couldn't be found in the strange labyrinth known as the House of Fourteen or the city of Los Angeles were new as well.

She was mesmerized by the way the herd moved. The sheep baahed, making a music unlike anything she'd ever heard. Strangely she was grateful that Hiker had forbidden talking. The peace that came with striding across the Expanse toward the Pond and watching the herd was a brand new experience.

The dark shadow that crossed overhead was gone by the time she snapped her head up. A figure, dark and majestic, swooped down on the herd of white fluffballs, making them scatter. It didn't matter because a second later, a large white dragon dove, grabbing a sheep with its claws.

The animal screamed, a sharp, pleading sound. The dragon's expansive wings flapped several times, carrying it higher. It brought its front legs up, its teeth ripping into the sheep's neck, spilling blood through the air. It splattered onto the pristine green grass below as the herd scattered to the other side of the hill.

Hiker halted, holding his hand up to shield his eyes as he watched the dragon's path toward the cave. "That's about as close as you'll get to one of the other dragons, Lunis."

As if the dragon had heard him, it changed trajectory, flying in their direction all of a sudden. Sophia was struck by the beauty of the creature. It wasn't even the piercing blue of its eyes that hit her, or how its shimmering white scales seemed to blur into the cloud-covered sky behind it. There was something about the dragon that was inherently beautiful, separate from the way it looked on the outside.

It landed only a few yards from them, wringing out the limp sheep's dead body as if for good measure. It dropped the carcass at its feet, turning its large face to the side as it studied Lunis as if trying to understand what he was. The dragon was at least twenty feet long and had to weigh three times more than Lunis, yet Sophia thought it was trying to decide whether it was safe to approach him.

Its head moved forward slightly, still at an angle. Sophia didn't get the impression that Lunis was nervous. Instead, she felt his pulse as if it were her own, steady and calm.

"Simi," Hiker said in an authoritative voice. "This is—"

"I know," the dragon replied, cutting off the leader of the Elite. "We've been waiting for Lunis to show up."

The dragon kicked the body of the sheep to the side as if it was in her way as she took tentative steps forward.

"You've been waiting?" Hiker asked. He held up his arm and let out a strange whistle through his teeth.

From the Cave, a large red-scaled dragon emerged, flying with incredible speed in their direction. The creature landed beside Hiker, her head turning to the side with a strange rhythm as she regarded the rider beside her, but then she switched her focus to Lunis. She sidestepped until she was right beside Simi.

Before Sophia could ask what was going on, two more dragons emerged from the Cave, one brown and the other purple. They landed on either side of their companions, their ancient eyes on Lunis.

He didn't move from Sophia's side, and nothing was said for a long moment. Hiker looked at the four regal dragons and Lunis as if listening to a strange conversation that Sophia couldn't hear. Finally, he centered his gaze on the youngest blue dragon.

"They know you," he said in disbelief.

"As I have known them for all my lives," he stated simply.

Hiker continued to look back and forth between the creatures towering like small buildings on the hill in front of them. "But they don't understand you."

Lunis nodded slightly. "I am different."

Sophia had so many questions that she finally couldn't hold them all in. "Lunis, what's going on? Why are they staring at you like that?" She wasn't sure if she should be worried for her dragon, who was much smaller and wouldn't last a moment if caught in a fight with four full-grown dragons.

As she'd seen the other dragons move their necks, he swung his head around to face her. "They aren't staring at me, Sophia. They are looking at you."

CHAPTER TWENTY-TWO

Sophia raised her hand to her forehead. "What? Why? You're the new dragon."

So only she could hear it, he said, *But we've known each other. You are the one they haven't yet met.*

"Yes, but..." she argued, staring at the strange and perfectly beautiful creatures in front of her who she didn't fear, although she knew that was the emotion they elicited from all other humans on Earth.

Hiker stumbled back several feet.

Sophia turned to face him. "Where are you going?"

"I'll be right here," he said, an urgent look on his face as he ushered her forward with a wave of his hands. "But Lunis is right. Bell wants to meet you."

Sophia spun to face her dragon. "But why?"

He simply blinked at her, an expression that said, "Why do you think?"

Sophia drew a breath and started forward, realizing she was doing something of great significance. When she was only a few feet from the dragons, she went down on one knee, bowing her head and making herself vulnerable in front of the oldest magical creatures on the planet. "It's an honor to meet you. I am—"

"The youngest dragonrider in history," the white dragon known as Simi stated. Sophia knew the dragon's name and that she was female without knowing how.

"The first female to ride," Bell, Hiker's dragon, added. She was also female.

"The only one to magnetize to an egg in the Elite," the purple dragon known as Coral stated. Another female.

The one with brown scales and eyes like amber stepped forward, kneeling like Sophia. His name was Tala. "And the one we've been waiting for. Welcome, Sophia Beaufont."

She looked up suddenly. "You've been waiting for me?"

The other three dragons kneeled, joining Tala and bowing their heads to the young woman before them. When they rose, Bell, the oldest of them, stepped forward. "Yes. You are the one who should change," her green eyes flickered to Hiker, "that which no others have been able to change, however they've tried."

Sophia didn't know what to say. She wanted to tell them they had her confused with someone else, or that they were putting too much importance on her, but as she regarded the wisdom of the creatures in front of her, she knew she couldn't.

Hiker took the spot next to Sophia once more. "She has much to learn. Lunis isn't even ready—"

A roar unlike anything Sophia had ever heard ripped from the brown dragon, scorching the ground as fire spilled from his mouth and stopped inches from Hiker's boots. To his credit, he didn't flinch at nearly being burned alive. Instead, he glanced up. Swallowed. Nodded.

"Very well," he said, unnerved. "But this changes nothing."

"We shall see," Simi said. She picked up the dead sheep and took off, flying toward the Cave. The other dragons sprang off up, changing their course once in the air and following the white dragon into the Cave.

Sophia watched as they disappeared, wondering what she'd missed and what had happened. She turned to Hiker to ask, but he simply waved them forward.

"Come on," he said, urging her toward the Pond.

The hike across the Expanse to the water took no time for Sophia. It was probably because her head was teeming with tons of questions. She suddenly was full of regret. Maybe she should have asked the dragons questions or said more. Or done more.

It had all gone by too fast. Over and over, her mind reviewed the beautiful details of the creatures she'd met. They were unlike anything she'd heard or read about. They were better in person. Although she knew Lunis, she couldn't fathom that he would one day be like them, and yet, she instinctively knew he'd be like them, but better.

When they were at the bluff that overlooked the Pond, Hiker stopped, looking out with great pride. He remained quiet for a long moment. Sophia somehow knew not to interrupt. Instead, she took the spot next to him and watched the placid water reflect the clouds overhead.

"You will start training tomorrow," he finally said.

She started inside but remained still on the outside. "I thought you—"

"Things have changed," he cut in.

"Once my training is complete, when do I start my missions?" Sophia asked.

"Missions?" Hiker shook his head. "There are no missions. Not anymore. Just be grateful that you'll start training."

"What do we do if we don't go on missions?" she questioned. "What does the Dragon Elite do?"

"We simply exist," he said, his hands behind his back as he turned and strode for the Castle. When he was a few yards away, he swung around. "Stay out here as long as you like. I suspect you can find your way back on your own."

Sophia nodded, knowing that sitting on this bluff with her dragon beside her was all she wanted for the next several hours. There was a lot to take in.

She glanced at the Cave in the distance. And there was a lot to process.

CHAPTER TWENTY-THREE

Sophia and Lunis sat on the bluff, gazing out at what felt like the edge of the Earth until the sunset. Not until they had started back for the Castle did Sophia realize she was starving, having skipped breakfast and lunch.

When she entered the Castle, she found the candles blown out in the dining hall. "We must have missed dinner too," she said with disappointment to Lunis. The front rooms of the Castle appeared deserted. "It seems no one was worried that we got lost out there or fell off the edge of the bluff."

"Ainsley set us out food in your room," he said, nodding toward the stairs.

"How do you know?" she asked.

"I can smell it," he stated.

"Okay, well, let's hope we don't get lost trying to find my room. I'll starve to death. You'll have to drag me to safety."

"Or leave you," he said matter-of-factly.

She gave him a look of offense. "Thanks a lot, my fair-weather friend."

"Hey, I'm hungry, too, and still growing."

"Yeah, sorry for keeping us out so long," she said as they climbed the stairs.

"Don't be," he offered. "You needed to process."

"I did," she agreed. "But I'd need another few days out there to do that fully."

"Whatever you need," he replied thoughtfully.

"Well, tomorrow training starts, so no more reflection for me," she said, looking back and forth when she got to the second-floor landing. Before, the hallway had split in two, and her room was to the left. However, there were three halls now. She could go straight, whereas that hadn't been an option before, and the corridor to the left didn't look like the one before with the statue of the centaur and the winged horse.

"Ainsley told me to appear to be lost for the Castle's benefit, but I don't think I'll have to pretend," she said, rotating in a full circle. "Do you know which way to go?"

"All hallways will get us there," Lunis stated.

Sophia gave him a frustrated expression, hunger getting the better of her. "Yes, they will also get us to Rome. But which is the most direct route?"

"Direct is a relative term," he replied.

"Seriously, are we going to have a philosophical conversation right now?" Sophia demanded.

"Well, it's true. One path might be direct but riddled with hidden dangers. The longer route might be smooth, without any delays."

She shook her head and went the hall that led straight ahead. A colorful light shone across the floor in front of her. From a distance, it appeared to be drifting water. When Sophia got close, she realized it was the moonlight cascading through a large stained-glass window. Similar to the one in the front door, this one also was a depiction of an angel, its wings spread and eyes staring up.

"What's the deal with Angels here?" Sophia asked.

"It is believed that they watch over and protect the riders," Lunis offered.

"What about everyone else, like mortals and other magical creatures?" Sophia questioned.

"Other entities watch over them," Lunis answered. "The House, for instance, presides over the magical world."

"And mortals?" Sophia asked.

He lumbered forward, not answering her question.

"I just love it when you ignore me," she said, dragging herself after him.

"Oh, good. I'll keep doing it, then," he joked.

Sophia's stomach rumbled when they reached a bend in the hallway. She sighed. This wasn't the corridor where her room was. "Ugh. I really don't want to hunt around all night for my room."

The hall in front of her blurred, making her blink to clear her vision. When things sharpened again, the statue of the centaur and the winged horse stood at the end of the corridor. She startled with disbelief. "Did the Castle just reorganize itself?"

"Well, you said you didn't want to hunt around anymore, and it appears to have honored that request."

Sophia smiled and hurried toward her room.

She was grateful to find a tray of roast beef sandwiches on the table in front of the fireplace when she entered. Also beside the hearth was a huge tray of meat. Lunis settled down, taking up more room than he had that morning. He wasn't going to fit in there much longer, and they both knew it.

Sophia didn't breathe properly until she'd finished two sandwiches. Then she picked up the book that was beside the tray, *The Incomplete History of Dragonriders*.

Randomly she flipped it open, strangely arriving at the chapter on angels.

Lunis pulled his face away from his dinner. "It's similar to Bermuda Lauren's book, *Mysterious Creatures*."

"It supplies the reader with what they are currently thinking about or most want to know?" Sophia asked, pouring a cup of tea. Her sister Liv worked with Bermuda, the giantess who was an expert on magical creatures. Her book, which was seemingly never-ending, was the premier source on all things related to magical creatures.

Sophia read the first passage on angels aloud. "As the adjudicators of the mortal world, dragonriders are thought to have an impeccable moral code. This, legend has it, is a result of the angel blood that flows through their veins."

She glanced up. "Wait, I wasn't descended from angels. I have the founders' blood. I'm from the original Seven of the House."

"Keep reading," Lunis said, licking a femur bone on the tray.

"When the Archangel Michael fell during a battle, his blood seeped into the Earth. It then spread, finding the thousand dragon eggs scattered across the planet."

She looked up. "Wait, there were once a thousand dragons eggs spread across the Earth?"

"That was how it started," Lunis explained. "That was how we began. With one thousand eggs. There will never be any more. Like a woman starts her life with as many eggs as she will ever have, the planet started with as many dragon eggs as it would ever have. No more will be created."

"Wow, so that's why many thought dragons were extinct," Sophia said, thinking of the other eggs she'd seen when she magnetized to Lunis' egg.

"Yes, but we aren't. And there are more eggs out there, but *when* they hatch is always the question."

She returned to the text. "The blood of the archangel infiltrated the dragon's eggs, all one thousand of them. It is believed that a dragon and their rider share the same blood once magnetized, therefore, the blood of the Archangel Michael flows in the rider's veins, protecting them in ways no other magical creature can be."

Sophia suddenly felt breathless. "So we're adjudicators. But what does that mean?"

"You're judges presiding over mortal affairs," Lunis offered.

"Like Judge Judy in small claims court?" she questions.

He rolled his eyes. "Yes, you're a sensational judge who uses fast quips to deal with trivial issues."

"Okay, I get that we're not like a television judge. I'm just trying to understand. This is the first time anyone has taken the opportunity to explain to me what the dragonriders do."

"Well," Lunis said, pushing the tray out of his way so he could lie down properly, "it seems as though you don't do anything presently."

"Yeah, about that," Sophia stated. "Why?"

"I think you'll have to do more investigating to find out." He indicated the crook he had created between his front and back feet. "Speaking of television, why don't you come curl up here, and we'll watch some YouTube?"

Sophia smiled. "My phone doesn't work here, remember? I need Liv to fix it."

"Try creating a hotspot," he suggested.

She laughed. "I can't believe the ancient dragon is offering tech advice to me. But your logic is flawed. If it doesn't work then how am I going to create a hotspot?"

"Again, I'm not your typical dragon," he stated. "And try using magic."

"Yeah, but the dragons today didn't seem to notice that you're different," she said, stretching.

"They did, but they don't know how to deal with it yet. It's very similar to how Hiker feels about you."

"Yes, I think I challenge that man on every level." Sophia nestled against Lunis but found that the floor under her was hard, especially after her long day of hiking and sitting on the bluff overlooking the Pond. She glanced around, looking for something to soften her seat.

When she couldn't find anything, she said, "I wished I had that beanbag from my room at Liv's."

"Summon it," Lunis suggested.

"I don't know," Sophia said carefully. "I'm not sure the Castle will like me filling it with modern furniture. Can you just imagine what a beanbag will look like in here?"

"Comfortable," Lunis said, gazing around the room.

She shrugged. "Fine. Castle, do you mind if I add a few personal effects to the space?" Sophia glanced around as if waiting for a reply. "It's not that I don't like your furnishings. It's just that I think it will make me feel more at home if I have something—"

As if in response to her question, the two tufted armchairs moved to the side, making room for a third. Sophia grinned and rose from her place next to Lunis. "Thanks, Castle. I think we're going to get along swell. You're very reasonable." She pointed to the spot beside her dragon and conjured the pink beanbag from Liv's place. It looked utterly ridiculous in the room filled with old furniture. However, when she settled into it, it felt utterly perfect, as if it absolutely belonged in the space.

"Okay," Sophia said, pulling out her phone. "Hotspot inside a Castle." She glanced up. "Oh, is that okay, Castle? Can I bring modern technology in here?"

Sophia waited for an answer. Lunis rested his heavy head on her shoulder and muttered, "I think that was a yes."

"I didn't hear anything," she stated.

"I did," he stated. "Shhh. Listen." The dragon then whispered from the corner of his mouth, "Do, it, Sophia."

She gave him a sideways expression. "Are you serious? You're trying to pull some ventriloquism weirdness on me."

"No," he lied. "That was the Castle."

"Fine," Sophia stated. "I'll create a hotspot, but if the Castle gets mad at me, you're taking the heat."

"Not a problem," he said, looking over his shoulder at the fire behind them. "Now pull up that video of the cat powering up his bite. That one always makes me laugh."

CHAPTER TWENTY-FOUR

The opening door woke Sophia. She'd fallen asleep lying against Lunis, his head in her lap.

Ainsley smiled as she magically opened the curtains and lit the fire. "Well, that is about the sweetest thing I've ever seen. Nothing like a girl and her dragon. Wouldn't kill the boys to cuddle with their dragons every once in a while."

Sophia yawned as Lunis raised his head, blinking awake. "Oh, we fell asleep watching YouTube."

The housekeeper nodded as if this made perfect sense. "Me too."

"You did?" Sophia asked, pushing up.

"No, actually." Ainsley shook her head. "I don't know what that is. I just wanted to relate. I fell asleep after reading the same book for the hundredth time."

"No wonder," Sophia related. "I'd fall asleep too if I read a book that many times."

Ainsley admired the still-made bed, not needing to do any work to straighten it. "Well, we are a bit limited on new materials here, although every now and again, I pick up something new to read in the village, not that their selection is very large. Hiker, of course, doesn't like it when I bring new things into the Castle. He says new stuff messes with the energy of this place." She looked around with a sigh. "Yes, the energy here is really in jeopardy of being hurt."

"Oh," Sophia said, a nervous expression on her face as she tried to hide the pink beanbag behind her.

"What's that?" Ainsley asked, pointing at the beanbag.

Sophia turned. "That?" she asked. "Oh, that's Lunis. He's a dragon. They are quite rare."

Ainsley laughed, then strode over and stood next to Sophia. "No, I think we both know I'm talking about the bright pink blob beside your dragon."

"Oh, that." Sophia raised her hand and directed her magic at the beanbag. "Well, that's nothing. I will just be sending it back to my old home."

Ainsley knocked Sophia's hand to the side. "No, don't. I'm curious. What is it?"

"Well, it's a chair of sorts," Sophia explained. "I curled up with Lunis last night, and we watched YouTube."

"Is that why it smells like magic in here?" The shapeshifter sniffed the air.

Sophia gave her a nervous expression. "Yes, I created a hotspot so my phone could work and we could watch cat videos on YouTube."

Ainsley nodded like this made perfect sense. "It costs you a great deal of magic to do that, it seems. Are you sure it was worth it?"

"You obviously haven't watched funny cat videos on YouTube," Sophia stated, pulling her phone from her back pocket. "Check this out."

Ainsley's laughter echoed all the way down the hall when they arrived at the bottom of the stairs. "I can't believe he just kept chasing his tail," she remarked to Sophia.

"Who?" Evan asked, looking up from the breakfast table. "Lunis? I guess that's normal for young dragons."

Sophia shook her head. "No. We were talking about…" Her voice trailed off, catching the serious expression on Hiker's face.

"Talking about what?" he asked, his eyes narrowed.

"Oh, there's this thing called YouTube on S. Beaufont's phone," Ainsley said, still laughing. "There are videos of cats doing the silliest things, as well as music videos of this girl named Taylor Swift. And S says there are these other videos of pandas being right pains in the ass to their zookeepers. I can't wait to watch those."

Hiker drew in a long breath. "Are you the reason the Castle has done this?" He pulled a Kindle from his pocket and slammed it on the table.

Sophia's eyes darted around. "I don't think so, but maybe."

"What is that?" Wilder asked, squinting at the device.

"I'm not sure, but when I went to my library this morning, all my books were gone. Hundreds of old, one-of-a-kind books had vanished, but lying on my desk was this thing," Hiker answered. "I'm guessing it's the Castle's doing, but it got the idea from somewhere."

"It's a Kindle," Sophia said, impressed by the Castle's knowledge of the modern world. She guessed it was connected to everything and therefore had the knowledge, even if it didn't usually use it.

"I once dated a girl named Kendal," Evan bragged.

"You did not," Wilder spat. "You stalked her by night, which is creepy and not what dating is, you loon."

"I was going to ask her out, but then she got married to some bloke with his own carriage and house," Evan stated sullenly. "Alas, it wasn't meant to be."

Hiker's fingers rapped on the table. "Do you want to explain this?" he asked, his heated gaze on Sophia.

She looked at Lunis, who had trudged in after her and Ainsley. He'd already settled in front of his platters of meat, and it didn't appear as if he were going to help her.

"Well," Sophia began. "I'm guessing that all your books are on the Kindle now. It's an electronic reading device that stores thousands of books. Makes for a really compact library. Isn't that cool?"

From the expression on Hiker's face, he didn't think it was cool. "Electronic? Device? Are you serious? Did you bring technology here?"

"And she's got this really cool beanbag," Ainsley said, excitedly. "I sat in it when I watched YouTube while she showered. It's really comfortable."

"Are you serious?" Hiker asked again.

"I know." Ainsley nodded. "She showers every day. Can you believe it? Fresh clothes on this one too. I can hardly believe it myself. She smells like summer rain."

Wilder leaned over, giving Sophia a whiff. "Very nice."

She grimaced at him. "Don't ever do that again."

"Until you beg me, I won't," he stated cordially.

She pulled a few pieces of bacon onto her plate, pretending she didn't notice Hiker's searing eyes on her.

"I don't want technology in here," he said finally, breaking the lovely silence building between everyone.

"I did ask the Castle first," Sophia stated, keeping her eyes low as she spooned potatoes onto her plate and grabbed a pastry. She wasn't going to skip breakfast again.

"The Castle isn't in charge here," Hiker shot back.

As if in rebuttal, something happened to his chair. He grabbed the table to steady himself, his eyes wide.

"Everything okay there, Hiker?" Ainsley asked, tilting her head to the side, hiding a grin.

"It's fine," he said, pushing to his feet and kicking the broken chair out behind him, where it fell to the floor. "And I don't want you filling your room with any more bean sacks."

"Beanbags," Ainsley corrected.

Hiker scolded her with a look.

She threw up her hands and made her way to the kitchen. "I'm just trying to help. I don't want you to look a fool when we finally enter the twenty-first century."

His eyes drifted back to Sophia. "We've been doing just fine with the things we've had, and without electronic libraries. They aren't good for the dragons."

"Actually," Mahkah cut in, but receiving a stern expression from Hiker, he shook his head. "I'll have to do more research on the matter, *actually*, is what I was going to say."

"Either way," Hiker began, looking straight at Sophia, "I'd appreciate it if you didn't bring any more things into the Castle that don't belong."

"How do I know what's on that list?" Sophia asked. "I simply brought in a chair from my old home. This morning, I conjured the clothes I'm wearing. I needed some female stuff also. Should I clear those things with you directly? Like eyelash curlers, body spray, and—"

"No, no, no," Hiker replied in a rush. "Fine, bring in the things you need. But limit it, would you? You're having an effect on the Castle. I don't even know how to find my books on this thing." He pointed to the Kindle, which was still lying on the table.

"I can show you," Sophia offered. "It's quite easy."

"I don't want you to show me," he spat. "I want my books back."

"I don't think she's hurting the Castle, actually," Wilder cut in. "I mean, for a nice change of pace, the..." The smoldering expression Hiker shot him silenced the rider immediately. Wilder shook his head. "As I was saying, Sophia, your voodoo won't be tolerated here. I, for one, am tired of the Castle illuminating the floorboards when I stagger to the bathroom at night. That was a really strange trick it did last night. Totally off-putting, if incredibly convenient. I didn't stub a single toe."

Evan laughed. "I thought I'd had too much whiskey. The Castle did that to me too last night."

"Those are nightlights activated by motion sensors," Sophia supplied. "We had them at my old home in Los Angeles. I don't know how it's doing it without electricity, though."

"It's called magic," Evan said, cramming his mouth with bacon. "It's like electricity, but better."

"What I'd like to know," Mahkah said thoughtfully, "is how is the Castle getting all this information from Sophia."

"It's pulling it from her subconscious," Ainsley stated, returning from the kitchen. "Or, more likely, from Lunis'. It's a very intuitive being." She looked up at the walls proudly.

"So just by being here, it's picking up on things from her modern life?" Wilder asked. Then seeing the still-annoyed expression on Hiker's face, he added, "Like those horrible nightlights, and thousands of books in a tiny little device?" He shook his head and looked straight at Sophia. "You are a witch of the worst kind. Shut your mind and keep your conveniences out of this drafty place, would you?"

Hiker let out a growl. "We will continue this discussion later. For now, I want you all off to training."

With that, he strode from the dining hall, just as Quiet entered. His cheeks were red and his clothes damp again, having returned from the Expanse.

"Last pastry, anyone?" Evan called, holding it up.

As before, Quiet waddled over to the table, inaudibly laying claim to the pastry.

"Oh, well, if no one wants it," Evan stated, and stuck it in his mouth, rising from the table and taking off after Hiker.

Sophia shook her head and handed her plate to Quiet when he sat. She'd eaten the bacon and potatoes, but sitting beside the crumbs was an untouched pastry.

CHAPTER TWENTY-FIVE

The Expanse was somehow even more beautiful than the day before. The unforgiving wind whipped through the trees, making the fields of grass look like green waves on the ocean.

Sophia stood on the front steps of the Castle, wondering where this training was supposed to take place. She'd charged out of the dining hall before the others and now didn't know what to do. Lunis was still finishing, leaving Sophia looking out at the Expanse, feeling very much alone in this strange place.

"We will set up over there," Wilder said, having arrived beside her soundlessly. He pointed to an area where barrels were set up with targets and various weapons lay on top of hay bales.

"Oh, so we're starting with combat, then?" she asked.

He nodded. "We always do combat first thing in the morning. Then dragon-training and care after lunch since they usually like to sleep in."

She blinked at him like he was pulling her chain. "What? Dragons sleep in?" Lunis had been on Sophia's schedule since the beginning.

He shook his head. "I actually don't know what they do. I just made that up. But that's the schedule, and has been since the beginning."

"So you've never been up to the Cave?" she asked.

He gave her a horrified expression. "No, of course not. Why? You're not thinking of going up there, are you?"

"Well, if that's where Lunis is going to live, I'd like to at least see it," she explained.

Again he shook his head as he led the way across the grounds. "You're going to get yourself into a world of trouble, aren't you?"

"That's not really the plan, but yeah, probably," she answered, studying the dragonrider beside her.

Wilder was tall but not too tall. She could tell he was strong from the way he moved, although his muscles were lean rather than bulky like Hiker's. While he had young features, there was old wisdom in his blue eyes. And the way his brown hair swept to the side, falling down in one eye, made him seem playful. The smile he flashed her also gave that impression.

"I've never seen anyone get under Hiker's skin quite like you," he said admiringly, as if that was a compliment.

"Well, I pretty much challenge him in every way possible, I guess."

Wilder laughed. "That you do."

"So, you guys just do the same thing day in and day out?" Sophia asked. "For how long?"

"Since I've been here," he answered. "So, close to a couple hundred years."

Her eyes widened in shock. "Are you serious? How have you all just existed like this without going insane?"

"We drink a lot," he replied with a laugh.

She joined in until his face turned serious once more.

"No, seriously, we do," he added. "And I don't know. I have Simi, and she keeps me young at heart. Patient. Humble. One day, all this training will pay off."

"I met her yesterday," Sophia said. "She's incredibly beautiful, but I guess I'm stating the obvious."

"You what?" he asked, surprised. "You mean, you saw her?"

Sophia shook her head. "No, she was hunting and headed back to the Cave when she saw me and came back. Then the others joined her."

He pointed at her, a strange expression on his face. "You, Sophia Beaufont, might be the strangest specimen I've yet to meet."

"Hiker was surprised by it too. I think the dragons were just curious since I'm the first new rider in a long time," she explained.

"No, dragons don't get curious. Well, maybe Lunis, but he's as strange as you are. Please tell Mahkah about this when I'm there. It's rare that he shows any surprise, and I have to see the expression on his face."

"Yeah, fine. But back to the riders' purpose."

He shook his head, pretending to be offended. "You and your one-track mind. Go on, then."

"Mortals can see magic now," Sophia stated. Reading *The Incomplete History of Dragonriders* had given her a lot of information about what the riders had been doing for the last several centuries, which was pretty much nothing. And it had told her why—because there was no purpose to it when mortals couldn't see them. But that had all recently changed. "I don't understand why the Dragon Elite are still hiding. You have concealed yourself for centuries, but it's okay to come out now."

"We're not ready," Wilder said, impersonating Hiker. "The world isn't ready for us."

She nodded. Things were starting to make sense. "So you have been hidden because mortals couldn't see magic. And now that this has changed, you're what, waiting until things calm down after the chaos?"

"Sure," Wilder stated, distracted as he picked up a thick sword, testing its balance in his hands. He shook his head as if the sword wasn't quite right. Picking up another, he swung it and again shook his head.

"What are you doing?" she asked, watching him.

"Well, all the swords are too big for you. They are meant for larger…" He tilted his head back and forth, apparently trying to find the right word.

"Men," she supplied.

He released a tame grin. "Yes, I guess that was what I intended to say. If you give me a few weeks, I should be able to make you something for your size."

"Thanks, but that's not necessary," Sophia said, summoning her sword from her room in the Castle where she had left it.

Wilder tilted his head to the side as she strapped her mother's sword and sheath around her waist. "What's that?"

"My sword," she answered, tightening the buckle and looking up at him.

"Wow, thank you, Mistress Obvious." He extended a hand to her. "May I see this thing you call a sword?"

Sophia pulled Inexorabilis from her sheath.

Wilder jumped back and his head went up in surprise. "Angels beside us, woman! Where did you get that thing?"

Her eyes cut back and forth. "It was my mother's. Guinevere Beaufont. It's elven-made."

He nodded rapidly, reclaiming the distance between them. "Yes, it's elven, made by none other than Hawaiki, one of the most skillful sword makers to ever live."

"She's still alive actually," Sophia said, giving him a careful look. "My sister visited her to unlock the memories stored in the sword. Why did you react like that?"

He kept his eyes pinned on the sword, intrigue swimming in his gaze. "For starters, I've never seen one of her swords in person. I've only ever heard of their craftmanship. Well, read about it, really."

"Then how did you know it was made by Hawaiki?" she asked.

"Because I'm highly attuned to weapons," he explained. "I can feel the maker's mark when I see them. I can feel the battles they've been in. I understand weapons better than people, I guess you could say." Wilder had suddenly turned serious, which somehow made his rugged features more pronounced.

"So when I pulled out Inexorabilis, you could feel it, or what?" she asked, still confused.

"Yes," he answered gruffly. "Your mother's sword has seen incredible things. It has been in battles I could only dream of." He held out his hands. "May I?"

Carefully, Sophia handed him the sword with the curved blade and intricate hilt that felt perfect in her fingers.

"Yes, Inexorabilis indeed." Wilder ran his eyes over the details of the sword.

"It means—"

"Unstoppable," he interrupted. "An appropriate name given by its maker."

"So, like Hawaiki, you can see the memories in the sword?" she questioned.

"I'm certain I can't see as much as she could, but yes. It is a gift of mine." His expression shifted with regret. "Well, it could be considered a curse. I had nightmares for the first few decades when I first came to the Castle.

"All those weapons decorating the walls throughout," Sophia exclaimed with a gasp.

"That's right," Wilder affirmed. "Whether my eyes were open or shut, I was inundated with visions of battles that the many weapons in the Castle had been in centuries before. I know how to shield myself now, but I wasn't prepared for your sword." He shook his head in disbelief. "No, I was utterly not ready for this."

"So you can see the battles my mother was in with Inexorabilis?" she asked, suddenly incredibly envious of Wilder's gift, even if he didn't see it as one.

"Oh, yes," he said, closing his eyes.

As she watched, they roamed under his lids like he was deep in REM sleep.

When his eyes snapped open, a smile sprang to his mouth. "You must be very proud to be the daughter of such an incredible warrior."

"Of course," Sophia said at once.

"And did your mum teach you how to fight before she gave you her sword?" he asked.

She swallowed. Her eyes drifted to the Expanse at his back. "No, she died when I was very young. I don't remember her. My sister Liv recovered Inexorabilis from where my mother dropped it on—"

"The Matterhorn," he cut in. "Yes, I saw that. She was murdered."

"Fighting for justice," Sophia said proudly.

"I'm sorry for your loss," he said, handing her the sword.

"We live in a world where it's inevitable to lose the ones we love. That's why we fight for justice. Or we should." Sophia glanced at the mountains, thinking of the world outside the Gullington that sorely needed dragonriders once again.

Evan was much less graceful when he approached, making enough noise whistling and stomping through the grass that there was no chance he could have snuck up on Sophia like Wilder had earlier. Beside him, Mahkah moved more like a wolf than a man. Slung over his shoulder was a bow.

"Shall we start with sparring?" Wilder offered when the other men joined them.

"Sure," Evan said. "I can teach the newbie the basics if you like."

Wilder thought about that for a moment. "Yeah, okay, but I'll supervise."

Sophia sheathed Inexorabilis and took a fighting stance. Evan stretched his neck from side to side.

"Don't worry, baby doll, I'll take it easy on you." He wriggled his fingers in invitation. "Show me what you're working with."

Sophia didn't move; instead, she kept her eyes trained on the large guy in front of her. Evan was built like a football player, with broad shoulders and thick legs.

He made several feints at her, but not once did she fall for his tricks. When he made his actual attempt, Sophia was ready. She blocked his hand, which was headed for her shoulder, deflecting it easily. Using his own momentum against him, she bent over, wrapping her arm around his waist, hoisting him over her arm, and throwing him on his back on the soft ground.

Evan coughed, slapping himself in the chest. "What the hell?"

Feeling a rush, she put her hands on her knees and looked down at Evan, who was still lying on the ground. "If you come at me like a bull, I'll simply use your weight and speed to my advantage."

"How were you able to throw me over your shoulder, Little Bit?" he asked.

"Magic," Sophia answered, extending a hand to him.

He didn't take it but instead sat up, pulling up his knees and giving her an expression of offense.

"I've told Evan many times that the strongest, biggest soldier isn't the one to be feared," Wilder said, standing in front of Mahkah, both with their fists up, although they didn't appear to be sparring. "It's the one who knows how to use the other's moves against them."

"That was an impressive move," Mahkah offered.

"Well, not really, but thanks," Sophia said. "When I blocked, he had too much momentum, thinking his attack was going to overwhelm me. I simply used it, helping him do a little flip, combined with a small incantation."

"I've never seen fighting like that," Mahkah stated.

"Yeah, using magic is cheating," Evan said, pushing up from the ground.

"In battle, there are no rules," Wilder said. "You two go again. Unless you're hurt, Evan, and want to go see the nurse."

He shook his head. "Come on. Now that I know that Little Bit uses trickery, I'm not taking it easy on her anymore."

Sophia batted her eyelashes. "Oh, whatever will I do? Just don't mess up my hair or chip my nail polish, please."

He blew out a breath and took a fighting stance once more. "I can't make any promises. The inner monster in me has been unleashed."

This time, Evan didn't hold back, rushing straight at Sophia and launching punch after punch in her direction. She nearly fell on her butt from deflecting the nonstop attacks.

Her flustered expression seemed to excite him. He let out a victorious laugh as he spun and launched a kick at her. She ducked, his leg swinging over her head. When it had passed, she popped back up, but he'd done some quick footwork and threw another kick from the opposite direction, which slammed into her midsection and threw her to the ground.

"Okay, break," Wilder said.

However, Sophia ignored him, rebounding off the earth and landing on her feet, surprising Evan with how quickly she bounced back. This time she beckoned to him to continue. He grinned and winked at her.

"Oh, Little Bit wants more," he sang. "That's exactly what she'll get."

He reached for Sophia and grabbed her by the arm, spinning her around and locking her in tight to his chest while holding both her arms down. "Quite the pickle you've gotten yourself into here," he said beside her face.

"Thing is," Sophia began, "sometimes you get yourself into a situation, and sometimes you put yourself there."

"Huh?" Evan asked.

She lifted her boot and stomped down hard on his foot. He yelled and released her at once. She spun while he was bent over cradling his foot and put him in a headlock. "I couldn't get in close to you for an attack until you locked me up next to you."

"So this was your attempt to get closer to me, eh?" He grunted, hardly able to open his mouth since she was partially obstructing the movement of his jaw with her arm.

She tightened her grip. "I wanted to remind you to invest in better boots. Those have seen better days."

"Thanks," he mumbled.

Wilder clapped. "Okay, I think that about does it."

Sophia released Evan, sidestepping at once to put distance between them in case he tried to retaliate.

He rubbed his neck, shooting her a dirty look. "She cheated again."

Wilder laughed. "Actually, I have to know…where did you learn how to fight? I've never seen moves like that. It was more a dance than a show of strength."

"It was strategy over physical prowess, which is perfect for a smaller rider to employ," Mahkah observed.

"Thank you." Sophia smiled. "My sister had me train daily with Akio Takahashi." She swallowed, the wound in her chest still fresh after losing the powerful warrior recently.

"Do you mean a Takahashi from the most acclaimed combat family in the magical world?" Wilder asked.

She blinked at him in surprise. "I'm shocked to hear you've heard of them inside the bubble of the Gullington."

He rolled his eyes. "You know, I lived outside this bubble at one point. And we know things here. The Castle sees to it, as does our commitment to education."

"My apologies, then," Sophia stated.

Wilder nodded. "Let's go again, then."

Evan rolled his neck. "Okay, but this time, Little Bit, no more Mr. Nice Guy."

Sophia scrunched her shoulders, clasping her hands to her chest. "Don't scare me, you big, strong man."

Wilder laughed, elbowing Mahkah. "I bet you she takes him down. What do you say?"

"I'm not taking that bet," he answered, his eyes drifting to the front of the Castle, where Hiker stood watching from a distance, the usual serious expression on his face.

CHAPTER TWENTY-SIX

At lunch, the dining hall felt airier without Hiker there. Ainsley informed them that he'd requested to take his meal in his study. She said he was inventing new swear words and trying to figure out how to operate the Kindle so he could find his books. Apparently, he'd pleaded with the Castle to put his office back the way it was, but currently, it wasn't complying, for whatever reason.

"If he'd just let me help, I could teach him how to use the Kindle," Sophia told Lunis as they strode toward the Cave, where Mahkah said the afternoon training would be held.

"I don't think he wants to learn," he stated.

"I don't think he wants me here," she added.

"Well, do you want to be here?" he asked her.

"Of course," she stated, not even needing to think about it. "And this isn't just about me. Do you want to be here?"

"Yes, as long as you understand that progress might look a lot like disappointment."

She narrowed her eyes. "What does that mean?"

"It means that things don't always go the way we think they will, but that doesn't mean they're not progressing."

"Oh, the riddle talk," Sophia sang.

A burst of movement flashed in her peripheral vision overhead. She halted, shielding her eyes as a tangle of purple and white rolled through the sky. It took a moment for her to realize that the ball of movement was two dragons wrestling in midair. Claws scratched and teeth ripped, the dragons filling the air with ferocious roars.

Coral, Evan's dragon, and Wilder's Simi split apart, staring at each other with heated gazes as they hovered at about the height of a two-story building.

The purple dragon shot a neat stream of fire at the white one, making Simi dart to the side to narrowly avoid the attack. She dove forward at once, wrapping her long neck around the other dragon's, tying her up like a ball. The pair plummeted to the ground, making it quake when they hit and then rolling one on top of one another.

They split apart again once they stopped rolling, leveling their gazes at each other as they sidestepped. Simi's white wings were held up beside her body, whereas Coral's were pinned to her body.

"Why are they doing that?" Sophia asked. "Dragons don't have to fight each other, do they?"

"We have, and I suspect we will again," Lunis answered. "But they are doing this because they are bored and have no other way of getting out their aggression."

"Yes, that makes sense," Sophia said, noticing Bell, Hikers' dragon, and Tala, Mahkah's, watching from a distance. "Several hundred years of no missions would make anyone crazy."

"Dragons who don't have riders are content without a mission," he explained. "However, once we elect to form a bond with a rider, we also subscribe to your world of productivity, purpose, and justice."

"She hurt her!" Evan yelled, rushing to Coral, who had a bloody gash on her neck.

Quiet was on his heels, as was Hiker.

The purple dragon hissed, unfolding her wings and holding them out to keep the others away from her. Sophia watched with her mouth open, assaulted by the strange sight, which was the farthest thing from normal. She had never fathomed that she'd be watching riders and a gnome try to subdue an injured dragon.

"She'll be okay," Mahkah said from beside her, startling Sophia.

She shook her head, hiding her surprise. "But she's hurt."

"Yes, and dragons heal quite quickly," he stated, nodding at Lunis. "Would it be all right if I accessed your dragon?"

"You will have to ask him," she answered.

"I already did," he said. "Now it's your turn to give your permission."

"Oh." Sophia gulped with surprise. "Yes, it's fine. What will this involve?"

Mahkah muttered an incantation, and gold dust hung in the air around Lunis. "I'm going to take some measurements to begin with. I'd like to track his growth since I've never seen a young dragon grow and don't know the rate."

"So, Tala magnetized to you when?" Sophia asked.

He gazed fondly at the brown dragon standing next to Bell. "When I was twenty-five, a memorable two-hundred and seventy-five years ago."

"Is that all?" Sophia asked sarcastically.

"Would you like to meet her?" he asked, waving his hand in the air, making the gold dust disappear.

Sophia smiled. "Thank you, but I had that honor yesterday."

"Oh, come on!" Wilder complained from behind her. "I told you to wait until I was present to tell Mahkah the news."

"News?" Mahkah asked, staring in awe at Sophia and Wilder. "So, you met the dragons?"

"They flew down to meet her, apparently out of curiosity," Wilder stated.

Mahkah shook his head. "No, they would never. But I believe

Sophia. How interesting."

Wilder elbowed her, leaning over and whispering next to her ear, "See that surprise covering his face?"

"Not really," she answered.

"Yes, exactly. That's about as close to emotion as the stoic warrior gets," Wilder stated. "That was why I had to be here for it."

"What did the dragons say to you when you met?" Mahkah asked, kneeling next to Lunis, who stood quite still and regal.

"I don't remember," she lied. What was she supposed to tell them? That she was a change agent? That sounded boastful and unnecessary. "I think they thought I was dinner."

Wilder laughed. "They don't eat humans…anymore."

"Very interesting," Mahkah stated, standing back and appraising Lunis.

"Is everything okay?" she asked.

"Well, I can't really say," he answered. "I don't know what to compare him to. He should be getting his fire any day now, and there are many other magical properties I expect he'll inherit."

"Like what?" Sophia asked as Lunis lumbered in the direction of the other dragons, seemingly bored with the human conversation.

"It's hard to know," Mahkah offered. "Each dragon's magic is unique to them and based on the element that ties them to the Earth. They inherited it from—"

"The Archangel Michael," Sophia supplied.

He nodded. "That's correct. His blood seeped into the earth and filled each dragon egg with unique properties. All dragons are related to an element, and when it is present, it makes them stronger. Tala, for instance, is connected to…" He tilted his head to the side, quizzing her.

"Earth, right?" she asked.

"Yes, you can tell both by his brown scales and her name, which means wolf," he stated. "She is strongest on the ground, rather than in the air."

He pointed to Bell, the largest dragon, who was red with green eyes. "She's governed by the sun, and is strongest on sunny days."

"Simi is connected to the wind," Wilder supplied.

Mahkah nodded. "And finally, Evan's dragon, Coral, is strongest around the ocean, flying faster than any creature I've ever seen."

"I think that's just because she's trying to get away from her rider," Wilder said with a laugh.

"So, Lunis," Sophia began, "will be stronger on full moons?"

"Yes, but beware, because there's always a drawback to their elemental connection," Mahkah explained. "It's hard to know what it is. Maybe on the new moon, he'll be weaker. Maybe on the night of a crescent moon? Then he might not fly as fast or high. It's hard to know yet."

"He doesn't fly," Sophia offered, watching as he interacted with the other dragons, looking so strange surrounded by the massive beasts.

"He will," Mahkah said with confidence.

"But when?" Sophia asked.

"Soon, I think."

"Then I'll be able to ride him, right?" she questioned.

He shook his head. "I can't say that for sure. It's up to him. Just because we're called riders doesn't mean we can. It's up to him."

"Right," Sophia said, a terse edge to her voice.

The other four dragons took off running for the cave. Lunis sprinted beside them, not keeping up, but rather catching dirt in the face as they left him behind. They sprang into the air, rising higher in unison. Lunis continued to run, his wings flapping but his feet staying firmly on the ground. He slowed when he reached the steep hill that was home to the Cave, looking up at the opening as the other dragons disappeared inside it.

Sophia's heart suddenly ached for all the things she and her dragon had to experience before they progressed, reminding herself that the process would look a lot like disappointment.

CHAPTER TWENTY-SEVEN

Maybe it was the exhaustion of a full day of training, or maybe it was simply overdue, but when Sophia settled into the armchair that night with *The Incomplete History of Dragonriders*, she was acutely hit with a piercing ache.

Lunis looked up suddenly, smoke puffing from his nostrils. "What is it?"

She clapped her hand to her chest. "I don't know exactly."

"You're in pain," he observed. "Did you hurt yourself during training?"

"No, but someone might want to check on Evan. I think I dislocated his shoulder, although he wouldn't admit it."

"Your pain is of the heart," he said after a moment as if he'd reflected on this before making the observation.

"I miss home," she said, finding it hard to admit that to herself. "It's not that I don't like this place, but..."

A knock at her door interrupted her thoughts.

"Come in," Sophia called.

No one entered. She sighed, finding her body sore all over

when she stood and trudged to the door. She would have used magic, but it was depleted by that point.

When she opened the door, there was no one on the other side. Looking back and forth in the hallway, Sophia didn't find a trace of anyone. Not even a little bird that was Ainsley.

She was about to close the door when a whisper down the corridor stole her attention.

Glancing at Lunis, she said, "Did you hear that?"

He stood, shaking himself like a dog after a bath but with much more grace. He'd grown yet again. "Do you want me to go with you?"

"Go with me?" she questioned.

"To investigate," he said.

"Oh…" She glanced at the hallway. "Do you think I should?"

"I think that when something knocks at your door, you need to find out why it ran off before you could greet it."

Sophia considered this for a moment. "Okay. But you stay here." She could feel his exhaustion and knew he wanted to rest.

"Okay, but if you need anything...well, I'm right here."

"Thanks, pal," she said, stepping out into the hallway. She heard YouTube fire up on her phone as she pulled the door shut.

She laughed as she strode down the hallway. The shadows in the Castle were strangely creepy tonight, making weird images on the walls as she passed.

When she came to a new corridor full of unmarked doors, she turned around, wondering if she'd gone the wrong way. Something told her she hadn't, though.

The whispering echoed from the far side of the hallway. It made a shiver run down Sophia's spine, making her feel like she was in a haunted house on Halloween.

She walked several yards before the whispers came again, this time from the other side of a door. Sophia pressed her ear to the door, listening intently.

"Hello?" she said in a hushed voice.

The whispering intensified. She rested her fingers lightly on the handle, sucking in a breath with indecision. Before she could change her mind, she opened it.

Sophia wasn't sure what she was expecting, but the bedroom strewn with papers and books wasn't it. She squinted into the darkness, finding it a bit easier to see than she would have thought.

Tentatively, she took a few steps into the room, which was about the size of hers.

"Hello?" she tried again.

Something brushed against her back and she spun, hands at the ready. Nothing was there, but the door had shut behind her. Suddenly she wished she'd had Lunis come with her.

A chill, like the wind that swept across the Expanse, passed through Sophia. Whispers erupted all around her. She swung around, looking for something. Anything to explain what was happening there. Although she wanted to run for the door, she didn't allow herself to.

Instead, she listened intently to the whispers, closing her eyes so she could hear the message in the chorus of words.

"Follow his path," the voices said.

"Follow his path. Follow his path. Follow his path," they repeated again and again.

Sophia's eyes sprang open, expecting to see a path illuminated in front of her in the disorderly room. There wasn't one, but she did notice a desk like the one in her room. On top of it were tons of newspapers. She strode over and picked up the first crinkled paper.

Her heart skipped when she read the date. It was from less than a week ago.

"Adam." She gasped, and the whispers ended suddenly.

She squinted at the newsprint. The dragonrider had circled an article on the front. She pulled out the paper under that one. Same thing. A headline had been highlighted. There were a dozen papers like that.

Gathering the papers in her arms, she looked over the room. "So, this is where Adam lived?" Sophia asked, feeling as though she was talking directly to the Castle. "You wanted me to see it, but why? You want me to follow his path?"

The Castle didn't respond in a way she heard. She held the papers to her chest, thinking she wouldn't know the answer until she studied the things Adam had circled.

Sophia made for the door, excited to tell Lunis about what she'd found. However, a portrait of a group of riders hanging beside the door made her halt. She recognized one of the faces without knowing how.

There were roughly a dozen men. Adam stood on one end, appearing much younger than in the portrait at the top of the grand staircase. Most of the other men didn't stick out, but there was one with a large beard in the center who grabbed Sophia's attention for some reason. She scanned the names in the caption, sucking in a breath when she read the one that matched the long-bearded fellow.

"Oscar Beaufont," she said, searching her memory for this person. She couldn't remember one, but this was no coincidence.

Turning, she looked at the room one last time before she left with the newspapers held to her chest.

Sophia was excited to tell Lunis what had happened and review the newspapers that she'd found. However, when she entered her room, she was assaulted by another surprise.

"I didn't do it," Lunis said when she halted and looked around the room.

The yellow bedspread and the curtains that hung around it were now pink, a bold contrast to the muted colors from before. Hanging on the wall between the fireplace and the door to the bathroom was a large flat-screen TV, but that wasn't the most striking change to the room. It was the words on the main wall in front of the hall door. They read *"Familia est Sempiternum."*

"That's my family motto," she stated.

"I know," Lunis said. "I closed my eyes for a brief moment, and when I opened them, the room had gone through a redesign."

She shook her head. "Well, Hiker's going to be pissed now, but I didn't do it this time."

"Yes, so since he's already going to be mad, we might as well curl up and watch some television."

Sophia laid the newspapers on the table. "I would, but I've got some studying to do."

"What did you find?" Lunis asked.

"I think it's something my long-lost relative wanted me to discover," she said, spreading out the newspapers. It would take her all night to review them, and that was completely fine with her. Fondly, she glanced at the words that had always decorated the main wall of where she lived with her family. Suddenly she didn't feel so lonesome for her old home. Wherever her family was, she'd be at home. She smiled at Lunis and settled in, pulling the first newspaper to her.

CHAPTER TWENTY-EIGHT

Sophia had showered and was dressed by the time Ainsley entered her chambers.

"You've already lit the fire and candles," the housekeeper complained, hurt in her voice.

"I'm sorry," Sophia said, gathering up the newspapers. "I was up early and needed the light."

"Oh," Ainsley said, looking around the room. "You've been busy."

"I haven't, actually," Sophia argued. "The Castle did this."

The shapeshifter morphed into Hiker, his hands on his hips. "There's so much color in here. I think I'm going to puke. How dare you bring something new and fun into this place? We prefer boring."

Sophia giggled. "If you think he was mad yesterday about the Kindle, just wait."

"What are those?" Ainsley asked, shifting back and indicating the newspapers.

"I want to tell you, but I have to wait." She hurried to the door, then turned back to the housekeeper, who was wearing a hurt expression. "I'm sorry. But on another note, is the Castle haunted?"

Ainsley nodded. "Is it haunted? That's an understatement. There are ghosts, poltergeists, and just about everything else you can imagine in here. And that's not even mentioning what keeps it alive. The Castle is a person of sorts. The ghosts are just like us, houseguests."

"Do you think Adam is here?" Sophia asked, looking around.

"Oh." Ainsley was taken aback as she glanced around at the wall with the Latin phrase *Familia est Sempiternum.* "I don't know. I don't think so. Not yet. Or maybe not. It's hard to say about these things. I'd hope if he were here, he'd pay me a visit. I miss him something fierce. But honestly, I bet he's transitioning. Or with the angels. I hope to see him at some point if he decides to return. It's always a choice for individuals, but who knows the parameters? Only the angels."

Sophia nodded. "Okay, well, thank you. I'm going to hurry down to breakfast."

"Does your hurrying have something to do with those papers in your arms?" Ainsley asked.

She looked at Lunis and smiled, having discussed the breakfast events with him in the middle of the night. "No, but yes. I just want to do something before the others get down there."

Ainsley smiled and leaned forward, whispering, "I love a good mystery, S. Beaufont."

"Thanks, Ains."

Sophia was seated with her plate full when the others made it down to breakfast.

Evan yawned loudly, rolling out his shoulder, a grimace making him jerk as if suddenly in pain. "I'm so hungry I could eat a horse right now."

"Me too," Lunis chimed in, having already polished off a great deal of food.

Evan glanced over his shoulder at him. "Your dragon is so…"

"Delightful?" Sophia asked.

"He's different," Evan stated. "I mean, I like it, but it takes some getting used to when you're accustomed to being thrown off your own dragon for making a joke."

"Or maybe Coral did that because you smell like sardines," Ainsley suggested as she swept through the dining hall.

"And that's on a good day," Wilder chimed in, taking the seat next to Evan. He sniffed and scooted down a chair. "Seriously, the water here flows like wine. Use it."

Evan yawned. "I forgot. What's the point, anyway? I'm just going to sweat again after breakfast, and later, it will be lather, rinse, repeat."

"The thing is that we all lather and rinse before we repeat," Wilder said, his eyes sliding to the stack of papers next to Sophia. She shook her head slightly, encouraging him not to say anything because Hiker had just entered the hall with Mahkah.

"Well, I don't care," Hiker said to him. "I want you to continue to research it."

Mahkah nodded. "Yes, sir." He smiled politely at Sophia, taking the seat on the other side of her as he normally did.

Hiker didn't acknowledge Sophia or any of the rest as he took the chair at the head of the table.

"It took me forever to repair that chair," Ainsley said, dropping a plate of fresh fruit on the table. "The Castle really didn't want you seated there, but I convinced it to give you another chance."

Hiker drew a breath as he poured himself a cup of hot coffee. "You're exaggerating again, woman."

"Am I?" she asked, with mock excitement. "Well, you know how I can be. All hysterical. Blame my uterus."

"Really? I'm about to eat," he said, pushing away his coffee before taking a sip as if she had spoiled his appetite.

"Uterus, uterus, uterus," she said with a laugh, going to clear the first of Lunis' platters.

"No fruit for me today," Evan said, pushing that plate out of his way as he reached for the overflowing platter of pastries. "I need to refill my reserves."

A shock zapped him when he reached for the pastry on top. He yanked his hand back, looking at the platter with offense. "What? What was that for?"

Ainsley turned around with a curious expression on her face. "That's strange."

"What's gotten into the Castle now?" Evan asked, shaking his hand like it still hurt.

Wilder reached around him to grab a pastry. He yanked a large one back with a smile. "Doesn't seem to mind me."

Mahkah gave the platter careful consideration before also making an attempt. He was successful, dropping a muffin on his plate.

"Well, that's unfair," Evan said, eyeing the platter with envy. "Must have been a fluke." He reached again and nearly toppled out of his chair when the platter sent electricity through him. "What the hell?"

Ainsley laughed, shaking her head. "That's bloody brilliant."

Evan stood, shaking. "What's gotten into the Castle? I haven't said a single mean thing about it all…well, in like a day."

The housekeeper drew in a breath, looking around. "I don't think the Castle is the one doing this."

Evan's brow scrunched in confusion before the reality dawned on him. He leveled his gaze on Sophia. "Then it must be Little Bit. Did you spell the tray so I couldn't have any pastries?"

"Maybe," she said casually, taking a bite of her muffin and closing her eyes as she chewed as if it were the best thing she'd ever eaten.

"Well, joke's over. Why don't you lift the spell, already?" he encouraged, waving at the platter but keeping his distance.

"I will," she said. "After Quiet has had his."

Evan growled, pointing at her. "Hiker, you have to put a stop to this. She's…she's…she's being…"

The leader of the Elite shook his head. "I'm not getting involved."

"When you decide to stop bullying Quiet, you can have pastries," Sophia said, articulating every word.

Evan rolled his eyes. "Oh, Quiet is just a—"

"Finish that sentence, and I'll knock out every one of your teeth so that Ainsley has to grind up pastries so you can drink them through a straw," Sophia threatened.

"Oh, great!" Ainsley said, throwing her hands in the air. "Now you are making more work for me!"

"No," Sophia said. "It was just… I'm not really going to knock out his teeth. That would be a mess. I don't want to make more work for you."

Ainsley smiled and curtsied. "Thank you, S. Beaufont. And nice work with the electrified platter. Simply brilliant." She waved her hand beside Evan. "You're still smoking, but it's an improvement over the other smell you were emitting."

He huffed, taking a seat back in his chair. "This is ridiculous. Just you wait, Sophia." Evan looked longingly at the platter of pastries.

"I'll wait," she said with a pleasant smile, turning her attention to Hiker. "In the meantime, I was up last night, and something led me to Adam's room."

"What?!" Ainsley yelled, turning around after picking up another empty platter from in front of Lunis. "That's been locked since his death. I've tried everything to get in there!"

Hiker held up a hand, silencing the housekeeper. "You went into Adam's room?"

"Well, I didn't know it was his," Sophia explained. "I heard whispering. I think the Castle wanted me to go in there as well since ghosts or whatever led me there. This is all new territory for me."

"Just wait until the Castle hides all your long johns," Wilder said. "That was new territory for me."

Hiker threw him a frustrated expression.

"You're right," Wilder said, returning his gaze to his plate. "My eggs are getting cold. Continue."

"Anyway, when I was in his room, I found all these newspapers." Sophia pulled the stack around and shoved them in Hiker's direction. "They are world events where two sides aren't getting along and need—"

"I know damn well what they are," Hiker said, his voice bordering on yelling. From behind the Viking, Ainsley had turned serious, shaking her head as if urging Sophia to abandon this.

She refused, though. "Okay, well, I didn't know what they were, but it appears that Adam was looking for missions for the dragonriders to go on. And now that mortals can see magic, well, I was just thinking—"

"Your dragon doesn't even fly," Hiker cut in, his face red. "He lays here eating beside us like a common hound."

"That's not fair," Sophia argued. "He's developing. How dare you?"

"I dare," he said through clenched teeth.

"And I'm brand new, but I know the men are looking for..."

Wilder shook his head minutely. Even Evan widened his eyes as if urging her to stop. "Okay, fine. It's my personal observation that the others here need a purpose. Adam seemed to be looking for that too. He found cases that you could be working on. Things where you could make a real difference."

Hiker lowered his chin, regarding her with a seething glare. "We aren't ready. The world isn't ready."

"I get that," Sophia continued. "But that's why we start somewhere small. Look." She thumbed through the newspapers.

"There's an oil dispute here. Land arguments. There are all sorts of places you could go in as adjudicators. And Adam—"

"Do not speak to me about him," Hiker interrupted, standing from the table, simply vibrating. "You know nothing about him."

"The Castle did lead her to his room and opened it," Ainsley said in a low voice.

Hiker moved his chin to the side, glaring at the housekeeper.

"What? Quiet?" she said, looking around as if she heard the gnome yelling for her. "You're stuck in the well? I'll be right there." Ainsley hurried toward the kitchen.

Hiker shook his head at Sophia. "There will be no more discussion about this. You will not go into Adam's room, and you will get rid of those newspapers. Have I made myself clear?"

Sophia wanted to argue. She felt as though it was her right to do so. However, the urgency in the eyes of the three men sitting around the table made her abandon this mission. "Yes, sir. I understand."

"Very well," Hiker said, striding out of the dining room. "Train, men. I mean, riders. I want you all to train hard today."

Evan wadded up his napkin and threw it on the table. "Oh, look. Today we get to train. It's so different from yesterday."

Quiet entered the dining hall, his cheeks red and confusion on his face since he had just been nearly run over by Hiker barreling from the room.

"Good morning, Quiet," Sophia said, feeling utterly defeated as she pushed away from the table, not having eaten much. "I saved you some pastries. I hope you enjoy them."

The gnome glanced at the platter piled high with pastries and smiled, muttering something she couldn't make out.

CHAPTER TWENTY-NINE

Before the others joined, Sophia was already on the Expanse, an axe in her hand as she stared at the target roughly twenty feet away.

She gritted her teeth. Held the axe behind her in one hand. With a guttural yell, she flung the axe overhead. It tumbled through the air and bumped into the target, then clattered to the ground.

None of what was going through her brain made any sense. Something had led her to Adam's room, which had been locked for everyone else. Sophia wondered…if it hadn't been, would Ainsley have cleaned up the newspapers, or would Hiker have gotten rid of them? And then she wondered who had led her there. Was it the Castle or the ghost of one of her relatives who had once been a dragonrider? More confounding than any of that was Hiker.

She picked up another axe and held it at the ready, then flung it at the target. This time it didn't even hit it, but rather continued past, landing in the grass.

"Although it appears you've mastered axe-throwing, I was wondering if I could offer you some tips," Wilder said from behind her, his hands pressed into his pockets and a roguish smile on his face.

Sophia sighed and walked over to retrieve the axes from the ground. "Sure. That would be great."

"Well, first of all," Wilder said, picking up one of the axes lying beside him on the hay bale, "you're a bit worked up."

"So I need to chill out first," she replied. "I get it."

He waited until she was beside him. With measured grace, he drew back the axe and launched it. It sped to the target and stuck straight into the bullseye.

"Hey, good job," she exclaimed, admiring his form.

"Well, don't give me too much credit. I have been practicing that pretty much every day for a century or two."

Sophia threw up her hands. "And all that skill and effort could be going to something. You could be out making a difference in the world instead of wasting time here in the Gullington."

Wilder's smile dropped. "Hey, now, I don't think any of my time here was wasted. It passes differently for riders. You'll see, young'un."

"It's cute that you call me that and totally doesn't make me want to throw an axe at you," she quipped.

"Fair enough," he said. "I have many, many years to tease you about being young and inexperienced. I'll sprinkle the jokes sparingly so that you don't tire of them in the first decade."

Sophia let out a hot breath, brought back the axe, and flung it at the target. It soared past it and stuck in the dirt.

"Well, you made it stick that time, so there you go." Wilder nudged her over, taking the place in front of the target. He threw the axe in his hand without even focusing on the target, making yet another bullseye.

Sucking in a deep breath, Sophia tried to calm her emotions.

"Soph, have you ever been in battle?" Wilder asked, studying her.

"Well, no, but I mean, I have…" She swallowed, resigning slightly. "No, actually. I haven't. But that doesn't mean I—"

He held up his hand to pause her, a sensitive expression on his face. "It's okay. I'm not judging you. If anything, I'm even more impressed that you became a dragonrider."

"You were in battles before you magnetized to Simi?" she asked.

"Oh, yes, loads of them," he stated. "But none since coming here."

Sophia opened her mouth to go on about Hiker again, but Wilder lifted his hand once more.

"We can get back to your righteous mission to put the dragonriders to use again, but first, if you wouldn't mind, I'd like to discuss emotions and battle."

"Yeah, okay," Sophia agreed, turning the axe in her hand over.

"Emotions are really valuable when you're in a fight. They are the difference between winning and losing. So no, I don't actually think you need to calm down to throw that axe. What you need to do is focus that energy and use it as fuel."

"So, I should picture the target as Hiker's face?" she asked.

He shook his head, whistling through his teeth. "When you do go into your first battle, I want to see it. You're feisty."

Focusing on the target, Sophia worked at honing her emotions, sending the energy out rather than allowing it to explode out of her in all directions. She drew her arms back behind her head, this time holding the axe evenly between both her hands. First, she released a breath, then the axe. It soared through the air, hitting the target and sticking in the outer top edge.

"Well, that's an improvement," Wilder said, striding over to the target and retrieving the axe.

"What happened to Adam?" Sophia asked.

Wilder's gaze dropped to the grass and he pressed his lips together, hesitant all of a sudden.

"Oh, good, more secrets," Sophia said, emotion ready to burst out of her.

"No," Wilder said, his expression softening. "The truth is, I don't know. None of us do."

"What?" She sucked in a breath, not having expected that answer.

He combed one of his hands through his hair. "One night... well, the one you appeared on the Elite globe, Adam and Kay-Rye crashed." Glancing out at the Expanse, he pointed. "It was out there, just past the Barrier. So close to home." He shook his head, obviously struggling with the memory playing in his head. "They were dead by the time we got there, and probably had been for a bit."

"I'm sorry," Sophia said, pressing her mouth to the side.

"Thanks," Wilder said, nodding to encourage Sophia to take a turn.

She launched the axe again. As before, it lodged in the top outer edge of the target.

"Adam and Hiker were really close," Wilder explained.

"And now I've gone into his room and pulled out his papers and Hiker will hate me forever, right?"

Wilder shook his head. "No, that's just the thing." He laughed suddenly. "You reminded me so much of Adam this morning. Put a beard on you, and I might not have known the difference."

"Uh, thanks?"

Another laugh spilled from his mouth. "I just mean you sounded like him, full of conviction. He and Hiker had been going at it nonstop lately. Adam knew it was time for the dragonriders to take back their role as adjudicators. Hiker was adamant that we weren't ready."

"That the world wasn't ready," Sophia added, impersonating Hiker.

"That's right," Wilder stated.

"But I thought you said they were close?" Sophia asked.

"They were," he explained. "Best friends for as long as I've been here. Hiker respected Adam more than anyone else, but we all know the person we love the most is usually the one who challenges us the most. And even before we learned that mortals could see magic again, the two were always arguing. That was just their way. Adam didn't think we should be confining ourselves in the Gullington, even when mortals couldn't see magic. He didn't like not learning about the world, and often ventured out. Took me on a field trip or two."

"And he had the newspapers," Sophia added.

"That's right," Wilder agreed. "I fear that when Hiker wouldn't allow us to go out on cases, Adam went anyway and found some trouble. He knew more about the world than any of us, but we are still sheltered here, and Adam was the oldest among us." He sighed deeply. "It's not that Hiker is right to keep us locked inside the Gullington, but he is right that we don't know about the modern world, and that takes time to learn about. Trying to understand it on our own has only led to confusion. I fear that whatever killed Adam was probably something he didn't understand how to fight. We need a new education on the world before we set out again...or for me, it will be the first time as a dragonrider and adjudicator."

A sideways smile graced his face, lighting his eyes. "If only we had someone who grew up in the present-day world and knew about technology, demographics, and whatnot…"

"Hiker would never allow it," she finally said.

"No, especially after the stunt you pulled this morning," Wilder agreed. "But time will wear him down, I suspect."

Sophia picked up another axe. "And what, in the meantime, we're just supposed to grow old?" She threw the axe, which grazed the bottom of the target.

"No, in the meantime, you need to work on your aim." Wilder strode over to the target and held out his hand, making a red apple appear in his palm. Turning around, he laid the large apple on the top of his head, backing up until he was flush with the target.

"What are you doing?" Sophia asked, horrified.

"The thing is that practice doesn't make perfect. When we

practice, I've learned, we have to have something at stake, just like when in battle, or we won't improve." He laughed. "Evan and I usually make a bet when sparring. Simi has been known to throw me off if I don't perform correctly. And you, Soph, need an extra motivator to get better as well."

"Then why don't we make a bet?" she offered, her hand with the axe in it sweating.

He shook his head. "That won't work. I have nothing you want since you can conjure just about whatever you like. Evan is horrible at that, so the stakes work."

"And what do you get if he wins?" Sophia questioned.

He sighed, a peaceful look on his face. "Quiet. He agrees to be quiet for a week. It never lasts, but those first couple of days are magical."

She laughed. "Okay, well, I'm not throwing this axe at your head, so forget about it."

"Please don't throw it at my head. Your target is the apple." Wilder appeared silly with the piece of fruit sitting on the top of his head. He smirked at her. "Come on, Soph. You did well with funneling your emotions. Now you just need the proper motivation to hit the target."

"You mean the apple," Sophia corrected.

"And once you've chopped it, we can have a snack, since I noticed you didn't eat anything at breakfast."

"Really, can't we do this another way?" Sophia pleaded. "Hover the apple in front of the target using your magic."

He shook his head, the apple nearly falling off until he corrected his balance. "No, there's no incentive there for you."

"But the idea that I might axe you is my motivation?" Sophia asked.

"Hey, if it helps, I believe you can do this," he offered.

She lowered the axe. "Aren't you scared?"

"More than a little bit," he said with a laugh. "But the best things in life are preceded by fear and usually followed by it."

She shook her head. "You dragonriders are sick, strange people."

He winked. "Welcome to the team. You're one of us now."

Sophia didn't think she was getting out of this, and she could see the logic in Wilder's method. Before, she was simply trying to hit the target. Now, she had an important goal: don't kill Wilder. That meant she couldn't just hit the target. She had to slice the apple.

She let out her breath. Focused her emotions. Honed her gaze on the apple.

When she threw the axe, she bit her tongue. Those seconds between when she released the axe and it hit the apple were the longest of her entire life.

The apple was split perfectly in half, one side landing in Wilder's hand. He grabbed the other from his head, laughing in pure relief. "Nice. I knew you could do it."

She wanted to scream. Jump up and down. Instead, she simply smiled as if this achievement was no big deal.

Wilder strode forward, holding out one of the apple halves to her.

She took it. "Thanks. Although unorthodox, I appreciate your teaching methods."

He took a bite. "It's nice to have a new student, and one who isn't as dumb as Evan."

CHAPTER THIRTY

"You've never let me aim at an apple on your head," Evan complained as they strode toward the area in front of the Caves.

"Because I'm not daft," Wilder replied. "You couldn't hit the target for a while. I'm not sure if you could hit a pumpkin sitting on my head at this point."

"Well, I'd like to at least be given a chance," Evan said, acting hurt. All through lunch, he kept glaring at Sophia. She was undeterred by his grumpiness. Bullies didn't deserve her sympathy.

"After careful consideration, I've decided that never, ever will I allow you to throw an axe at my head," Wilder offered, sounding generous.

Evan flashed him a smile. "Okay, well, keep thinking about it, and let me know when you have changed your mind."

"Let's start with riding today to give Sophia an idea about how it works," Mahkah stated when they approached. He held his arm out to the field, where Lunis was racing back and forth, flapping his wings. "I've already gotten Lunis started on some exercises."

It warmed Sophia's heart to see her dragon sprinting and

trying hard to grow stronger. "What should I do?" she asked Mahkah.

"Watch," he commanded, pointing at Coral and Simi, who landed next to the other men.

Both Evan and Wilder snapped their fingers in unison. A second later, leather saddles appeared in their hands. They were sleek, a thin piece of leather for the main section with ropes and thick braided straps dangling off it.

Mahkah indicated the other riders. "I will make you a saddle when Lunis is finished growing and you're riding him."

She nodded, watching as the other two guys threw the saddles into the air. They vanished and then reappeared, snuggly tied in place around their dragons. "I don't think I saw how they fastened the buckles around the underbelly."

Mahkah released the smallest of smiles, barely showing his amusement. "We used to put on the saddles manually. It was quite cumbersome and usually resulted in a slower reaction time. I came up with that spell. It almost always works for getting the saddle on quickly and correctly."

"You've been here as long as the others, right?" Sophia asked, watching as Wilder mounted his dragon by first stepping on the wing Simi spread from a hunched position. Then in swift movements that flowed together, he stepped up, swinging his leg over and straddling her back. It reminded Sophia of a rider on a horse, if the horse was incredibly old, one of the most beautiful creatures she'd ever seen, and much larger than any horse.

"I've been here for maybe three hundred years," he stated matter-of-factly.

"So you haven't been on any missions either, then?" she asked.

He cut his eyes at her, hesitation in his gaze. "Tala and I have never been in a battle together or on a mission, but she's seen much, and so have I."

"I realize that," she said quickly. "I'm not trying to downplay the importance of what you've been doing here."

"Some of us require a few hundred years to prepare for what the world will need from us in the future," Mahkah said, his hands behind his back and his chin held high as he looked out at the Expanse. "And then there are some who will be ready much quicker."

She studied him, wondering if he meant her. Instinctively, she liked Mahkah. He was reserved, unlike Evan and Wilder. For some reason, she knew she could trust him. This was a man of pure virtue.

He pointed as Simi began to move. "The takeoff is the hardest for riders to learn. Pay close attention."

Wilder bent down on his dragon, his hands holding tight to the reins, boots locked against her sides. Simi started forward, her powerful legs moving so fast they blurred. Her wings lifted slowly but then flapped down rapidly. Again and again this happened, until Wilder yanked back on the reins. Her head pulled up as she pushed off the ground, the beat of her wings increasing. Wilder seemed to disappear into his dragon as they soared into the gray sky, vanishing into the clouds. Coral and Evan were not far behind them.

"He told her when to take off," Sophia said, surprised by this realization.

"That's right," Mahkah said proudly. "Do you know why?"

She suddenly wished she had spent the night reading *The Incomplete History of Dragonriders* instead of reviewing Adam's newspapers. "No, I'm not sure I do."

"A dragon, as you know, can fly without a rider," he began. "However, when the rider joins the dragon, they become one in flight. They can't take off until the rider is ready. The dragon might be the one who flies, but when connected to their rider, they are governed by their control. It's what bonds us. The dragon is the most fierce and independent creature on this planet, but they give up that freedom to partner with their rider. Like any good relationship, we have to give up a part of ourselves to become whole with another."

"He didn't hesitate," Sophia observed, watching as the two dragons whipped into and around the clouds, vanishing behind them and then reappearing.

"No, and if he would have, Simi would have made a false start, which often results in injuries."

Sophia gulped, her eyes drifting back down to Lunis, who was continuing the race across the Expanse, Bell and Tala watching him from close by. She never wanted to hurt him, and the idea that she could by not being a good enough rider from the beginning made her heart ache.

"And landing?" Sophia asked. "Is that as tricky as the takeoff?"

"It's similar," he answered. "The most important thing for you to remember is that your dragon will do what you tell him, whether it's in his best interests or not. He will trust you implicitly. Mistakes happen with riders who don't believe in themselves. The confidence of a rider becomes the fate of the dragon. Evan might be teased a lot for one thing or another, but make no mistake about it—when he's on his dragon, he has the confidence to impress. That's why Coral will follow him wherever he asks."

Sophia caught sight of the dragon and rider cutting across the sky, Evan hunched low. Coral spiraled through the air, and he didn't budge even when the dragon rotated upside-down. When she soared straight up like a rocket, he held his face to the wind, courage radiating off him.

"Now, you have a question for me," he said, returning his focus to the Expanse.

"Ummm…" It seemed like such a loaded way of inviting her to ask him something. She didn't want to say something dumb, so instead, she chewed her lip, thinking.

She watched as Lunis sped across the ground beside Bell. The larger dragon left him behind easily. Sophia wanted to run over to her dragon. Cheer him on. Tell him he would get stronger and faster. But she stayed cemented to the ground next to Mahkah, watching helplessly.

Finally, something occurred to her. "Is it true that electronics and electricity affect the dragons?"

He arched an eyebrow, turning to her. "I don't think so."

"You don't?" She wondered if her desire to get that reply had made her brainwash Mahkah into saying that. When she was a child, she'd had to be careful. Because she got her magic so early, it was hard for her to control it. On the rare occasion that she was around other children, if they disagreed with her, she found it easy to manipulate the situation with her magic. As soon as she became aware of that, she had worked to stop it.

For Sophia, even as a child, making people do something they didn't want to didn't feel right. What was the point in someone agreeing with her or complying because she made them? She only wanted others to do things because that was how they felt intrinsically. Anything else was cheap.

"No, I don't think electricity or devices affect the dragons," Mahkah stated. "I've been looking into it recently at Hiker's request. The information we had before was around the time that technology was budding. I've been doing my own experiments, and I think the belief came out of a fear of things changing."

He drew a breath, deliberating. "Dragons and their riders are probably the most powerful magical creatures to ever exist. We can also be very stuck in the old ways. I think that's because the history of dragons is a part of their consciousness from the beginning. It must be hard to accept the new when the old cascades across their memories. However, Lunis doesn't have a problem with this as much as the others. I'm guessing it's because he has been with you since hatching."

"And before hatching," Sophia stated. "We used to curl up on the couch together when he was still in the egg and watch *Beetlejuice* and *Sabrina the Teenage Witch*."

Mahkah gave her a curious expression. "Please excuse me for not understanding what you're talking about."

She blushed, feeling strangely silly.

"Nothing, just a popular culture reference from about thirty years ago," she said. "Even I'm not totally up on the times."

"Well, to answer your question, then," he continued, "I don't think you have anything to worry about. Honestly, whether we want it to or not, the world will push us into the modern era. I think that's part of your mission, although I'm certain you'll have many other important purposes when it comes to the Elite."

"So, does that mean you're going to tell Hiker that electronics in the Castle aren't all that bad?" Sophia asked, hope laced in her tone.

"I think," he said, drawing out the word, "it doesn't matter what I tell him. Some things we have to decide on our own."

Sophia nodded, watching as Bell and Lunis took off again. However, this time, she didn't leave him behind as fast. He actually kept up with her nicely, his wings pressed into his body and a keen focus on his face.

"Woohoo!" she yelled, feeling his pride rebound in her chest. That was what it was like to be a dragon and rider. His victories were hers, and hers…well, she hoped he felt them once she actually had them.

"And there's the other thing to be aware of," Mahkah stated proudly.

"The bonding of our feelings?" Sophia asked, thinking of the moment they'd just shared.

"Yes, that," he answered. "But also, soon you will notice that you two aren't just stronger because you're training, but because you're together. Your eyesight will become so advanced, you'll be like an eagle. That is the gift of the dragon."

"And I'll live longer, like you all," she added.

"Yes, but your dragon will also feel emotions more keenly. That's the contribution of the rider," he explained. "You see, when the dragon chooses a rider, they choose companionship, loyalty, and a bond like no other. They give up freedom, but in return, we both receive gifts from one another."

"So I'll be stronger and faster too?" she asked.

He gave her a measured glare. "If you're not already. I'm not sure I've met many who mastered axe-throwing in a single session."

Again she blushed, watching as Evan and Wilder descended through the clouds, their dragons with their heads down and front legs extended. It reminded Sophia of an airplane landing, but organic and flowing, not the way a stiff craft could ever do.

Like they were one with the Earth, the dragon and rider slid onto the ground, not having to brace for the landing. It seemed as simple and complex as landing on a cloud.

Sophia tensed, suddenly glad she had time to get ready to ride Lunis. It seemed to her that it would require much more faith than skill. Much more confidence than prowess. And certainly more imagination than courage.

Surprisingly, she smiled at this realization. This might not have been the way she saw dragon riding going, but now she didn't want it to be any other way.

CHAPTER THIRTY-ONE

For weeks and weeks, Sophia awoke, showered, and got ready, receiving praise from Ainsley for the small tasks. She made it down to breakfast early every single day, protecting the pastries from Evan for Quiet. He hadn't had a single buttery, sweet treat in weeks. She would have given him another chance, but every time she considered it, he'd say something smug and earn another week of punishment.

All the while, Hiker remained stone-faced, as if he wasn't sure whether to commend or punish Sophia for her antics. During every breakfast, which was the only meal he was at regardless, he seemed conflicted.

Sophia could have sworn that a few times she'd seen Hiker actually grin about the ways she had kept Evan in check. However, the glint in his eyes disappeared when she gave him a questioning look.

She learned to ignore Hiker, and he seemed to have perfected that with her as well. The two moved like ghosts around each other, not talking to one another and never acknowledging each other's presence.

Even after a couple of weeks, she didn't notice him rolling his eyes at her pranks. She didn't even notice him standing on the front steps of the Castle, watching her spar with Wilder. And she never saw him lurking in the distance as she watched the dragons by Mahkah's side.

The young rider had gotten so good that Evan refused to battle her during combat training. Mahkah always stated he had to go check on the dragons. That left Wilder to clink swords with her, which always resulted in both of them being breathless, one of them bloody, and both of them sore as hell.

"You've gotten good," Wilder said one morning, gripping his side.

"Good?" she said, heaving to breathe.

"By good, I obviously meant you just beat my ass and should stay back, for the love of the angels," he said, holding up his sword like she was going to charge him.

"Thanks," she said, grateful she didn't have to try to kick his ass again. She was worried she wouldn't survive the effort, but she'd do it even if it killed her.

Training with the dragons had progressed, but apparently not like before, since there had never been a newborn. Lunis had learned how to fly. Watching him soar over the Expanse with Bell and Tala on either side of him filled Sophia with a love she'd never felt before. She didn't even miss the fact that she wasn't on his back. He had said he wasn't strong enough to carry her yet, and she had understood at once.

It was strange because Sophia had wondered in the beginning how the men hadn't gotten lonely living inside the Gullington all these years. However, as her bond with Lunis deepened, she realized that the love she felt for him would keep loneliness at bay for the rest of her life.

Sophia didn't do much during dragon training except watch. However, she had grown accustomed to her increased eyesight, which did take some getting used to. Using her enhanced sight, she'd watched Wilder mount and take off on Simi so many times that she did the actions in her sleep, hungry for the moment she could ride Lunis.

He was still small by dragon standards, though. However, he hardly fit in her room anymore. When he laid down at night, he took up most of the open space. The other furniture had been moved out, and at night, he laid his head on her bed, his gentle breathing putting her to sleep like a draft through the windows.

In a few weeks, Sophia had grown stronger. Her dragon had, too. The ones around her didn't tense when she entered the room. Well, besides Hiker, but he didn't curse as much anymore either, according to Ainsley.

Sophia strangely began to think of the Castle as home. She didn't know why, but the Castle gave her something she'd never felt at the House of Fourteen. It strangely supplied her with something she hadn't realized she was missing—a connection.

However, she was still restless. Training was good, but it wasn't good enough. To Sophia, training was supposed to lead up to something, but every day rolled into the next with no end in sight. It was starting to hurt her heart.

On one such morning, she'd tortured herself on the subject for so long that she was late to breakfast for the first time in several weeks.

She arrived to find Evan hovering over the platter of pastries, a victorious smile on his face when he looked at her.

"Well, well, well. Look who slept in," he said, holding onto the tray and angling his shoulders back and forth.

"Save it," she said. "I think you've learned your lesson. Don't be a jerk. Share the pastries. End of story."

His tongue wiped across his teeth. The other men looked at the two of them as if waiting for the next move. "Oh, yes, I've learned my lesson, and here it comes right now."

Sophia turned to find Quiet entering late, as usual. He never came to breakfast until the flock was settled.

She rolled her eyes and returned her gaze to Evan. "Seriously?"

He laughed. "Yeah. Seriously, S."

Hiker kept his eyes on his cup of coffee.

Wilder and Mahkah remained stone-faced. However, Ainsley set down her tray and stepped back as if waiting for the show.

Sophia shook her head, ready to take her usual seat, but Evan picked up the only pastry left lying on the platter and held it high in the air.

"Oh, hey there, Quiet," he called. "Would you like this?"

Quiet's chin lifted. He mouthed, "Yes, I would."

Sophia sighed. "Don't, Evan."

"Don't what?" he argued. "Do what I want. After you've taken that from me for so long?"

"Don't," she encouraged.

He held the pastry high. "How about this? If the little guy can reach it, it's all his. Come on, Quiet. Jump for it. Would you?"

The gnome thought about that. His eyes shifted to the platters of fruit and scraps of overcooked meat, then he positioned himself under the pastry. He bent his knees, about to jump, his eyes shifting back and forth.

"That's right, little guy," Evan said. "Show me how much you want it."

"Stop," Sophia argued, but it did little good.

Quiet jumped, but his heels barely came off the floor.

"Oh, good try, but I think I'll take a bite since you didn't get it, little guy," Evan said, picking up the pastry and putting it near his mouth.

Sophia couldn't restrain herself any longer. She grabbed a knife on the table and threw it across the room. With impressive precision, it struck the pastry an inch from Evan's face and pinned it to the wall.

With his hand still beside his face like he was holding the pastry, Evan's eyes widened. He screamed like a little girl who had been pinched hard. It was a loud sound that went on for a while.

So long that the gnome retreated several steps and Hiker covered his ears from the screeching.

Everyone froze, taking in the strange sight of Evan frightened. Sophia's hand was still in the air, having released the knife. Quiet wore an expression of victory.

And then it all erupted.

For the first time since Sophia Beaufont arrived at the Gullington, Hiker laughed. A loud sound, full of joy. It filled the dining hall, infecting the space. This seemed to put the rest at ease, and Wilder, Mahkah, and Ainsley joined in, laughing at Evan's expense.

Quiet, however, had jumped up on a chair and grabbed the pastry from the wall, taking a bite and winking at Sophia.

"You nearly hit me in the face," Evan complained.

"The knife was yards from your face," Sophia said, joining in with the others, finding the laughter healing.

"No, it nearly got me!" he complained.

"It was miles away," Wilder said, shaking his head.

"But it did nearly graze your head," Ainsley added.

"And your expression," Hiker said, his cheeks beet-red from laughter. "That was the best thing I've seen in centuries."

Everyone halted their laughter, looking at their leader, realizing all of a sudden that things had changed at the Castle in the Gullington.

CHAPTER THIRTY-TWO

Not in all the time that Sophia had been at the Castle had she visited Hiker's office. The men, apparently, hung out there many evenings, drinking and discussing whatever they discussed. She only knew this because Ainsley had told her. When she pursed her lips, looking left out, the housekeeper had waved her off.

"Oh, you don't want to be a part of that bore-fest." The shapeshifter had spent a lot of time watching YouTube with Sophia, and her lingo showed it. Hiker had mentioned that he couldn't understand half of what she said anymore.

"Well, you never listen to me anyway, so who cares?" Ainsley had retorted.

One evening, though, Sophia was surprised to get a message from Hiker, stating that he requested her presence in his study. She didn't even know where the office was, but that didn't matter in the Castle. All she had to do was think about where she wanted to go, and it would lead the way. That had been problematic a few times when she'd been exhausted but still tried to drag herself to her trainings and the Castle kept leading her to her bedroom. No matter how many times she tried to find the front door, it hadn't worked. Every door led to her bedroom.

On this occasion, thinking of Hiker's office brought her there straight away. That had to be because she was entirely intrigued by what he wanted to discuss with her. She wouldn't have told Ainsley, but she hoped the other guys were there and she'd been invited to the "boy's club," as the housekeeper called it.

Hope made her walk faster when she considered that maybe he was going to start sending the riders on missions again. She could hardly breathe, thinking of the possibilities. The guys would definitely go on the missions until she and Lunis were ready, but they'd return with stories, and this would be the beginning of a new era of dragonriders.

She quelled her excitement at the door to his office, poking her head around the corner. "Sir, you wanted to see me?"

Hiker glanced up from his desk, the Kindle in front of him and a scowl on his face. The office was large, with a long bank of windows that showed an incredible view of the Pond. The sun was setting over the water, producing a beautiful glow that shimmered for miles.

"Yes, come on in," he said, returning his gaze to the Kindle.

The office sort of looked like he had started to pack up, all the shelves along the walls completely bare. Sophia knew Hiker hadn't packed up a single book, but rather the Castle had done something with them, replacing the volumes with the Kindle. She had no idea how the Castle did half the stuff it did. It was magic unlike any she'd ever seen.

"Have you figured out how to use it?" she asked, pointing at the Kindle.

He shook his head. "No, it's not a magic I can comprehend. I don't even know what spell will get it working."

Sophia kept her smile locked inside. "Actually…" She pointed at the device but paused, reading his expression.

"Go on, then," he said, seeming to resign a bit.

"Well, you just need to turn it on, sir," she offered. "There's a button on the side."

"Button?" he questioned, looking the device over. Finding the on switch, his eyes widened. "Who comes up with these things?"

"Mortals," she answered, releasing a grin.

The Kindle awoke, glowing brightly in the Viking's hands. He set it down and pushed it away.

"Sir, why don't you just ask the Castle to give you back your books?"

He gave her a petulant expression. "That might work if I was you, but the Castle doesn't do a damn thing I ask anymore."

"Hmmm. I wonder why?" she mused, trying to keep the glee out of her tone.

"Who knows?" he stated, looking down at the Kindle.

"You'll want to scroll through the list of books and pick the one you want to read," she said, leaning forward and staring at the device.

He gave it a cautious look, hovering his finger a few inches from the screen as if afraid it might shock him the way the pastry platter electrocuted Evan each morning.

Sensing that he didn't want her watching him, Sophia turned her attention to a giant globe that sat in a beautifully intricate stand beside his desk. She knew at once that it wasn't a normal globe.

Her fingers traced the surface until she found where she thought the Gullington was, somewhere in Scotland. Hovering over the green mass of land were five red spots.

"This globe?" she questioned, her eyes still studying it.

"It's the Elite globe," Hiker stated. "It tells the position of our riders and gives me an indication if they are in danger."

Sophia nodded, having guessed this. She then turned the large globe until she found the west coast of the United States. Her finger brushed Los Angeles, thinking of her old home. "So, there are more of us in the world?" she asked Hiker, her eyes staying pinned on the globe.

"You mean, as far as dragonriders?" he asked.

"Yeah," she said, remembering that *The Incomplete History of Dragonriders* had made it sound like there were once dozens of them.

"We are the Elite," Hiker explained. "When a new rider magnetizes to a dragon, the globe sometimes tells me. It was a bit late informing me about you, so I have my doubts about its reliability."

She didn't think it was a good idea to tell him that her sister'd had giants putting protective wards around her and Lunis so Hiker couldn't find her before she was ready to leave the House of Fourteen.

"In the past, before you, there have been other riders, but if they chose not to be a part of the Dragon Elite, they disappeared from the globe," he continued. "I can still find them, but I chose not to use my magic for such things. I don't want anyone here who doesn't absolutely want to be here." There was an edge to his voice.

"So, there are other riders out there?" Sophia asked.

"Yes, of course."

"And do they go on missions?" she questioned.

"I have no idea."

She glanced up, sensing the tension in his voice. He was studying her, his eyes flicking down to where her finger was still resting on Los Angeles on the globe.

Hiker pointed. "That was actually why I asked you here tonight."

Sophia looked down at the globe, her brow wrinkling. "Because of Los Angeles? Do you have a trip planned? Stay away from the 101."

He shook his head. "What's the 10...never mind. No, you mentioned before that you were a Royal for the House of Fourteen and in line to be Warrior."

"Yes," Sophia answered. "But Liv is the current Warrior for the House."

"I also understand that you are next in line, and there are not any other eligible Beaufonts," he stated.

"Right…" she said, drawing out the word and wondering where he was going with this.

"My question to you is, what will you do if something, angels forbid, happens to your sister?"

She blinked at him. "Well, I'd go home. I'd take her position. Family first, always."

He nodded. "That's what I thought."

"But why does that matter?" Sophia asked, sensing his disappointment. "Liv is the best Warrior the House has ever had. She works directly for Father Time. I don't think she's going anywhere for several hundred years, and when she does, hopefully she'll have offspring who can fill her role. Either that or my brother Clark will."

He cleared his throat. "I just need to know if you're sticking around here for good."

She tilted her head, confused. "Why should it matter?"

"Because I like to know what to expect," he replied.

"Well, you can expect me to be here," she stated. "So, if you were trying to get rid of me, it's not going to work."

"Get rid of you?" he questioned. "That's what you think?"

"Only since the moment I arrived," she answered.

"Well, I won't say it has been easy, but I think we're making progress."

She nodded. "Yes, and in a few centuries, I hope to get a case, and we'll go from there."

Hiker picked up a piece of paper lying on his desk. "Why do you want to go on missions so badly?"

"Because that's what we're here for," she said with conviction. "We're supposed to be out there helping the world, not shut up in here."

He sighed. "And that's why I believe that if given the choice, you'll go back to the House of Fourteen. Maybe your sister will get tired of being a Warrior and step down. You're old enough to replace her now, so how do I know your loyalty is to us?"

She squinted at him as if she suddenly couldn't see him clearly. "My loyalty? I've been here every day doing everything you've asked."

"That's only been for a few weeks. Give it a few years and see if you still want to do this."

Sophia shook her head. "That's not fair. I'm here because I want to be. I'm a dragonrider. I was chosen. And yes, I want to be useful and go on missions that help the world. I want to take back our role as adjudicators, and I want that much more than to police the magical world, as my sister's role requires of her."

He shook his head, handing her a piece of paper. "I don't believe you. I think that once you get a taste for action, you won't want anything else. I think you want to be out there doing things more than in here preparing to do them."

"Well, what you think is wrong." She snatched the piece of paper from him. "What's this?"

"That," he began, "is your first case."

"My what?" She couldn't believe it. "But why?"

"Because I don't want you here if you would rather be one of those rogue dragonriders, not on the Elite globe. The men are here because they believe in me as their leader. Others have left to do their own thing, and you might decide to do that as well, or go on to the House of Fourteen and be a Warrior. The decision is yours, so I'm giving you a case. When you complete it, come back and see me. Tell me if you can stay here and train, knowing there are missions you could be doing. Or leave here and do it on your own."

Sophia didn't know what to say. She was getting what she wanted, but not in the way she wanted. If she liked going on missions, if this fulfilled her, then Hiker wanted her gone. And if she didn't...well, she couldn't even fathom that. She wasn't sure exactly what was going on, but this seemed like a trick.

CHAPTER THIRTY-THREE

The next morning, Sophia was out of the Castle with Lunis before the sun was up. The piece of paper Hiker had given her was in her hands, although she'd already memorized its contents.

"Hiker is trying to give me the most boring mission in the world to either break my spirit or reset my expectations," she said, watching the sun rise over the mountains.

"Our jobs can't always be glamorous," Lunis stated, towering over her now, having grown a great deal in the past few weeks.

"Please tell me when our jobs have ever been glamorous? Was it when you crash-landed in the Pond and got tangled in that net, and I had to cut it away from your horns? Or was it when Coral accidentally dropped the sheep from mid-air and you had to dive and push me out of the way before I was crushed?"

"We're still training," he said simply.

"You sound like Hiker," she fumed.

"He isn't wrong."

"Well, why the boring mission, then?" Sophia asked.

"I think he doesn't want you here if you're going to be restless. He wants you to be like the other men or leave."

She shook her head. "How many has he done this to, pushing them out when they asked to have a purpose?"

"There is no way for me to know for sure," he answered.

"The others won't tell me," she grumbled. "And I know that Adam was different since he was here before Hiker even."

"I think he gave you this mission because it's close by and not too complicated, since you are still relatively new as a rider," Lunis stated.

"It isn't far, but I don't really want to hoof it," she said, looking out over the Expanse. The mission involved resolving a dispute between two horse breeders just east of the Gullington, only a few miles away. Apparently, one had a herd of horses, but the other neighboring rancher had laid claim to them, saying they actually belonged to him. The two had been bickering for quite some time, doing really mean things to retaliate back and forth.

"Should I give you a head start?" Lunis asked.

"No, what you should give me is a ride," she complained.

The dragon shook his head. "I wish I could, but you're too big."

She scoffed. "And there you go, calling me fat again."

"I'm not calling you fat," he said dully. "I'm simply not big enough to support your weight during flight yet."

"Well, instead of giving me a complex, maybe you need to work out more," she suggested.

"I train for hours every single day," he argued.

"Yeah, but it's obviously not working. Maybe try changing your workout."

"Like how?" he asked, his chin down and blue eyes shining with skeptical speculation.

"I don't know. Maybe add something like Pilates to the mix."

Lunis shook his head and started forward. "You're ridiculous, Sophia." After a few long strides, he launched into the air, spread his wings, and soared toward the sunrise.

"Okay, well, when you get there hours before me, wait, would you?" she yelled.

Sophia was winded by the time she reached the hilltop where Lunis was perched, looking down at the two farms. From a distance, they appeared almost idyllic, with smoke billowing up from their chimneys. The white fences that separated the two farms seemed inconspicuous, but Sophia knew the barriers were important for a lot of reasons. They kept the horses on one farm, displaying them for the other rancher to seethe about.

"So, are those the horses in question?" she asked, hands on her knees, trying to breathe after the long climb to the top. It was a herd of roughly twenty horses, grazing in the green pastures.

"Do you remember the first rule of dragonriders?" Lunis asked, his focus on the homes below.

"First, in any dispute, the adjudicators get the sides to come together and talk," she said, her hands going to her hips.

"And second?" he asked as if quizzing her.

"We get them to negotiate," she answered.

"That's right," he said. "How do you want to proceed?'

"We call the sides out to talk," Sophia said, uncertainty in her voice.

"Okay," he offered. "Call them."

Sophia muttered an incantation. Two scrolls materialized in the air and hovered before her face, then shot down to the two farms in the distance. She watched from a mile away as the two breeders opened their doors. Both of their faces were surprised when they opened the door to find a scroll hovering in the air before them. Her eagle vision gave her the chance to see this like it was happening right in front of her.

They opened the scrolls and read, and Lunis and Sophia exchanged curious expressions.

"Ready for stage one?" she asked.

"How about you go first?" he suggested.

"What is your role in this?" she asked, rolling her eyes.

"I'm here for when it all goes wrong," he stated.

"This is an open-and-shut case." She shook her head as she hurried down the hilltop. "That's never going to happen, so take a vacay, dragon."

It took Sophia less time than she'd expected to cross the fields to the farmers' houses. She picked up on a strange energy when she crossed the property line but dismissed it, earning the attention of the men. They joined her on either side of the fence when she arrived, having read the note she had sent to them. A black dog ran around behind one of the ranchers, herding free-range chickens.

"Hello," she said, turning to face both men alternately. "Thank you for joining me."

"Why are we here?" Mr. Lightbody asked.

"Yeah, I don't like to look at his face," Mr. Hopper added.

"Well, I have a way of resolving your dispute, and—"

Sophia was immediately cut off by the chorus of bickering from the two men. They yelled so loudly across her that she knew there was no magic that would get them to quiet down. Sophia glanced at them, wondering if she'd already failed.

On the heels of her thoughts, Lunis flew down, cutting the men off immediately. They both straightened, turning to face the majestic dragon as he shook out his wings, his chin high.

"Whoa!" Mr. Lightbody yelled, clapping a hand to his forehead.

"You're..." Mr. Hopper said, all the color having drained from his face.

"I thought you all were gone." Mr. Lightbody's voice shook. "My great-grandfather said—"

"We're back," Sophia said, striding out to where Lunis was. "And we're here to help."

"Well, there's nothing to be done," Mr. Hopper stated matter-of-factly. "He wants what belongs to me."

"But there is obviously a problem," Sophia stated. "What's going on?"

Mr. Lightbody pointed at Mr. Hopper. "He stole my horses long ago. He stole them from my great-grandfather, and I want what belongs to me. Those are some prize-winning horses."

"He's wrong, and won't listen to reason. Our grandfathers had an agreement," Mr. Hopper argued. "The horses were to stay on my property. It was very clear."

"How do you know?" Sophia asked. "Do you have the agreement?"

"No. My granddaddy told me," Mr. Hopper answered. "They had an agreement for a reason. He said the horses were to remain over here. He was very specific about that."

"Well, I have no agreement, and want my horses back," Mr. Lightbody stated.

"Okay," Sophia cut in. "I think we can come to a new agreement here."

The men studied each other, not looking close to agreeing.

Lunis growled, making both of them start. It was a low rumble that echoed in Sophia's core, vibrating something primitive inside of her. By the expression on the men's faces, it did something similar to them.

Lunis' eyes now shimmered, and smoke streamed from his nostrils. It was the smallest show of power, but quite effective, based on the expressions that crossed the men's faces.

"An agreement," Sophia stated again. "I want you two to talk."

The men talked for a long hour, going back and forth, sometimes yelling, sometimes threatening each other. Sophia didn't let them leave, and her show of magic earlier, and definitely Lunis' presence, made them take her seriously.

She was about to make threats of her own, when Mr. Hopper's demeanor changed, becoming slightly resigned.

"I guess I have had the horses a long time," Mr. Hopper stated, his eyes on Lunis. "What if I let you have them for a while?"

Mr. Lightbody nodded cordially, a tentative expression on his face as his gaze also swiveled to Lunis. "Okay, and I will let you have them in a year."

Mr. Hopper clapped. "That's a good plan. You have them every other decade. We can divide."

The two smiled at each other and shook hands.

"Okay," Sophia stated, ushering Lunis to the field where the horses were. "Let's move them. We have an agreement."

She smiled, realizing she'd settled her first mission faster than she thought possible. It did fill her with an urge to do it again. Maybe Hiker was right, and she needed to leave the Dragon Elite. Maybe she needed to be with those who wanted to make change rather than be overly deliberate?

She nodded as Lunis herded the horses over the border from one farm to the other. Yeah, it seemed like she wasn't cut out for the Elite. She needed a place where she could do what she was doing here—making a real change.

CHAPTER THIRTY-FOUR

"We'll put them in this pasture," Mr. Lightbody stated, indicating the fence on the other side of his house.

Sophia waved her hand, opening the gates that divided the pastures and undoing the locks without a problem. Another small spell encouraged the horses through the gates and hustled them across the yard. She'd watched Quiet employ that specific spell many times to corral the sheep. What he did seemed subtle, but over time, she'd noticed that it was more of an art form, taking care of the grounds and flock.

Lunis stood to the side, watching the horses with a strange expression. He tilted his head like he saw something that wasn't quite there.

"What is it?" she asked him. The farmers had moved over to the horses, working together for probably the first time in all their lives.

"That was too easy," he said.

She rolled her eyes. "Did you see them argue for an hour? There was nothing easy about it."

"Yes, but there's something not right about this," he stated. "I'm also picking up strange energy around this place."

"Yeah," Sophia agreed, scanning the pastures. "I picked up on something when we first came down here."

"It has to do with dragons," Lunis said, narrowing his eyes and sniffing the air.

"What do you mean?" she asked.

He shook his head. "I don't know. I just sense that there's a curse on these lands that has to do with dragons."

"Well, the Gullington is only a few miles away, so that makes sense," Sophia stated, watching Mr. Lightbody lead the group of horses to the opposite field. The first had almost made it to the other pasture. "But Hiker didn't mention anything in the report he gave me."

"That's mostly what bothers me about this," Lunis said. "I have a feeling something was intentionally not disclosed here."

"Why?" Sophia questioned.

"Because if there was a curse on lands this close to the Gullington, Hiker would certainly know about it."

Sophia nodded, her eyes on the horses as they filed into the pasture. Mr. Lightbody slapped one on the rear end, making it charge forward and hurrying the others in front of it.

If Sophia hadn't been looking closely, she wouldn't have noticed the smallest of details that indicated something wasn't right. The horses that had filed into the pasture already were acting strange, tossing their heads. Whinnying as if suddenly in pain.

Then the changes began to ripple through the horses, starting with the ones that were the farthest into the pasture. The muscles in their necks rippled, and then as if under an X-ray, the bones became visible.

Sophia pulled her sword, and Lunis stood suddenly. "What's happening?" she asked him.

"I don't know, but we have to stop them from going any farther," he said urgently.

The two farmers who hadn't gotten along for decades were now working seamlessly together, moving the horses into the area rapidly.

They didn't notice that the horses in the front were transforming. Light vibrated down their bodies, making them convulse. Sophia could see their skeletons and also their flesh. Parts of them appeared rotten, like they were corpses.

She sucked in a breath. "What are they?"

"Zombies," Lunis answered, his chin down.

"What do we do?"

"We get them off that land," he stated.

Simultaneously, Sophia took off running as Lunis launched into the sky. The flapping of his wings sent a surge of energy through the air, making the possessed horses gallop forward at lightning speed. The first few barreled through the wooden fence on the other side, intruding on a pasture of grazing cows.

The ranchers had noticed the commotion now, their eyes wide at the bizarre sight of the horses trampling through the fields.

"Get them back!" Sophia yelled to the men.

They froze, obviously not knowing what to do for a moment. For mortals who had just seen magic, this must have seemed like a strange nightmare.

"Go!" Sophia exclaimed, pointing at the open pasture the horses had come from. There was definitely a curse on this land, but who knew why it affected the horses and not the other animals like the chickens, cows, and the loose dog. As soon as the question occurred to Sophia, the two horses in the front tore after a cow that was regarding the charging monsters with pure terror.

"Lunis!" she screamed.

From the air, the dragon had already seen the potential disaster. He opened his mouth, shooting out a thick stream of fire and cutting the beasts off. The cow mooed loudly and ran in the opposite direction.

Lunis swung around in the air, moving in a way Sophia had never seen before, changing directions on the spot. Hovering right in front of the charging horses, he shot another stream of fire at them, hoping to encourage them back the way they came. However, the undead horses weren't afraid and trampled straight into the flames, catching fire at once.

They sprinted through the fire, now ablaze, and streaked through the pasture, catching grass on fire. It spread wildly. The flaming creatures were a strange sight, barreling through the pasture, flames streaming behind them like flags in the wind.

In unison, the possessed creatures jumped the next fence, headed toward some homes.

"Stop them!" Sophia yelled.

Lunis sped forward, moving faster than ever before. He shot through the air like he'd suddenly been hit with a power boost. It was inspiring for Sophia to watch, but she knew she couldn't risk the distraction. She pulled her gaze away.

Another group of horses that had shifted was headed in the direction of the farmers, who were surrounded by chaos as unchanged animals circled them, bucking and throwing their heads, about to transition.

Sophia halted, throwing her hand up and reversing the spell she'd used to herd the horses. They seemed to be dragged back in the direction they came from. The ones that had changed resisted the most. One barreled forward, picking up a chicken and tearing it to shreds. Not having ever seen horses attack like this, it challenged every part of Sophia's perception. It was too bizarre to be happening, and yet she knew what she was seeing was real.

She couldn't save the chicken, but when the horse, now covered in blood from its feast on the chicken, galloped toward Mr. Lightbody, Sophia moved quickly. She threw herself in front of the farmer, holding her sword steady as the zombie-horse charged her.

Narrowing her eyes, she didn't budge when the monster drew closer. Instead, she positioned herself carefully. When the beast was upon her, she had no choice but to thrust her sword through its chest, yanking it up and to the side.

The horse screamed and rolled over on its side. From up close, Sophia noticed how deformed the monster was. She could look straight into its body at exposed flesh and its ribs. It smelled horrible, like it had been rotting in the sun for days, and yet the eyes of the creature were alive and filled with rage.

"I'm sorry," Sophia said, full of regret that the innocent creature had been possessed and would suffer for her mistakes. She grabbed Inexorabilis with both hands, holding it high above her head. A guttural scream echoed from her mouth as she plunged the blade deep into the monster's chest and straight through its heart. It went still immediately, but Sophia was granted no respite.

Around her was chaos. Zombie horses were feasting on chickens. The two on fire were spreading flames as they streaked toward the mountains with Lunis on their heels, shooting more attacks at them. In the pasture that had infected them, two of the monsters were feasting on a moaning cow, tearing at its entrails and yanking its intestines into the air, seeming to savor every bite.

Sophia looked over her shoulder. The only good news of the morning was that the farmers were working together for once, wrangling the rest of the horses back into the first pasture. The black dog was barking wildly at the horses, scaring them into submission.

She walked with purpose, unafraid, toward the two zombies devouring the poor cow. She was hyper-aware that she was being stalked by another set of horses that were circling the perimeter.

"First things first," Sophia said to herself, holding up a hand and sending a powerful spell at the first horse. It picked him up from the ground. She threw her hand through the air, making the animal fly through the sky, landing in the safe pasture and rolling several times. The creatures writhed as if in pain, but to her relief, its zombie appearance began to melt away, safely transforming it back to its original appearance. However, Sophia didn't think her magic would allow her to do that again. Picking up the beast had cost her greatly.

The other zombie looked up, his face covered in blood and a crazed expression in his soulless eyes. Sophia spun her sword through her hands, not just as a show of power, but also a way to prepare for what she'd have to do next.

The monster barreled in her direction, mouth wide and mane streaking behind it. When it was close, Sophia jumped, spun in the air, and landed on the beast's back.

It immediately tried to buck her off. Pressing her legs into the soft flesh of the zombie made Sophia's stomach churn. Still, she put her arms around the animal's neck, her sword in a position to slit its throat if it came to that, although she didn't want to kill the innocent creature. She wanted to save it, but that required getting it to safety.

Although she'd never ridden a horse or a dragon, it strangely felt normal, especially after all this time watching the others ride. Sophia steered the zombie horse, somehow keeping it under control, both using magic and steering it with her hands and knees.

Several times it tried to buck her off, but she held on, her boot looped into its open chest cavity. It was not something she had ever pictured herself doing, but she didn't hesitate, screaming as she braced herself and made the horse speed over the border to the farm and into the safe pasture.

The animal transformed under her, throwing her off when its skin became healthy once more. Sophia soared over its head, rolling several times when she hit the ground.

Sophia didn't take a moment to breathe when she came to a stop, lying flat for less than a second. Instead, she bolted to her feet, seeing Lunis returning, having charred the other two zombie-horses he'd been flying after. There was only one more left, and it was barreling toward a cow who was trying to get away from it.

There was nothing for Sophia to do but watch in awe as Lunis dove toward the ground, his claws extended, intensity burning in his eyes. He zipped through the air, dropping suddenly, picking up the possessed horse, and rising back into the air. Quickly he soared overhead, came back down, and dropped the creature into the pasture where it had been before.

Sophia used her magic to close the gates, locking the horses back inside the safety of the pasture where they'd been for quite some time. Suddenly she knew exactly why, as she mopped sweat and the blood of a zombie-horse from her forehead.

CHAPTER THIRTY-FIVE

The fires around the pastures had started to die. The fear in Mr. Hopper and Mr. Lightbody's eyes, however, looked to be far from receding.

They stood looking at the chaos the zombie-horses had left, bewilderment covering their faces.

"How?" Mr. Hopper asked.

Sophia shook her head as Lunis landed next to her. "I don't know, but I'll do everything I can to ensure it never happens again."

"The agreement," Mr. Lightbody said, his gaze distant as shock overwhelmed him.

"Yes, that must have been why our ancestors required we keep the horses over there on my land although they belonged to you," Mr. Hopper said.

The other farmer combed his hand through his long beard, shaking his head. "I've never seen anything..." His voice trailed away as his eyes connected with Lunis, who seemed to be glowing after his first battle. Covering his head with his hands, he shook it. "I think I could use a drink."

"Me too," Mr. Hopper agreed. "Come on, neighbor. I'll pour us a few."

They both ambled off for the house, neither looking back at Sophia or the wreckage the zombie-horses had caused.

Sophia's reserves were low after this first battle on her own. However, she wasn't going to leave the mess for the innocent men to clean up. It was bad enough that they'd lost many animals. Working with Lunis, they cleaned the farms, not even leaving behind a blade of stained grass.

When they were done, Sophia turned for the hills that divided this area from the Gullington. She sighed. "I really wish you could carry me," she said, hiking toward the ridge.

"I wish you could carry me," Lunis said, staying on the ground and moving beside her.

"Hey, I saw you pick up that horse," she exclaimed.

"Yes, and I saw you ride that zombie," he replied proudly. "Good work."

"Thanks," she stated. "However, if you can pick up and carry a horse, why can't you let me ride you?"

His eyes cut to the side. "It's different."

"Really?" she questioned, her feet moving although she wanted to lie down, the exhaustion close to overwhelming her. "I don't weigh nearly as much as a horse."

"It was a zombie horse," he stated.

"And that makes it different how?" she questioned.

"They have fewer parts," he reasoned.

She shook her head. "Nope, I'm not buying it."

"Well, I guess it was the adrenaline of the moment, but there's no way I could carry you now."

"Fine," Sophia acquiesced. "But good work. For our first battle, I think we did well."

"Although the entire thing was a disaster?" he posed.

"Yeah, although that," she said, looking over her shoulder at the farmers' houses. "At least Mr. Hopper and Mr. Lightbody get along now."

"And know not to allow those horses out of that pasture ever," Lunis replied.

Sophia still couldn't believe what she'd seen. It didn't seem real in her mind's eye. She tried to process it all the way back to the Gullington. Even when she crossed the Barrier, she could still hardly comprehend what they'd seen and been through.

Once in the Castle, Sophia didn't stop to say hi to Ainsley. Instead, she went straight to Hiker's office.

"It's good to see you, too," Ainsley said, replying to Sophia's non-greeting. "How are you, Ainsley?" the shapeshifter said, taking on the form of Sophia. She then shifted back. "I'm very well, S. Beaufont. Thanks so much for asking."

Sophia halted on the first landing of the stairs, aware she was covered in zombie-horse blood. "Sorry, Ains. Let's catch up later. For right now, there's a Viking I need to rip in half."

The housekeeper ran her eyes over Sophia. "Well, tell him I said hi, and that he's two decades behind on my pay."

Sophia tilted her head to the side. "He is? Why do you stay?"

Ainsley laughed. "That's a good one, S. Why do I stick around? Because getting another position with my only reference being Hiker would work out really well." She waved her off. "Be sure to soak those clothes, would you? Zombie blood is really tough to get out, although it's been a while since I've had the challenge. Thanks for bringing the spice back into my life."

Sophia regarded the shapeshifter like she was an alien. "You're very strange."

"Why, thank you," Ainsley said, curtsying. "I think you're absolutely bizarre."

Sophia shook her head, then headed in the direction of Hiker's office.

Sophia didn't wait for Hiker to acknowledge her. Instead, she strode into his office, standing straight in front of his desk.

"You tricked me," she said bitterly.

He hardly looked up from the Kindle in front of him. "I gave you a case. It's what you asked for."

"You could have told me that moving the horses would cause them to transform," she argued.

He tilted his head back and forth. "Details you didn't ask about."

She clenched her fists. "That's not fair. You set me up for failure."

"No," he said, finally looking up. "You set yourself up for failure. Did you ask questions about the agreement?"

"They didn't know the details," she answered.

"Did you try to find out?" he questioned.

"How was I supposed to do that?" she argued. "I thought it was easy enough. Get them to share the horses, and everyone is happy."

"But in order to be successful in negotiations, we as adjudicators have to know all the details of the case. Otherwise, we will always do more harm than good."

"You know," Sophia began, "you could have told me that in the lengthy training you've given me on the subject."

He scowled at her. "I haven't trained you in negotiations."

"Exactly!" Sophia fired back. "You have me do combat and watch Lunis and read *The Incomplete History of Dragon Riding*, but have you taken a second to sit down and tell me anything that you're sharing now?"

"You're not ready," he seethed.

"That seems to be your answer to everything," she hissed between clenched teeth.

"What happened with the horses?" Hiker asked, looking her over as if the answer wasn't obvious by her appearance. "Did you kill them all?"

She flinched, shocked by his question. "No. Of course not. We took great care to wrangle them back, only having to slaughter a few. Unfortunately, we lost a couple of cows and chickens as well."

One of his eyebrows lifted in surprise. "Is that all?"

"Is that good?" she asked.

"Well, it's been a long time since anyone tried to resolve that dispute, but the last one resulted in the massacre of all of the horses."

She lowered her chin. "What do you mean, the last time you tried to resolve that dispute?"

"Well, it was before the current farmers," he said, casually pushing the Kindle around on the desk.

"Do you give this case to new riders to break their spirit?" she asked.

He slid back from the desk, giving her a look of offense. "Of course not. I give it to them so they know how tricky adjudication is. That it is never straightforward. A solution for both might mean the death of everyone. Usually, a compromise means everyone loses, but you wishful thinkers believe you can just go out there and strike a deal, and everything will be great because you've got a majestic dragon beside you. I'm here to tell you, sweetheart, that things aren't so easy in most dragonrider negotiations."

"So these others, they left, didn't they?" she dared asked.

"They thought they knew better," he answered.

She threw her hand in the direction of the Elite globe. "And they are out there doing what? You don't know because you wrote them off."

"And should I write you off?" he questioned. "Or are you ready to recognize that this will take much more training on your part? That the world isn't ready for us? Otherwise, those ranchers wouldn't have panicked, would they have?"

Sophia shook her head. "I'm not ready to answer that line of questioning yet, actually. I want to know why those horses change when they cross the property lines."

He shrugged. "It's an old spell. Those horses are a part of an agreement. They will live, but if they cross territories, they transform."

"You did that, didn't you?" she realized. "You made those horses. It's just a way for you to test riders. Eliminate them."

"I haven't had to eliminate any riders in quite some time, not since Evan," Hiker explained, sounding tired all of a sudden. "Between Wilder and Mahkah, there were quite a few. But yes, in the past, I've had to train men…I mean, riders, about how complex our jobs are."

"Well, I don't want to leave," she said with finality.

"Then you will quit asking for cases," he stated.

She dared to shake her head. "No. I want to learn more about how riders negotiate. More about the rules of adjudication. I want you to teach me."

"Fine," he stated. "But no cases."

"None for me, but what about the others?" Sophia questioned. "They can go on cases. They are ready. The world can see dragons and magic. The world has problems the others can help resolve."

He shook his head. "No, the world isn't ready."

"You keep saying that, but you don't really believe it."

"Of course, I do," he hissed.

"No, and don't you want to know what killed Adam?" she asked. "Because it's out there, and we could be using this time and effort to find it."

His eyes narrowed at her. "How dare you!"

"I dare," she fired back. "Something killed him, and you're not even investigating. And there were all those cases he'd researched in the newspapers, and you don't even want to look at them, although you have three strong riders who have nothing to do."

"You will mind your place," he stated.

"Or what?" she asked. "You've already tried to trick me into leaving."

"I try to get rid of anyone who doesn't want to be here," he replied.

"Well, things have changed. I want to be here, but not under the current circumstances," she replied.

Hiker stood, placing his hands on the desk and leaning forward. "You don't get to dictate the circumstances at this Castle."

"Even if you stick your head in the sand and pretend there is nothing we could be doing to help the world?"

"Watch yourself," he warned.

She shook her head. "No, you're trying to get rid of me because you know I'm right. You got rid of other riders because they weren't content with sitting around, but I'm not going to allow you to do that. There's something beautiful about the Elite, and I want to be a part of it, but only if you give us back our reins. Make us who we were once."

"You know nothing about what we were," he said in a rush.

"No, maybe I don't, but I know what the history book says."

"It's incomplete," he replied.

"Yes, hence the title, *The Incomplete History of Dragonriders*. I've read most of it," she said with confidence. "But I also have a dragon who sees the past. Who knows there is a world where we can make a difference."

"Then leave and make that difference," he said through clenched teeth.

"No," she said firmly. "I'm staying. I want your training. I want you to lead. I want—"

"Get out of here!" he yelled.

"No," she refused. "I won't leave your office until you hear me."

Hiker pointed at the door. "I meant the Castle. Get out of the Castle, and do not ever come back. I don't need people like you, trying to spoil what we have."

She fumed and took a step back, not believing he'd kicked her out.

"I mean it," he said, vibrating. "Get out. Take your self-righteous know-it-all attitude and get out. Take what you think you know about this world and go fix it on your own. Take everything you've brought into the Castle and leave here. We don't want your type."

Sophia opened her mouth to argue, but she realized it was useless. Hiker was never going to hear her. She'd failed. She'd failed herself. She'd failed Lunis. She'd failed her family.

And she had nowhere to go, but she knew she had to leave.

CHAPTER THIRTY-SIX

Sophia charged down the grand staircase, nearly knocking into Evan, who was seated, sharpening a knife on the middle stair.

"Hey, what's your deal?" he asked, sounding offended.

She turned at the door with the stained-glass angel window. "Sorry, but I'll make your life easier right now."

"How's that?" he asked.

"I'll leave," she replied. "That is what Hiker has wanted all along. That was what you wanted too, right? And probably everyone else here."

Evan stood, shaking his head, his dreads hitting him in the face. "No, I'd be upset if you left. I haven't had this much fun since...well, I can't remember. You don't put up with anything, and it's actually pretty refreshing."

"But I kept the pastries away from you for weeks," she said, surprised.

"I was a jerk who wouldn't share," he argued. "I bullied poor Quiet. I've been thinking about apologizing."

"Really?" she asked.

"Well, it might take me a few years to actually do the apologizing, but I want to, and that should count for something."

"Why are you such a jerk?" she asked, shaking her head.

"I was the youngest of seven," he explained. "They always picked on me. I guess I took my first opportunity to pick on Quiet because I could."

Sophia didn't know what to say to that. Her heart felt like it was about to burst right out of her chest as she stared around the Castle, the place she was about to leave for good.

"I've never been good with being myself," he continued. "The guys make fun of me, as they probably should. And I guess I'm always trying to overcompensate. But..." he looked around and then finally back at her, "I like that you put me in my place in a crafty way. You're one of a kind, Sophia Beaufont. If you tell anyone this, I'll deny it, but I'm glad you're here."

It was like the final nail in her coffin. She backed up. "Well, then, I have some bad news..."

She glanced up to the top of the grand staircase where Hiker was standing, looking down at them.

Evan peered up. "What's going on?"

"I'm leaving," Sophia said, and before he could object, before she could change her mind, before her heart broke any worse, she opened the Castle door and ran out and onto the grounds of the Expanse, just as it began to pour.

Within thirty seconds, Sophia was soaked. She didn't care, though. It felt like the universe, or maybe the angels, or whoever looked over her was trying to wash away her problems.

She glanced toward the Cave, but in the storm, she couldn't see it. That might be where Lunis was. He hadn't come into the Castle, and she felt that after his first battle, he might want to be with the other dragons, although usually, he spent the night with her even if he visited the Cave.

She knew she couldn't leave without him. Well, technically she could by using a portal, but she'd never do that. She had no plans to leave anyway, although she didn't know what to do with herself. Going home to the House of Fourteen wasn't an option at that point. She would feel like she'd let herself down. Like she'd let everyone down.

That was why, even though she had no idea where she was going or what to do with herself, she strode into the Expanse, her chin held high, the rain rolling down her face and dripping over her cheeks.

Sophia didn't dare call Lunis to her. She had to be alone with her problems, not burdening him with them. In the morning, things would be better, or at least, she hoped they would.

When she came to a large rock on the grounds, Sophia settled down, thinking she could sleep there. It wasn't the best place she'd ever slept. Actually, it was the absolute worst. And although it wasn't night, the storm made it feel that way.

Sophia felt her boots sink into the mud and knew that soon she'd be sitting in inches of water. Still, she didn't allow herself to fall into despair.

So what if she'd been kicked out and lost the only friends she'd ever had? So what if she was alone and her dragon was warm in the Cave? So what if she wasn't going to train with the Elite? And so what if the world was going to hell while the dragonriders at the Gullington wasted their days?

She placed her arms on her knees and leaned forward, pretending she didn't care.

The rain got harder, but Sophia told herself it would soon let up.

"Just another five minutes," she muttered, tasting rainwater.

When the rain stopped abruptly, Sophia thought she was psychic.

Then she looked up, noticing the shadow over her, and her heart lightened. Sitting next to her in the mud, having arrived soundlessly, with no whoosh or anything else, was Lunis. He had one of his wings extended over her, shielding her from the rain, which she could hear thundering overhead and hitting him, although he kept her dry.

"Thank you," Sophia said. "I didn't want to disturb you."

"Sophia, if you were across the world, I would feel your heart breaking, as it is now," he said, both aloud and in her head.

"Lun, I tried, but he…"

Lunis shook his head, looking down at her over his wing. "He isn't ready."

She giggled at that. "That's Hiker's line."

"It's appropriate for him. That's why he says it," Lunis explained.

She snuggled closer to her dragon. "I just don't know what to do. I can't give up."

"I know," he stated. "That's why you're here, and I think options will find you. The thing I appreciate about you is that you create paths well before you need to walk down them."

"I don't know what you mean," she replied.

He indicated with his head a small lantern that was growing closer in the rain. Someone was coming nearer, the light swinging back and forth. It was someone small who waddled when they walked.

Sophia could hardly believe it when she saw the groundskeeper Quiet approach through the storm, making his way to her and Lunis.

CHAPTER THIRTY-SEVEN

Sophia watched through the rain as Quiet drew closer. He stopped, his lantern swinging in the wind, when he was only a few feet away.

He opened his mouth to speak, but she couldn't make out a single word he said over the drumming of the rain. She doubted that she could have otherwise either since he was so soft-spoken.

"Come closer," she urged, offering the cover of Lunis' wing.

The gnome glanced up as if asking for permission from the dragon. Lunis nodded once, beckoning the gnome under the wing.

When he was close, Sophia didn't know what to say. It was such an awkward place to find herself, nose to nose with the gnome in a torrential downpour. She simply blinked at him in the darkness, waiting to find out what he was going to say.

Finally, he said in almost a whisper, "I have something to show you."

Sophia tilted her head to the side, wondering if she'd heard him right. "Me? Are you sure? What is it?"

He shook his head. "I want you to see it for yourself. I don't know how to explain. Will you follow me?"

Sophia stood, and in unison, Lunis lifted his wing, making room for her. "Yes, of course. Where are we going?"

Quiet turned, pointing to the mountains that couldn't be seen through the rain and clouds, but Sophia knew they were out there. She'd memorized these hills. The Expanse. The Gullington.

"Past the Barrier?" Sophia questioned.

Quiet nodded.

"Okay, is it safe?" she asked.

He simply stared at her, strange wisdom in his eyes.

"Okay, well, I'll follow you wherever, Quiet," she told him.

He nodded. "That's not my name."

"What is it?" she asked.

For the first time ever, he smiled. "I'll tell you one day, but you have to stay to learn it."

Sophia wanted to cry. To scream. To tell him she'd do anything to stay with the Dragon Elite. Instead, she simply returned his smile. "Okay, I'll do my best. Until then, lead the way, Quiet."

<hr>

They hiked for several hours, no one saying anything. Sophia didn't think it would matter if they did. She couldn't hear Quiet unless he was really close. She knew what Lunis was thinking, and him her. And really, the whole mission was a mystery, and she was okay with that.

When they'd come to a ravine that was tough to negotiate, the rain finally let up like it was giving them a break, given the arduous path they had ahead of them. The terrain was slippery, and many times Sophia lost her footing. Still, she followed Quiet, impressed by how the gnome crossed the slick earth, never making a misstep.

She was prepared to follow the gnome without question for another couple of hours when he abruptly turned to her.

"Here," he mouthed. She saw his words rather than heard them.

Sophia squinted in the darkness, not seeing what he was referring to at first. Her eyes took a bit to adjust, but as soon as she did, she sucked in a breath.

"What's this doing here?" she asked, running her eyes over the crashed aircraft. She wasn't that well versed in technology such as airplanes and whatnot, but she recognized this one well enough, although she stayed back from the cockpit where she knew someone was rotting, having died long ago.

"Adam," Quiet said. "This."

Sophia gasped, looking between the wreckage and Quiet. "This is what killed Adam? By mistake."

She suddenly thought it must have been an accident. He was flying too high. It all made sense. He was out of his territory. This was exactly why the world needed to know about dragonriders. Well, and also because they could fix the world.

Quiet shook his head. "No, on purpose."

"What?" Sophia asked, looking to Lunis before returning her gaze to Quiet. "How do you know that?"

As if he always spoke at a normal level, the gnome said. "Over that ridge, you'll find what Adam was investigating. This came from there. I thought you could help…"

Sophia drew in a deep breath. "Of course, I will." Although she'd said it, she had no idea how to help. "Have you showed this to Hiker?"

He shook his head. "It's because of him that I know about this. I followed him here the night Adam died."

Sophia pulled back, shocked by this news. "What? He knows what killed Adam?"

"Yes, but he tried to cover it up," the gnome explained. "He glamoured this so it couldn't be seen, but I've finally been able to undo his spell."

Sophia looked to Lunis, who was wearing a grave expression like Quiet's. "Why would he cover it up?"

The groundskeeper simply shrugged.

"Okay, well, I'll help to investigate. Lunis and I will do it together," Sophia said with real conviction.

She pulled out her phone and began snapping pictures of the crashed aircraft. Adam had been murdered, as they'd expected. But by who? And what lay on the other side of the ridge? All Sophia knew for sure was that she needed reinforcements. She needed information. She couldn't do this on her own, and one thing was certain—she had to do something.

CHAPTER THIRTY-EIGHT

The entrance to the House of Fourteen was in Santa Monica, right on the boardwalk. It was disguised as a two-story palm-reading shop that was always closed. The tourists and hipsters never noticed the strange people who entered the store, and no one had any idea that the modest building was the façade for a multi-story house that morphed and transformed constantly, based on the people inside it.

Even those in the magical world didn't know this was the location of the House of Fourteen. If they did, it would compromise the safety of the most important figures who helped to protect magical creatures and mortals alike. The House represented justice, which was something many wanted to destroy.

Sophia held her hand up to the door, pressing her palm into it. The door, which would only open for Royals, peeled back a few inches, blackness spilling out of the House to greet her.

Sophia Beaufont couldn't think of a better reason to return home. She couldn't have come back to Los Angeles when she got kicked out of the Elite. She couldn't come back when she didn't belong at the Gullington. But to come back for answers? Well, that made sense to her, and it felt right. No one knew how to solve a mystery like her sister, Liv Beaufont.

They'd agreed that Lunis would stay behind. He was too big for the mortal world...well, and also the magical one, probably. Sophia knew he craved the Cave and his own. She didn't fault him for that or envy that he got along well with the other dragons, unlike her with the riders. She knew their situations were different. They were one and separate, as they would be forever.

Entering the House of Fourteen after those long several weeks made Sophia feel like a lifetime had passed. The entryway was different, as Liv told her it would be. The House of Fourteen changed based on who was in there and their role. For instance, Warriors saw the House differently, according to Liv. When Lunis' egg had been in the House, it had grown in size to accommodate the dragon that would one day hatch. That was one reason they'd had to move him to Liv's place, and later to Rory's.

Sophia held her breath as she took a step into her childhood home. She didn't remember having much of a childhood and that was completely fine, but she still felt a wave of nostalgia pass over her. The language of the Founders was plastered across the golden walls of the entryway, messages that she wouldn't be able to read until she was a Warrior, which she hoped never happened. The foreign language was comprised of symbols that sparkled in the light of the torches on the walls. Sophia ran her fingers over the symbols, watching as they twirled and danced as if coming alive under her touch.

She stopped abruptly between the entryway to the Chamber of the Tree where the Royals met and the residential wing. Sophia hadn't thought past that moment. She had planned to enter the House of Fourteen, find Liv, tell her about the complications with the crashed aircraft, and then move on.

However, she hadn't considered how to find Liv. Her sister was always there when she needed her. All Sophia ever had to do was want her sister, and Liv would appear, but things had changed. Liv probably had moved on. She wasn't used to being at Sophia's beck and call anymore. And that was as it should be, she thought, turning back toward the entryway, trying to consider another option.

Only Warriors and Councilors could enter the Chamber of the Tree, where the meetings that oversaw magical matters were held. There was no way for Sophia to get in there. She glanced at her phone. Liv hadn't answered her messages, which meant she was in a meeting. Sophia slumped, feeling slightly defeated momentarily.

"Sophia?" a voice she recognized said in disbelief. "Is that you?"

She turned, expecting to see Liv, but it wasn't her. Still, it was a friendly face.

It was another Royal. Hester, a healer who was also a Councilor.

"I'm okay," Sophia said at once, although she wasn't sure why.

"I can plainly see that, although you're drenched," Hester replied.

Sophia glanced down at her clothes. She'd portaled out of Scotland immediately, not even taking an opportunity to change her soaked and bloody clothes. She could only imagine that she looked like quite the sight right then.

"Is Liv…" Sophia asked, letting the question trail away.

"Yes, she's in the Chamber of the Tree. They are just wrapping up. She will be out soon," Hester informed.

Sophia smiled at the healer, returning her gaze expectantly to the chamber.

"Oh, and Sophia?" Hester said, walking for the other door that led to the residential wing.

"Yes?" she answered.

"It hurts now, but it will hurt a lot more later," the healer said thoughtfully.

"Oh," Sophia said, grasping her chest like her heart would fall out if she didn't. Of course, Hester felt her pain. It was radiating from her, and the healer was also empathic. "A lot more later?"

Hester nodded. "I'm afraid so. Trudy has seen it in a vision."

Unable to respond, Sophia dropped her gaze to the floor. Trudy, a Warrior for the House, was Hester's sister, and also a seer. Few knew this, however, since even in the magical world, seers were shunned.

"I only tell you this so you learn how to shoulder the pain," Hester went on. "It won't kill for your heart to ache, but it can ruin you if you're not careful."

"Okay, thank you," Sophia said as the healer disappeared through the other door.

She turned her attention back to the door to the chamber, her heart drumming with impatience. The entrance to the Chamber of the Tree was known as the Door of Reflection. To Sophia, it appeared like a shimmering mirror of water, reflecting her rippling image. Apparently, when Royals passed through it, the door served up that person's worst fears. The idea was to cleanse them before each meeting. Liv had said it wasn't actually all that cleansing, but incredibly intimidating.

Sophia couldn't help the groan that escaped her mouth when a familiar figure stepped through. She wasn't just disappointed that it wasn't Liv. The man who exited the Chamber of the Tree was one of those people she didn't have the patience for right then.

"Oh, my gods!" King Rudolf Sweetwater exclaimed. "It's little Sophia."

"Hi, Rudolf," she said, angling her head to peer around him to see if anyone else was coming through.

The king of the fae was by far one of the most attractive people on the planet, with his wavy blond hair and blue eyes. None of his features were too big or too small. His face was a perfect balance, making him a pleasure to look at. His maroon wings shimmered behind him, framing him in the dark hallway. Rudolf was drop-dead gorgeous, the king of an entire magical race, and had the IQ of a plate of spaghetti.

He smiled at her. "Sophia, look at how much you've grown. I remember when you were just this tall."

He held his hand only an inch off the floor.

"No, you don't," she said dully. "When I was that small, I was a fetus."

The fae wagged his finger at her. "Oh, don't sass your elder. Of course, I remember. I've been around a long time."

"But you weren't in my mother's uterus," she retorted.

"Wasn't I?" he asked seriously.

Sophia pointed at the chamber. "Is my sister in there?"

"Sister?" he asked seriously, drumming his fingers on his chin. "You have a sister? Describe her to me."

"Yes, I have a sister," she said, rolling her eyes. "Remember memory banks? She's the girl who helped you to become king, and who helped you to get your wife back, and who saved your ass several times."

He continued to appear puzzled. "That's not ringing any bells. Is she tall, with brown hair and wide hips?"

Sophia sighed. "No, she's short, blonde, and can kick your ass."

Rudolf shook his head. "Never met anyone by that description. Are you sure you have a sister?"

Every day was a new day for Rudolf Sweetwater. Sometimes Sophia wondered how he'd lived so many centuries without drowning in his soup. "Liv Beaufont, Warrior for the House of Fourteen. The best man at your wedding, and the godparent to your unborn triplets."

Rudolf slapped his forehead. "Triplets. I'm having triplets?" He cradled his stomach. "No wonder I keep feeling like I'm getting kicked in the spleen."

"No, your wife Serena is. Never mind."

"And yes, I remember Liv now." Rudolf pointed to the Chamber of the Tree. "She's in there creating all sorts of problems. She's just not happy unless we are stopping every single bad guy. It's annoying if you ask me."

"Okay, well, thanks," she said, smiling politely.

"You're so welcome, Symphony," Rudolf exclaimed.

"My name is Sophia," she corrected.

"Right, right, I can't keep up with names. Anyway, I have to go and do Kegel exercises."

"But you don't have... Never mind."

Sophia was so relieved when the next face that came through the door belonged to her sister, the only person she wanted to see right then. Sophia ran, throwing her arms around Liv, hugging her before she knew what was happening, nearly knocking her over.

Liv automatically wrapped her arms around her sister, holding her in tight in a way Sophia hadn't felt in too long. "Soph, you're back." She peeled back several inches, looking her over. "What's going on? Are you okay?"

Only then did Sophia break for the first time, telling her sister everything. When she was done, she had no more tears left to cry, and she felt immeasurably better. And then her sister told her the one thing that would give her hope for the future.

"You are going to return to the Gullington," Liv said, scanning the pictures that Sophia had sent her on her phone. "I'll start researching this aircraft and find out who it belongs to."

"But I don't have a home there," Sophia stated.

Liv nodded. "No, but you want one there, don't you?"

"Of course," she exclaimed.

"Then go back and find a way to make it work. Don't give up," Liv stated. "I'll give you answers when I have them."

Sophia backed up, not knowing what to do right then. "Liv?"

Her sister looked up, confidence in her gaze. "Yes, love?"

"What would you do if you were me?" she asked. "I mean, how would you make things work? How would you fix everything?"

Liv smiled. "I'd convince them I had to stay if that was what I wanted with all my heart."

Sophia laid her hand on her heart. "You already know what's in my heart, sis."

"Then go, love. Create that reason," Liv urged. "Make them glad you're there."

CHAPTER THIRTY-NINE

It was time to put everything Sophia and Lunis had learned to the test.

The sun was rising over the ridge when she stepped through the portal, clean and wearing fresh clothes, although she hadn't slept. The crash site of the aircraft that had killed Adam lay before her. Lunis wasn't there yet, but he would be within a minute, she suspected.

At first, Sophia had considered going back to the Castle and confronting Hiker about why he'd covered up the crash site. However, that would only make him angrier. Instead, she knew that she needed to finish what Adam had started. That was the way to find answers. That was the way to earn the loyalty of the Dragon Elite and their leader.

She didn't believe Hiker was a bad person. He was scared, maybe. Reluctant, for sure. And absolutely petrified when it came to venturing out into the modern world. Of course, he didn't want anyone to know what had killed Adam because then they'd have to face it, and *he* wasn't ready. That was plain and clear to Sophia upon reflection.

Maybe whatever took down Adam would kill her too. He was a much more skilled rider than her. She couldn't even ride her dragon yet. However, the Castle had led her to Adam's room for a good reason, she believed.

She might be new and inexperienced, but Sophia reminded herself that she was the youngest dragonrider in history for a reason. It was time she reinforced her confidence. She remembered Mahkah's words: "The confidence of the rider becomes the fate of the dragon." She was beginning to understand that, and it didn't relate solely to riding. There was so much more to the dragon and rider relationship than she'd thought.

Mahkah, during their many training sessions, had begun to teach her about summoning her dragon. It wasn't as simple as he made it out to be, where she simply called Lunis with her mind and he found her wherever she was on the globe. Instead, it required a laser-sharp focus, or he couldn't locate her or even hear her call. They were bonded and shared feelings and thoughts, but when tension was high that connection could be muddied by the stress.

She closed her eyes, blocking out the worry and doubt and focused on Lunis, who was somewhere in the Gullington.

Lunis, find me. It's time we embark on a mission, she thought, sending the dragon a clear message.

The many times she'd practiced this during training, she hadn't been able to get his attention from a distance. However, just as Wilder had taught her, if there are no stakes, there was usually no progress.

Everything was at stake for Sophia. Her place with the Dragon Elite, her future as dragonrider, and a potential evil that could harm mortals and her friends.

Sophia was about to try to reach Lunis again when she felt the brush of wind on her face and the backs of her hands. A shadow passed overhead. Before she could even look up, Lunis had landed next to her, a proud expression in his ancient eyes.

"You called me to you," he said, surprise in his voice.

"And you came," she remarked, her chest filling with pride.

"Of course," he said. "I'll always come. But why here?"

She pointed to the ridge. "I have a plan."

"You think we need to investigate?" he asked.

Sophia nodded. "Yes, Adam was onto something."

He motioned to the wreckage. "It might be bigger than us. Bigger than what we can deal with."

"I guarantee that it is," she affirmed. "Will you still go with me?"

He bowed his head, giving her a look that was an expression halfway between love and annoyance. "Do you even have to ask?"

She smiled. "Always. I won't ever take your loyalty for granted. I won't assume you'll follow me without question."

"Well, then you have much more training to do, Sophia," he stated.

"But what if I'm wrong? Will you follow me blindly?" she asked.

"Then we will be wrong together," he answered. "That's how it should be. When a dragon doesn't comply with his rider, it's like severing yourself from your soul. There's no way to feel complete if you aren't connected to who you are at your essence, so even if you are wrong, we do it together. Otherwise, you will go into a battle and possibly die, and I wouldn't live much longer anyway."

"If I die, then you do too?" she asked, astonished. She hadn't read about this in *The Incomplete History of Dragonriders*.

"In a way," he said. "It is more figurative than anything. But yes, sometimes the death of a rider causes the literal death of a dragon and vice versa. That's why we're better off together—always."

"Okay, well, since you won't carry me—"

"Can't," he corrected. "Not won't."

"Right, because I'm heavier than a horse, and now I have a serious weight complex."

He grinned at her. "Go on, then."

"Well, I was thinking that I should open a portal," she stated.

"But you don't know exactly where you're going," he replied. "It is never advisable to portal somewhere when you don't know the location or what could be waiting for you on the other side."

She sighed. "So, I have to hike."

"You're not alone, though," he stated. "I'll hike right along with you."

She shook her head. "No, I think you should go up and see what we're walking into."

"Are you sure?" he asked, looking into the sky.

Sophia wanted to say no. That she was making it up as she went along. However, she remembered that the key was confidence. "Yes, and please report back when you get a visual. I'll meet you on the other side of this mountain."

He nodded. "Very well, Sophia."

The hike over the ridge was one of the hardest Sophia had done. At one point, the incline was nearly vertical, making her have to climb to get to the top. When she reached it, she had a view unlike any other.

The mountains surrounded by mists and the view of the rising sun weren't what took her breath away. That was beautiful and would have filled her heart with love if it wasn't for what was stretched between the mountain ranges. A factory definitely covered by a glamour sat between two ridges. Sophia had worked with Lunis to see through the magic. Smoke billowed into the air from the many buildings, polluting the clean Scottish sky.

She couldn't tell much from a distance, even with her enhanced vision, but she could feel something about the factory that wasn't right. It made her stomach turn. Made her raise her lip in disgust.

"So this was what Adam was investigating," Sophia stated when Lunis landed next to her.

"It appears so," he said. "I found two more jets down there like the one at the crash site."

"What else?" Sophia asked.

"They are polluting the streams by dumping waste into them." He indicated the rivers that ran around the mountains.

"Do we have any indication of who they are?" Sophia asked. "Or why they are here? So close to the Gullington."

"I'm certain the Gullington has nothing to do with it," he answered. "I think the remote location was the reason for this spot. The fact that it's near the Dragon Elite's headquarters is most likely coincidence."

Sophia raised an eyebrow, skepticism heavy in her gaze. "I don't believe in coincidences."

"Then I don't either," he said at once.

"You do think for yourself, don't you?" she joked.

"Only when you tell me to." Lunis winked at her.

"What's the security like down there?" Sophia asked.

"I didn't get that close," Lunis said. "Cloaking would be necessary."

"Especially because we know they fire to kill," she said. "Can you do it?"

Just as Sophia had struggled with calling Lunis, he'd had problems learning to cloak during training. It wasn't a problem for him to hide. The issue came with maintaining it, which created bigger issues. What was the point of sneaking in somewhere while you were invisible and randomly popping up when the shield came down? That created bigger problems, putting those unsuspecting of a dragon in their midst on edge when it randomly appeared.

She offered Lunis a calm expression. "You can do it. I know you can."

"And if I don't?" he questioned.

"We're in this together, and I'll step in and save you," she replied.

He nodded and took off, flying toward the factory below. When he was halfway there, the dragon disappeared in the sky, soaring to places Sophia couldn't see with her eyes, but she could definitely hear his thoughts about it since he was close by.

There aren't many in the factory, maybe since it's so early, he said in her mind, using his heat-sensing vision.

"They must come through using portals," she muttered.

Still, I'm getting the impression that there are some people down there, he continued. *And something else.*

What? Sophia asked.

Security cameras. Technology. The place seems to be run by automated precautions, he explained.

But why? she wondered. *What do they do down there?*

Nothing good, he replied to her question. *I can feel that much. If dark has a feel, then that place is pure evil.*

Well, I need to get in there, Sophia said. *That's the only way to get answers.*

I'll watch from above, Lunis stated.

Sophia nodded, hiking down to the factory that held more questions than answers for her. Why were there fighter jets there? Why had they gone after Adam? And what did this place produce?

CHAPTER FORTY

Up close, the factory was much more disconcerting than viewing it from the hilltop. The smell nearly made Sophia cough, but she stayed quiet, sneaking between the buildings. She'd already spied several security cameras, blowing them out with her magic.

She thought Adam wouldn't have known to look for those. That would have been one way that his presence was detected by whoever was running this place. She also wondered if he even knew what the jets that followed him and his dragon were. Like Wilder had said, learning about the modern world secondhand usually resulted in confusion. He wouldn't have known how to fight the aircraft or what it was capable of.

Sliding up against the largest building in the center of the factory, Sophia checked around her. The place was quiet, although she could feel the hum of machines vibrating the ground and wall at her back.

There was a door only a few steps away. Sophia thought about disguising herself, but she didn't know what persona to take. She would just have to risk it and be prepared for the fallout if she was caught.

In the air, still cloaked, Lunis seemed okay with this approach. It was haphazard at best, but she was out of options.

Quietly, she opened the metal door, finding it unlocked, surprisingly. She guessed that was because of the remote location.

Lunis had said there were people here, but so far, she hadn't seen any.

Inside the building, the smell of chemicals was strong. It burned her eyes and nose. Whatever they were doing in there, it wasn't healthy.

Now inside the factory, Sophia could hear people moving. They made strange swishing noises. There were hydraulics constantly going off. Heavy breathing. The clanging of metal. And only a small bit of chatter, mostly hushed voices.

Sophia paused at a corner, preparing to peer around the other side. She could have used magic and had seriously considered it. However, after the long hike and little sleep, she knew it was better to reserve her magic for when she absolutely needed it.

The hallway where she stood was dark, but the factory she was about to glimpse was covered in bright overhead light. Letting out a breath, she took a chance, peering around the corner.

What she saw wasn't what she expected. It was horrible; that much she *had* expected. But the slaves who were working, chained at the ankles and supervised by robots? That was the stuff of fiction and nightmares.

CHAPTER FORTY-ONE

A robot swiveled its head to where she was when Sophia peeked out. She slunk back around the corner, sucking in a breath.

It was too late, though. She'd been spotted. She knew it. And worse than that, she could hear the hydraulics of the machine as it made its way over to her.

Her brief glimpse had told her the robot was holding an automatic weapon. No wonder the people who were chained and wearing rags were working so hard, their heads down and defeat heavy in their eyes.

Sophia braced herself as she heard the robot get closer. It was just around the corner when it paused. She gripped Inexorabilis and held her breath.

The robot seemed to have concluded that it was a false alarm. She heard it retreat at the exact same moment she had an idea. She decided to take a risk and poke her head out again, whistling softly.

The machine halted and spun. It had red eyes and a sleek chrome body like a skeleton's, all bare bones. However, she didn't doubt for a moment that it was incredibly strong, not to mention, it had one of its metal fingers resting on the trigger of its gun.

There were few times in her life that she prayed, but that was one of them.

Angels, if you watch over us, please help me to survive right now.

She stepped back into the dark corner, holding her breath and waiting for the robot to come around. When it did, the machine made a zipping noise like it was accessing the area. Maybe sensing her, it came forward for further investigation.

That was when Sophia raised her hand, coming out of the shadows, and hit the robot with a compact yet powerful spell. It impacted its chest, sending a spray of electricity over the metal armor and making it convulse. It teetered from side to side before hitting the wall and crumpling to the floor, making more noise than she would have liked.

Sophia didn't waste a single second. She pushed the robot out of the way using her magic as she simultaneously took on its appearance. This use of magic would cost her greatly, but anything less would get her killed.

It was strange to look down at her body and see metal, but she moved the way she'd seen the robot do, striding out as she heard other robots headed that way. They had probably heard the commotion and were checking. She didn't know what protocol regulated these machines, but she was going to pretend she did until she figured out more information.

As she suspected, the other robots responded to her presence at once, turning back and taking their positions monitoring and guarding the slaves. Now that Sophia could look around freely, her stomach tied itself into knots. The people who were chained stood in front of conveyor belts, assembling things that appeared to be weapons.

They all had dirty faces and appeared starved. It was easy to peg them as slaves.

Many cut their eyes at her as she strode by in the form of a robot holding a gun. She didn't know what these slaves were doing here or who had them under their control, but there would be time to figure that out later. Right then, she had to get them out. Something told her the factory would only grow busier as the morning hour waxed, so this was her chance. That meant she'd have to take a deadly risk.

She glanced around the large factory and counted three other robots. That was more than she had the magic to deal with, but she knew from her training at the House of Fourteen that when reserves were low, strategy was the most important.

She focused on Lunis, who was flying somewhere overhead. *I need a diversion,* she communicated to him.

The wait for his reply went on too long, making her certain she didn't have a strong enough connection to him.

When he responded, she nearly yelped but stopped herself.

Where? he asked simply.

Stay cloaked. North side of the largest building. I need you to draw out three robots and then fry them to hell, she told him.

Robots, he responded. *Interesting.* Lunis, a dragon raised in the modern world, knew about robots. She'd even gamble that he knew how to deal with them, unlike Adam and Kay-Rye. They'd never had a chance, she realized now.

They are disgusting, Sophia replied. *Enslaving people.*

Then we will take them down. Consider it done, he told her. *I have just the way to do it.*

Sophia didn't know what that meant, but she trusted that Lunis would come through. She continued pacing like the other robots, holding her gun and watching the terrified and demoralized slaves work, their eyes cutting to her, anger radiating from their gazes.

CHAPTER FORTY-TWO

Something rocked the side of the building, making all the robots and slaves jerk their heads up.

The machines searched the area, strange scanners on their faces automatically scanning the building. Sophia copied their actions. One of the robots made a show of encouraging the slaves to get back to work. Sophia did this too, brandishing her gun, although it hurt her soul to bully the slaves.

Still, she kept her eyes on the door where the other two robots were headed. Once they were out there, another assault hit the side of the building. An explosion followed, rocking the ground underfoot. The blast sent heat through the factory.

Now they had drawn some attention—maybe more than they wanted.

This caused the third robot to hurry toward the door.

Sophia didn't waste a single second. This was her chance. She looked around the factory, finding the many cameras and knocking them out one by one. When she was certain there were no evil eyes on her, she dropped her disguise, feeling her magic pool in her chest, allowing her to breathe easily once more.

The slaves around her startled.

"It's okay," Sophia explained in an urgent whisper. "I'm here to help. You have to tell me who did this. I've got to get you out."

The scared faces simply stared at her, shaking their heads. They continued to work like chaos wasn't happening right outside the building, making many questionable noises.

Sophia didn't have much time. She cleared her throat. "I don't know who is behind this or why you're here, but I'm going to get you out. But you have to be fast and cooperate."

She turned to the open space behind her. She had to create a portal to a place in the world to send these people. Without knowing their story, she didn't know where safety would lie, but she knew that there was one person she trusted more than all the rest. And she knew without a doubt that she'd help without question.

Sophia opened a portal that emptied into a park half a block from Liv Beaufont's place in West Hollywood. "Come on. You have to go!"

No one moved. They all regarded her like it was a trick.

She nearly screamed. The assaults on the side the building cut her off, though. "I'm not kidding. I'm here to help." Sophia looked at the portal. "I know this is weird, but if you go through this portal, you'll be safe. I'll send someone to help you. Please."

A woman right in front of her stepped forward. "You're not with him?"

Sophia shook her head. "I don't even know who *he* is."

"We don't either," she said. "We just know he stole our lives. He stole us."

Like a zombie, the woman strode forward and disappeared through the portal.

Like a domino had been tipped, the others marched forward, making a cacophony of noise as their ankle chains clanged. Sophia urged them to move faster. She kept glancing at the door, where noise continued to erupt.

She had to get to Lunis. To help. But her first priority was the slaves.

She pulled her phone out of her pocket and sent a message to her sister: "Go to the park. Help the people I've sent. I'll be in touch."

CHAPTER FORTY-THREE

When the last man was about to step through the portal, he turned to Sophia. "I don't know who you are, but I thank you. I don't know why, but you saved our lives."

She shook her head, adrenaline burning in her chest from the many noises emanating from outside the building. "I don't know what's going on here. Get through before it's too late."

The man rushed through the portal just as the largest blast yet hit the building, nearly sending Sophia to the concrete floor. She closed the portal, rushing for the open door.

What's happening? she asked Lunis.

There was no answer, which she didn't take as good.

Sophia wanted to put on the disguise as a robot again, but her reserves from opening the portal and everything else were too low. Cautiously, she approached the door and peered out.

What she saw was strange, to say the least. Fire streamed through the air, delivered by an invisible source.

So Lunis has remained cloaked, she thought. *He's okay, at least for now.*

On the ground, shielded behind other buildings and debris, were the three robots.

They were firing at Lunis, many of their attempts seeming to get dangerously close. No wonder he couldn't respond. He was trying to stay alive, but it had to be difficult to hold off the attacks and keep up the cloak.

You can quit, she encouraged, shouting to him in her mind.

The fire disappeared.

The robots looked around, not knowing where to shoot since the fire had stopped. They had few clues about their attacker.

Great, Sophia thought. *Now I just have to get out of here.*

She retreated through the building, going back the way she'd come and through the other entrance. It emptied out on the other side of the factory, which was deserted, for the most part.

I'm headed for the mountains, Sophia told Lunis.

No! he yelled in her mind.

She had already run straight into the open lot when she got his message. She halted as a jet unlike anything she'd ever seen roared to life behind her. It hovered off the ground a few feet like a helicopter. This was no normal aircraft. Sophia knew at once that it was magical tech.

If she'd had a chance, she would have opened a portal, but the terror bursting in her heart prevented it. She made eye contact with the pilot, reading the deceit on his expression before she spun and ran for the edge of the property.

It was a dumb attempt, she knew. But what else could she do?

The craft might have been playing with her, but it didn't start after her right away. Instead, it let her get away several hundred yards before it zoomed in her direction.

No! Lunis yelled in her mind. A stream of fire shot between her and the aircraft, cutting it off and making it divert. She only allowed herself a moment to look over her shoulder, gauging the assault.

"I'm almost there," Sophia said aloud, and also in her head. "I'll portal as soon as I get a chance."

You'll never make it, he answered.

Just hold them off, she stated.

The aircraft similar to the one that took down Adam was circling.

Overhead, Lunis' form flickered in the air.

Sophia's heart dropped.

All at once, his cloak dropped, and he was solid. A target for the robots and the aircraft.

"Go!" Sophia yelled. "Get out of here."

No, he argued. *Not without you.*

Twice Sophia tried to create a portal, but she couldn't do it while running. That was the only thing keeping her alive, she knew as bullets rained down around her feet.

The aircraft took off after Lunis, gaining on him fast. The robots were still firing. Sophia knew she had few options. She turned, throwing the rest of her magical reserves at a vehicle sitting in the lot. Aiming directly at the gas tank, she sent an igniting spell at the vehicle. It exploded immediately, blowing up into the air and sending fire all around, knocking her back at least twenty yards

The explosion sent the robots across the lot too, many of them flying into a warehouse. The aircraft also retreated, not daring to fly through the fire rising high into the air and sending smoke everywhere.

The blast had sent Sophia into a metal wall, and her head hit hard. Blood gushed into her eyes, and her magic was completely depleted.

She closed her eyes, wishing she had the strength to communicate with Lunis. But at least he was safe. He could get away. The slaves had gotten away.

But Sophia's role as a dragonrider was over almost as soon it began, her second mission taking her out.

CHAPTER FORTY-FOUR

A strange swishing sound sought to wake Sophia from a horrible dream.

Not a dream, she realized as she tried to open her eyes. The light burned. Her head ached. Her heart felt raw.

"This is a terrible place to take a nap," a voice said.

Sophia brought her hand up to shield her eyes as she tried to peel herself off the hard surface under her. She could barely spy the form of Ainsley standing over her, holding a broom and sweeping like there was no more important job in the world right then.

"Ains..." Sophia said, relief in her voice, and also bewilderment. She was safe. She was at the Castle. Inside the Gullington. But she had no idea how she'd gotten there.

She started trying to stand, but the attempt was useless. Her immediate thought was of Lunis. *Where was he? And was he safe?*

"Oh, you're bleeding all over the steps," Ainsley said, clapping her hand down on her thigh with annoyance. "And I just cleaned them."

Sophia went to touch her head, but finding that it was mostly exposed flesh, she pulled her hand away.

"Ains," she tried again. "Lun…"

"Oh, he's all right," she said, her voice soothing now. "I saw him fly to the Cave earlier through the window up top. Then I came down here to sweep and found you taking a nap on the stairs."

"I-I-I…" Sophia didn't know where to begin, and the more she tried to think, the less she felt like keeping her eyes open.

"You're going to pass out," Ainsley stated. "And that will make my job horribly difficult. I don't want to have to sweep around you. I have to do that when Evan passes out here after staggering home from the Pond totally wasted. I won't do it with you, S. Beaufont. You're better than that. And really, drinking this early? You should know better."

Sophia tried again to stand, but she couldn't find the strength.

"Oh, fine then," Ainsley said, relenting slightly. "I'll help you."

"Thank you," Sophia replied, her voice nearly a whisper.

"Wild!" the housekeeper yelled so loud it felt like it would cut Sophia's head in two. "That girl you were all worried about is here, bleeding everywhere. Come and get her, would you?"

A moment later, Wilder appeared, his face in front of Sophia's, worry in his eyes. "There you are? We've been concerned. You disappeared."

"I was kicked out," she said, finding her voice suddenly.

Ainsley laughed. "Oh, did Hiker kick you out?"

Sophia nodded as Wilder supported her back, keeping her from toppling over.

"And you listened to him?" Ainsley asked with a laugh.

Another nod.

"He fires me every day," Ainsley related. "And he kicks Evan out at least once a week."

"He's told me to leave at least a dozen times," Wilder added.

Ainsley continued to laugh. "We never listen because he's just a hothead who loves us in his own sick and demented way."

"What?" Sophia asked, confounded by the reality that the eviction she'd received wasn't one. It made everything she'd just done seem strange and out of context. *But it wasn't,* she told herself. She and Lunis had saved people. She knew things she wouldn't have known otherwise. Quiet had helped her. It had to all have been worth it, but she knew she wouldn't have done any of it if Hiker hadn't kicked her out. Made her fight for what she wanted most—a place in the Dragon Elite.

"Come on, let's get you upstairs," Wilder said, supporting her weight. "Ainsley, would you help me? I'll need your medical expertise."

"Yes, sure," the housekeeper said. "Let me just finish up here." She continued to move the broom back and forth on the stairs.

"Come on, really!" Wilder complained. "She's got a head wound."

"Oh, fine," Ainsley said, striding in behind them. "But I want the full story while I patch you."

Sophia was about to say something but her eyes connected with Hiker, standing at the top of the stairs. Her mouth fell open when he disappeared, an angry expression on his face.

CHAPTER FORTY-FIVE

"What do you mean, you're not going to tell us?" Ainsley said, removing the bloody rags from beside Sophia's bed.

"I just think I need to talk to Hiker first," Sophia related.

"The man who kicked you out of here?" Ainsley asked. "I can't believe you took him seriously. But good on you. It took me several years to get under his skin enough for him to fire me. Evan, well, it took him at least a year." She glanced up at Wilder, a proud expression on her face. "I think this is a new record."

"She's pretty efficient," he agreed, nodding.

"I know how to piss him off," Sophia said, trying to get comfortable on her pink bed.

Wilder pointed to the television. "How do you turn this on?"

"Magic," she replied. "And currently I'm a bit depleted."

He shrugged, defeated. "Okay, next time. I want to see those cat videos."

"Oh, you should," Ainsley said, hurrying out the door. "That one with the cat hoarding baby dolls under the bed is simply priceless."

Sophia shook her head and immediately regretted it. "I think we need to get Ains out more. Or out at all."

"I think we all need to get out," Wilder said. He was sitting on the side of her bed, looking at how the Castle had redesigned her bedroom. Every day there was something new. The newest thing was a bouquet of pink roses. Ainsley had said it was her get well present. She quickly added, "I've never gotten one of those, but then again, I'm never sick or sporting a head injury."

"So, you're really not going to tell me what happened to you?" he asked.

"I want to," Sophia said. "But I have to make things right with Hiker first. I need him to trust me, and I'm only going to get that if I try to do things his way."

He shook his head. "You might be better than all the rest of us."

"No," she argued. "You all are here because you didn't challenge him. You didn't go on the fake mission to save zombie horses."

Wilder laughed. "Oh, gosh, he sent you to the farmers to settle their dispute."

"You know about that?" she asked.

"Of course," Wilder said. "I've heard of other riders being sent on that mission before me."

"You ever asked to go on a mission?" Sophia questioned.

He shook his head. "No. I should have, maybe. But remember, mortals were only recently able to see magic again, which kind of changed things for me. But also I like it here. And those other riders? Well, when they left, they were all alone. I never wanted that. I gave up everything for this. For Simi. And I would again, but I don't want us out there alone. So I've swallowed my pride and done as Hiker wanted. Maybe that was wrong, but you have to know that for a long time, there hasn't been any point. Only recently were missions even a possibility for me. And now I see you and your passion for it. I guess I might want that soon."

She rubbed her head and immediately regretted it. "I don't know. It's not all it's cracked up to be."

They were quiet for a moment. Sophia stared out the window. "So, do you know how I got to the Castle? I sort of passed out after cracking my head open."

He shook his head. "Quiet will know. Nothing happens here without him knowing."

She nodded. "Yes, I think he's underestimated."

Wilder winked at her. "Good thing he counts you as an ally."

Ainsley returned with a tray of soup. "Okay, I've got everything you need to get better."

Sophia sat up. "Oh, thank you. I'm starving."

"Not this," Ainsley said seriously. "This is my lunch. Just thought I'd bring it here so I can keep an eye on you. But I brought you a couple of aspirin."

"First off, the best you've got in a magical castle is aspirin?" Sophia asked. "And I don't get to eat?"

Ainsley laughed, setting the tray down beside Sophia. "I'm kidding. The soup is for you, and there's no aspirin. The Castle says it knows what to do for you." She backed up, pointing to the door. "Wild, get out. She needs her rest. And the Castle, well, apparently, it has its own home remedy."

"What is it?" Sophia asked, looking around.

"Eat your soup," Ainsley encouraged. "It's not for me to say."

Without another word, the strange housekeeper pulled the door shut, leaving Sophia alone.

CHAPTER FORTY-SIX

Immediately upon finishing her soup, Sophia was hit with a wave of exhaustion unlike any she'd ever felt before. She didn't even push the tray away before she passed out on her pillows, falling into a dream all at once.

Wind whipped her face, pushing her hair back and making her feel more alive than ever before. She felt the power under her and relished in the connection she had to the dragon she was riding.

Lunis soared through the air, cutting through clouds and sliding around patches of blue sky. The green of the Gullington blurred in Sophia's vision. She knew the tears in her eyes were because of the wind, but also because of the joy she felt in her heart.

The dragon glided down when they got to the Pond, soaring only feet from the glass-like surface of the water.

Clenching the dragon with both her legs, Sophia released her grip on the reins and angled back, dipping her fingers into the Pond and relishing in the way the water skimmed over her hands.

The rush was intoxicating. It made her feel alive. It made her feel brand new. More than anything, it was a healing experience.

The sound of knocking nearly made her fall off her dragon. Sophia started awake, not even realizing she was asleep. Disappointment hit her when she realized she hadn't been riding Lunis. She rolled over suddenly, making the tray with the soup crash to the floor, but she caught herself before she fell off the bed with it.

Sophia was bewildered, trying to remember where she was as she took in her room in the Castle. It all came back to her. She blinked, suddenly feeling better, her head not aching.

Hiker stood in her doorway, a strange expression on his face as he took in the room.

"Why does it look like a pink monster threw up in here?" he asked, a strangely casual tone in his voice.

"Was that a joke?" she asked, pulling the covers up to her chest when she realized she was wearing pajamas. "I think that was a first."

"That was the first joke you've heard me tell," he said, striding into the room even though he hadn't been invited in. "I've been around for five hundred years. I've told a joke or two in my time."

"Oh, well…" Sophia said, watching him look around her room. "I didn't do all this. Just the beanbag. The Castle did the rest."

He nodded, not saying a word.

That gave Sophia a chance to think about the strange dream she'd just experienced. It felt more real than any dream she'd ever had before, so much so that it seemed to fix her from the inside out. She peered at the walls of the Castle, knowing it had everything to do with her dream, which had healed her, oddly enough.

"So this?" he asked, pointing at the television. "Is this what you call a VT?"

"TV," Sophia corrected. "And yes. Again, I didn't do it."

He turned to face her. "Then tell me, what did you do?"

She sat up more. "Why did you cover up who killed Adam?"

Hiker let out a long breath, and his gaze dropped to the floor. "I didn't want to, but I didn't know what to do about it. If something was strong enough, whatever that thing was—"

"An aircraft," Sophia informed.

"Yes, if that aircraft was strong enough to kill Adam, the best among us, well, we don't stand a chance."

"So you simply covered it up and what, you were going to forget that it happened? That he'd been murdered?" Sophia asked.

"No, it's just that it's complicated," he reasoned.

"Is it?" she probed.

"Look, I'm not good at this…"

"Good at what?" Sophia asked.

"At telling anyone, especially you, that maybe you were right," he said reluctantly. "I've lost my confidence over the years. Adam knew it. My men probably do as well. I've gotten complacent. When I saw what took Adam down, I closed up even more. And then you came here, and you challenged me on every front. I just don't know what to do at this point."

Sophia nodded. "I went to the site the aircraft was from."

Hiker looked up suddenly. "That's where you got the head injury?"

Another nod. "Yes, Lunis and I went in there."

"That was foolish!" he boomed. "Th-th-that was something Adam would have done."

"Well, I have no regrets," Sophia said proudly. "I don't know who runs it, but they had slaves working in chains. There were these robots that…"

The confusion on Hiker's face made her pause.

"Robots," she continued, "they are like men made out of machines."

He shook his head. "This is what I mean. I'm not sure about this world. I thought we'd be out for a few years when mortals couldn't see magic anymore, and then one year rolled into a decade, and then into a century, and then another, and so forth. Now the world has changed too much. It will never accept dragonriders. We are archaic. I know that much."

"They won't accept us if we don't try," Sophia agreed.

"So, these slaves?" Hiker questioned. "You saw them?"

"I freed them," she stated. "And I blew up some stuff. I think Lunis was pretty amazing too, although I need to talk to him about it."

"You saved them," he said, apparently needing to digest that.

"Well, I couldn't leave them there," she replied.

"Right," he chirped. "Of course, you couldn't."

"I know you kicked me out and that you don't want me here, but more than anything, all I want—"

"I was wrong," he said, cutting her off.

Sophia paused. Brought her chin up. Forced herself to remain quiet and listen.

"You have to forgive an old man for being set in his ways," he began. "Adam, my elder, tried to change me. You would have thought losing him would have done it, but it only made me more afraid of the world outside of the Gullington. Then you, Sophia Beaufont, came along. The riders have been ignored for a long time. I don't know how to enter the world again. I told myself we weren't needed anymore, but maybe this strange, modern world does need us after all. I won't make any promises, but I'll try to change things. I'll try to get the world to see that dragonriders are the way again. We are the judge, the jury, and the executioner, after all."

If Sophia wasn't so exhausted, she might have bounded out of bed and hugged the large man before her. It was probably better that she was tired. That might have ruined everything.

"So…." she began.

"So, we will try," he agreed simply. "And maybe you can help since you know something about this modern world."

"Of course," Sophia answered. "And I'm looking into leads about who owns the aircraft that killed Adam. My sister has taken the slaves, and we can send the guys to the factory..." Her voice trailed away after she received a tentative look from Hiker.

"Small steps, right?" she asked, shrugging.

"I appreciate that you didn't tell Ainsley and Wilder about the aircraft I covered up or anything else," he stated. "You could have, but now I see you're someone who garners trust. That's the most important part of being a dragonrider. Some would have you believe you have to be strong, courageous, and a risk-taker, but they are wrong. That's not the most important attribute for a dragonrider. You can't fix people's problems if they can't trust you."

For the first time ever, Hiker Wallace made Sophia smile. Not because of his tense attitude or his unyielding ways, but because she saw, deep within his tough exterior, that he was a man she could grow to like, just like the life blossoming all around her in the Gullington.

CHAPTER FORTY-SEVEN

The next morning, Sophia was out of the Castle before breakfast was even served, leaving Evan and Quiet to figure out the pastry battle on their own for once.

She enjoyed the peace of the Expanse as she strode in the direction of the Cave. The Pond shimmered with morning sunlight reflecting off it, and the flock was a sea of creatures grazing in the ancient pastures.

For a girl who grew up in a magical house in a congested city, she couldn't picture a better place to live. The Gullington was quiet. It was peaceful. And it was on the brink of changing forever.

Sophia wanted to be a part of that change. And although Hiker hadn't committed to drastic changes, she knew he was more receptive than before. That was progress. For men who didn't change a lot in a century, that was good enough for her.

When Sophia was roughly a hundred yards from the Cave, she sat on the grass and waited.

It only took a minute before Lunis poked his head out, his horns catching the morning light. She couldn't believe how much she'd missed looking at him. It had only been a day, but that was too long. He had moved into the Cave permanently, now much too big for the Castle or sleeping in her room anymore. She was happy for him but grieving the past.

When she locked eyes with Lunis, her heart leapt in a way she'd never experienced before. She'd read books about people falling in love, and that was what her affection for Lunis was akin to. It wasn't romantic love, though. It was much deeper. It was the kind of bond that transcended centuries. It was an unconditional love she'd die to protect and do anything to keep.

He glided down to her, landing soundlessly in the grass.

"You're alive," he said casually.

"You had doubts?" she joked.

"I think we both know I didn't."

"It's strange, because I somehow ended up on the steps of the Castle, although no one knows how I got there," she mused. "I was passed out and don't remember a thing."

He looked at the flock, a hungry expression in his eyes. "That is weird."

"What do you remember?" she asked. "You were there."

"There was an explosion," he recounted. "Lots of fire. And chaos. Robots and aircraft. The usual."

"And then what?" she asked, hiding her laughter.

"And then a flying ambulance took you to safety," he answered. "Or so I'm guessing."

"They have those out here?" She had to really work to keep herself from laughing.

"I guess," he said, covering his expression.

Sophia decided not to push the issue. She and Lunis had to go through their own evolution. Who knew how long it would take? She hoped it wasn't another century.

"Hiker has agreed to look into missions," she informed him. "But I think there is preliminary work to do."

"And reconnaissance," he stated. "But that's good progress."

Sophia nodded. "Yes, and we have to figure out who was behind Adam's death and the factory and the slaves."

He stood nobly. "It seems we have our work cut out for us."

"It seems so," Sophia said, smiling out at the Expanse, enjoying the morning breeze on her face.

"Well, I hope you don't mind, but I'm off to grab breakfast," he said.

"Not at all," she answered, watching as her dragon took a few steps before launching into the air, his expansive wings flapping, carrying him gracefully across the sky.

He had grown so much, and yet, as she watched him dive to grab a sheep with his claws, she knew he would grow more. They both would.

One day, he'd grow enough that she'd be able to ride him, even when she wasn't unconscious.

CHAPTER FORTY-EIGHT

Cigar smoke circled through the air behind Thad Reinhart as he strode down the dark corridor, flicking ashes on the ground. He was unconcerned about the mess he left behind.

Messes were other people's problem. Thad Reinhart didn't clean up messes, his own or other people's. He made them. He had for over five hundred years, and he planned to do it for another half millennium, the angels willing.

At the entrance to the dungeon in his castle in North America, he turned, taking a puff on his cigar. He could never stand the stench in the dungeon for long. That was why he prepared himself, looking at one of his many trophies that lined the walls in the long corridor.

The stuffed head of the dragon on the wall still appeared as lifelike as when he'd slaughtered it centuries ago. This one was named Stellar. Her rider had died shortly afterward, although Thad hadn't had him taxidermized.

He drew in a breath and entered the dungeon, the stench and thick air making him sneer. The dungeon, just like the entire castle, had been modeled after his original one in Scotland.

That had been his home before the dragons and their riders had destroyed it. They thought they'd destroyed him too, but nothing could be farther from the truth. What the Dragon Elite did when they sought to bring Thad Reinhart down had only spurred him on and made him stronger.

When Thad had rebuilt himself, he planned to destroy the Dragon Elite. However, someone had done that for him—whoever made it so mortals couldn't see magic anymore, making the riders completely useless. He couldn't have devised a better punishment for them. Being marginalized was a far better fate for those who thought as highly of themselves as the Dragon Elite.

Yet, whatever had made it so mortals couldn't see magic anymore was gone. They had returned to the world of magic, and Thad worried that meant the Dragon Elite would as well.

His worries had become reality when someone recently nearly destroyed the Chainley facility, releasing all the slaves. Someone the few witnesses at the facility said was with a dragon. Thad could believe that, since he knew Adam Rivalry had gotten close recently. However, this rider wasn't described as being like Adam, nor did the dragon match Kay-Rye's appearance. Baffling to Thad was that the person in question was supposedly a woman.

The Chainley factory was in close proximity to the Gullington for a very good reason. It pulled from its magical reservoir to fuel the magical tech inside the facility, although no one knew that.

It satisfied Thad very much to know that the one thing Hiker Wallace struggled with most—technology—he was unknowingly fueling. The location of the Chainley facility was also important because things that were right under Hiker Wallace's nose, he never saw.

Thad Reinhart had spent centuries trying to find the exact location of the Gullington. Trying to figure out how to break through the Barrier. Although he'd been mostly unsuccessful at this, he still knew the approximate location. In time, he'd find it and destroy everything that was part of the Gullington.

The floor was sticky under Thad's dragonhide shoes. He made a mental note to throw them away after this. He had many that could replace these shoes, having used Stellar's hide to make multiple pairs. Her horns had been used in the inlay throughout the castle.

Abruptly, Thad halted in front of the chained prisoner one of his men had brought in that morning. It was a man who owned a farm close to the Gullington. Recently, one of the pilots for the Chainley facility had spotted a very curious incident at two neighboring farms. The pilot had been searching for an aircraft that had gone missing.

It didn't make any sense to Thad that his magical tech-inspired aircraft had simply disappeared. There were too many tracking devices on the craft, which meant another brand of magic was in play. The whole thing reeked of Hiker Wallace.

And then, one of his pilots had mentioned seeing scorch marks in the farm's pastures and animals that appeared to have been attacked.

Immediately, Thad had demanded that the farmer be brought in for questioning. Mr. Hopper hadn't wanted to cooperate, even after being shoved through a portal and intimidated by some of the best interrogators Thad employed. That was why he'd had to stop what he was doing to intervene and do it himself.

"Mr. Hopper," Thad began, puffing on his Cuban cigar and blowing the smoke in the kneeling man's face, "I understand you've been less than forthcoming. I'm here to change that."

The old mortal shook his head. "I have nothing to tell you."

Thad laughed, a hollow sound lacking any joy. "Really? What happened at your farm recently?"

"Nothing," the man lied. "It was nothing."

"Who burned the fields?" Thad asked, losing his patience.

"That was me," he said, his Scottish accent growing deeper.

"And you slaughtered your own cow in the middle of a field?" Thad questioned.

"I-I-I think dementia is overcoming me, the same as my father," he stuttered.

"Yes, your father," Thad said. "Strange things happened at the farm when he owned it, too."

What Thad couldn't figure out was why this man was protecting the Dragon Elite. It seemed that a spell was at play. He could use his magic to undo it, but that might fully erase the man's memory. He believed the man *was* probably suffering from dementia, but only because he'd been spelled too many times by Hiker Wallace. That was Thad's guess, anyway.

The best way to break the spell was through a conventional method, he figured. Thad grabbed the man's hands, which were constricted by chains, and held the lit cigar an inch from the back of one. Fear was by far the best spell anyone could employ.

Mr. Hopper tensed. Tried to pull away. Pleaded.

Thad shook his head. "Tell me what happened at your farm."

"Please," the man said, tears in his eyes. "I don't remember."

"But you can," Thad said, putting the end of the cigar straight down on the man's skin, searing it and sending the smell of burned flesh through the air.

Mr. Hopper screamed. Tried to yank his hand away. Cried.

Thad didn't release him, even after he pulled the cigar from his burned skin. "Now, unless you want that to happen again, you will tell me what happened at your farm."

"I-I-I," the man stuttered, "I don't re—" He looked around like he suddenly saw something that wasn't there a moment before. "Dragon." The man blinked up at Thad, tears running down his face. "I saw a dragon."

"What else?" Thad demanded.

"There was a-a-a—"

"What else!"

"A girl," he nearly shouted. "I remember a girl. She came to negotiate a dispute between Mr. Lightbody and me."

"Is that right?" Thad said in almost a whisper.

"I don't remember anything else," the man said, cradling his hand.

"I don't need to know anything else," Thad stated. This farmer had told him what he suspected.

"Please let me go," Mr. Hopper begged. "I've told you what you wanted."

Thad released a small smile, which looked all wrong on his face, due to the many scars that had deformed him. Smiles made him look like the monster he was.

"You have done very well," Thad said, striding toward the exit, He wanted to be away from the smell of rot and death in the dungeon.

"So you'll let me go?"

At the door, Thad turned back. "Oh, no. I can't do that."

"Please! Please! *Please!*" the man yelled as Thad pulled the door shut once more, enjoying the fresh air in the corridor. Thankfully, Mr. Hopper's screams were drowned out immediately.

Thad glanced up at the head of Stellar, looking down on him with a powerful glint in her eyes.

So he was right.

Dragons were back.

They were taking their role as adjudicators. They were meddling in affairs Thad had ruled over for centuries. It would only be a matter of time before they discovered that he was behind the most controversial matters, ruling through power, money, and magical tech, as he had since the fall of the Dragon Elite.

And Thad now believed what he'd long feared—when the Dragon Elite rose again, they'd try to ruin everything for him.

CHAPTER FORTY-NINE

Sophia clenched her eyes shut, trying to focus even though everything around her seemed to be trying to distract her.

What do you see? Lunis asked in her mind.

"Blackness," she answered out loud and in her head.

What else? he barked, annoyance in his voice.

"A grass-covered meadow," she began. "It's sprinkled with cottages. There's a billowing haystack next to you, and a slab of meat that you just caught. Oh, and nice job with the dozen villagers who are circled around you, worshipping."

Lunis growled in her head so loud, it felt like it rumbled the ground under her feet. *Making up things, however creative and flattering, won't work on me,* he answered.

Sophia sighed, opening her eyes. "This is useless. I can't see what you see."

She peered around, half-believing that Lunis was somewhere close, staring at her from a nearby hilltop. Her guess proved correct. He sprang off the nearest mountain and glided down to her.

"You have to really try if you want scrying to work between us," he encouraged when he'd landed with a breathtaking grace, his wings sending wind across her face.

"I *am* trying," she argued. She looked at the blue dragon, who was even larger than a few moments prior. She'd heard of growth spurts, but they did little to explain what happened to her dragon when no one was looking. One minute his body, not counting tail and neck, would be twenty feet long, then it would grow by a foot. He would soon be bigger than even Bell, the oldest and largest of all the dragons at the Gullington.

Lunis shook his head. "If you were trying, when we are in battle, you'd be able to see everything I saw. That's crucial for our survival."

"Fine," Sophia spat. "Why don't we try it in reverse? I'll do it, and you tell me what I see."

He coughed, smoke billowing from his nostrils. "I really think you need to master it before I attempt it. That way, we won't confuse things."

Sophia narrowed her eyes at her dragon. "Or are you nervous that you'll struggle with it as much as me?"

"No. Maybe…no. Okay, yes, that's totally it." He gave her a look of guilt.

"We might have telepathy down," Sophia complained, "but this scrying business is really difficult. It's more than getting into your head. It's sharing your senses."

"Which is why you need to focus," he encouraged. "It's crucial that you're able to scry through me in battle."

She gave him an angry glare. "You know what else is important for battle?"

Lunis, who was solely a carnivore, began nipping at the grass underfoot. "Vigilance?"

"Nope," Sophia stated.

"How about courage?" he posed casually.

"Yep, super important, but not what I'm really looking for when thinking of dragonriders," she stated.

"How about perseverance?" Lunis questioned.

"Yeah, no," Sophia said, tossing her head to the side.

"Oh, well, I don't know then," he stated. "I'm totally stumped."

"It's cute that you say both the words 'totally' and 'stumped' like a teenager from LA," she mused.

"Cute. Yes, that's a word all dragons like to be described using," he said with a growl. "So, what was this thing you thought was important for us in battle?"

"How about riding an actual freaking dragon?" Sophia asked. "Where does that stack up in dragon battles?"

"Low," he stated.

She lowered her chin. "Are you sure?"

"Don't question me. I know things," he argued.

"Seriously, Lunis, I'm a dragonrider. When will I be able to ride my dragon?"

"When you're ready," he stated.

"But *you're* obviously ready. You're big enough to pick up livestock, and yet you can't carry me?"

"As I said, when you're ready," Lunis repeated.

"You're giving me nothing," she muttered.

"Well, it's just that the time isn't right," he said, giving her an inconspicuous glance.

"Fine," Sophia said, picking up her bag and striding toward the Castle.

"Where are you going?" he asked, sounding insulted.

"To the Castle." Sophia continued walking.

"Why?" he asked. "We're still training."

"I would tell you, but you're not ready," she fired back, knowing it would burn him up.

CHAPTER FIFTY

Ainsley held her finger to her lips when Sophia strode down the wide corridor of the Castle on her way to Hiker's office. It had moved again, and she was hoping it was around the next bend since she'd been searching for it for half an hour.

Sophia tensed, holding up her hands and shrugging. She didn't think she'd been making any noise.

The housekeeper peered into a room and shook her head before shutting the door.

"What?" Sophia mouthed.

"It's the Castle," Ainsley answered in a whisper. "It's asleep. I've been ordered to fetch Hiker's books, but I have to find them first. Who knows what the Castle did with them?"

Sophia regarded the elf with a confused expression. "How do you know it's asleep?" She looked around, not noticing anything in particular that would give her that impression.

Ainsley scoffed. "Isn't it obvious?"

Sophia's eyes slid from side to side. "Not especially."

"Where are you headed?" she asked her.

"To Hiker's office for a meeting," Sophia answered.

"And how long have you been looking for it?" The shapeshifter had a knowing expression on her face.

"Well, longer than usual," she answered honestly.

"That's because when the Castle sleeps, it does it in his office since that's its favorite room. You won't be able to find it until it awakes."

Sophia sighed with annoyance. "Well, then I'm going to be late for the meeting."

Ainsley nodded. "As will everyone else." She snickered. "Hiker is probably pissed, wondering where the lot of you are. He never knows when the Castle sleeps. He's so dense."

"So, you're looking for the books?" Sophia asked. "I'll help you search. Do you know how long we have?"

She nodded. "Until someone wakes the Castle. As long as everything remains quiet, it should be out for a few hours. It's been months since it's taken a proper nap."

"Okay," Sophia said, drawing out the word. "'Cause that's not weird."

"Well, *you* need to sleep," Ainsley argued. "So why is it so weird that the Castle should too?"

"Because it's a building," Sophia stated.

Ainsley gave her a look of offense. "With feelings."

"Right," Sophia said, offering an apologetic smile. "And why... I mean, how does it sleep in Hiker's office?"

Ainsley threw up her hands, exasperated. "Like I'd know. I don't have the place all figured out."

"Sorry, I just thought that since you're so in tune with the beautiful creature that is this place, you'd have some insights."

Ainsley smiled sweetly at her. "Oh, lovely S. Beaufont. You are truly my favorite." She ran her hand affectionately over the nearest wall. "I think the Castle stuffs its conscious form into the office and closes it off from the rest of the rooms so it can recharge. Just you wait; when it wakes, it will have a renewed sense of spirit. The last time it napped, it rearranged the entire kitchen like it had a new zest for everything to be organized. I couldn't find anything for years. Apparently, it had put everything in the *other* kitchen."

"There are two kitchens?" Sophia asked, watching as Evan approached from behind Ainsley.

"Well, there are now, after the last nap."

"What? Did you say nap?" Evan asked, not whispering like they were.

"I did," Ainsley hissed softly, her eyes scolding.

"Oh, hell, nah! The Castle can't nap!" he yelled, lifting his chin to the ceiling.

Ainsley growled. "Well, it's not anymore, thanks to you."

"Good. The last time it did, all the furniture in my room ended up spread across the Expanse," Evan complained loudly again.

"I think the message there was clear," Ainsley said, sticking her nose into the air.

"I get it," he seethed. "The Castle doesn't want me here, but I'm not leaving, so it can just deal with it."

"Oh, yes, now you've done it," Ainsley said, looking around. "It's awake now for sure. I'll never find those books, which means Hiker will keep complaining like a schoolboy every time he tries to use that Kindle." She turned to face Sophia. "Why is it so difficult for that big ole lug to figure out technology? I'm as old as him, and you don't see me struggling to use your electric razor."

"You use my electric razor?" Sophia asked.

Ainsley's eyes bulged as she turned and strode down the corridor. "You two better get to Hiker's office. He'll be livid that you're late."

Sophia shook her head, giving Evan a commiserating expression.

"She's a rare gem, don't you think?" he asked her with a wink.

"I adore her, actually, even if she uses my stuff," Sophia said honestly.

"Me too, but it would be great if she didn't rummage through my belongings and then blame it on the Castle," Evan seethed. "I know it was you who went through my closet!" he called after the housekeeper.

Ainsley held up her hand as she continued down the hallway. "I can't hear you. I'm way over here. And I adore you too, S. Beaufont."

Evan sighed loudly. "Well, shall we?" He held up his hand, directing the way. "I think we should be able to find Hiker's office now. Makes sense this blasted place was napping. No wonder I couldn't find the office."

"You know," Sophia began as they walked, "if you call it names, I think it will just keep kicking you out."

He shrugged. "It's sort of our thing. Like you and I have a love/hate relationship."

"What?" Sophia spat. "I don't hate you."

He blushed. "Oh, well, ignore that note someone slipped under your door the other day, then."

"What?" Sophia asked. "That was you? You think I'm a stuck-up snob who wants to teach everyone around here manners?"

"Nooooo." Evan dropped his gaze to the floor.

"I don't try to teach anyone around here manners!" she argued.

He shook his head. "I said to ignore the message someone else obviously put in your room. I, for one, appreciate the class and modern edge you bring to the Castle and to the Dragon Elite."

"I thought you were going to be on better behavior," she snapped, not letting it go.

"And I thought that you weren't trying to teach us all manners," he fired back as they rounded the corner and stumbled unexpectedly into Hiker's office.

CHAPTER FIFTY-ONE

"Finally!" the leader of the Dragon Elite yelled when Sophia and Evan entered his office, the first to have arrived. "I was starting to wonder."

"Sir," Evan began, bowing slightly. "The Castle was napping."

Hiker Wallace's eyes fluttered with annoyance. "That makes sense now. It never likes anyone to leave or enter my office when it takes a nap in here. I've been meaning to track you lot down for an hour, but every time I tried to leave here, I'd think of something I needed to do at my desk. Bloody, sneaky old place."

"If it helps," Evan began, "Ainsley hasn't had any luck locating your books."

Hiker dropped his square chin, regarding Evan with even more annoyance. "I don't think you understand the phrase, 'If it helps.'"

"Oh, I probably don't." Evan looked at Sophia. "Maybe Ms. Manners will teach me about language after we cover table etiquette."

Sophia ignored him, but Hiker shook his head and glanced at her. "I'm afraid you have an impossible task."

"Do you want my help with the Kindle?" Sophia asked.

"No!" Hiker exclaimed. "I'd like my books back." He gestured at the long rows of empty shelves. "Thousands of irreplaceable texts, and I can't get to them."

"Well, you can, actually," Sophia offered, pointing to the device sitting on his desk, appearing completely out of place in the office full of antiques. "They are all on there, and it might be easier to find things now that you have a search function."

The glare the Viking gave her made her pause.

"You know what?" she said, changing her tone and pointing at the door. "How about I help Ainsley find your books?"

Hiker shook his head. "No, I want you in here for this meeting. It's your bloody fault I called it."

She gave a false smile. "It's so nice that you're embracing this."

He tilted his head at her, narrowing his eyes. "I'm trying. Don't expect progress overnight."

"Or in a decade," Evan added with a laugh.

"Here it is!" Wilder said, rounding into the office, relief on his face. "Bloody hell, it took me forever to find this place." His eyes widened in horror as the realization took over. "Oh, no, the Castle napped, didn't it?"

Hiker nodded. "Yes, so finding my office should be the least of your concerns. We won't be able to locate anything for years to come."

Wilder ran his hands through his loose brown hair, knocking it out from in front of his eyes. It fell back immediately, stubborn as him. "Maybe this time, we'll actually get that pool we've been asking for."

Evan shook his head. "No, I want a wraparound balcony. That way, I can shoot from up high."

"You do know you have a dragon for such things?" Sophia said dryly.

He jerked his thumb in her direction. "This know-it-all. She doesn't know what it's like to ask for things and have the Castle ignore you year after year. A balcony and a pool. Is that too much to ask for?"

"I just want my damn books back," Hiker said, thundering behind his desk, as Mahkah strolled into the office, not appearing hurried. He had the same poised expression on his face that he normally did, and his long black hair was braided down his back.

"Well, now that we're all here," Hiker continued, waving at the chairs in front of his desk. "Go on, take a seat."

Evan quickly slipped into the nearest chair, as did the other two men, leaving no place for Sophia to sit.

Wilder popped up at once. "Oh, you can have mine."

She shook her head. "I'm fine. I've been sitting most of the day."

"Oh, because Lunis has allowed you to ride him, has he?" Evan asked, sitting back in his seat and crossing his legs.

"No," she answered. "I'm fine with standing, though." Sophia straightened and put her hands behind her back. "Sir, you called us here?" There was an expectant quality to her voice that she hoped would move things forward and get everyone's attention off her.

Reluctantly, Wilder took his seat again, but he still stared at her, as if wondering if she'd change her mind.

"It's fine," Sophia said, tired of receiving looks from him.

"She's so nice," Evan sang. "You just don't want to meet her evil twin."

"Dragonriders don't have twins," Hiker stated.

"I have a twin," Sophia stated.

"What?" Evan threw up his arms. "She gets everything. A phone. Knowledge of the modern world. Summoning abilities."

She shook her head at him. "He's dead. Jamison died at birth."

"Oh," Evan said, sinking down in his chair.

"Jerk," Wilder said, casting a rude glare at the other rider.

Hiker, on the other hand, appeared momentarily struck. "Y-y-you had a twin?"

Uncertain why this was a concern, she shrugged. "Yeah. I mean, I, of course, didn't know him, so there isn't really anything to talk about. But why would riders not have twins?"

He cleared his throat. "It's not important."

"It seems important," she argued. "Is it okay that I had a twin?"

Hiker nodded, pushing his shoulder-length blond hair behind his ears. "Yes, anyway, we're moving on. As you all know, I'm going to attempt to—"

Sophia coughed slightly, politely giving him a hint.

He caught her gaze. "As I was saying, I'm going to meet with the leaders of the major nations to make them aware of the Dragon Elite. That will be the first step in making our presence known once more."

Mahkah sat forward. "That is a formative step, sir."

Hiker agreed. "Yes, I think so. They need to know we're back and ready to intervene, taking up our role once more. But I don't want to rule without consent. I believe it would be better if we get the endorsement of the major leaders, like the President of the United States and so forth and so on."

"What do you need from us, sir?" Evan asked. "I can go to the United Nations for you."

Everyone in the office erupted in laughter.

Evan sat up. "Come on, guys. I can be polite and professional."

Hiker shook his head, still laughing. "Please, Evan, don't fool around. We need to focus. Actually, I just need you all to hold down this place, so you should keep doing what you've been doing."

"Oh, good…" Evan said dryly. "More training."

"Well, once the path has been set for the Dragon Elite, we will have missions," Hiker said with confidence. "So get ready, men…I mean, riders."

Sophia didn't really care that Hiker wasn't used to her being there and confused his pronouns. They were making progress.

Hiker was willing to go to the world leaders to make the Dragon Elite's presence known. That was enough.

"There is something I need from one of you, though," Hiker said, his mouth twitching.

Evan stood. "At your service, sir. What do you need? I'm on it."

Hiker blinked at the young rider. "Not from you."

Wilder stood, saluting. "Do you need a guard? Simi and I would be happy to accompany you."

"No," Hiker said, his gaze skipping over Mahkah and going straight to Sophia. "Actually, as a Royal for the House of Fourteen, I was hoping that you, Sophia, would go there and tell them about us."

"Her?" Evan asked in surprise.

"Well, can *you* get into the House of Fourteen?" Hiker asked.

"I haven't tried," he replied.

"You can't," she stated. "Only Royals can enter. And even then, I'm not a Warrior or a Councilor, so I can't get into the main chamber."

Hiker tilted his head to the side. "I believe you can. There are few places a rider can't get into. If the House allows you in, you should have access to everything."

Sophia blinked at him in surprise. "So, you want me to go and do what?"

Hiker pushed out his chest with pride. "Tell them we're back. We're ready to take our roles as adjudicators back again, and that we would appreciate...no, we *demand* their support in all matters. There's new blood in the House of Fourteen now, but they should know the truth, which is that we are the ones who govern the mortal world. They own the magical one, but we have dominance over the mundanes. We are larger than any nation, any leader. We are their allies, but we will be their greatest enemies if they aren't careful."

Sophia couldn't breathe properly for a moment. She couldn't believe it. A few weeks ago, Hiker was petrified to do anything, and now, he was back. Taking the role that was rightfully the Dragon Elite's in the mortal world.

She wanted to believe this was the beginning of a new era for dragonriders, but a part of her deep down inside knew there were many more obstacles to face before the Dragon Elite could reign.

CHAPTER FIFTY-TWO

In a room no one had ever entered in the Castle of the Gullington, a book appeared out of nowhere.

There was nothing else in the dark room, and the space had only just been created to house that particular volume.

It hovered in the air for a moment before landing softly on the stone floor, lying inconspicuously in the shadows.

Dust particles formed above the book like snowflakes and floated down, covering it completely, until the words printed on the front couldn't be read. One would think that this book had been lost for centuries, it was so thickly coated in dust.

The Castle hummed peacefully to itself, pleased that even if its housekeeper found the books from the library, she wouldn't find *this* particular one.

There would be a time for that.

Just not yet.

CHAPTER FIFTY-THREE

It wasn't that Sophia didn't enjoy Ainsley's cooking. She just missed cheese and fried foods. Well, and Asian foods, too, as well as things in Los Angeles that were often described with the words "fusion" or "gastropub."

And if Sophia were absolutely honest with herself, she was tired of just meat and potatoes. She'd never considered herself a snotty foodie, but she could have used a bit of bearnaise sauce on her steak, although she wouldn't dare mention that to Ainsley.

Evan had asked for some salt the other day, and his plate magically got picked up and tossed across the dining hall, his peas rolling all over the floor. There were no offers for replacements that evening, and he went to bed without dinner, despite his sulking.

"Don't you think that's too much to order?" Sophia asked, lowering her menu and staring across the table at her sister and brother.

Liv pursed her lips. "That's just for me. What are you getting to eat?"

"Ha-ha," Sophia said, looking around the bar and grill in Santa

Monica. She felt strangely out of place among all the hipsters with their shorts and button-up shirts.

It hadn't been that long since she'd removed herself from modern culture, but it easily felt like ages. She suddenly sympathized with the men at the Gullington who had been outside societies' influences for much longer.

She realized then how easy it was to forget that the world went on outside the Barrier, and in very different ways from how they lived.

The Castle provided everything they needed, and Ainsley took care of everything else. All matters outside the Castle but inside the Gullington were Quiet's domain.

In a way, their lives were pretty minimalistic, which was nice—right up until the point where Sophia found it hard to assimilate back into regular society. That was when she had to remind herself that she'd never really been in the real world. She'd grown up as a protégé of sorts in the House of Fourteen, which no one, not even those in the magical world, would say was normal.

Clark slammed down his menu. "None of this stuff has any nutritional value. I could be making us something from scratch at home with organic ingredients."

Liv cut her eyes at her brother. "And I could be slaying demons, but we all have to take a break sometime. Sophia is here for a visit. Just try to have a good time."

The grimace that swept across her brother's face made Liv shake her head. "Okay, have an okay time. Not fun, dare I suggest. Just an average, acceptable time. Will you?"

He sighed. "Of course, I'm having fun. Sophia is back, and it's wonderful to see her." Clark smiled at her. "I just don't like all the greasy food options."

A basket of fries arrived right then, with three sides of Ranch, two ketchups, and a spicy mustard, all at Liv's request. She pushed the basket between her and Sophia. "Well, then I'll take these off your hands, Clarky-poo."

His eyes roamed longingly over the crispy fries as their smell wafted in his direction. "I wasn't saying that *all* greasy food is bad. It's just that—"

"What?" Liv asked, chewing. "I can't hear you over the deliciousness."

He shook his head, used to his sister's antics. "So, Soph, tell us how things are going."

She wiped her mouth. "It's good. But honestly, I'm here on business, not to socialize. Sorry."

Liv scoffed. "How dare you lure us to this bar and make me drink under such pretenses?"

Sophia giggled. "I wanted to talk to you before I met with the others. Hiker asked me to get the House of Fourteen's support."

Liv sat back, making room as the waitress brought a large plate of nachos dripping with melted cheese and piled high with toppings. "Hell, yeah."

"Liv, you can't really eat all that," Clark said, disapproval heavy in his voice.

"Why?" she asked seriously. "As magicians, food fuels our magic. And not only that, but we can't get overweight if we exercise our powers every day. *And,* if that wasn't reason enough, nachos are the best thing in the world."

"Do you know how much saturated fat is in those? It's not good for your heart," Clark stated.

Liv leaned across the table, her face suddenly serious. "Do you know how much your words kill the joy in my heart?"

He sighed, picking up a fry with reluctance. "Fine, we can indulge tonight, but we're eating vegetarian for the rest of the week."

"I'll eat a vegetarian," Liv said, sticking a nacho covered with grilled chicken into her mouth.

An abrupt laugh burst from Sophia. The comment distinctly reminded her of something Lunis would say. It was strange that she missed him already, although it hadn't been long since she'd left him at the Gullington.

She'd wanted him to accompany her, but it was decided it was best for him to stay behind. He had much training to do, and Hiker didn't want dragons flying around and getting attention before the Dragon Elite had the support of all the major world governing bodies.

And even though Lunis could use his magic to enter the House of Fourteen, it wasn't necessary for him to be with her to prove her point. She was a Dragon Elite, and that title should be enough to get the respect she deserved without her dragon beside her.

"The House of Fourteen's support?" Clark asked curiously.

Sophia nodded and then explained what all had happened recently with the leader of the Dragon Elite. Liv knew a lot of it since she'd counseled Sophia about it. However, more had happened since then.

Liv pushed the plate of nachos away, having done them justice. "He's going about it all wrong if you ask me."

Clark gave her a look of offense. "What are you talking about? He's trying to get the support he needs behind him."

"Well, for one, he thinks he's the biggest and baddest entity out there," Liv began.

"He has dragons," Clark argued, cutting her off.

She rolled her eyes. "In a modern world full of missiles and rocket launchers. Dragons used to be amazing." That earned her a contemptuous look from Sophia, and she held up her hand. "They still are, Soph. I'm not saying that they aren't. It's just that the world's different than when Hiker ruled it. That means it takes a different approach."

"So…what?" Sophia asked, confused, but also feeling like she absolutely knew where Liv was going with this and agreed with her already.

"Well, for one, asking for support when you think you're the biggest governing body seems weird," Liv continued. "It's like

Mom and Dad going to their children and saying, 'Hey, is it cool if I tell you what to do from now on?'"

"Yes," Sophia agreed, cramming a French fry into her mouth. "Exactly."

Clark gave them both a look of uncertainty. "He's just being polite."

Liv shook her head. "When are you going to realize there are no niceties in politics?"

"Coming from the one who is friends with everyone from brownies to giants? Really, Liv?" Clark questioned.

She shook her head. "That's different. I'm nice to people because kindness can't be overrated. But I'm not nice to get my way. That's plainly and simply called 'manipulation,' and even the dumbest person will see through that eventually. I, for one, hate suck-ups more than assholes. At least with a jerk, you know what you're getting. Suck-ups don't have a genuine bone in their wimpy bodies."

Clark lowered his chin, regarding Liv. "Why don't you tell us how you really feel?"

"Well, there was this one guy who used to always tell me I was much stronger than him because he was afraid I'd beat him up," Liv began.

"Hey, don't make this personal," Clark cut her off.

Sophia waved her hand between them. "If you two don't mind…"

Liv shook her head as if coming back to the present conversation. "Right. Anyway, as I was saying, I think Hiker also needs to be careful. The Dragon Elite is technically a higher governing body, according to everything I've read. But you can't just show up after a few hundred years and exert your dominance over a world that has survived without you. I think strategy is key here."

Sophia nodded, chewing her lip. "Right."

Liv reached across the table, grabbing Sophia's hands with her greasy fingers. "You can't tell Hiker how to do his job. That's already gotten you into issues with him. He's your leader, and butting heads with him constantly will only lead to bigger problems."

"That's funny, coming from you," Sophia said with a chuckle.

"I know," Liv agreed. "I'm not saying you can't argue with him, but it's about finding a balance."

Sophia nodded. There was no way she wasn't going to oppose Hiker on some levels. They were just too different, and that was apparently by design.

"However," Liv continued, "he's given you a chance to do this with the House of Fourteen your way. So…" She shrugged, smiling at Sophia. "You're going to do great. Just follow your instincts. Address the Council the way *you* think is right, not the way he told you to."

Sophia swallowed, trying to process. She knew Liv was right, and strangely, she wasn't supposed to challenge Hiker too much or overstep his leadership totally, but in this, she was allowed to run the show her way.

Sophia finally realized the fine lines in politics at that moment. It was a messy business, but someone had to be part of it to lead toward a better world in the future, and that was Sophia's destiny.

CHAPTER FIFTY-FOUR

Standing outside the Chamber of the Tree in the House of Fourteen, Sophia began to question everything.

What if Hiker was wrong, and she couldn't enter the chamber? she wondered. That was key to her plans.

What if she entered the chamber, but they promptly kicked her out since she wasn't technically one of them?

And the fear that circled back through her thoughts most rapidly was, what if she failed entirely? What if the Council rejected the Dragon Elite because of her? This was the first real task Hiker had given her.

Liv and Clark had headed into the Chamber of the Tree ten minutes ago, leaving Sophia staring at the Door of Reflection by herself.

She strangely wished that the Door of Reflection would work for her the way it did for Councilors and Warriors, serving up their worst fears so they could cleanse themselves of them before entering the Chamber of the Tree.

Since she wasn't sure if she could actually enter the chamber, she didn't know about the Door of Reflection. Liv and Clark didn't think it would work for her since she wasn't technically a member.

Sucking in a breath, Sophia tried to push away the doubt. Suddenly, she wished Lunis was beside her, offering words of wisdom. She envied Liv in this way because Plato, her lynx, could follow her wherever she went.

Sophia heard Lunis' words in her head: "If you could learn how to scry, I could be with you, no matter what. I could see what you see. I could hear what you hear."

She sighed. He didn't have to be beside her for her to know what he would say. However, at that moment, she wished he was there to tell her something encouraging.

Realizing that she was stalling, Sophia stepped through the rippling surface of the Door of Reflection. At first, she thought she'd been prevented from entering the Chamber of the Tree because the reflective surface felt exactly like stepping through water, pushing her back slightly. However, her intention drove her forward, carrying her to the other side.

No nightmarish visions gripped her the way Liv described the Door of Reflection working. Instead, she simply entered a circular room with a domed ceiling. It was covered in thousands of twinkling lights, which represented magicians all over the world.

Standing in a half-circle were the Warriors for the House of Fourteen, all dressed similarly to Liv in combat clothes, with weapons strapped to their sides or across their backs. Completing the circle were the Councilors, who sat at the back of the room. The council now included Royals, as well as the Mortal Seven. Each of the mortals had a chimera in the forms of different pets, making for a strange menagerie milling about the room.

On either side of the bench were two other creatures who belonged to no one. A large white tiger stood on one side, and a small black crow on the other. They represented truth and lies. Good and evil. Yin and yang. Jude was the tiger and Diabolos was the crow, and they both glanced at Sophia when she stepped forward.

The Warriors all turned to face her and the Councilors regarded her with confusion.

"Who are you, and what are you doing here?" Councilor Bianca Mantovani asked, a pinched expression on her face.

Sophia's gaze darted to Liv, who was standing in the center of the Warriors. Her sister held her face firm, true confidence in her eyes.

"I-I-I..." Sophia stuttered.

Liv lowered her chin, her expression seeming to say, "I taught you better than that."

Sophia cleared her throat. "I'm a Dragon Elite."

"How did she get in here?" Lorenzo Rosario asked in a questioning tone. He was another Councilor, who, like Bianca, objected to Sophia being there.

"Did you hear what she said?" Hester DeVries asked, leaning forward from the bench.

"Dragon Elite..." Raina Ludwig answered, her tone full of awe. "I thought they were—"

"Extinct," Haro Takahashi mused. "Yes, that was my understanding as well."

Sophia's gaze drifted to Clark. Like Liv, he didn't appear ready to step in and help her. She couldn't blame them. They both knew Sophia couldn't rely on her name and status as a Royal to help her there.

She needed the House of Fourteen's support because she was a Dragon Elite and not because she was a Beaufont. If her siblings explained things for her, well, it would only make the Councilors continue to see her the way they had the last times—as a child. But Sophia was anything but that.

Although she didn't have Hiker's five hundred years of experience, magic had made her equal in maturity to someone half his age. She often felt it flowing through her veins, awoken by the chi of her dragon.

"The Dragon Elite aren't extinct," Sophia said, striding forward and taking the spot in the center of the round room between the Warriors and the Councilors. "When the mortals were prevented from seeing magic, it inhibited us significantly."

Hester combed her hand through her short gray hair. "Yes, I can see that. Mortals wouldn't have been able to see dragons."

"And without seeing dragons…" Raina continued.

"It would make it impossible to serve as adjudicators," Haro stated.

"Exactly," Sophia stated, her confidence building. "But mortals can see magic again, so we are back to take on our role presiding over their affairs."

"Well," Hester said, smiling slightly, "this will be quite a help, I think."

"I wouldn't jump to conclusions," Bianca fired back.

"When have you ever jumped?" Liv questioned. "Or gotten off your high horse?"

Bianca's nostrils flared. "Would you try to act civilized? We have a guest here, one who isn't used to your insulting ways."

Liv bowed low to Sophia. "My apologies, representative for the Dragon Elite. Please don't take offense to my rude nature. B is trying to teach me manners, but I ain't used to her cultured ways."

Bianca sighed with annoyance.

"If you *are* a Dragon Elite, that explains why you could enter the Chamber of the Tree," Lorenzo stated with skepticism.

"Of course, she's a Dragon Elite," Raina stated. "I'm not up on the laws, but I believe their powers supersede ours."

"Which means this young lady outranks all of us," Hester said, impressed. She winked down at Sophia.

"That's precisely why we need to look into the laws," Lorenzo stated. "A dusty old organization of riders who have been out of practice for a few centuries can't hold power over us. We didn't lie down and die when mortals couldn't see magic."

"No, we simply turned a blind eye to the whole thing," Liv said dryly. "I do believe it was one of our own who created the whole issue, cursing mortals and erasing our memories and the history."

Sophia worked to keep herself from laughing at her sister's usual antics, which were obviously making Clark flustered. Some things never changed. "I can understand your concerns, which is why I'm here. And although the Dragon Elite numbers have dwindled, our leadership is strong, and we're ready to take back on our role as adjudicators for the mortal world."

"Are you the leader of the Dragon Elite?" Haro asked.

Sophia shook her head. "Oh, no. That's Hiker Wallace."

"Why didn't he come to ask for our support?" Bianca asked. "That's why you're here, isn't it?"

"Yes," Sophia said, her tone faltering. "He sent me because…" Her voice trailed away, and she hesitated to tell them who she was. "Because…"

"You're a female," Hester stated with a gasp as if she had finally realized this obvious detail.

"Yes, that's true," Sophia said, blushing.

"I was going to mention that too," Haro stated.

Raina nodded. "The Dragon Elite might have been hiding for a long time, but they've progressed, it seems. I don't remember learning about any women riders."

"No," Sophia stated. "I'm the first."

To her surprise, all of the Warriors took a knee and bowed to Sophia, their weapons clanging as they moved. Liv smiled proudly before catching herself, kneeling beside them, her head low.

"Would you get up!" Bianca stated. "We aren't kneeling to a body of magicians who are pretty much here to tell us they are back and ruling over us, as well as their own affairs."

"I don't think that's what this rider said," Hester argued before looking at Sophia as the warriors rose again. "I'm sorry, what exactly *are* you saying?"

She cleared her throat nervously. "We would like to have the support of the House of Fourteen, to start with."

"Yes, and then?" Haro asked.

"Well, it is true that centuries ago, we were the highest governing body," Sophia continued, her eyes sliding to Liv.

Her sister gave her a sturdy expression, encouraging her to go on.

"And although things were run a certain way in the past," Sophia said, "we recognize that things have changed. We want you as our allies."

"So, you're not here to tell us your judgments supersede ours?" Lorenzo asked.

"I'm here to ask for your support as we reenter the mortal world," Sophia stated. "We should work together for a better world. Mortals can see magic. Their affairs have gone without our help for a long time, but we are back and ready to make the world a better place."

"But what if we don't agree on something? If push comes to shove," Bianca began, "who overrules who?"

Now Sophia wasn't nervous. She was angry. Lowering her chin, she stared at the Councilor. "If you are going to insist, then if push comes to shove, our say would be final. We are the Dragon Elite. Our desire is for peace, justice, and cooperation. Yes, we have been gone, but we are back. We appreciate the strides you've made. We are grateful that mortals can see magic again. We have always been the strongest entity on Earth, but it is our hope that we can work with the House of Fourteen, not rule you, forcing you to abide by our dominance. How you proceed is up to you, but I beseech you to think long and hard about it. We would like partners, not enemies. Our goals are the same, but if ego comes into it, you will find yourself at the epicenter of a war."

Liv looked to be restraining the smile waiting to burst forth on her mouth. Clark lowered his head while waiting for the response from the council.

All the tension building in the chamber was broken when the first mortal stood up, slowly clapping. It was John Carroway, the first of the Mortal Seven. He was quickly joined by other mortals, each of them standing and clapping until it was a chorus of noise.

"What are you doing?" Bianca asked, looking at the mortals standing around her.

"Endorsing the Dragon Elite and welcoming them back as the supreme ruling force overall," John stated matter-of-factly.

"But you can't do that," Bianca objected.

"Oh, but as mortals, the largest of the populations, we can," John argued.

"They are the ones the Dragon Elite serve," Hester said proudly, "so if the Mortal Seven endorse them, I think we should wise up."

She stood, bringing her hands together and clapping. The Councilor was soon joined by Raina, Clark, Haro, and the Warriors.

"Oh, this is ridiculous," Bianca said, but she was drowned out by the overwhelming support of the House of Fourteen.

Sophia bowed her head appreciatively. "Thank you. Hiker Wallace will be grateful to know you've given us your support."

"Now, since we are happy you've returned," Haro said, reviewing a tablet in front of him, "we have our own affairs that could use your help. There's something that has recently come to our attention, and it could use the assistance of a Dragon Elite."

"Actually, they are exactly who we need," Hester stated. "I don't know how we could find *her* without one of them."

"And it would be a good way to build goodwill between magicians and the Dragon Elite," Raina added.

Haro nodded. "Yes, I agree. It's perfect, actually. We endorse the Dragon Elite, but if they help with this, it will be publicized to the magical races, gaining their favor as well."

"Excuse me," Sophia said to regain their attention. "Who is this 'her?' And *what?*"

Hester nodded. "We have something we'd like your help with." She waved her hand, and a scroll materialized in front of Sophia. "Please take this to Hiker Wallace and ask for his help. If he is willing, well, then we will be on our way to a new partnership, as you put it, which I like very much."

Sophia swallowed and took the hovering scroll. "Very well. I will do that."

"Now, I think that about does it," Haro said, looking around at the other Councilors. "Is there anything else?"

"Well, yes," Raina said. "We were very rude and a bit distracted. I didn't get your name, although it has been a real privilege to meet the first female in the Dragon Elite."

Sophia smiled at Liv and then the others in the room who recognized her. She bowed her head slightly. "But we have met. I've met all of you, actually."

"What?" Hester asked, glancing around.

"I'm sorry for the confusion," Sophia said. "I looked much different the last time you saw me. My name is Sophia Beaufont."

The hush that fell over the chamber had been well worth waiting for, and if Sophia wondered if she had the support of the House of Fourteen before, it was plain and clear now. In unison, the entire council stood, even Bianca and Lorenzo, their chins held high, although bewilderment covered many of their faces.

"A Beaufont, as well as a rider," Haro said with pride. "If I had any doubts before, they are gone now, Sophia. We trust that you as a Royal will help forge this partnership between the new Dragon Elite and us."

CHAPTER FIFTY-FIVE

"I wouldn't go up there," Ainsley said, fondly petting the banister as Sophia passed her on the grand staircase.

She paused, watching the housekeeper run her hand back and forth. "Ummm…first of all, what are you doing?"

"The Castle was upset that you left, so I'm comforting it," she said, leaning close to the banister and continuing to stroke it. "See there? She's back." She put her ear next to the wood. "I know she'll leave again, but don't worry, she'll be back. She lives with us now." The shapeshifter seemed to listen and then nodded. "Exactly, just like she's our prisoner. But we allow her to leave, right?"

Sophia's eyes drifted between the banister and Ainsley. "What did it say?"

Ainsley turned away from the banister, her hands on her hips as she shook her head. "I shouldn't have given it the idea of holding you prisoner. If you can't get out of your room tomorrow morning, don't worry, I'll be up to fetch you."

"Okay," Sophia said, drawing out the word. "And don't worry, Castle. I'll always come back."

"Well, unless she dies," Ainsley said matter-of-factly.

"Right," Sophia said with hesitation. "Unless I die. Thanks for that reminder."

Ainsley waved her hand at her dismissively. "But that won't happen because you're braver than all the men in this house and absolutely my favorite, which is why I keep spiking your food with that potion."

"Wait, what?" Sophia asked.

The elf's eyes slid to the right. "Nothing. Anyway, are you headed up to Hiker's office? If so, I'd change my plans."

"Why is that?" Sophia asked, opening the bag strapped across her chest.

"He's in a foul mood," Ainsley answered. "He's been thundering back and forth in his study ever since he returned from the mortal world."

"Oh," Sophia said, pulling a bag of Doritos from the backpack. "Well, maybe I can help him make sense of things. Here, I brought you a present from the modern world."

Ainsley reached out and pinched up the bag with two fingers, holding it up in the air and studying it. "Wow, it's fantastic. What is it?"

"It's chips," Sophia said. "They are called Doritos, and they're my favorite."

"Thank you, S. Beaufont. They look delicious," Ainsley said, sticking a corner of the bag into her mouth and trying to take a bite.

Sophia shook her head. "No, you don't eat that. That's the bag. You open it, and the chips are inside."

"Oh, thank the angels," Ainsley said with relief. "I was thinking that food like this would give me an awful stomachache." She opened the bag and inhaled. "Wow, that smells really strange."

Tentatively, she picked out a single chip and held it up, studying it. "What a strange color for food to be. Is the chip covered in carrot dust?"

Sophia shook her head. "No, I don't think there are any real vegetables in Doritos, actually. Since over processed corn doesn't really count. Try them, though."

Ainsley popped it into her mouth, a hesitant expression on her face as she chewed. "Oh, I can see the appeal now. It's crunchy, cold, and overly salty. I can see why you've missed the food from your world."

"I don't either," Sophia said, blushing.

"You do too," Ainsley argued. "The Castle told me."

Sophia sighed, realizing it was no use arguing. "I enjoy your cooking, Ains. Really."

"No, it's fine. The food I make is fresh and hot and from scratch. Why would you want that when you can have bags of these things?"

She picked up another chip and eyed it as she strode downstairs.

Sophia continued to Hiker's office, pulling out another treat she'd brought from the modern world.

The sound of stomping echoed from Hiker's office. Sophia thought about giving him some time to cool down about whatever had him angry but decided not to cower. She had news and also something that might lift his spirits.

In the doorway to his office, Sophia held up a bag of gummy bears. Hiker halted his pacing.

"What's that?" he asked, narrowing his eyes at the bright package.

"Candy from the mortal world," she answered.

"I just got back from that blasted place!" he yelled. "I don't need you bringing me things to remind me of it!"

"Okay," she said, tossing them on his desk. "But in case you change your mind. Gummy bears are super good and will lift your spirits."

"Gummy what?" he asked, eyeing the package on his desk.

"Gummy bears," she stated. "They are little candy bears."

"Have you ever eaten a bear?" he asked seriously. "They aren't good at all."

She gave him a hesitant expression. "Ummm. They aren't real bears. Just sugar, mostly. And they are only in the shape of bears because kids like to pretend with them. I used to bite their heads off when I was little."

"When you were little?" he asked. "So, you mean last week?"

Sophia rolled her eyes. "No, not like last week."

"And you ate their heads off. That's very strange." He scooted the package to the corner of his desk. "You can take these back with you. I don't want them."

Sophia held up her hands. "I can't take them back. They are for you. It's not nice to not accept a gift."

Hiker growled. "Yes, I'm so concerned about being nice."

She strolled into the office and took a seat in one of the armchairs across from his desk.

His eyes fluttered with annoyance. "Please come on in and have a seat."

"Do you want to talk about what happened?" Sophia asked casually.

"No!" he exclaimed, biting off the one word.

"So, it went well then?" she said casually.

"No, it went horribly," Hiker continued to pace. "Security removed me from the President of the United States' office."

"You didn't just show up there, did you?" Sophia asked.

He halted and stared at her. "Well, of course, I did."

She nodded. "Yeah, that was probably your first mistake."

"You could have told me that," he said, continuing his pacing.

"Excuse me. I didn't realize that you were going to portal into the President's office uninvited," she said.

"Well, they locked me up, but the last laugh is on them since I simply portaled out," Hiker said with a cold laugh.

"Ha-ha," she said with zero inflection.

"And then I went to the United Nations to explain things, and they all laughed at me," he said, his face turning red.

"Because of how you're dressed?" she asked.

He peered down. "What's wrong with how I'm dressed?"

"Well, you look like a five-hundred-year-old Viking," she said a bit sheepishly.

"That's exactly what I am!" he hollered.

"Right, I get that. It's just that..." Sophia's voice trailed away since she was discouraged from continuing by the angry expression he was giving her. "Anyway, the United Nations..."

"They said that although dragonriders used to be adjudicators, we were obsolete now," Hiker explained, his voice frustrated. "Can you believe that? Obsolete."

"Well, in the modern world, I can see how dragons could seem a bit old-school," Sophia mused. Catching the furious expression on Hiker's face, she quickly added, "But they are wrong, of course, and we will simply have to prove that."

He shook his head. "No, this was a waste. I know I said I'd look at returning to our roles, but we aren't ready. And more importantly, the world isn't ready for us."

"There will never be a good time for this," Sophia argued.

"There will," Hiker fired back. "And right now, this modern world thinks they don't need us. Apparently, there are governments in place, and police, and other forms of law enforcement. We are just going to wait until all those systems fail and they are begging for our help once more."

"I'm not sure that will work," Sophia countered. "They don't even know enough about us to ask for our help. Instead of asking for permission, I think we just need to intervene. Take the power you know belongs to us. Stand up as the judge and jury, exerting our influence. Then they will see that the world is a better place with us in our former positions."

Hiker shook his head. "I don't want to force this. I want the world to welcome us into our roles."

Sophia sighed. "The world has changed. Dragons were thought to be extinct. People can't appreciate us because they don't even know we exist."

"Then we wait," Hiker suggested.

Sophia pulled out her phone and brought up the recent news. "Look at all these cases we could intervene on. There are property disputes between different groups, oil embargos, foreign rights issues, and—"

"I don't even know what half those things are," he complained.

And there it was, Sophia thought. Hiker was, understandably, reluctant to enter a world that was so strange to him. It didn't take much for him to want to quit.

"If we simply step in on disputes, we will show our power immediately," Sophia stated. "Before long, the United Nations and the world leaders will be begging for our help. Right now, no one knows about us. They have no idea who we are or what we're capable of."

He shook his head more forcefully this time, his blond hair knocking him in the face. "No. Back in the day, nations knew how valuable we were. That's how it should be. We were asked to intervene, and that's the way it will be once more."

"But things aren't like they were," she argued. "You have to realize that. You're starting over from scratch. How was it in the very beginning?"

He scratched his head. "I don't know." He looked at his empty bookcases. "If I had my books, I could look it up."

She pointed at the Kindle, still lying on his desk. "Well, I can look them up for you. Tell me the name of the book."

"No," he replied at once. "I don't even remember which book it is in."

Sophia thought he was probably lying but decided not to push the matter. "Well, if it makes you feel any better, the House of Fourteen has acknowledged us and stated that we have their support."

He narrowed his eyes at her. "How did you accomplish that?"

She drew in a breath. "Well, I told them we were back, and although we are the supreme ruling force, we wanted to work with them. They were open to the idea, although they did ask for a favor."

More adamantly than before, he shook his head. "No, the Dragon Elite doesn't do favors. Others work for *us*. They do *our* bidding."

"Again, the world has changed," Sophia argued. "We can't assume we are the most powerful force. People won't respond to that. We have to build our reputation anew."

Sophia pulled the scroll the council had given her from her bag.

"What's that?" Hiker asked skeptically.

She handed it to him. "It's from the council. It's a request for us. They need our help with something, and I think it would be a good opportunity to build bridges."

He snatched it from her hands. "Bridges. The Dragon Elite doesn't build bridges. We sit on an island, and others build bridges to come to us."

"That was the old way," Sophia said.

The Viking unrolled the scroll, running his gaze quickly over it. "Oh, they have lost their minds. Even if we could…"

"What is it?" Sophia asked.

He lowered the scroll. "Didn't you read this?"

She shook her head. "No, they said it was for you."

"And you… You're a very strange person, Sophia," Hiker stated.

"Evan would have read it, right?"

He nodded. "They want us to find Mother Nature. Apparently, their seers have forecast that we will need her help with something very soon, and since we're the only ones who can find her, well, they are relying on us."

Sophia leaned forward, her brow furrowed. "I don't think I understood half of what you just said. We can find Mother Nature? Like, she's a real person?"

"As real as Father Time," Hiker answered. "And I'm not sure we can find her anymore. It's been a long, long time. But if anyone can, it's us."

"Why?" Sophia asked.

"Who do you think we work for?" Hiker questioned.

"Mother Nature, obviously," Sophia said with uncertainty.

He nodded. "Yes. She's the only one above us. Do you see why this United Nations business is difficult? We are the second-highest entity in the world, and they are just laughing at us. We should be regarded with great reverence."

"I think it would be the same if Mother Nature showed up to the United Nations, to be honest," Sophia explained. "The modern world doesn't know that there is an actual person who is Mother Nature. Most think it's a metaphor. I believe it because I've met Father Time, but—"

"You what?" Hiker asked.

"Well, my sister works directly for Papa Creola," Sophia stated. "Anyway, maybe taking on this task is exactly what we need to do. We find Mother Nature, find out what this issue is that the House of Fourteen foresees, and get her support on everything else. Then we will gain favor with the House. It's killing two birds with one stone."

Hiker stroked his chin. "Maybe. I haven't seen Mama for a long time. She might know how to handle this problem."

Sophia stood. "Great! I can go and find her for you!"

He shook his head. "No. No, you can't."

"Why?" she argued. "Because I'm new?"

"There's also that issue that you don't ride your dragon," he stated.

She grunted, having expected that response. "But I want to do *something*. Let me at least try to help to find her."

"No, and when you can fly on Lunis, there is another excursion I will send you on," Hiker said.

"Oh?" she asked curiously.

"Yes. Each new rider goes to the great library in Tanzania. That will be your first journey."

"Okay, but you'll send one of the guys after Mother Nature?" Sophia asked.

"Sure," Hiker said casually. "I'll send Evan. He's annoying me, and it will be good to get him out of here for a bit."

"Evan?" she asked. "Are you serious. This is important. It's our first opportunity to—"

"Evan can handle it," he argued. "Or he can't, and it won't matter."

"Why do I get the impression you want this to fail?" Sophia asked.

"I don't," he refuted. "It's just that finding Mother Nature is no easy feat, and the House of Fourteen knows it. We could spend decades on the search. I'm not going on some wild hunt for all this. Evan will go, and you will continue your training. No other missions."

Sophia opened her mouth to argue, but he held up his hand, a stern look in his eyes.

"Do you understand?" Hiker asked her.

She nodded, hesitation living deep inside of her. "Yeah, okay."

CHAPTER FIFTY-SIX

The morning sunshine had melted the frost, making the grass mushy as Sophia stomped out to the combat area in the Expanse.

The others had already gotten started on the daily exercises by the time she joined them.

Evan took one look at her and strode to the opposite side of the field, sensing her frustration. "What's that, Mahkah?" he called to the rider practicing archery in the distance. "You need me to teach you how to aim? I'll be right there."

Sophia shook her head at Evan, grateful he was smart enough to keep his distance, although he wouldn't know yet that he'd gotten the case she wanted. She wasn't sure why she wanted to go on a mission again. More than anyone, she was aware of how much training she needed. But freeing the slaves from the facility not too far in the distant past had awoken something inside her. Before she'd been hungry for an adventure. Now she was starving for one.

Desperately, she'd wanted to return to that strange facility full of magical tech and investigate more. However, Hiker had asked her not to. He had agreed to make progress, and she didn't want him to change his mind, even though he did seem to be caving already to the strangeness of the modern world.

As Sophia swung Inexorabilis, she felt stronger than even the day before. She was progressing, and she knew it was important to remember that. Even if she couldn't ride Lunis, she was developing into a stronger rider.

"So did my treat from the modern world get lost?" Wilder asked, approaching, swinging his own sword to loosen his shoulders.

Sophia flashed him a rebellious glare. "Patience is a virtue."

He laughed. "I've been hanging out at the Gullington for almost two centuries. I think I got this patience thing down."

"Your treat is in my room," she stated. "And you know you're not a prisoner here. You could leave and have your own adventures in the mortal world. Or are you like Hiker, and against such things?"

Wilder regarded his sword with speculation. "I get out. Just last week, I went to Tanzania."

"What is the deal with that place?" Sophia asked, practicing a block on a straw dummy they had set up for practice.

"It's like a secondary headquarters for dragonriders," he explained. "It's hard to explain what happens there. You'll just have to see it for yourself."

"Oh, are there other riders there?" she asked.

Wilder shrugged. "I've never seen any, but if a rider doesn't want to be seen, well, they aren't."

"Like a lynx," Sophia mused, thinking of Liv's sidekick Plato.

"Yeah, I guess," Wilder said, giving her a questioning look. He observed her as she took out some aggression on the dummy. "And Hiker is in quite the mood as well. You seem to have woken up on the same side of the bed as him."

"The gummy bears didn't help, then," she joked.

He shook his head. "No, but Ainsley seems to like the chips you gave her, although she's making a great show of despising them. What did you bring me?"

"Reese's Pieces," she answered, pivoting and swinging Inexorabilis, catching the dummy's shoulder.

"Who is Reese? And why is she in pieces?" Wilder asked with a laugh.

Sophia's chin dropped suddenly without her consent as old memories washed over her.

Wilder's head tilted to the side with curiosity. "What is it?"

"Nothing, it's just that Reese was my sister's name," Sophia said, feeling like it was last week she had helped her kooky sister make experimental potions.

"She's not alive anymore, is she?" he asked.

She swallowed the old pain. "You're much older. I'm sure you've lost many more than I have."

He nodded. "Maybe, but I've outlived many of my family due to the fact that I'm a dragonrider. You will, too."

"Right," Sophia said, looking into the distance.

"Anyway, my point was going to be that you have lost a lot in your short life," Wilder stated. "Whereas I've lost those I would have expected to lose, based on my years."

"Still…" Sophia argued.

"And," he continued, "I haven't been very close with anyone in my family since joining the Dragon Elite."

"Right," Sophia said. "Do you ever think about going home?"

He pursed his lips and shook his head. "There isn't anything left for me there. I came from a small family of magicians. I'm not royalty like you."

"I'm not royalty," she argued.

He pointed to her sword. "I've seen every battle Inexorabilis has been in since its creation. You come from royalty."

"I'm not sure why the battles have anything to do with me," she stated.

"Because your mother was a Warrior, and it is because of her and your family that we have the potential of coming back as the Dragon Elite."

She shook her head. "Yeah, but not if Hiker doesn't…" Sophia's voice trailed away; she realized she shouldn't complain to Wilder about the Viking. It wasn't right. It wasn't respectful, and as angry as she was at Hiker, she wasn't going to disregard him.

"What?" he pressed.

"Nothing," she said, chewing her lip. "It just seems like he's waiting for permission to take the world back over. It doesn't make any sense to me, but maybe I don't understand things like I should."

"Hiker comes from a different time," Wilder explained. "As do I, and I think you're here to help us progress. As you have so astutely observed, it's difficult for us to leave the Gullington. We've gotten comfortable and complacent."

"I get it," Sophia said, parrying another attack and diving away from the dummy's imaginary attempts to pin her.

"I also think there's a possibility that we will be instrumental in *your* development," Wilder said, watching her from the sidelines.

She gave him a sideways expression. "Yes, I'm sure of it. Maybe you can help me by persuading my dragon to allow me to ride him."

He shot her a knowing smile. "Here's something I find curious. Your advice to Hiker is that he needs to stop waiting for permission to take back our role as adjudicators, and yet, that's exactly what you're doing with Lunis. You're waiting for him to grant you permission to ride him."

"Well, it's different with him," Sophia argued. "We have a partnership. I can't force him into anything."

"But you think Hiker should force the mortal world to accept us?" he posed, a discriminating expression on his face.

"Well, that's different," Sophia said. "We are at the top of the hierarchy, and Hiker is waiting for the world to acknowledge that."

He shrugged. "It just seems to me that your situation with Lunis and Hiker's with the world isn't all that different."

Sophia sheathed her sword. "Did you wait until Simi granted you permission to ride her?"

He laughed. "No. She picked me up by the back of my shirt and slung me over her head. I had a split second to make a choice. Grab hold and ride or fall to my death."

"So, what happened?" she asked, a serious expression on her face.

He shook his head. "Obviously, I died. But every dragon is different. Simi was ready. I was the one who was nervous. Maybe you and Lunis have your roles reversed. While I'm observing these things about you, it would appear that Sophia Beaufont isn't reluctant about anything. Does nothing scare you?"

She stared out at the mountains in the distance where the facility that was responsible for Adam's death was located. "Giving up scares me. I never want to get to the point where I'm okay just surviving when thriving is an option."

He came around to stand next to her, putting his head beside hers and following her gaze. "What are you looking at?"

Sophia shook her head, remembering that she'd promised Hiker when they discussed Adam's death recently that she wouldn't mention anything to the men about it. Hiker had covered up the cause of the rider's and dragon's death, afraid of what had taken them down.

After talking with Sophia, they'd concluded that Adam had gotten mixed up with something that he didn't know how to fight. They still didn't know how to fight it, though, since the aircraft were definitely powered by magical tech.

Sophia didn't know much about the facility, but she'd promised Hiker that she'd let it go for now, as long as he made strides toward getting the dragonriders out. There was much about the world to learn. They obviously moved at different speeds, though, because he hadn't made much progress, and she was already antsy to do more.

"It's nothing," she lied. "I'm lost in thought, I guess."

"Right," Wilder said, not convinced. "And I agree about thriving, but remember, that hasn't been an option for the Dragon Elite for a long while."

"So?" she questioned, sensing he wanted to say more but was trying to be diplomatic.

"So be patient with those of us who have had to sit out for a long time," he stated. "It's not as easy as you think to reenter the game."

She nodded. "Fair enough. I guess the one who needs to learn patience is me."

CHAPTER FIFTY-SEVEN

"Yeehaw!" Evan yelled, running after Coral as she sprinted across the Expanse.

Sophia thought that he would get left in her dust, but to her surprise, he caught up with her, diving and grabbing one of the spikes on her back. He then pulled himself up, swinging his leg over the saddle as she sprang into the air.

"Showoff," Sophia seethed, turning to Lunis. "Should we try scrying again?"

"It won't work when you're angry," he stated matter-of-factly.

"What?" she asked. "Me? Angry? No, I love not riding my dragon. Remember that one part in *How to Train Your Dragon* when—"

"It's probably better if you don't relate our experiences to a cartoon movie," Lunis stated dryly.

"Well, it's the closest experience I have to dragon-riding," she shot back.

"How about this?" Lunis began. "If you catch me like Evan just did with Coral, then you get to ride me."

A spark shot through Sophia's chest. "You have yourself a deal. Tell me when to go—"

Without warning, Lunis took off, his legs carrying him at lightning speed across the Expanse.

"Hey," she complained, taking off after him but slowing when he kicked a mound of dirt into her face. She coughed, waving her hand in front of her mouth, slowing, and coming to stand next to Mahkah.

"What is that dragon's deal?" Sophia asked, shaking her head as Lunis launched into the air, flapping his large wings and soaring majestically across the sky.

"Did he say that you could ride him if you caught him?" Mahkah asked, standing with his arms behind his back, proudly looking out as the others practiced.

"Yes, but Evan did it," she stated.

"Do you think Coral was running at full speed?" Mahkah questioned.

She sighed. "Of course, she wasn't. I realize now. She was simply running so they could practice a fleeing take off, weren't they?"

He nodded. "Here's something you won't find in any book about dragons. Nor will you hear me say this in front of Tala."

The rider had her attention now. "Yes?"

Mahkah cleared his throat, speaking in a whisper. "Dragons can be deceptive."

"Go on," Sophia encouraged.

"Well, they are quite persuasive when they want to be," he continued.

"Which is what makes them great as adjudicators, right?" she questioned.

He nodded. "Exactly. A dragon will be eating livestock with a foot hanging out of their mouth and tell someone they are a vegetarian. And most will believe them."

Sophia giggled. "Persuasive? They are downright liars."

"For them, truth is relative," he explained. "And a dragon will never, ever lie to their rider. Not really. They may withhold, but that's not lying."

"So if I did catch Lunis, he would have allowed me to ride him?" Sophia questioned.

"I think so," Mahkah answered.

"Why is he being so difficult?" she asked.

"I don't think he is trying to be difficult," Mahkah began slowly. "You and Lunis aren't typical by any standard. Maybe he doesn't think you're ready. Maybe he isn't ready. No one but a dragon and their rider can determine that. There is nothing I can offer or do to hasten this for you."

Sophia huffed out a breath, blowing her blonde hair out of her face before the Scottish winds sent it straight back around her cheeks. She pulled a hair tie from her wrist and attempted to corral her long locks back. "I think I need to work on my patience. In all things. I haven't been at this for very long."

Mahkah offered her a tame smile. "I think you're used to things happening on a different timeline than the rest of us. Try not to be so hard on yourself. We were all born for a certain time."

Lunis landed soundlessly, arching his head as he folded his wings against his body. "Shall we try again, Sophia?"

She shot Mahkah a hesitant glance. "Do I dare play the game of a vegetarian?"

"If you wish," he answered. "But remember, you and Lunis are two of the same."

"So you mean, I'm a deceptive liar?" she joked.

"I mean, you're as persuasive as he is," he stated. "And you also can't lie to your dragon. It is physically impossible for us."

She blinked at him, stunned that the magic bonding them prevented her from being dishonest with him. That seemed like the most wonderful magic in the world. Sophia wanted all beings to be bonded in that way, but would it change the significance of the bond between riders and dragons? Diminish it? Things that were rare were special.

"Okay, Lunis," Sophia said, striding in the direction of her dragon. "Let's try this again, but this time, I get a head start."

The blue dragon, which was almost as big as his brother and sisters around him, regarded her with a curious glare. "Very well, Sophia. Go on, then."

She gave him a skeptical glare over her shoulder as she started forward. Seconds later, Lunis thundered up beside her, passing her easily and taking off into the blue sky. Sophia dove for him as his front legs launched into the air. The force of his wings sent her to the ground immediately, knocking her to the side, where she ate dirt.

She rolled over on her back, looking up at the underbelly of her dragon as he circled in the air. There wasn't a mischievous look on his face. Strangely, it was one of love and concern. He was helping her. She just didn't know with what.

CHAPTER FIFTY-EIGHT

Sophia threw the bag of Reese's Pieces across the dining room table to Wilder. His eyes went wide at the sight of the orange cellophane.

"Don't eat the bag," Ainsley warned. "The food is inside."

"Thanks," Wilder said, giving her an odd look. "I sort of figured that."

"Heads up, Mahkah," Sophia said, tossing jelly beans at him.

He caught them with a confused expression.

"You eat them," she offered.

He nodded like he totally knew this, although his expression was uncertain.

"What about me?" Evan asked.

Sophia snapped her fingers, and a bag of sunflower seeds in the shells materialized in front of him.

"Are you serious?" he asked, picking up the bag. "I have to work for my food? And I have had sunflower seeds before. I'm old, but not that old."

Ainsley plucked the bag from his hands. "I'll take those since I don't want you spoiling your appetite. I'm serving dinner now."

"Thanks," he said without real gratitude. "I was worried I was going to ruin my appetite, shelling tiny little seeds and eating them."

"Me too," she said, buzzing off to the kitchen.

Quiet materialized inconspicuously, as usual, looking at the colorful treats in Wilder's and Mahkah's hands.

"I have something for you too," Sophia said, snapping her fingers again. A large, flat box materialized on the table in front of the gnome. On the front, it read, Krispy Kreme.

He sniffed the air and looked at her in disbelief.

Sophia smiled. "Go on, then. Open it."

The gnome pulled the lid off the box and sat back in his seat like he couldn't believe the contents. Colorful and shiny donuts lay before him, their sugary smell wafting through the air.

"Oh, man!" Evan complained. "Are you serious? I get a bag of seeds, and he gets a bunch of donuts?"

Sophia clapped her hand to her chest. "Do you not like the gift I got you?"

Evan crossed his arms over his chest. "No, I don't like it." He leaned over, eyeing the donuts. "You're not going to eat all those, are you, fellow? Can I pinch one?"

Quiet narrowed his eyes at Evan, muttering something inaudible. Ainsley laughed; she was carrying a tray of roasted duck from the kitchen.

"Quite right," she cackled. "I think he could stand to miss a bit more than that."

Evan looked at Ainsley and the groundskeeper. "Why can you understand him, but no one else can?"

Hiker began carving the bird once Ainsley set it down. "I understand him just fine."

"I do, too," Wilder chimed in.

Mahkah simply nodded, tucking a napkin into his collar.

Sensing all eyes were on her, Sophia nodded as well. "Yeah, of course, I understand him."

Evan scoffed. "No, you don't. You are all full of it."

Ainsley picked up the box of donuts. "I'll have these sent to your room."

Quiet muttered inaudibly again.

"Oh, don't worry about that," Ainsley said. "He doesn't even know where to look."

"Was that about me?" Evan questioned, his eyes shifting between Ainsley and the gnome.

"No, we were talking about the other Evan who lives here," she remarked.

"How odd," he said quietly. "I haven't met him."

"Speaking of you," Hiker said, cutting into his meat, "I have a case for you, Evan."

Everyone at the table jerked upright. Ainsley dropped the tray she was carrying.

"Did you say 'case,' sir?" Mahkah had asked the question waiting to burst from everyone's mouth.

"Yes, I did," Hiker began. "I need you, Evan, to go and hunt down Mother Nature."

Evan looked around. "You mean, me? As in, this Evan?"

Hiker's eyes fluttered with annoyance. "There is only one of you in the Castle."

"But, Mother Nature?" Evan questioned. "Are you sure?"

"Yes, are you sure?" Ainsley asked.

"Of course, I am," Hiker said, annoyance dripping from his tone.

"Well, it's just, this is the first case in..." Ainsley began to count on her fingers. "Well, a really long time. "And it's going to..."

Hiker shook his head. "Evan is capable. He gets a bad rap, but I trust that's only because he needs to be pushed through the rest of his growing pains."

"'Growing pains?'" Evan questioned.

"Sir," Wilder began, "Ainsley is right. This is the first case that...

well, you've assigned since I came here. Can I at least go with Evan?"

"No," Hiker said at once. "I have cases for you and Mahkah, as well."

"I believe you could have led with that," Wilder said with relief.

"Well, they're not as glamorous as finding Mother Nature," Hiker stated.

Wilder shook his head. "You're not selling this like you want to."

"The cases I have for you and Mahkah require a bit more..." Hiker looked around, as if trying to find the right word, "shall we say, 'diplomacy?'"

Wilder elbowed Evan. "He's saying you're an unmannered git."

"That's not what he's saying," Evan retorted.

"I sort of am," Hiker cut in. "But like I said, Evan is one of us, and he simply hasn't had the opportunity to grow. I have every hope that after this mission, he will come back seasoned, and dare I say, a bit humbler."

"Mother Nature, huh?" Ainsley asked. "Where are you even sending him to find her? I hear she's harder to find than a silver snail in the Pond."

Hiker tilted his head and squinted at her. "I haven't heard that expression before."

"Expression?" Ainsley asked. "Sir, that's a real thing. There's one silver snail that...never mind. Now, Mother Nature. Where is she?"

"Well, I don't know," Hiker stated. "But if anyone can find her, it will be a dragonrider. And as the Elite, we are in the best position." He looked to Evan. "I trust you will rely on your education to know where to look for her."

"Of course, sir," Evan said, looking like he'd swallowed his meat without chewing.

"And any obstacles you encounter, well, I trust the century of training will aid you," Hiker said proudly.

"No doubt about that, sir," Evan said, slightly squirming with unease.

"And us, sir?" Mahkah asked.

"Well, you and Wilder will be diplomats for the Dragon Elite," he stated. "As you know, I'm trying to make our presence known to the world once more. I'd like you two to take certain excursions on Simi and Tala, riding over populated areas, gaining interest, and more importantly, favor."

"Good idea, sir," Wilder said.

"And there will be meetings with world leaders," Hiker continued, catching Sophia staring at him with interest. "It's small steps, but I trust that in time, they will get us where we want to go."

"You all sound like you're parading yourself around like show ponies to get attention," Ainsley said.

Hiker jerked his head around, giving her an angry scowl.

"I for one think it's a brilliant idea," Ainsley sang, heading for the kitchen.

"What will Sophia do while we are all off on missions?" Wilder asked.

Everyone turned to look at her.

"She will train," Hiker said plainly.

Evan shook his head at her. "Did you give him sunflower seeds too?"

"Yes, but his aren't poisoned," she said with a sneer.

He shook his head. "Well, I guess you will need to train a lot more since you're currently doing the equivalent of walking your bike with Lunis."

She fumed. "He's simply not ready yet."

"Well, until he is, you can sit around the Castle and wait for us real men to come home," Evan said, yawning.

Sophia narrowed her eyes at him. "I'll be waiting for you to return as well."

Wilder and Quiet both laughed.

"Oh, yeah," Evan said, returning her seething glare. "Well, while you're waiting for me to return, you can make jewelry that you sell on Itty."

Sophia immediately regretted telling Evan anything about the modern world. He was like the little brother she'd never had, nor wanted, who was incidentally older than her. "It's called Etsy. And I don't make jewelry."

"No?" Evan asked. "But you knit, right? Make me a scarf, would you? I'll need something thick for when I'm off riding my dragon."

She held up her hands like she was going to choke him. "How about I measure your neck real quick? I want to ensure I get it just right."

He shook his head, pointing at his thick neck. "That's okay. Just use your own. We're about the same size."

Sophia was about to retort, but Hiker's chair scraping on the floor cut her off. "I trust that you will all get to bed at a reasonable time. I expect everyone who's on a mission to set off early tomorrow morning. Especially you, Evan."

"Yes, of course, sir," the men muttered in unison as the Viking strode from the room.

When he was out of earshot, Wilder spun to face Evan. "So, your education and training have well-prepared you for this? Where are you going to hunt for Mother Nature?"

Evan slipped down in his chair, covering his face. "I haven't got a clue."

CHAPTER FIFTY-NINE

The four dragons taking off from the Expanse were quite the sight. Bell led the way, Hiker crouching on the red dragon. Behind him, in perfect formation, were the other three riders, climbing higher and soaring through the clouds, their traveling cloaks rippling behind them.

"That's a first," said a voice behind Sophia she didn't recognize.

She turned from the second-story window in the long corridor to find Quiet standing beside a large tapestry on the opposite wall.

"What?" she asked.

His lips moved, but Sophia couldn't make out what he said, although what she'd heard before had been clear and loud.

She leaned forward. "I'm sorry. Did you say, 'that's a first?'"

He nodded, opening his mouth and muttering something she couldn't understand.

"Wait, what?" Sophia asked, craning to hear him.

The gnome smiled. "And that's why you're so important."

She shook her head, wondering if she'd heard him correctly that time. "Why am I important?"

He opened the satchel strapped across his chest and pulled out one of the Krispy Kreme donuts she'd given him. Holding it up, he smiled at it fondly before taking a bite. A look of pure joy crossed his face as he turned toward the dark corridor and strode away.

"Quiet?" Sophia called. "What? I couldn't…" She sighed, wishing she'd heard what else he'd said.

A second later, from the shadows, a twin version of Quiet stepped out from behind the tapestry with an uncharacteristically mischievous expression on his face. Sophia recognized the scar on his temple.

"Ainsley," she scolded. "What are you doing?"

The elf morphed into her normal willowy appearance, wearing a sour expression on her face. "I was just trying to be part of the fun."

"Well, you could be part of it without impersonating people or hiding behind tapestries," Sophia argued.

Ainsley shrugged. "Where's the fun in that?"

She came over to stand next to Sophia and peered out the window. "Oh, I see what Quiet meant." The dragonriders were still streaking across the sky, although they were growing smaller by the second.

"What did he mean?" Sophia asked. "What did he say?"

Ainsley gave her a confused expression. "It was as plain as day. He said, 'That's a first.'"

Sophia nodded. "Yes, and then what?"

The housekeeper sighed. "Then he said, 'blah, blah, blah, and that's why you're so important.'"

"Yes, but what was the 'blah, blah, blah' part?"

"Really?" Ainsley asked. "I mean, you were right there in front of him. Anyway, it is a first to see the men all taking off together, leaving the Gullington. I can't remember the last time I saw such a thing."

"Well, things are changing," Sophia said, glancing out the window as rain began to splatter the glass.

"Things are always changing," Ainsley reasoned. "Hiker is amazing at ignoring change. But thankfully, you're not."

"Yeah, well, I think he left just to get away from my nagging," Sophia said.

"Oh, no, S. Beaufont," Ainsley stated. "If he could be driven away so easily, he'd have left long ago. I'm a world-class nagger."

"Well, do you need help with anything?" Sophia asked, staring out at the rainstorm, which was pounding harder by the second. "I don't have any plans."

"Yes, I do, actually," Ainsley said, quite seriously.

"Yeah? What's that?" Sophia asked.

The shapeshifter's eyes drifted up to the right as if she was listening for a sound over the noisy rain. "I need you to fetch a couple of buckets from the fifth floor."

"There's a fifth floor?" Sophia asked, sure there were only four stories, and the top one was only in the turrets at the corners of the Castle.

"Sure, there is." Ainsley let out an impatient sigh. "No wonder you can't hear Quiet properly. Remember what I told you about the Castle?"

"Which part?" Sophia scratched her head, trying to recall all the strange things Ainsley had told her about the Castle.

"Well, the unseen part," Ainsley stated. "You have to tell yourself that you can see the unseen. And with Quiet, you need to hear the unheard. With all things in life, you need to be open to knowing the unknown. It's simple, really."

"I'm not sure I even understand what you're talking about," Sophia stated dully.

"Well, I get that. It's more about openness," Ainsley explained. "You know, most wake up constructing their world from what they experienced the day before. When we look out expecting what we've always gotten, then that's exactly what we get. But if we want something new, then we have to regard life with fresh eyes, ears and a mind open to possibilities."

Letting out a tired breath, Sophia nodded. "So, you need pails from the fifth floor? Is it to catch leaks?"

Ainsley shook her head, starting down the hallway. "Heavens no. The Castle has no leaks. It's because I want to send you on a wild goose chase." She hurried down the corridor. "Fifth floor. Look for the buckets."

"Right," Sophia said, peering back out the window. She would have gone out to find Lunis but didn't think that anything had changed with the dragon. For whatever reason, he was being difficult about her riding him. Since her spirits were low, having to stay behind at the Castle while the others went off, she started in the opposite direction as Ainsley, looking for the fifth floor.

"I can see the unseen, hear the unheard and know the unknown," she said, trying to keep her mind open. It all seemed like a silly game. However, as she walked, she started to forget where she was going. For a moment, Sophia actually forgot where she was.

As if she were on autopilot, she took a set of stairs she didn't remember going up before. She hummed as if she was deep in thought, her mind drifting as if lost in meditation.

"Here," a voice whispered.

Sophia spun, sure she'd find Quiet lurking in a shadow again. Instead, she found a small door that possibly only the gnome could have stepped through without having to duck.

She squinted around, realizing suddenly that she was in a different part of the Castle. The windows a few feet away showed that she was higher up than she remembered being before.

"The fifth floor…" Sophia muttered, turning back to the door. She regarded it with indecision for a moment. Then, deciding to go for it, Sophia knelt, and, finding it unlocked, opened the door.

It creaked when she pushed it back, and a musty smell wafted from the recesses of the room. Sophia tried to peer into the darkened space, but she couldn't see anything. She tried to send lights through the door to illuminate what was on the other side, but they kept extinguishing.

She looked down the hallway before deciding to duck and squeeze through the small door. As small as she was, she found it a feat to fit through the narrow opening.

On her elbows and knees, she inched into the black room, hoping there wasn't a large spider or some other strange animal ready to eat her when she got to the other side.

As if waiting for her to join them, the lights Sophia had sent in suddenly glowed, bouncing around beside the walls. At first, it was just faint lights, but they grew in intensity until the small orbs illuminated the room.

In the middle of the empty space was a piece of paper, its edges frayed as if it had been ripped from a larger section.

Sophia studied the space and noticed that the door she'd come through had reshaped to be normal-sized.

"Ha-ha, Castle," Sophia said with no amusement. "So, was all that just for your entertainment?"

The floorboard creaked under her foot, making a strange noise that sounded like "Maybe."

Sophia shook her head, then peered at the piece of paper on the floor. It was a newspaper article, and it was from *that* day.

Carefully, Sophia picked up the clipping. She read it twice before the realization hit her.

"You want me to do this?" she asked the Castle aloud.

There was no answer, but Sophia felt she knew the truth.

CHAPTER SIXTY

Since Sophia wasn't allowed to enter the Cave, she stood on the Expanse, signaling to Lunis and hoping he wouldn't keep her waiting too much longer. She was already soaked to the bone and shivering violently. However, she wasn't going to quit just because of the cold and rain.

Sophia was about to try another approach, such as yelling out loud rather than summoning him with her thoughts, when she felt a presence at her back. When she turned, she was unsurprised to find Lunis staring down at her with a knowing expression in his eyes.

"Are you sure about this?" he asked, obviously having read her thoughts.

Sophia nodded. "The Castle sent it to me, and I can't stay around here while the others are off saving the world."

"But your training?" he remarked.

"Well, are you going to allow me to ride you?" she questioned.

His expression said, "No."

"The rain is preventing me from doing much training," she

reasoned. "So either we go on this mission, or I'll go back to my room and read."

When Lunis didn't answer her, Sophia turned around and headed for the Castle. She was cold, wet, and starting to get a bit frustrated with her dragon, which she knew he felt all too well. It wasn't strange to feel upset at him. Instead, it seemed like she was mad at herself, as if she'd done something she knew wasn't good for her but had to accept and deal with anyway.

"Where are you going?" he asked.

The rain was pouring harder now. "To the Castle. I'm going to go watch videos of that dog who calls his owner Linda and says 'heck you' to her when she tries to feed him 'trees of doom.'"

"I'd say much worse things to you if you tried to make me eat broccoli," Lunis said.

She sighed with defeat. "Well, I'm not trying to make you do anything. So go back to whatever you were doing before."

"I was waiting for you," he stated.

"You were?" she questioned.

"Of course," he answered. "The Cave is awfully boring right now without the others. And this isn't ideal flying weather, and your sulking is making my insides ache."

"I'm not sulking," she argued.

"And I'm a vegetarian," he retorted.

"Ha-ha. Okay, so you're in?" she asked.

"Just open a portal, and we'll be on our way," he said.

"Is it safe?" she asked, remembering that before when they'd gone on missions, she'd trudged the whole way since it was dangerous to portal into unknown areas.

"I think because the Castle is leading this one, it is fine," he stated. "And besides, I'll be with you."

Sophia couldn't help but smile at that. She might not understand why the dragon was acting the way he was, but she knew that no matter what, he loved her as he loved himself. They were one and the same. He was her and she was him, and forever they were intertwined.

341

CHAPTER SIXTY-ONE

The Amazon rainforest wasn't any place Sophia or Lunis had ever been in real life. For dragons, it was sort of relative, since they experienced many of the memories of those who came before them. But those were considered references, rather than lived memories.

Sophia looked at the lush green trees and dense foliage all around them, wondering which way to venture first. That was when she heard a high-pitched whizzing sound. Instinct commanded her to drop to the ground, so, without hesitation, she threw herself down face-first, to land in a puddle of mud. It splattered into her eyes and covered her body.

Looking over her shoulder, she spied Lunis as some sort of strange illusion that was much skinnier than he should have been. She blinked at the dragon, and like a balloon, he inflated once more.

"I guess you've mastered that condensing spell," she muttered, spitting out mud as she pushed to her knees.

"I hadn't until now, but that's the reason missions are important," he explained. "There are things one can never do in practice because they don't have the urgency."

"Like riding their dragon?" she muttered dryly.

"That wasn't what I meant," he stated.

Lunis had been working on the condensing spell for a while. It was something dragons could employ sparingly to allow them to squeeze through small spaces when flying. Or as in this case, it allowed him to avoid whatever projectile had just passed over their heads.

"What was that?" Sophia asked, looking around as she stayed low.

"A dart," he answered, peering over his shoulder. "But I think we're okay right now."

"Why?" Sophia asked, glancing back and forth, trying to see what he saw while also staying vigilant about what lurked around them.

"Because," he simply said. On cue, a dozen faces covered in war paint peeked through the foliage, the shooters in their hands pointed directly at them.

Sophia braced herself, her hand on Inexorabilis at her side.

A man in the middle stepped forward, wearing a large head-dress and holding a spear decorated with beads and feathers. Sophia sucked in a breath as the nearly naked man approached.

She wasn't sure what to say to him, so she simply pulled out the newspaper article she'd found in the Castle.

"Hello. We come in peace," she said to the man, but her words didn't sound at all like she expected.

Glancing sideways at Lunis, she gave him a questioning expression. *Riders and dragons can speak all languages at will,* he explained in her mind. *How else can we be adjudicators for the world at large?*

She nodded, turning her attention back to the man. Holding up the article, she pointed at it. "Is this your tribe? Are you the ones having territorial disputes with the local Brazilian military?"

Again, she didn't recognize her words. They were a series of strange vowels and clucks, but beautiful and enchanting none-theless.

The man, who seemed to be the chief of the tribe, scanned the article and nodded. "You work for the militia? We will not stand down?"

Sophia gave Lunis a curious expression. *I'm guessing that the translation app we use works both ways, then?*

It's not an app, it's magic, he explained. *And yes.*

Apps are magical, she replied.

"We aren't with the Brazilian government," Sophia explained. "We are an impartial third party, here to help." Proudly, she looked at Lunis. "We are—"

An old woman with long gray hair pushed through the men crowding the jungle behind the chief, swaying like she was lost. Sophia realized as she neared that she was blind.

"The dragonriders—the great adjudicators—have come once more," the woman said. "We are saved. They will bring peace to our battles. They will ensure no more bloodshed. They will do what is right."

The chief turned to the woman, "Mother, what do you mean? These people are the ones you once spoke of?"

The blind woman pointed straight at Lunis. "Don't you see the dragon, son?"

"Well, yes," the chief said, "but we see magic these days, and with it, many strange things. The dragon was why I ceased fire, though."

"And beside the dragon," the woman stated, "isn't that a rider?" She pointed at Sophia.

"Yes, but she's not riding the dragon, so how do we know she's what you say?" the man asked.

Sophia offered a timid smile. "I rode him all the way here. He's all tuckered out. I think some walking will do me good."

The chief gave her a skeptical expression but was interrupted by the woman swaying in Sophia's direction.

"I knew you'd come," she said in a misty voice. "I dreamed about it, and here you are. Ready to save us and our lands."

Sophia looked at Lunis tentatively.

He bowed his head to her. *Well, what's next for your plan?*

I don't know, she answered telepathically. *I hadn't gotten that far. What about you?*

I'd help, but I'm all tuckered out, he replied.

CHAPTER SIXTY-TWO

For over an hour, Sophia and Lunis listened to the tribe's leader, Grosso, explain the situation. Unsurprisingly, a lot of pertinent details had been left out of the newspaper article, which mostly told the military's side of the story.

The Anacombre were peaceful people unless provoked, which was exactly what had happened when the military expanded one of their bases, impinging on the tribe's sacred land. They retaliated, attacking soldiers and destroying property. In turn, the military pushed back the tribe using deadly force such as guns and cannons.

Now the Anacombre were miles from the land they so dearly prized. Grosso was fed up and defending their borders with a new intensity, unwilling to be pushed even farther out of their homelands.

"We simply want what belongs to us," Grosso explained. Many of his men were crowded around him.

"You aren't giving them the full story," his mother said. She was standing beside him and was much shorter than her son.

He cut his eyes at the old woman. "That's not important."

"I think it is," she replied.

"What is it?" Sophia asked her.

"We consider it unlucky to live on the sacred land," she explained.

"Wait, I thought you said they pushed you off your land?" Sophia argued.

"We used to live next to it," the woman stated. "The disputes pushed us away from it, but we are nomadic in nature, so that isn't the issue."

"What is, then?" Sophia asked. "If you don't want to live on the land, why do you want access to it?"

"There are two sacred ceremonies that must be held on the land every year," the woman explained. "We believe that if we live on this property, the gods will curse us."

"Are you okay with others living on it?" Sophia asked, giving Lunis a knowing look. He seemed to understand her intention.

"What others do is up to them," Grosso cut in.

She nodded, thinking. "Okay, I need to meet with the other side, but if I can help you, will you agree to meet with them?"

"We will have our weapons. We will defend ourselves if necessary," Grosso stated with conviction.

"I understand," Sophia said. "But my goal is that it won't come to that again."

CHAPTER SIXTY-THREE

Sophia knew from reading *The Incomplete History of Dragonriders* that first impressions were crucial for setting the stage for the negotiations. The majestic appearance of the dragon, mixed with the unyielding courage of the rider, was a combination that put the odds in their favor.

The first rule of adjudication, according to the book, was to get the two sides to come together to talk. The second was to get them to engage in negotiations. Like many opposing sides throughout history, the Anacombre and the military had skipped those stages and gone straight to battle. That was actually the last stage of adjudication, and only happened when all other solutions had been exhausted.

Those were the bloodiest battles in history. Not only because they usually involved dragons, but because two sides who resorted to that were bent on destruction rather than peace. However, Sophia had learned that war was sometimes inevitable. It was impossible to always reach a peaceful resolution because too often, peace wasn't what others wanted. They wanted land, resources, or power at the expense of all else.

"I should warn you," Lunis began as they hiked through the unforgiving Amazon rainforest, "this military force will be resistant to our efforts."

"I didn't expect this to be easy," Sophia said, tugging on her ankle, which was currently tethered by a thick vine.

"They will shoot first and ask questions later," Lunis continued.

"Like the Anacombre, who just shot a deadly dart straight at us?" Sophia asked.

"They only shot once, and quit upon seeing me," Lunis stated.

"So what, you don't think the military will have the same reaction?" Sophia questioned.

"I think that whereas the Anacombre stopped out of awe, the military will attack out of fear," Lunis said.

"First off, how do you know this?"

"Dragon's advantage," he imparted simply.

Sophia rolled her eyes. "How should we proceed, given your information?"

"First impressions will be important," Lunis remarked.

"So, I should ride you when we enter."

When the dragon rolled his eyes, it was more effective. "You sure do get stuck on things, don't you? And that's not what I had in mind. I think you should enter alone."

Sophia faced him. "Are you serious? You're sending me into hostile territory on my own? Is the idea that they'll shoot at me, giving you the chance to make a majestic entrance?"

A slight smile formed on the dragon's face. "And here I thought you would be opposed to my brilliant idea."

<h1 style="text-align:center">CHAPTER SIXTY-FOUR</h1>

Feigning annoyance, Sophia shook her head at Lunis before stepping through the barrier of trees that bordered the military base. She'd officially set foot on the property the Anacombre held so dearly.

Sophia could tell immediately that it wasn't land the military was actually using. It appeared to be a buffer zone around their main base. It angered her that land that was of such importance to the tribe was not being used, but in a way, this might be perfect.

The main base was surrounded by a high fence reinforced with barbed wire. Guard towers stood on either side of the area, and behind the fence, large weapons were on display, as if for intimidation.

Sophia shook her head at the sight of the howitzer on the tarmac in the distance. "That's definitely a show of power."

The cannon sat on a base on wheels on the ground, menacingly pointed into the sky, as if ready to send a blast at the Anacombre at any minute. Many soldiers were milling around it. However, as Sophia strode out of the jungle, they all came to attention, drew their automatic weapons, and pointed them at her.

Some knelt, taking aim. Others rushed forward. The guards on the towers did exactly what Lunis had stated and began shooting.

Sophia sighed dramatically, as if the gunfire was an annoyance rather than a lethal danger. Thanks to Lunis, she'd created an impenetrable shield. It wouldn't last long, especially at the rate it was being assaulted by bullets, but hopefully, they wouldn't need it for too long.

Already, Sophia was getting the reaction she was going for. The guards had stopped firing and were now regarding her with skeptical interest. Maybe it was because their bullets had ricocheted off her round, invisible shield. But also probably because she was holding her hands in the air.

She yelled the same thing she'd said to the Anacombre tribe. "I come in peace."

The ground forces moved closer to the gate. She was hoping there wouldn't be more attacks, since she'd felt her shield come down. The men crowded along the fence, glaring at her menacingly.

She must have been quite the sight to them—a young woman in traditional armor, with a sword at her side and a determined look in her eyes, marching up to a heavily defended base.

Or I look like a looney tune, she thought as the men parted, making way for a single individual.

The red sash that ran diagonally across his chest told her he was in charge. The heated expression in his dark eyes told her he thought he was more powerful than her.

CHAPTER SIXTY-FIVE

These rogue militia forces were no joke, Sophia concluded as she drew closer, taking in their gritty appearance and trigger-happy expressions. She'd used magic to get to this point, but from here on out, she was going to have to rely on her wit and charm. She glanced down. *And my appearance.*

She'd used her magic to put herself in something fashionable and elegant because every occasion called for the best dress. Her appearance seemed to be having a two-pronged effect. She was both fashionable and disconcerting, according to the expression on the militia man's face.

"Who are you?" the leader exclaimed in a foreign language Sophia understood, although she recognized it as different.

She sheathed her sword, lowered her chin, and glanced at the men flanking the leader.

They had opened the gates to about the width of a two-car garage. So far, everything was going to plan.

"I'm Sophia Beaufont, a dragonrider and adjudicator for the Dragon Elite," she stated with brand-new confidence. It was exhilarating. It was thrilling. And the sound of the weapons cocking, all pointed at her, was absolutely terrifying.

"What do you want?" the man called.

"I'm here to mediate the land negotiations between you and the Anacombre," she said.

He laughed, placing his hand on his belly and throwing his chin skyward. The men around him laughed as well, most of them faking it.

"We have nothing to discuss," the man stated. "The land is ours, and when we want more, we will simply take it."

"It isn't, actually," Sophia stated. She didn't flinch, although she thought she might pee on herself at any moment, but she hid that fear.

The leader held up his hand, stopping them. "Before, you deflected our bullets. How?"

"I'm a dragonrider," she stated simply.

"Then where is your dragon?" the man asked, laughing and holding his arms out wide.

The men around him joined in again.

"He's busy," she stated with no inflection.

"Busy?" the man asked, still amused. "Does he have a doctor's appointment?"

"He's running an errand for me," she replied.

"Go back and tell the Anacombre that this is our land," the man said, no longer laughing. "We will not negotiate. We are the stronger power." He gestured to the base at his back. If you or they dare to attack us, we will squash you, dragon or no dragon."

"Thing is," Sophia said, tilting her head back and forth, "it doesn't take much to turn everything in our favor, making you the one easy to squash."

The man's laughter rang out again. "You are a little girl, and your dragon is nowhere that I can see. Those savages only have darts and spears, which can't stand up to our guns and cannons."

"True," Sophia said. "But imagine if you didn't have cannons? That would make you all just a bunch of little old men."

The man's laughter was starting to wear on Sophia's nerves. "But there is no point in arguing about things we do have. Like our cannons. And our gun—"

An explosion behind the men made them dive forward, many of them dropping their guns to cover their heads. The blast was more severe than Sophia was expecting, but the militia's reaction was absolutely perfect.

The leader shielded his eyes to take in the plume of smoke billowing from the nearest building before calmly turning around to face her. "What did you do?"

"I leveled the playing field," she stated. "As you know, your armory just went up in flames."

He looked ready to murder her, but something was restraining him. "That's fine. We still have our howitzer."

Sophia's mouth twitched to the side. "Thing is…"

"What?" the man barked.

Lunis' invisibility shield wore off, making all the men around the leader shriek and run for the opposite side of the fence.

The sight of the dragon wasn't going to have much effect on them, Lunis and Sophia had concluded. She'd believed this was most likely attributed to the fact that she wasn't riding him.

Lunis, however, had thought that it would be more attributed to the militia's hardened nature. Dragons and their riders just weren't enough for these men, who hid behind their big guns and weapons. But take those from them, and they were just men once more. Those were the types of people they could reason with.

When Lunis appeared, he was straddling the howitzer, having already chewed up the main part of the artillery, destroying it like it was a common dog toy. The long barrel creaked as it swung back and forth, seemingly hanging by a string before it dropped to the ground, sending up dust all around the base of the cannon.

The dragon's face seemed to say, "Oops." As majestically as

ever, Lunis disembarked from his position, standing tall and casting the men in front of him in shadows.

"*You* did this?" the leader yelled, glaring at Sophia.

Fire soared from Lunis' mouth, blasting the backsides of many of the men behind the leader, sending them shrieking for the fields, as they covered their butts and screamed.

"Yes, and we are prepared to do more," Sophia said, her expression unwavering. "But luckily for you, we are also willing to help you cooperate with the Anacombre."

The man's face twitched. "I don't have to—"

"Should I remind you that you're running out of weapons?" Sophia asked.

"Sir," a man said, tapping the leader on the shoulder. "The dragon destroyed our howitzer."

"I know that!" the leader yelled.

"Okay, just pointing it out," the man said. "Because the dragon is headed this way."

Lumbering forward, Lunis had his head and tail down, which took up a great deal of room since they swung unnecessarily back and forth as he made his way over to where Sophia stood.

"F-fi-fine," the leader stammered. "What do you want?"

Sophia smiled as Lunis made his way to her.

"It's actually simple," she began. "We just want your cooperation with a plan we think will suit everyone."

CHAPTER SIXTY-SIX

The leader of the militia was named Baro. He wasn't an easy man to talk to, and not because the language translator was faulty. This became even more evident when Grosso was pulled into the mix.

However, with Lunis beside her, Sophia was able to get the two opposing leaders together.

"You both need something here," Sophia began. "You, Grosso, want access to the sacred land twice a year." She turned to the militia leader. "And you, Baro, want that property to protect your own, year-round."

"There is no compromise, then," Baro argued.

"And yet," Sophia said, "I think there is."

"If I don't agree, are you going to blow up more of my hard-won weapons?" Baro asked.

"I think we can all conclude they've been stolen," Sophia said dismissively. "And no. If you don't agree, you two are going to destroy each other, and the land will belong to no one."

"I want to hear her solution," Grosso said, his blind mother poking him in the back with her cane.

Baro agreed half-heartedly. "Fine."

"My solution is easy," Sophia said. "We think that you, Baro, should allow the Anacombre people access to their land on the two days of the year they desire. You will have it for the rest of the time. The solution is easy."

The two men, who had been battling each other for months, didn't seem amenable at first. Given a few more weeks, their people would slaughter each other. What Sophia and Lunis had proposed was easy. It made sense, and if it didn't work, there would be war.

Baro stiffened, sending his chin to one side and then the other. "We can't allow them on the property unsupervised. We have too many things at risk."

Sophia was about to argue but felt a gentle nudge in her mind from Lunis. She found herself smiling. "Then accompany them. Escort them onto the land on the day they chose and off at the end." She turned to Grosso. "If you agree, then on all the other days of the year, you'll stay away from this land."

Grosso's mother nodded at once. "We don't want anything to do with it otherwise. The gods will haunt us if we do."

"What did she say?" Baro asked, apparently not understanding the old woman's language.

"She said that would be fine," Sophia paraphrased.

"So, we have a deal then?" Lunis spoke for the first time, making everyone stiffen.

Everyone nodded. No one consented verbally, but strangely, gold dust appeared in the air between Grosso and Baro, wrapping around and linking them, ready to seal their agreement.

Sophia was so astonished that she didn't know what to say until Lunis beckoned her back to reality in her mind.

That's what happens when dragonriders resolve a dispute, he said, snapping her back.

Why didn't it do that before? she asked. The two men seemed just as perplexed as she was.

Because there was no real agreement; it was all made up by Hiker. The farmers and zombie horses were a ruse, Lunis explained. *But this? This was our first resolved dispute.*

On our own, she stated with pride.

She turned to Grosso, offering him her hand. He didn't seem to know what to do with it for a moment but finally extended his own. She didn't take it but instead turned to Baro, who put out his hand. It didn't take the two long to realize what she wanted and they shook each other's hands, fusing the gold dust and making it sing as it wrapped around their hands, binding their agreement.

Sophia and Lunis looked at each other fondly, realizing they had completed their first real case together in the way of the dragonriders.

It wasn't like most cases, where one or more people were in danger, then were saved and a bad guy slaughtered. That happened, and it was usually the way.

However, in the cases with the dragonriders, there weren't always bad guys and good guys. Instead, there was one party and another who were opposed, and they tortured each other until a dragon and their rider came along and made them cooperate and see eye to eye, then negotiate and form an agreement by one means or another until there was peace once more.

The Dragon Elite had seen its fair share of war, but the history books didn't talk about the many battles that had been avoided because of them.

That was the tradition Sophia and Lunis were bent on continuing.

CHAPTER SIXTY-SEVEN

Grosso and Baro might not have agreed on much, but they both apparently wanted to see Sophia ride off on Lunis. When she opened the portal to leave, they objected in unison.

"Dragonriders are supposed to ride dragons," Grosso dared to say. "Why aren't you leaving on your dragon?"

Baro nodded in agreement, pointing to his people lined up in the trees behind them. "They were hoping to see the dragon in the sky with his rider."

Sophia smiled meekly, giving Lunis a begging expression. She heard a firm "no" in her head. "I'm sorry to disappoint, but isn't traveling through a portal pretty magical to see?"

Both men shrugged like they'd grown bored with seeing people traveling through a magic portal across thousands of miles.

She sighed. "Well, we really must get going. Lunis is pretty spent after demolishing all those weapons."

This didn't go over well with Baro, but she ignored him as she and Lunis disappeared through the portal.

Upon returning to the Gullington, Sophia knew something was wrong right away. Not just because Ainsley was waving madly from the front steps of the Castle some twenty yards away. It was mostly because Hiker was standing only a few feet away from her portal with his chin down, arms crossed over his chest and a murderous glare in his eyes. That was what gave it away.

"Well, I've got to go," Lunis said, flying toward the Cave.

"B-b-but," Sophia stuttered, thinking she could maybe dive back through the portal and live with the Anacombre. She could get used to wearing tribal paint and sleeping in a hut. However, the portal closed, making this no longer an option.

She wasn't surprised that Lunis had abandoned her as she was facing the murderous rage of Hiker. He had said before that he wasn't getting mixed up in rider politics with the Dragon Elite leader, and she understood. Her disputes with Hiker might have been about the Elite, but they were of a human nature. Apparently, dragons didn't have the same disagreements because they simply did what they wanted, and as long as it didn't hurt anyone else, it didn't bother the others.

The majestic blue dragon sped toward the Cave, not looking back even as Sophia pined for a way to get out of the trouble she was definitely in with Hiker.

"Hey," she tried casually. "So, you're back. Welcome."

"And you are too," he said through clenched teeth. "Although I remember expressly telling you not to leave the Gullington."

"Actually, I think you told me to stay here and train," Sophia argued, daring to walk past him like she had an important meeting at the Castle. She did have to pee, but she wasn't going to use that as an excuse to get out of the argument just yet.

"And did you stay here and train?" he asked, stalking right beside her.

"I was going to," Sophia began. Ainsley continued to wave frantically from the Castle's steps. She picked up her speed, thinking something must be wrong, but Hiker didn't seem to notice since he apparently knew what was going on. "But you see, the Castle led me to this room on the fifth floor, and—"

"There is no fifth floor," he cut in.

"That's what I said," Sophia said, offering the Viking a chuckle he didn't return.

"S. Beaufont," Ainsley said in a hushed voice as they neared the Castle. "Hiker is on the warpath and looking for you because you left the Gullington."

"Thanks," Sophia said dryly, angling her head in his direction. "I believe he found me."

"Oh," Ainsley said as if seeing Hiker beside her for the first time. "I didn't know she'd left, Hiker. Seriously."

"How did she find out about the case?!" Hiker bellowed.

"Case?" Sophia stopped on the top step, turning to face the hulking man. "How did you know I went on a case?"

"We will get to that later," he said, still fuming.

Ainsley clapped her hands. "A case! Oh, how exciting. I want to hear all about it."

"You will not," Hiker said. "Especially since I sense you were behind this."

"I was not," Ainsley argued, sounding offended.

"No, she wasn't," Sophia said, entering the Castle. "I found the information on the case on the fifth floor. The Castle led me to it."

Again the housekeeper clapped, delighted. "Oh, you found the fifth floor! That's lovely. I knew you could do it."

Hiker looked at them, his expression growing even angrier.

A guilty look rose in Ainsley's eyes. "Oh, well, I did tell S. Beaufont how to find the fifth floor, so maybe I'm sort of responsible."

Hiker thundered across the threshold, stalking after Sophia, who was trying to get up the stairs and to her room as fast as she could. "You come back here. I'm not done with you."

"Hiker Wallace!" Ainsley scolded from the doorway. "You're tracking mud everywhere. You're the one who needs to get back here and clean your feet."

Sophia and Hiker both paused, turning to the housekeeper. He had indeed left muddy footprints across the entryway.

"She has mud on her boots too," he argued, pointing at Sophia.

"Yes, but she's not stomping around and leaving it everywhere," Ainsley said, her hands on her hips. "Besides, the Castle likes her. It cleans up her mud before it even falls off her boots."

Sophia glanced down at her boots and found that the housekeeper was right. Her boots appeared mostly clean, although she knew they'd been caked in mud from the rainforest moments prior.

"And it apparently gives her cases," Hiker exclaimed, looking around at the entryway. "You do realize that I'm in charge here?"

Ainsley curtsied. "Of course, sir."

"I'm talking to the Castle!" Hiker yelled.

"And I'm responding for it," Ainsley said with a sneaky grin. "It says that it knows you're in charge and has left a peace offering in your office."

Hiker huffed, calming slightly. "Fine. Follow me to my office, Sophia."

He said her name like it was a bad word.

She gave Ainsley a cautious look when Hiker thundered past her, as if looking for the shapeshifter to rescue her.

"Don't worry," Ainsley said in a loud whisper. "I can most likely hear you scream from his office. I'll be up there to fetch you if it sounds like he's close to killing you."

"Thanks," Sophia said with zero inflection.

"No problem," Ainsley sang, toddling toward the kitchen, smiling proudly. "She found the fifth floor. Years and years I've been telling the men there's a fifth floor, but do they believe me? Oh, no. S. Beaufont is as sane as me, and the rest of the lot are all crazy. Soon they'll see, won't they, Castle?"

Sophia turned back to the staircase, shaking away the ridiculous behavior of the housekeeper.

She thought about buzzing down the hall to the bathroom but decided she better not anger Hiker any more than he already was. When she climbed to the top of the stairs, she found him standing squarely in the doorway to his office. Even with his back to her, she could tell he was restraining his anger, his back rising and falling rapidly like he was breathing fast.

"Peace offering," he spat. "I should have known. You twisted Castle, you." He strode forward, giving Sophia a chance to see what he was talking about.

The bank of windows that took up one wall and usually showed the Pond, glistening and stretching for miles, was gone. Without the light from the windows, the large room felt cramped and dark.

"Maybe the Castle is trying to tell you—"

"The Castle is bitterly angry at me," Hiker interrupted her, snapping his fingers and lighting all the candles and lanterns in the space. They sprang to life, filling the room with light. "It has been for a while, waking me up in the middle of the night, trying to send me on scavenger hunts. But I refuse to be baited anymore. And it took all my books." He threw his arm wide to indicate the empty and dusty shelves. "And now, it's redesigning my office."

"Well, maybe you'll find your books if you go on these scavenger hunts?" Sophia offered.

"I won't," he fired. "I've tried that. It always sends me to the dungeon, as if trying to hint that I should be punished. But you—" He pointed an accusatory finger at Sophia. "It sends you to this supposed fifth floor, where it gives you a case. Or it sends you to Adam's room, again offering information that is none of your concern, and entirely outside your ability to deal with."

"But I did complete the case it gave me," Sophia argued.

"I know that!" Hiker pointed to the globe, which Sophia noticed was glowing in the area of the Amazon rainforest she'd just come from. The gold dust she'd seen wrap around Grosso's and Baro's hands was whirling around this area.

"Oh, so that was how you knew I completed a case," she said timidly. "That's a cool globe, to tell you that."

"Yes, and it tells me where all my riders are, and if they are in danger, dead, or successful," Hiker said tersely.

Sophia then noticed red dots on the globe in various places, representing the other riders.

"How does it tell you if they are in danger or dead?" she asked.

He sighed. "The dots beep if a rider is in danger, and that beep is continuous if they die until the dot turns black."

"Oh," Sophia said, noticing the labels on the dots that told which rider they were.

"Imagine my surprise when I returned from a very unpleasant meeting with mortals to learn that you, one of my riders, had left the Gullington and was on a case that you'd taken upon yourself without my permission?"

"I'm going to guess you were a bit frustrated," Sophia stated mildly.

"Yes," he hissed. "I was just a bit frustrated."

"But again, I completed the case," Sophia argued. "Doesn't that count for anything?"

"No!" he boomed. "You're not ready, and I have enough problems going on without having to worry about what you're getting yourself into."

"Lunis and I resolved a dispute between two warring groups," Sophia stated, starting to squirm from having to pee.

"Great," Hiker said, not sounding at all happy about the achievement. "And what problems did you create in the meantime? Like, with the facility close by? Now aircraft keep circling the Gullington, looking for something."

"They can't see us," Sophia stated. "And I freed those slaves."

"Just because you were successful, it doesn't mean you should be doing anything," he went on. "You can't even ride your dragon. And there's a difference between doing things and being successful and doing things the right way."

"That doesn't make any sense." Sophia started to do the *I've got to pee dance.*

"What are you doing?" Hiker barked at her.

"Nothing," she said, swaying back and forth. "It's a girl thing."

He lifted a skeptical eyebrow. "Are you saying that to get out of this?"

"No," she said, throwing her hands up. "You're mad because I went off and made progress on the first case the Dragon Elite has taken on in ages. Obviously, I'm a horrible person who needs to be punished. Send me to the dungeon."

"I'd do that, but the Castle would probably fill it with treats and comfortable furniture for you," he said. "And again, just because you were successful doesn't make it right. We aren't to be doing cases until we get the approval of the mortal world, and more importantly, their governments. As of right now, they think we're a joke."

"Then stop asking for their permission to be an adjudicator." Sophia threw her arms wide. "We need to just intervene. Show up to a war that's about to break out and fix things. Then everyone will see how valuable we are and beg for our help."

"That's not how it works," Hiker argued. "We will do this with the blessing of the people we are to serve."

"But they don't get it," Sophia stated. "And how can they? Things have changed. You keep going to these meetings with politicians, and of course, they'll think you're nuts. But what if you and Bell showed up on the front line of a war? You'd get everyone's attention, especially when you created peace, where before war was the only option."

He narrowed his eyes at her. "I will do things the way I see as right, which means garnering the support of leaders first."

"Leaders don't always—"

"Finish that sentence, and you're out of here for good," Hiker threatened.

Sophia shook her head. "Fine. Never mind. You know best. I'm just a dumb kid."

He sighed. "You're not dumb. You're just impatient. Now, I'm leaving again to meet with diplomats."

Sophia had trouble containing the growl begging to spill from her lips.

"I'm serious this time. You are to stay here and train," Hiker ordered. "Don't leave, not even to get gummy bears from the candy shop."

"I'm not twelve years old."

He stopped at the door before turning to face her. "No, you're eighteen years old, with the brain of a brownie."

"Hey, I know some brownies who would resent that statement."

CHAPTER SIXTY-EIGHT

The Castle knew Sophia was sulking, so it dimmed the lights in the torches on the wall as she walked down to the dining hall.

She found Quiet and Ainsley sitting at the long table, sharing a plate of crackers and cheese.

"What's going on?" Sophia asked. "Are we not having dinner?"

"Well, we are, but it isn't the usual fare," Ainsley stated. "Since the others aren't here, I decided not to cook. Quiet and I usually have something easy for dinner when everyone is gone."

"Wait," Sophia said, looking around. "Isn't this the first time in a long time that the men have all been gone at the same time?"

Ainsley thought for a moment. "Why, yes. That makes me sort of overdue for a break from cooking, don't you think? I've cooked dinner every night for centuries."

Sophia nodded. "Yeah, I'm fine with that." She eyed the cold crackers and cheese, listening to her stomach growl. She was hungrier than usual after the long adventure in the Amazon rainforest.

"Actually…"Sophia interrupted as Ainsley and Quiet both lifted loaded crackers to their mouths.

"What?" Ainsley asked, pausing with the cracker not far from her lips.

"Well," Sophia began, "what if I was in charge of dinner tonight?"

Quiet's eyes widened. He didn't have to say anything for his hesitation to be clear.

"I get that I can't cook," Sophia cut in. "But I have an option that doesn't involve me cooking or the overworked Ainsley having to lift a finger."

They both lowered their crackers, giving her skeptical expressions.

"You do?" Ainsley asked.

Quiet mumbled something that, unsurprisingly, Sophia couldn't make out.

"I was just about to ask that same thing, Quiet," Ainsley said to the gnome.

"What?" Sophia asked, looking at the two.

"What he said was as clear as day," Ainsley stated, waving in Quiet's direction.

Sophia gave her a reluctant expression.

"Oh, so you can find the fifth floor, but you can't hear Quiet?" Ainsley asked.

Sophia gave her a look that said, "Pretty much."

"Fine, then," Ainsley said, waving her hand. "What's your solution for dinner tonight if you're not cooking? I didn't think you could magic food?"

"I can't," Sophia stated, pulling out her phone. "But I have an app that's pretty much magic."

"Aren't all apps magic?" Ainsley asked.

Sophia sighed. "That's what I told Lunis." Pulling up her Uber Eats app, Sophia scrolled through. "So if I get something from

Magical UberEats, what do you all want? They deliver pretty much anywhere."

The elf and the gnome exchanged confused expressions.

Sophia shook her head. "Never mind. I'll get a smorgasbord. Just give me twenty minutes."

"It's going to take twenty minutes to get dinner?" Ainsley asked.

Sophia lowered her phone. "Is that too long? We can do something else."

The elf shook her head. "No, that's short. I think I'll be ordering from this app more often, and the men won't be any the wiser."

CHAPTER SIXTY-NINE

The only flaw in Sophia's plan was that UberEats, no matter that it was a part of the magical branch, couldn't deliver to the Gullington. Sophia had to meet the "driver" at a local hilltop a safe distance away. That was easy enough, so she had hot food ready for the housekeeper and the gnome within the promised twenty minutes.

"Here you go," Sophia said triumphantly, dropping the bags of food on the dining room table in front of Ainsley and Quiet.

They both jumped back at the sight of the crinkled bags.

"What is this witchcraft?" Ainsley asked, holding up a piece of sage in defense of the bags.

Sophia scrunched up her brow. "What do you mean? It's food."

"But what is it in?" Ainsley asked, staring at the bags like they were made of demons.

"That's plastic," Sophia stated.

"Plastic," Ainsley said slowly. "Like the chip bag? What kind of magic is that?"

Sophia tilted her head to the side. "It's not. It's a material used for different things." She dove into the to-go containers, handing out the various options. "I ordered from a popular Los Angeles Mexican eatery. We have nachos, tacos, quesadillas, and—"

Ainsley's and Quiet's muttering cut her off. She raised her chin and stared at them, waiting for them to look at her.

When they both gave her their attention, she asked, "What?"

Ainsley said politely, "We just don't know what you're saying? Can you speak English?"

"Oh," Sophia said, smiling, opening the container of nachos. "These are Mexican foods."

Ainsley copied Sophia's polite smile and reached for one of the nachos. "Well, I'll try to keep an open mind, but I'm certain this Mexican food is not to my liking."

Quiet mumbled, reaching out as well and grabbing a chip.

Hiker strode past the dining room and then doubled back. He narrowed his eyes as he took in the sight before him.

Sophia wiped her mouth and sat up. "I'm here, sir."

"Yes, I see that," he said, staring at the two passed-out figures beside Sophia. "Tell me, why are my housekeeper and groundskeeper in comas?"

Sophia cast a backward glance at them. "Oh, that? Well, they are not very good at handling carbs."

"What did you do to Ainsley and Quiet?" he asked, his frustration growing.

"I gave them Mexican food," she admitted, holding up a nearly demolished quesadilla. "Want some?"

Hiker stepped back at the sight of the food like she'd offered him head cheese. "This is what you gave them that's made them sick?"

"Well, actually, they loved it, but they ate too much, and they might have stomachaches now."

Quiet rubbed his stomach, mumbling in his sleep.

Ainsley did the same thing, stirring from her food coma. "Oh, man, I'll never be the same. I'm ruined."

Hiker lowered his chin. "Sophia, what have you done?"

"I fed them something delicious," she answered. "They loved it, sir. Seriously. They will sleep well and be happy tomorrow."

"If they are even moving then," Hiker said, snapping his fingers at her and pointing to the stairs. "I believe you've done enough. Up to your room."

Feeling like a child being scolded, Sophia narrowed her eyes at him. She couldn't win for losing. Sophia strode past the Viking and headed toward her room, wondering when she'd catch a break.

"And," he said at her back. She halted. Waited. Turned to face him.

"I'll be heading out again, so…"

"I'm not to do anything but train," she said, finishing his statement.

"That's right," he answered. "And?"

"And I won't feed the staff ever again," Sophia said.

"And?" Hiker said in an expectant tone.

"I won't allow the Castle to send me on any scavenger hunts," Sophia answered.

"Very well," he said proudly, dismissing her with a wave of his hand.

CHAPTER SEVENTY

A loneliness Sophia had never felt before crept into her stomach as she lounged in her beanbag chair next to the fire in her room. She'd never been prone to such things, having spent much of her childhood isolated from others.

Actually, going for long periods of time without social interaction was easy for her. So much so that she had often forced herself to "go out" and be around other people. But suddenly, she felt the need for friends like it was vital to her wellbeing.

She pulled her phone out of her pocket and messaged her sister Liv.

Hey, are you busy?

A few seconds later, a message came through.

I've got a demon in a headlock, but not really. How are you?

Oh, well, that sounds like it needs your full attention. Text me when you're free.

No, he's a pansy who totally doesn't require much effort. I'm pretty much holding him with my pinky.

Why don't you kill him?

I will, as soon as he tells me where to find a labyrinth that holds the fountain of youth, Liv answered.

Oh, you're going to take a drink from it?

I'm going to destroy it on Father Time's orders.

Sophia laughed. **Do you ever have a boring day at the office?**

Not that I can recall, but yesterday was sort of slow.

Because?

Because I only had to teach a troll table manners.

Sophia curled her legs up.

That sounds pretty tame compared to your usual tasks.

Oh, it was, until the heathen turned the table upside-down and yelled in my face, Liv messaged.

Then what did you do? Sophia asked.

I told him that if he can't sit at a table like a well-mannered troll, I wasn't taking him to the Hard Rock Café.

Wait, what?

That was the agreement, Liv messaged. **If I took him to that restaurant, he'd tell me where to find the demon I'm currently choking.**

Oh, so I guess he figured out how to be polite and have table manners, then.

Yes, he's a big fan of rock and roll and cheese fries, Liv replied.

And how is the demon-choking going? Sophia questioned.

He's still not talking yet, but demons can pretty much hold their breath forever, Liv responded. **So how are you? How is Crispy McToasterbreath?**

Sophia laughed. **Lunis is okay. He's grown a lot.**

Tell him I said, "What's up, bro?"

Sophia sent her a picture she'd recently taken of Lunis.

Whoa, he's gotten big. What is it like to ride him? Liv asked.

I wouldn't know, Sophia answered.

Oh?

Sophia sighed, her emotions welling to the surface. **Yeah, my ride is broken.**

How?

He's got a bad attitude.

Well, I'll send you a broom if you want something to ride that doesn't talk back.

It felt good to smile. Liv was great at picking up Sophia's mood. **Magicians don't ride brooms.**

No, they don't, Liv responded. **That was just an old wives' tale we told mortals because it was funny to watch them run around with the broom between their legs, trying to impersonate us.**

How is the demon? Sophia asked, thinking she should probably let her sister get back to things.

He's bleeding on my boots, which really pisses me off. This is my third pair this week.

What happened to the others?

A troll ate the first pair, she answered.

The one who likes rock and roll? Sophia asked.

No, his brother, who doesn't like cheese fries but loves leather boots. That was his payment for giving me the location of Arggg.

Arggg is the name of the troll with table manners?

Yep, Liv responded. **The second pair got scorched when I had to cross a lava pit.**

Because?

Because demons live in hell. Duh.

Right, Sophia responded, searching for another question to keep Liv on the phone.

So what's wrong? her sister asked as if reading her thoughts.

Why would you think that something is wrong?

Sophia could almost hear her sister sigh. **Because I know you.**

Well, Sophia began, **Hiker hates me.**

That's because he's a bitter old man who doesn't want to change, and you're the essence of evolution.

Sophia pressed the phone to her chest with fondness before typing her reply. **That's my new title: Essence of Evolution.**

Because you've already outgrown the title of dragonrider?

Well, and I don't ride a dragon, Sophia answered.

What else has you down?

The guys are all off on missions and I've been forbidden from leaving the Gullington. Apparently, Dad has grounded me, Sophia explained. **I'm currently watching the mist float across the mountains.**

That sounds lovely, Liv replied.

It's what I plan on doing tomorrow too.

You know what you should do? Liv asked.

Practice my sword skills?

Nah, Liv replied. **You should eat nachos.**

Sophia giggled. **I just did. I gave some to the housekeeper and the groundskeeper.**

Good girl. Spread the addiction.

Stretching out her feet in front of the fire, Sophia typed out another message. **I got the staff sick with stomachaches. Now Hiker hates me even more.**

They just can't handle the cheesy gooeyness. Liv's message was followed by another one. **And Hiker doesn't hate you. He just needs time to appreciate how badass you are.**

Hard to show that to him when I've been grounded, Sophia complained.

Well, I'm certain an adventure is in store for you soon.

Why is that?

Because the demon I'm about to slaughter told me. Apparently he was a seer in his past life, Liv responded. **He says the dragonrider I'm talking to should take a stroll through the Castle.**

Sophia sat up suddenly. **That's bizarre.**

Yes, but you should probably do what he says, Liv texted. **I'm going to bring him some more pain since he's still not talking.**

Well, good luck, Sophia said.

Thanks, Liv responded. A moment later, another message came through. **And Soph...**

Yeah?

I love you.

CHAPTER SEVENTY-ONE

Not only did Sophia feel much better after her conversation with Liv, but her heart was full of love. For some reason, Liv's affection was better than anyone else's by far. It made Sophia high. Feel invincible. It inspired her in ways no one else could compare to.

Sophia knew that she wasn't alone in feeling this way. Many were magnetized to Liv Beaufont. That was why she was such a successful warrior for the House of Fourteen. Well, and also because she could kick serious ass.

"I did promise Hiker I wouldn't go on anymore scavenger hunts that the Castle sent me on," Sophia said to herself as she strode tentatively down the long, dark corridor.

The torches lit as she walked, illuminating the path ahead little by little. Sophia wondered why Ainsley came in to light her candles and fire each morning since the Castle could obviously do it. Then she reminded herself that questioning why the Castle or the housekeeper did anything was a recipe for a headache. It was better to just go along with things.

"And I'm not really going on a scavenger hunt that the Castle is sending me on," Sophia reasoned, still talking to herself. "I'm going on a late-night walk because a demon seer told me to."

She nearly laughed, hearing herself talk.

Impersonating Hiker, she put her hands on her hips, "Sophia, why were you out of your room exploring the Castle when I forbade you from doing anything but breathing?"

"Because, sir," she said, changing her voice back to normal, "there was this demon who knows where the fountain of youth is."

"Oh, and it's in the Castle, is it?" she asked in a deep voice.

"No," she responded. "Actually, while being choked for the information, he said I should walk about the Castle."

"And you listened to the demon?" Sophia questioned, furrowing her brow the way Hiker always did when talking to her.

"Well, he seemed like the knowledgeable type."

Sophia sighed. "I don't have to do anything if I find something while exploring."

She nodded, liking this compromise. "Yeah, I'll just look around and take note of anything I find. When Hiker returns, I'll give him the newspaper article or whatever other mystery the Castle serves up to me. I won't get in trouble, and Hiker will trust me once more. Win-win."

Sophia had been so busy talking to herself that she hadn't even realized that she'd made it all the way to the front of the Castle.

A weird beeping caught her attention. There weren't any electronics in the Castle aside from her own and the Kindle, but she reminded herself that all this was subject to change, depending on the mood of the strange place. The beeping definitely belonged to an electronic.

For a moment, Sophia thought it was a smoke detector alerting them that its batteries were low. She laughed, thinking about smoke detectors lining the ceiling of the ancient castle.

After another few paces, Sophia realized the beeping was coming from Hiker's office.

"Of course, it is," she said with a sigh.

Maybe it was his Kindle making the noise, Sophia reasoned.

She halted at the entrance to Hiker's office and took a deep breath. "I'll just see what it is and make a note to tell Hiker about it later. Nothing else."

Sophia nodded like she'd just made a deal with herself, then rounded the corner, peering into the leader of the Dragon Elite's office.

It didn't take her long to determine that the beeping was coming from the Elite globe next to the wall that used to have windows.

She approached carefully, as if worried that the globe was a bomb that would go off at any moment.

On the globe, she could plainly see the dot in Scotland that was labeled S. Beaufont.

She turned the orb, finding three more dots in various places throughout the world: Mahkah, Wilder, and Hiker. All of theirs appeared normal.

Sophia continued to rotate the globe until she found the last red dot. This one was labeled Evan. It was blinking rapidly and emitting the beeping sound.

Sucking in a breath, Sophia remembered what Hiker had told her about the globe.

"The dots beep if a rider is in danger, and that beep is continuous if they die and the dot turns black," he had told her.

"Evan," she exclaimed, covering her mouth. He was in danger. The globe was telling her that much.

She looked around, wondering what to do. It didn't feel right to leave a note for Hiker about this.

She imagined how that note would read:

Dear Hiker,

Evan is in mortal danger. Just wanted you to know. I'm going back to my room, where you banished me. See you later. Hope Evan doesn't die.

Sincerely,

S. Beaufont

aka the dragonrider who doesn't ride

She shook her head at the dark thought, continuing to comb through her options. It was hard to think with the incessant beeping.

"Why doesn't Hiker have a cell phone?" she wondered aloud. "Then I could call him, tell him about the situation, and be done with it."

Peering at the globe, she tried to determine where Evan was. It wasn't far, but what did it matter if he was close or on the other side of the world? She couldn't get to him without a dragon since portaling into the sky was probably not an option, and he was most likely riding Coral.

Even if she could get to him, she wasn't allowed to leave the Castle.

The beeping seemed to try to squash her resolve.

Sophia sorted through the issue, trying to remain objective.

"Evan is in danger," she began, "and I'm the only one who knows about it. I'm therefore the only one who can help him." She tilted her head back and forth. "But I can't ride my dragon. And even if I could, Hiker will be angry if I leave again."

Very distinctly, she heard a voice behind her echo through the Castle. It didn't spook her, although it probably should have because it was her voice. The words were the ones she'd said to Hiker:

"Stop asking for permission and just intervene. It's time that we demonstrated our greatness. The world will see it and accept us as adjudicators once again."

Sophia turned toward the door, knowing with total conviction what she had to do next, even if it got her kicked out of the Dragon Elite. Sometimes one should mind the rules and obey their leader, but sometimes, when others were in danger and needed help, action had to be taken with no regard for consequences.

CHAPTER SEVENTY-TWO

Sophia had to work to hide her surprise when she exited the Castle to find Lunis standing on the Expanse as if he'd been waiting for her.

With a renewed sense of confidence, she strode over to her dragon, none of the rejection and frustration she'd felt recently taking up any of her thoughts or feelings.

"Evan is in trouble," she said, hurrying over to him.

"I know," he replied calmly, a hint of something different in his eyes.

"How?"

"Because it's screaming in your thoughts," Lunis stated.

"Oh," Sophia said, still not used to having someone else in her head. Lunis couldn't always read her mind, but when there was something monopolizing her thoughts, it came to him without her even trying to telepathically communicate with him. "Well, no one else is here. We're the only ones who can save him."

The clouds moved, showing the full moon hanging high in the sky. The round orb seemed to glow brighter than ever before. "He could save himself."

She growled at her dragon. "Is that what we do when others are in danger? We let them save themselves? Maybe we curl up and watch Netflix because we can't be bothered to risk our lives for each other?"

He actually shrugged. "Maybe."

"Look," she began with pure conviction, "I get that Evan is a total pain in the ass. He might not risk his neck for me, but how others treat me won't dictate how I treat them. He's off trying to find Mother Nature, and something has happened to him. I don't know what or even where to look specifically."

"Sounds like a lost cause," he said simply.

Sophia screamed with anger. Stomped. Clenched her fists. "No, it absolutely isn't. I know you think I'm not ready to ride, but nothing is farther from the truth. I was born to be a dragonrider, and specifically to ride you, Lunis."

"I'm not arguing that," he related casually.

"I know Hiker forbade me from leaving the Gullington."

"Yes," Lunis replied. "He will be furious if you leave again without permission."

"Then he will be furious. I'm done asking for permission from you and Hiker." Sophia stuck her hands on her hips, her passion drumming in her chest.

He shook his head. "If you're asking to ride me, it's not going to work."

"No!" she exclaimed. "I'm not asking. I'm telling you. Whether you think I'm ready or not, tonight, I will ride you. We're going to find Evan and Coral and bring them back. I will deal with Hiker's wrath upon returning, but right now, time is of the essence, so get ready."

Sophia braced herself for Lunis' reaction. She felt something hot start to build in him and wondered if she might be the first rider to be killed by her own dragon.

He opened his mouth and she resisted the urge to run, worried he was about to scorch her. Instead, though, he lowered his head as if bowing to her. "Now, Sophia, you are ready."

She blinked at him in confusion. "What?"

"We are a team and must never exert undue influence on each other," Lunis began. "I would never force you to do something, nor you me. However, there will be three times during our lives that you will make a demand of me. This is the first."

Sophia's mouth was suddenly dry. "So, you were waiting for me to demand to ride you?"

"The first ride is the most important," Lunis explained. "It's like a christening. Without a fire burning in your belly and indisputable conviction in your heart, the maiden voyage can't be undertaken. I was waiting for you to get to the point where no wasn't an acceptable answer for you to hear."

"Why?" Sophia asked, still confused.

"Because most fall on their first ride."

Sophia gasped. "What? Mahkah didn't tell me that."

"Because it would have made you nervous," Lunis stated. "Are you?"

She thought for a moment. Shook her head adamantly. "No, who has time for that? And speaking of time, we must make haste. Evan's life is in danger."

Lunis extended one wing, making a step for Sophia. "There is no saddle, which will make things more difficult."

"Maybe for you," Sophia said, striding forward. "My butt is boney."

"The spikes on my head and neck are sharp," he added. "Try not to get impaled by them."

"Don't worry about me," she said, taking a deliberate step onto the dragon's wing. He immediately hoisted her up to his back.

At first, Sophia thought the momentum would send her over the other side of him to land on the ground, but she caught herself, gracefully swinging her leg over and straddling her dragon.

Without a saddle, she would have to hold onto him. Still, as she felt the magical creature underneath her preparing for flight, Sophia wasn't at all nervous. For some reason, this felt as normal as walking for her. The only thing she wished at that moment was there was someone there to witness her taking her first ride.

Everything she'd learned from Mahkah about riding sped through her head. She was in charge while she was on her dragon. It was Sophia who dictated when take-off happened and the direction they chose. Above all else, confidence was key.

She pinned her boots to dragon's sides to secure her balance. Lunis turned around, giving her a look that seemed to speak of his great wisdom. In an instant, Sophia understood more about the dragon than she had in all the time they'd had together. Never had she felt closer to him, and she knew this connection would only deepen through the years.

She returned it with a serious expression that spoke of her readiness.

Lunis turned around and sped forward. Sophia wasn't forced back by the sudden rush. She leaned down, feeling the incredible power thundering under her. The drumming of the dragon's feet speeding across the Expanse was in perfect unison with the rush of her heartbeats.

When Lunis' wings spread out, Sophia rounded her back, purely on instinct. Her hands were pressed only slightly into the neck of her dragon, and as they sped up, there was no urgency to tighten her grip. Sophia wasn't going anywhere. She felt magnetized to her dragon. He could turn upside down in the air, and she wasn't going anywhere. That might have been magic, but she wanted to believe it was love—which was basically magic, the most powerful kind in the world.

The wind from the rush of Lunis' wings sent Sophia's long hair spiraling around her face. That didn't distract her, though. She was pure focus.

Again, using her instincts leading the way, Sophia brought her chest up, and in unison, Lunis launched into the air, taking flight.

Rapidly, they rose, the Gullington quickly disappearing behind them as the dragon and his rider flew toward the full moon ahead.

CHAPTER SEVENTY-THREE

The gnome who went by the nickname Quiet watched from the front of the Castle as Lunis and Sophia took their first flight. He'd seen many a rider take that first trip on their dragon. Never had he seen one not use a saddle, or do it completely unsupervised.

He had also watched many fall or get thrown off, especially as the dragon took off for the first time. However, S. Beaufont was as steady on her dragon as if she were riding with a saddle and reins. Like a seasoned rider, the two moved as one, Sophia's thoughts steering the dragon and leading him confidently across the Expanse.

S. Beaufont represented many things for the Dragon Elite. She was the first female rider. She was the youngest. And she was now the first who brought a tear to the groundskeeper's eyes as she and her dragon soared across the sky, moving faster than Lunis had ever flown before.

The full moon gave Lunis a speed he'd never experienced. The rush of wind over Sophia's face was exhilarating, and when she looked down at the hills glowing with moonlight, she simply smiled, not an ounce of fear in her heart.

So, not a big deal, she began, telepathically communicating with Lunis.

But you don't know where to go, he said, finishing her thought with his own.

I know generally where to go, she replied. *North.*

Evan and Coral went to find Mother Nature, he offered.

Yeah, and I'm not sure where they were going.

Thankfully, I think I do, Lunis stated with confidence.

Oh, did Coral tell you? Sophia asked.

No.

Is it a dragon thing? She questioned. *Like, you know where to look for Mother Nature through the collective consciousness of the dragons?*

Nope, he answered again.

Well, I give up then, she said, scanning the hillsides for clues. *How do you know where to go?*

Lunis lowered his neck, giving Sophia a view of the area in front of him. She had to lean down to keep her balance, which must have been why he was flying with his head up before, instead of elongated, as usual.

In front of them was a large peak that looked like it was straight out of a horror movie. Like a gnarly stick, it rose into the air, twisting at strange angles. At its top, it came to a sharp peak, looking like a needle meant to spear enemies.

Flying around the mountain, distress evident in every one of her moves, was Coral, with no Evan riding her.

CHAPTER SEVENTY-FOUR

Sophia's gaze searched the ground, thinking that Evan was lying somewhere on the mountain hurt. She didn't see him anywhere.

However, Coral spotted them right away, streaking in their direction with urgency. The purple dragon was radiating fear as she neared.

Lunis didn't slow as he approached the dragon. At first, Sophia thought that they'd fly headfirst into the other dragon. But in a show of agility she'd never witnessed before, he veered at the last moment, Coral did the same thing, and the two began to circle, their bodies making arcs that created a perfect ring.

"Where is Evan?" Sophia yelled to the dragon. "Is he okay?"

"Yes, but he's severely injured," Coral said, nodding in the direction of the peak. "He's in the mountain. I can't get in there."

"What happened?" Sophia asked.

"I don't know," the dragon answered. "He entered through the cave at the top, and immediately I was alerted to a problem. But all communications with him have been cut off for a reason that's unclear to me."

Sophia looked to the cave opening. "It's too narrow for dragons, isn't it?"

"Yes," Lunis answered simply.

"There isn't anywhere for Lunis to land," Coral said, the two dragons continuing to circle.

"So, the entrance to the cave is how we find Mother Nature?" Sophia asked.

"We think so," Coral answered. "But I sense there's a trap set, and not by Mother Nature."

"Okay, can you get me close enough that I can jump?" Sophia asked Lunis.

"Of course I can, but you better make it," he said a warning in his voice. "That mountain doesn't look forgiving if you aren't precise."

Sophia gulped. Nodded. "My concern isn't with making it into the cave. It's facing whatever is in there that took Evan out."

CHAPTER SEVENTY-FIVE

I can't get you any closer, Lunis communicated to Sophia, flapping his wings to keep them steady.

The jump to the mouth of the cave looked to be at least fifteen feet, and Lunis was right that precision was key. If Sophia didn't make it, the fall wouldn't be short or smooth. Like the peak at the top, the mountain was covered in sharp, unforgiving spires. A fall from a misstep would send Sophia to her death, impaled by the rocky spikes of the mountain.

They were hovering just above the mouth to the cave. Sophia couldn't see anything in the dark opening.

Are you sure about this? Lunis asked, no hesitation in his voice, but rather calculated caution.

As with most things in life, it appears I'll have to take a blind leap of faith, Sophia answered. *And yes, I'm absolutely sure.*

Then whenever you're ready, Lunis said. *I'll be here with Coral.*

Bracing herself, Sophia pulled her other leg over so she was perched on her dragon. He had been beating his wings gently, keeping them aloft. At her silent command, his wings fell still, held out stick-straight.

They hadn't discussed it, and she didn't know she was going to do it until that moment. As Lunis began to slowly descend, Sophia took off at a sprint, running across the wing of her dragon and then leaping. For a second, it was just her and the air, her arms and legs flapping as if she could fly on her own.

Time slowed down. Sophia's heart paused. She held her breath as something became quite evident.

She wasn't going to make it.

The edge of the cave was five feet away. A whole five feet away, and she was quickly falling, losing height and speed.

She reached for the cave, throwing her head forward to try to cross the distance. But even as she did it, she knew the effort wouldn't get her there.

And then a rush like a gale-force wind hit her in the back, pushed her hard. To her surprise, Sophia caught the lip of the cave with her hands, and she held onto the rocky cliff. Her heart started again, pounding hard in her chest.

She dared to look over her shoulder as Lunis flew away, not wanting to knock her down with the wind from his wings. But it had been that same wind that saved her—at least up until that point.

Sophia still didn't know what she was facing, and she was worried. If it was powerful enough to take out an experienced dragonrider, did she stand a chance?

CHAPTER SEVENTY-SIX

Grunting, Sophia tried to pull herself up over the lip of the cave. She kicked and dug her feet into the mountain, using every advantage she could harness. The sharp rocks cut into her fingers but she ignored the pain, finally pulling herself up enough that she was able to swing a leg over the side.

Looking down had been a mistake, she realized immediately. Or maybe it was exactly the motivation she needed to push herself harder, getting the rest of her body into the cave mouth.

Sophia rolled over on her back, taking a moment to simply breathe as she blinked at the inky sky.

In her peripheral vision, she saw the two dragons streaking back and forth. And in her heart, she felt Lunis' relief that she'd made it into the cave.

Not granting herself another moment of respite, Sophia rolled over, cautiously looking into the cave where Evan had disappeared. She only spied darkness, but she thought she heard the hum of electricity.

They weren't far from the Gullington, and this mountain had appeared completely deserted—nothing around it for miles. It didn't make any sense that there would be electricity there, and yet, as she got to her feet, she felt static, as if she'd just dragged her feet across a carpet and was about to shock someone.

There was definitely electricity here, but whether manmade or of Mother Nature's doing was yet to be determined.

Evan might not have felt the electricity, and even if he had, his limited experience in the modern world might not have prepared him. However, Sophia halted before proceeding, an idea suddenly occurring to her.

She closed her eyes and magicked a full-sized rubber catsuit. She sucked in a breath as the tight suit replaced her armor. It was a bit snugger than the clothes she was used to, but she could no longer feel the electric static that filled the air.

Holding out her hand, she summoned her sword, which had disappeared when she changed clothes. Methodically, she strapped her sword around her waist, trying to prepare herself for the unknown she was facing.

She snapped into the blackness in front of her, creating an orb of light that hovered beside her. When she took a step, she was grateful to see the orb move with her.

Sophia had only taken a few steps when her suspicions were confirmed. Electricity shot around the cave walls like scurrying spiders as she progressed.

She magicked a pair of rubber gloves, not daring to take any chances. Something about this didn't seem right.

Mother Nature might have obstacles, but this felt more like magical tech. That meant a magician was behind it, not one of the most powerful entities in the world.

Sophia descended through the cave, walking a great distance without seeing much besides the electrical pulses streaking over the walls.

She met several bats flying and rats scurrying underfoot but kept her calm. Sophia had jumped through the air to this cave. She wasn't about to scream because of a rodent, even if they looked to be protected by magic, the electricity radiating off them.

Well? Lunis asked in her mind.

Nothing yet, she answered. *But there is a lot of electricity in this place.*

That's odd, Lunis stated.

My thoughts exactly, she replied.

Keep me posted, Lunis said, and for some reason, his voice made Sophia feel more confident.

I will, she said, swallowing as she came to a room that smelled like water.

She halted. Water and electricity—the worst combination she could think of.

And then she saw him, trapped like a fish in a pond, convulsing.

CHAPTER SEVENTY-SEVEN

There were many benefits to having Liv, a warrior for the House of Fourteen, as a big sister. Right then, while Sophia watched one of her fellow riders trapped in a puddle of electricity, it wasn't that her sister worked for one of the most powerful entities in the world or influenced so much in the magical world. It was separate from who Liv was as a magician and had everything to do with who she had been before becoming a Warrior.

Liv Beaufont had worked in an electronics repair shop before taking on her role for the House of Fourteen. There, she'd learned about electronics and how to repair them so they didn't end up overfilling the landfills. Once she'd unlocked her magic, she'd learned about magical tech, later teaching Sophia many of the things she knew.

That was how Sophia knew the cave was infected with the stuff. She'd sensed it before, but now she knew it at her core. And unlike with natural electricity, magical tech would be powered from a main source, most likely a power box of some sort.

Magical tech had fewer limitations than regular electronics, but it still was confined by certain restrictions. For one, it couldn't exist separate from a power source. And it had a practical aspect that could be overpowered without using magic.

Sophia searched for the source. It might not be in this room, but since it was the first one she'd come to and the one where Evan had been caught, she thought it might. This was a trap meant to keep anyone from going farther.

She tried to not look at Evan's convulsing figure, realizing he was one of those people halted from making progress.

Lifting her hand, Sophia intensified the light orb, making it illuminate the large cave room. Then she could plainly see that electricity ran over the walls more frequently here as if there were conduits every foot.

The puddles that were spread across the space made this a death maze. Evan hadn't stood a chance. He'd walked straight into electrocution.

Sophia just hoped he was still alive. It was hard to tell at this point. She shook off the concern, but only briefly. Her focus needed to be on finding the power source holding Evan hostage.

Her eyes continued to scan the walls. She was about to abandon searching this room and risk progressing to the next one when she decided to look up, and there in the center of the ceiling of the cave was the power source.

It was a round box, with wires snaking out in different directions and disappearing into thin air, sending their electrical impulses throughout the cave.

This wasn't Mother Nature. Whoever was behind this had a great knowledge of well-constructed magical tech. And one thing was certain—they didn't want anyone getting to Mother Nature.

That begged the question of why.

CHAPTER SEVENTY-EIGHT

Using magic to disable the power source might make matters worse, sending a surge that would kill Evan.

Sophia knew she needed to shut it down. Desperately she wanted to message Liv and ask for a solution, but there was no time for that. Also, this was Sophia's time to stand on her own two feet and create her own solutions.

It wasn't about pride. It was about taking what she'd learned and applying it.

"I just have to shut down the source," she said to herself, quickly adding, "Not using magic."

For a girl who had relied on magic from a much younger age than most, that was a challenge.

Sophia's brain searched for an option, something that would short out the power source without creating more problems. She knew the solution had to be at her fingertips.

Her hands tingled. She moved them slightly, watching as the water in the puddles bubbled, responding to her movements.

Could it really be so simple? she wondered.

Water and electricity didn't mix, and she knew from experience that pouring water on a power strip made it short, blowing the breaker attached to the circuit. That was exactly what she needed.

Sophia muttered an incantation as she lifted her hands into the air. Following the path of her hands, the water rose out of the puddles, gathering in the air as if contained by a huge balloon.

Stepping back into the corridor, Sophia continued to concentrate, raising her hands higher. The water rose as well, now inches from the power source.

Timing was important. And if this was going to work, Sophia was going to have to make it happen quickly. She clenched her eyes shut and shot her hands straight up. The water followed that path, splashing upward and drenching the power source.

Sparks rained down, making Sophia shield her eyes and duck. The room displayed a strange array of lights and colors as electricity and water battled.

In the end, water won, killing the power source and sending all the electrical surges away.

That only left Sophia with one final important task—she had to get Evan out and quickly.

CHAPTER SEVENTY-NINE

Rushing forward, Sophia checked the other dragonrider's pulse.

He was breathing. That was good. But his breath was shallow and his pulse faint.

It was obvious he needed immediate medical attention.

I've found him, she communicated to Lunis.

And? he asked.

He's alive but won't make it without help. Meet me at the Barrier, she stated, grabbing his hand and pulling it around her shoulder. He was much heavier than she would have thought.

Clenching her teeth, Sophia grunted, pulling the man twice her size up even though he was unconscious. It wasn't easy, but she used magic to aid her, and soon she had him to his feet and a portal open right in front of them. She'd never been so happy that portal magic worked in this strange place than when she stepped through, carrying the passed-out man with her.

When they got to the Barrier, Sophia realized how exhausted she was from the effort and dropped Evan. He rolled onto the grass in front of the Barrier.

She spun, grateful to see the two dragons speeding toward her. Lunis was making incredible progress, the moon at his back seeming to cheer him on.

Coral landed, her face grief-stricken at the sight of her unconscious rider. However, she scooped him up immediately and hurried toward the Castle. Inside the walls of the Castle lay the cure that could save Evan at this point, and they all knew it.

Sophia didn't hesitate but instead jumped onto Lunis like it was something she'd done a thousand times. He rose into the air at once and flew beside Coral.

They were about to land when Sophia realized that standing in front of the Castle was a figure. Two, actually. She blinked. Three.

It was hard to make out Quiet sometimes since he blended into the shadows. Hiker, however, stood out like a sore thumb. And based on the look on his face, he was absolutely aching with irritation.

Beside him, Ainsley was shaking her head as if she sensed an inconvenience approaching.

Sophia didn't realize it was her first landing on Lunis until it was already done and she had stepped off as smoothly as if they'd practiced for centuries. Her legs carried her straight over to Coral, who still had Evan clutched in her grasp.

"What's happened?" Hiker bellowed, striding forward.

"He was electrocuted," Sophia explained. "Trying to find Mother Nature."

"Get him into the Castle," he ordered, pointing at the door. "Now!"

Ainsley and Quiet went straight to work, hauling the young man's body in through the Castle doors.

Hiker looked at her, his face twitching with annoyance. "You and I will discuss this later. For now, I have to go save his life."

The Viking turned, striding into the Castle, where the others had already disappeared.

Sophia turned and gave her full attention to Coral. She could feel the dragon's pain like it was her own for a moment. Sophia clasped her hands to her chest, shooting Lunis a questioning expression.

The chi of the dragon bonds you to all of us, not just me, although more to me than the others, he explained in her head.

So that's why I can feel her pain, Sophia stated.

You can feel anyone's pain if you try enough, he said. *You just want to feel hers right now.*

Sophia lifted her hand tentatively, a question in her eyes. Coral looked up, her dark eyes overflowing with emotion.

Sensing that it was okay, Sophia ran her hand down the side of the dragon's face. "He will be okay. I'll do everything I can to help, and I'll give you an update first thing."

"Thank you, S. Beaufont," Coral said, pressing her head into Sophia's offered hand. "If he has any chance of living at all, it's because of you."

CHAPTER EIGHTY

For many hours, no one said anything. The Castle was trying to repair Evan. Ainsley was its assistant, doing everything it told her. Hiker supervised, offering silent support that felt oddly like magic. Sophia watched from the corner, noticing how pale Evan's dark skin was, his long, black dreadlocks scorched in places.

If anyone dared to actually say anything, they wouldn't say what everyone was thinking—that if something happened to Evan, it was very likely to also harm Coral.

The death of one usually brought the end of the other, but that was the beauty and tragedy of the rider-dragon connection.

After hours of sitting quietly next to Evan's bed, Ainsley stood suddenly.

"He will be okay," she said, her brow sweating.

Sophia stepped forward. "He will? Are you certain?"

"Yes," the housekeeper said, serious for the first time ever. "He just needs to rest. It was a close call, but I believe he will be fine. Another minute of electrocution and he would have been irrecoverable."

Sophia sucked in a breath as she turned toward the door.

"Where do you think you're going?" Hiker asked.

"To give the information to Coral," she explained.

"She will already know," he stated. "She probably knew before we did."

Sophia nodded, exhaustion making her head heavy. "Okay, well, I'll just—"

"Go straight to my office," Hiker interrupted. "I'll be there in one moment. Head there now."

Sophia swallowed, wishing she could rest before having to face Hiker's wrath. But she had known this was coming and she'd face it, even if it meant the end of her life as a dragonrider. "Yes, sir," she said, hurrying out the door and to his office.

She sighed when she entered the space, finding that the windows were still absent.

"Oh, Castle," she groaned. "Hiker is really angry at me. You think you can give him a window, so he's not so pissed?"

In reply, the Castle made a tiny window in the center of the far wall, one that wasn't even large enough to stick one's head through.

Sophia sighed. "Thanks, but that might just make him madder."

She was about to negotiate with the Castle some more, hoping to get the books back as well as the windows, but Hiker thundered into his office. Sophia moved to the corner.

He threw his traveling cloak on the chair behind his desk and shook his head, his hair flying back and forth. His heated gaze swiveled until it found Sophia, feigning her best casual smile.

"So, good news about Ev—"

"Tell me exactly what happened!" Hiker exclaimed, his face blossoming to a bright shade of red.

"Oh," she replied, hiccupping on the word. "Well, I was minding my own business when I noticed that your Elite globe was beeping loudly."

"Minding your own business in my office?" he said, nodding along, irritation heavy on his face. "That seems about right."

"Okay, well, I couldn't sleep, so I was walking around the Castle," she stated. "I was not on a scavenger hunt. Promise."

"And you heard the globe alerting about a fallen rider?" Hiker asked.

She nodded. "And you weren't here, nor was anyone else who could help, so I went after Evan. I know you're going to fire me for going off to that mountain after you told me not to leave the Gullington, and I'll take your wrath. But in my defense—"

"You rode Lunis," he interrupted.

She paused. "Well, yeah. I mean, I demanded that he let me ride him, and I guess that was what he was waiting for."

Hiker regarded the paperwork on his desk like it had insulted him, shaking his head. He let out a loud growl. Turning to face Sophia, his eyes were full of hostility. "I've never been so livid at one of my own in all my life."

Sophia knew that was bad. Really bad. But also, quite the achievement. Hiker had been around for a long time and had overseen many riders, and she had made him madder than all the rest. That should deserve a bit of respect in a weird and morbid way.

"Sir, I know. I'm sorry. It's just—"

"And conversely," he interrupted, "I've never been more impressed by one of my own. I don't know how you do it."

Her mouth slammed shut. She stood rigid, watching as the large man stalked back and forth in front of her, stroking his beard. "You do what you want regardless of what I tell you." He threw up his hands. "Yet, in this instance, if you hadn't, Evan would surely be dead right now."

"Ummm..." Sophia tried to cut in, but one punishing glare from Hiker made her quiet.

"And you went to the Nocturne entrance of Mother Nature's temple on your first ride," he went on.

"What?" Sophia asked, confused.

"The mountain peak where you found Evan," Hiker explained, still fuming. "It's one of the entrances to Mother Nature's temple. I told him about it before he left, sensing he didn't know where to look."

"Right," Sophia said. "I'm sorry. I shouldn't—"

"On your first ride!" Hiker yelled, looking around like something had angered him all over again and he was looking for the cause.

"I'm sorry, sir—"

"You made that jump and survived," he said, looking at her in disbelief.

She halted, standing unmoving. "Huh?" Sophia finally asked.

"The jump to the entrance to the mountain," he explained. "I've met riders who can't make that after decades of riding, and you did it on your first try."

He clenched his fist and shook his head.

"Again, I'm sorry…" Sophia didn't know what she was apologizing for anymore.

"That's just the thing," Hiker said, calming slightly. "If it wasn't for your quick thinking, Evan would be dead. You rode Lunis for the first time and rescued Evan, and I can only imagine the obstacles you faced. Well…"

Sophia didn't know what to say, so she decided to not say anything.

"Tell me about what electrocuted Evan," Hiker finally ordered.

She cleared her throat. "It was magical tech, sir, and—"

"It was what?" he asked.

"Magical tech," she repeated. "Technology that's fueled by magic."

"I know what magical tech is!" he roared. "I might be behind the times, but I'm aware of these things."

"Sorry. Of course," Sophia said, looking down at the floor.

"What was it doing in the entrance to the temple?" Hiker asked, seeming to talk to himself.

"I'm not sure, sir," Sophia answered. "But it was advanced. It appears that someone didn't want anyone finding Mother Nature. That's my best guess, anyway. It felt like a booby trap because I don't think Mother Nature would put something like that out as an obstacle."

He nodded, his eyes off in thought. "Yes, you're right. She doesn't use technology, as you would guess. And I'm certain that Mother Nature is the only one who knows why or who is behind this magical tech. The House of Fourteen seems to have been right to have us track her down, but someone is thwarting our efforts."

"Oh, well, maybe one of the other men will have a better time getting past the obstacles," Sophia stated. "Especially now that they know to be on guard."

"Other men?" Hiker asked, giving her a confused expression.

"Yes, like Wilder, or Mahkah," Sophia stated. "Whoever you send after Mother Nature next."

He waved her off. "I'm not sending one of them. They have diplomatic roles, and that's important if we're ever going to make progress with the mortal world, which isn't looking good."

"I'm sorry," Sophia said, thoroughly tired of apologizing.

"Well, your stunt with the land dispute didn't help matters much," he seethed.

"Again, I'm sorry."

"Oh, no," Hiker stated. "It did exactly what you wanted, and now they want us to intervene in every little squabble."

"Isn't that a good thing?" Sophia asked.

"No," he refuted at once. "We are the Dragon Elite. We adjudicate global matters, not tiny land disputes in the middle of nowhere."

Sophia scratched her head. "Okay, so we're being acknowledged but not on the level you want. Is that right?"

He sighed. "We used to run this planet. Our orders were law. And now they want us overseeing trivial matters? I want to be recognized as the world's adjudicators, but the higher powers still insist they have politicians and governments to do that." He shook his head. "It's just not the same world I left, and I don't know what to do about it."

Sophia pressed her lips together, willing herself to stay quiet. If she had dared to speak, she would have said that proving their worth in small matters would graduate them to larger ones, and they'd be world leaders once more. But she sensed that Hiker wouldn't welcome such input right then…or maybe ever.

"Now, since you can ride Lunis, I'm sending you to Tanzania," Hiker stated.

"Oh, to do research on riders?" Sophia asked.

He shook his head. "Usually, I would send a new rider there for such things, but you need to find a different entrance to Mother Nature's temple since that one has apparently been laid with traps."

"Really?" Sophia asked, surprised. "You want me to research that for you?"

He tilted his head to the side like he wasn't hearing her correctly. "No, I want you to research it for you."

"Why would I research Mother Nature's temple entrances for me?" she asked, feeling exceptionally slow, maybe due to the exhaustion.

"Because when you find them, you're going to go and find her," he answered.

Sophia's mouth popped open, cueing him to shake his head.

"I know, but don't get excited," he said, backing up. "Evan is out of commission for a while. The others have jobs. And well, that landing on Lunis? It was just about the best first landing I've ever seen a rider perform on their dragon."

"The landing?" Sophia asked, astonished. "It was just about the best?"

He shook his head. "No, that's not right."

She nodded, thinking she had gotten ahead of herself. Sophia worked to corral her excitement, putting it back in the confines of her heart.

"It was without a doubt *the* best first landing," he stated. "That was your first landing on Lunis, correct?"

Deciding to finally enjoy a success, Sophia smiled broadly. "Yes, sir, it was. But I'm sure it was only because of the emotions and urgency."

"Yes, we wouldn't want to give you credit for being an exceptionally good rider from the beginning," he said, hiding a tiny smile.

"So, I get to go to Tanzania and then track down Mother Nature?" Sophia asked, trying to keep her excitement at bay.

He let out a long sigh. "I don't see why not. You are entirely a pain in my ass, disobeying me at every turn and arguing with me about things no one has ever dared to. Well, except for Adam. And yet, you, Sophia Beaufont, are…well, you're deserving of a mission, I guess. Even if you *are* young, inexperienced, and—"

"Completely a pain in the ass," she said, interrupting him this time.

He nodded. "But first, you have to make it to Tanzania, and finding information about Mother Nature won't be easy. So don't get your hopes up just yet that you'll be going on the mission to find her."

Sophia backed toward the door, deciding it was best to take her leave before he found another reason to tear into her. "I understand, sir. And thank you. I won't let you down."

"Failure, I've come to expect in my lifetime. It's what you'll do that I'm *not* expecting that worries me," he said, turning and regarding the tiny window on his wall and grunting slightly at the sight.

CHAPTER EIGHTY-ONE

It wasn't that Sophia thought Hiker believed she'd fail to find entrances to Mother Nature's temple. He obviously had his doubts, but she had more and knew she needed to leverage every single one of her advantages to be successful. And since her last conversation with Liv, her sister had been blowing up her phone, obviously wanting an update on the "adventure" she had gone on.

As soon as she had rested, Sophia called Liv from her four-poster bed. She didn't even care that her sister would see her on Facetime with her hair matted to her head and large bags under her eyes. Liv had seen her at her worst, and that was one of the best parts of sisters—they loved you no matter what you looked like or what you'd been through.

"There you are," Liv said, answering the phone right away. She conversely looked very put together, her long blonde hair draped over her shoulder and warmth in her Beaufont blue eyes. Sophia missed her intensely.

"Yeah, sorry, I had to go rescue a dragonrider from electrocution," Sophia said, smiling.

Liv sighed. "If I had a quarter for every time I heard that."

"You'd have a quarter?" Sophia asked.

"Exactly," she answered.

"How is the demon you had in a headlock?"

"Dead," Liv stated. "I made it as painless as I could."

"After you tortured him for information," Sophia added.

"Well, yeah," Liv said. "It took me twenty whole minutes to get the location for the Fountain of Youth out of him. I think I'm losing my touch."

Sophia stretched out of bed. "Have you destroyed the fountain, then?"

"I was just about to. Want to watch?" Liv turned the phone around to reveal a large, mesmerizing golden fountain surrounded by statues of men, women, and animals. It reminded Sophia of the Trevi fountain in Rome, although there was something more magical about this one.

"You're going to destroy it now?" Sophia asked, having mixed reactions about getting rid of something with such a reputation.

"Well, now is better than later since I have a date with a hot demon hunter," Liv said, turning the phone back around to show her face. "And you know that Father Time isn't a patient man. He always wants stuff done an hour before he orders me to do it. Completely unrealistic expectations, but what can I do? He's sort of in charge since he's one of the most powerful entities in the world."

"How are you going to destroy the fountain?" Sophia asked.

A glint of mischief sparked in Liv's eyes. "Magical tech, of course."

"Speaking of which," Sophia began, "did you ever figure out anything about those pictures I sent you of the aircraft that killed a dragon and rider?"

"Yeah," Liv stated. "They are fueled with magical tech."

Sophia sighed. "Right. I sort of found that out afterward when one chased me. I was hoping for a source on their maker."

"I know," Liv said, her tone filled with disappointment. "Whoever is behind that is brilliant at covering their tracks. I haven't been able to determine anything that leads me to a magician or organization."

By snapping her fingers, Sophia started the fire in her hearth and lit the candles around the space, cutting through the chill in the room. "Yeah, I have a feeling that whoever is behind this isn't an amateur. Either it's a coincidence or not one at all, but we've found some more pretty advanced tech in one of the entrances to Mother Nature's temple."

Liv narrowed her eyes in speculation. "That doesn't sound like a coincidence."

"Remember that the House of Fourteen asked the Dragon Elite to track down Mother Nature?" Sophia asked.

"Yes," Liv answered.

"Well, do you know why?" Sophia questioned. "Besides that the seers think we will need her help with something in the future?"

"I think it has something to do with Earth," Liv replied.

Lowering her chin, Sophia gave her sister an annoyed expression. "Thanks."

Liv laughed. "I get that's obvious at this point, but I've heard rumors about some toxic things going on around the planet that will no doubt lead to pollution. We've looked into it, without any success. Whoever is behind this is a bazillion steps ahead of us, and also, it's a bit outside the House of Fourteen's domain."

"I thought you cleaned up all things magical?" Sophia questioned.

"Yes," Liv retorted. "But these matters are on a more global scale and involve mortals heavily."

Sophia chewed her lip. "Which falls under the Dragon Elite's domain."

"Of course," Liv began, "I'm always happy to lend help. Wouldn't it be cool if we could go on a mission together at some point? You, me, and No-Rides McGooFace."

Sophia giggled. "Actually, I rode Lunis yesterday for the first time."

"How did it go?" Liv asked.

"I fell off and died," she joked.

Liv blinked at her. "Not funny."

"Okay, sorry. Poor joke. It was incredible." Everything had been happening so fast when Sophia rode Lunis that she hadn't had time to enjoy it or even reflect on it. Suddenly she just wanted to bound out of the Castle and take another ride. "Apparently, Hiker was surprised too. He's assigned me to go to this place for riders in Tanzania to find alternative entrances to Mother Nature's temple."

"Oh, the Great Library of Zanzibar," Liv said at once.

"Wait, you've heard of it?" Sophia questioned. "It's a resource for dragonriders."

Liv shook her head. "No, it's a resource for all magical creatures. It's the main library for all things magical."

"How come I've never heard of it?" Sophia asked.

"Well, if it makes you feel better, I only recently learned about it," Liv explained. "Its location was hidden from magicians, and many other magical creatures simply forgot about it during the period of time when mortals couldn't see magic."

"Because it holds information on the real history that was covered up?" Sophia asked.

"Bingo," Liv stated. "Apparently, only those on a quest for specific information can enter, with a few exceptions."

"So, it's not like a public library where anyone can go and browse," Sophia offered.

"Right again," Liv affirmed. "But it sounds like you have a mission."

"Yes, but I think all new dragonriders get to visit the Great Library of Zanzibar," Sophia said. "And the riders were the only ones not affected when memories were wiped to make everyone forget that mortals could see magic, so they've visited the library in the recent past, according to the men."

"Did Hiker tell you how to find it?" Liv questioned, a skeptical expression on her face.

"No, why?" Sophia asked.

She sighed. "That's what I figured. That tricky man might be testing you."

"Well, he did say that finding the entrances to Mother Nature's temple is difficult, which is why I was going to see if you could help."

"I'm sure finding those is nearly impossible, and that's after you find the library," Liv explained.

Sophia slumped with defeat. "I suddenly don't feel as charged about this whole thing anymore."

"Don't worry, Soph. I've got someone who can help you find the library. He's been there many times, and is one of those exceptions who can enter it without needing a reason."

Sophia brightened. "Really? That would be amazing. But then, once I'm in the library, I still have to find the entrances. Any help there?"

"I don't know much about the library," Liv explained. "I do know that there are certain areas reserved for dragonriders, though. And, of course, there are other areas reserved for other races like giants and gnomes. Maybe my friend can help with that too. I'll contact him and message you where to meet him."

"Okay, thanks." Sophia pushed her hair out of her face, feeling hopeful. "What's the friend's name?"

The phone shook, making Liv's face blur. "Oh, you're breaking up, Soph."

She leaned forward. "It looks like you just jiggled the phone. I was asking who this friend is you're sending to help me."

"Yeah, I can't understand you at all," Liv said, averting her eyes from the screen.

"That's weird because I can hear you just fine," Sophia said, narrowing her eyes at Liv. She could always tell when she was fibbing.

"Must be on my end," Liv said, smiling at her sister. "I'll message you later."

"The friend?" Sophia tried once more. "Who is it?"

"Gotta go. Love you, Soph. I'll message you with details," Liv said before shutting off the phone.

CHAPTER EIGHTY-TWO

Sophia had stopped by to check on Evan before breakfast, but he was still resting. She skipped the actual meal and headed out to the Expanse, excited to ride again.

The green of the hills was somehow brighter than the day before. The air smelled sweeter, as if it were laced with the scent of the flowers that bordered the Pond, and she could definitely see farther than she had yesterday, her vision even better than before.

"I hear you rode Lunis," Mahkah said from her side, although she hadn't heard him approach.

"You're back," she stated with excitement.

"Briefly," he answered, looking out at the Expanse, as she'd been doing moments prior. "Your senses…are they heightened?"

"Yes!" she exclaimed, grateful it wasn't just her imagination.

In true Mahkah fashion, his expression didn't give anything away. He simply nodded. "Yes, after you actually ride, your senses heighten again. They should be at full strength now."

Sophia cocked her head, hearing birds in the trees on the hills in the distance. She could easily distinguish that noise from the sound of the Pond gently lapping on the rocks behind the Castle.

That was separate from the sound of schoolchildren playing in the nearest town.

"This is incredible," Sophia said with a gasp.

"Well, please note that it can be quite overwhelming," Mahkah warned. "Meditation will help you to hone it even more, so that you use your senses for that which is most important for you. Otherwise, you will be distracted most of the time, inundated with things that shouldn't be taking up your focus. I can lead you in meditations if you'd like."

"I thought you were off on another mission soon?" Sophia said.

"I am," Mahkah stated. "But I'd like to work with you this morning on riding techniques as well as get you a saddle for the interim. When I return from the next tasks, I'll make you a custom one."

"Okay," Sophia said. "I'm actually off to Tanzania today. Do you have any advice for once I get there?"

Mahkah held up a finger. "Actually, that's what I'd like to work with you on this morning. You could fly there, but it would take a long time. I'd like to teach you and Lunis portal magic while flying."

"Absolutely," Sophia said, bounding toward the Expanse. "I'll call him now, and we'll get started."

"I'll just need to retrieve a saddle for you," Mahkah said, backing toward the Castle. "I have some options inside that will work for the time being."

"Thanks," Sophia said, nearly skipping in the direction of the Cave.

To her surprise, she could hear Lunis breathing in the Cave as she stood on the Expanse. She knew it was his breathing, although she could hear the other dragons in the Cave as well. There was something different about it, although she couldn't describe what.

She was about to call him down when she felt someone approaching. Turning, she noticed Wilder striding in her direction from the Castle.

Yes, meditation would be important for honing these senses, or she would be overwhelmed by all the information constantly vying for her attention.

"I heard you saved Evan's life," Wilder said, halting beside her. He looked to have just returned, still wearing his traveling cloak, his hair windswept like he'd just slid off his dragon.

"I just responded to the Elite globe's warning," she explained.

"How come adventures seem to find you?" he asked.

"They don't, actually," she argued.

"Oh, really?" He scrutinized her, his green eyes piercing in the morning light. "How about when you showed up here mysteriously on the steps of the Castle with your head busted open?"

"That was…"

"Yeah, you're still not talking about that incident, are you?" Wilder asked, a persuasive quality in his voice.

"There's nothing to talk about," she said, looking away. Sophia didn't like lying, especially to her friends. But she wanted Hiker's trust more than anyone else's, and she knew he had no idea what to do about that facility at this point.

"Right," he said, not sounding convinced. "I just find it interesting that some of us have been lounging around the Gullington for a while, then you show up, and now there are all these exciting missions."

"Super-interesting," she deadpanned. "Hey, you've been to the Great Library of Zanzibar, right?"

"That's pretty much all that I've been to during my time as a rider, up until this week." He flourished his arm and bowed slightly to her. "Thanks to Sophia, the bringer of adventures."

"Well, is it hard to find?" she asked, thinking maybe she didn't need this guide Liv was sending her. She wouldn't disclose his name, which made her super suspicious.

He pursed his lips. "Not really."

"Oh, good," she said, thinking she'd text Liv and cancel the help.

"It only took me six weeks to find it the first time," Wilder stated.

"What?" Sophia turned to face him, disbelief on her face.

"Well, it took Evan eight weeks," he said. "The second time was much easier. I think it was only two weeks then. They change the path to keep us on our toes, but it's worth it once you get into the library. Just you wait."

"Who is this 'they?'" she asked.

He shrugged. "I don't know."

"I can't waste six weeks trying to find this place," Sophia commented. "I need to learn the other entrances to Mother Nature's temple." She looked up suddenly. "Hey, do you happen to know where they are?"

He shook his head. "I was only aware of the Nocturne, but that sounds like a no-go now."

"Yeah, it's been compromised, apparently."

"Well," Wilder began, "six weeks is nothing to a rider. That's like a second in mortal years."

"I get it, but there's someone out there who is damaging the planet, and only Mother Nature can tell us more. I don't want to waste six weeks trying to find the library."

Wilder offered her a sympathetic look. "I'd go with you, but Hiker has me—"

"It's fine," she interrupted, waving him off. "My sister lined up a mysterious guide who can apparently get me there faster. I just don't like that it's a mystery and I'm not sure who I'm going to end up with."

"How bad can it be?" Wilder asked.

She gave him an impatient expression. "Given my sister's friends, bad."

He laughed. "Well, you're making some pretty awful friends too." He winked at her. "Just wait—one day, you can send me to your sister to help her with a mission, and I'll annoy the hell out of her. And then there's Evan. He's pretty much in your debt for like a few years or something."

"Is that all?" Sophia questioned.

"Well, we kind of get used to saving each other's butts after a while," he said. "It goes with the territory."

"I thought you hadn't been on missions until recently?" she questioned.

"Well, I did a lot of studying during my times in the Great Library," he answered. "Dragonriders save each other. If we didn't, well, we wouldn't last very long. We are fierce when teamed with our dragons, but the problems we are meant to face are bigger than a single rider and their dragon."

A chill ran down Sophia's arms, making her shiver. "That's sort of beautiful, actually."

Wilder smiled wide, a dimple she'd never noticed surfacing on one of his cheeks. "Yeah, I think so, too."

"So, once I'm actually in the Great Library," she began, "any ideas on where I should look first for the entrance locations to Mother Nature's temple?"

He laughed, but catching her scathing look, he quelled himself. "Sorry. It's just that not until you get there will you understand what a ridiculous question that is. Again, I apologize, but you're on your own. However, if anyone can make quick work of this, my guess is, it will be you."

"Thanks," Sophia said, hoping he was right. She had no idea what she was facing or how she'd get through it, but she knew success had to be imminent. There was no other option. She could thank her sister for that mentality.

"This should work," Mahkah said, appearing next to her holding a leather saddle. "It's not designed for Lunis or you, so it won't be perfect, but until I can make you something custom, it will get you by."

"Like to Tanzania and back?" Wilder asked, one eyebrow arched with skepticism.

Mahkah's eyes widened, and he cocked his head. "No, you'll need something much better for that."

"It will be fine," Sophia said, taking the saddle. "I'll make it work, and I'll have a guide in Tanzania."

"Oh," Mahkah said, relief on his face. "You might be okay, then."

"Thanks for this," Sophia said, examining the fine craftsmanship of the saddle.

"Yes, but first, I need to teach you portal magic and technique while riding," Mahkah stated. "And before that, you need to learn the spell for saddling your dragon."

Sophia smiled, thinking about how strange and wonderful her life was that this was part of her daily lessons.

CHAPTER EIGHTY-THREE

The hills of Scotland streaked by Lunis and Sophia as they soared, gaining speed and height.

The saddle definitely made riding much more comfortable, and having the reins was nice. Sophia realized after the first ride that she didn't much need them. Maybe she would in high-octane combat, but Lunis responded to her whims before they fully registered for her. He was essentially an extension of her.

She thought "turn," and he did just that. It was the same with all other directives, but the reins made it easier to hold on. That gave Sophia the freedom to look around and explore, something she didn't have a chance to do before.

When the pair soared into the clouds, Sophia prepared to portal. She'd practiced it all afternoon with Mahkah. It wasn't as easy as portaling on the ground. For one, they were moving fast, and if she created a portal like she normally did, they'd be well past it before it was ready. Therefore, she needed to project the portal forward by several hundred yards. Then the problem was other complications like birds, aircraft, or something else flying through the portal. The key was to project it forward and then shield it, which wasn't as easy as it had sounded to Sophia.

As she prepared to create a portal to Tanzania, she wasn't entirely confident she'd do it successfully. So far, she'd only practiced with going places within the Gullington. If her shield didn't work, they would pass right through the portal, wasting valuable energy. The distance a portal took the user burned tons of magical power, which was why Mahkah had her practice portaling inside the Gullington.

Here's the real test, she said to Lunis.

You can do it, he encouraged, flying with expert elegance.

Sophia lowered her chin to her chest and stared at a gray and white area of clouds, projecting out her portal. It showed up instantly, a gorgeous shimmering of blues and greens hanging in the open sky. As Lunis sped toward the portal, she shielded it, making it so only they could enter. That was something she'd never learned as a magician, but dragonriders were thought to be more advanced in these things—although a magician would never admit it.

As they approached the portal, Sophia held her breath, hoping she'd done everything right. Otherwise, Lunis would hit it like a bull hitting a brick wall, sending them both to the ground.

When they were feet from the portal, Sophia closed her eyes and clutched her dragon, holding him in tight to her—a silent apology in her heart if she had failed.

The cool air soaring across her cheeks suddenly turned warm, and the soothing darkness of the clouds was replaced by bright sunshine. Sophia knew she was no longer anywhere near the Gullington.

CHAPTER EIGHTY-FOUR

The sun in Tanzania was so bright, it burned Sophia's eyes when she opened them. It was the sun, but also the reflection off the Indian Ocean that seared her corneas, so accustomed to the gray skies of the Gullington.

The blues of the waters were unlike anything that she'd seen before. And Lunis, for all his collective memories and wisdom, was charged by the sight as well. Without warning, he folded his wings and spiraled toward the pristine waters. Sophia held onto the reins, but she felt no fear. Instead, a smile spread on her mouth as she enjoyed the salty air.

Even as they turned upside-down, she remained firmly connected to her dragon, riding him as though he were a wave below and she was a fish, at one with the water.

Twice more, Lunis streaked through the sky, joyriding over the beaches of Tanzania. It was beyond beautiful, reminding Sophia that a feast for the eyes nourished her heart as well.

Sophia pointed up the coast, more because she'd just recognized their destination than because Lunis needed direction. "There. That's where we are headed."

Stone Town, he answered, referring to the assortment of buildings crammed together on the coast. She narrowed her eyes, searching for the one Liv had said was where she'd meet her guide.

It took her only seconds to locate the Old Fort, the oldest building in Zanzibar. It was huge, taking up much of the real estate on the seafront. Sophia knew Lunis had spotted their destination as well, heading straight for the round part of the structure, where they were supposed to meet the guide.

With an expert grace, Lunis landed on a round stage in the middle of a stone amphitheater. The tourists in the area all turned, horrified looks on their faces. After a moment, they all turned back to what they were doing, seeming to forget about Sophia and Lunis. Apparently, that was part of the magic of Zanzibar. It was less to protect the many magical creatures who visited and more to keep the mortals from finding the Great Library. If they remembered the magical creatures or could see them for long, they might follow them, but due to the wards, they were ignored.

Sophia slid off Lunis, pulled off her gloves, and looked around the strange stone structure. "So this is Tanzania. I just wait for my guide."

"No need to wait any longer," a flamboyant voice Sophia recognized said.

She clenched her eyes shut, feeling the presence at her back.

Do you want me to kill him on the spot? Lunis asked in her mind.

No, she answered with reluctance. *He's dear to my sister, and will probably be of help to me.*

Suit yourself, Lunis said. *I'm going fishing.* The dragon took off with a gentle swoosh, disappearing before Sophia turned to face the person Liv had sent to help her.

When she opened her eyes, she wasn't surprised to find the king of the fae standing in front of her, his arms wide and a toothy grin on his face.

"Hello, Rudolf."

CHAPTER EIGHTY-FIVE

Thankfully, the tourists were spelled to not pay the magical creatures much notice. Otherwise, they most certainly would have noticed the majestic fae with his large wings and winning smile. There was no one more attractive than Rudolf Sweetwater, and probably only a few who could lose to him in a game of Go Fish.

"Sophia Maria Beaufont," Rudolf said in a fake Spanish accent. He grabbed her hand without permission and yanked it to his lips, where he kissed it gently. "It is a pleasure, as you say in your language, to make your acquaintance."

"Ummm…" Sophia said, pulling her hand back and wiping his saliva on her pants. "First off, Maria isn't my middle name. Secondly, my language is your language."

He laughed, good-naturedly. "So you say. So you say."

"Anyway, Liv sent you to help me." She put her hand on her forehead, realizing immediately why her sister hadn't been more forthcoming about who she was sending.

Rudolf was great if you needed someone to sing karaoke with or pretend to be your boyfriend at a ball where your ex was parading his trashy date. But otherwise, Rudolf was a mixed bag. He could be helpful, and had been, but it always came with certain complications, and Liv damn well knew it.

"I'm at your service, my lady," he said again in the horrible Spanish accent.

"What's with the accent?" Sophia asked.

He laughed. "Do you like it? I thought I'd try it out since we are in Madrid."

"Zanzibar," she corrected.

"Right." He nodded. "Which is off the coast of Spain."

"Tanzania, actually," she stated.

He shrugged. "Same thing."

"Are you sure you're going to be able to lead me to the Great Library?"

"Of course, my lady!" he exclaimed.

"This year?" she clarified.

"Oh, I didn't realize you were in a hurry," he said, pursing his lips. "I thought we could stop and get some tapas, maybe have a glass or two of sangria, and finish things off with a bull fight."

"Again, we're not in Spain," Sophia said, making a note of all the bad names she was going to call Liv later.

"Well, no, we're not." Rudolf leaned in closer. "But we could be," he whispered. "I have a very pregnant wife who hates me, a kingdom I've got no idea what do with, and you? Well, you've got that large reptile who wants to eat you. I say we take a holiday until everyone gets a better attitude."

"That's my dragon Lunis," Sophia corrected. "He loves me and would never… You know what?" She shook her head. "I'm not having this conversation. And if you've got a really pregnant wife, shouldn't you be with her? Isn't she having your triplets?"

"Yes, but she's kicked me out of the castle, which we also call the Cosmopolitan because that's actually what it is on the Las Vegas Strip," he explained, not abandoning the accent. "I'm bunking with Liv until Serena has the babies and allows me back in my kingdom."

"There are so many things to address in those statements," Sophia said, feeling her head cramp. "Of course, Liv sent you to help me. She wasn't trying to get rid of you at all."

"No," Rudolf said, shocked. "She loves having me there. I tell her how horrid her outfits are every single morning, and when she walks through the door at night, I ensure I'm plastered, so she has someone to laugh at. It has really been a thrill. We have this cute game where she strides past me, pretending I don't exist, then slams her bedroom door in my face when I tell her that she's looking a little chunky. Isn't that cute?"

"Oh, for the love of the angels," Sophia said, thinking that maybe taking six weeks to find the Great Library wasn't so bad. Eight weeks was still probably okay. She could work with that.

"Now, since you don't want to have any fun, very much like your sister," Rudolf began, "how about we go and find the Great Library?"

"Can you actually do that?" Sophia asked, overflowing with skepticism.

"Of course, I can," Rudolf said, clapping a hand proudly to his chest.

"Today?" she clarified.

"Well, since you're being so pushy, I guess so," Rudolf said, narrowing his eyes at her. "What's the rush? Do you have an emergency?"

"Yes," she answered briefly.

"Oh." His eyes widened. "You lost your magic sparkles too?"

"What?" she asked.

"Well, the last time I was here, I had to visit the Great Library to find out how to get my magical sparkles back." He turned and flapped his wings, making the sparkles on them glitter in the sunlight.

"Wow, so you have been here before and know what you're doing," Sophia said in relief.

"Of course, I do," Rudolf said. "I've been to the Great Library so many times I can get there in my sleep. It will take me a few minutes longer, though."

"What do the sparkles do?" she asked.

He shrugged. "Nothing, but I look awful without them."

She sighed. "Right."

"Anyway, do not fear, my lady," Rudolf stated. "I can get you there, and since I'm the king of the fae, I'm allowed into the library no matter what."

She scratched her head. "Is it ironic that you who are never quiet can get into the most prestigious library on Earth?"

"I didn't understand most of those words you said," he remarked, batting his eyelashes at her.

She drew in a long, calming breath. "No worries." Sophia held out her hand. "Please lead the way."

Rudolf started forward before stopping abruptly, making Sophia run into his shoulder. "I was going to say, 'Be sure to keep up,' but I guess that shan't be a problem for you."

"Continue on," she urged, trying to keep her anger at bay.

CHAPTER EIGHTY-SIX

The narrow alleys were full of exotic smells and strange noises. It was overwhelming for Sophia with her heightened senses, but she forced herself to stay focused, speeding after the fae, who moved surprisingly fast.

They had taken several turns, and Sophia was already lost in the convoluted alleys that all looked the same. She didn't want to admit it, but without Rudolf, she would no doubt have difficulty finding anything in this strange place.

"I agree," he called over his shoulder to her.

"You agree with what?" she asked, thinking she hadn't heard him say anything before that.

"I can read thoughts," he explained. "I heard what you just thought, and I absolutely agree."

"You can?" she asked, wondering if he'd heard her think she'd be lost without him. If so, she'd need to monitor her thoughts more closely. It wasn't that Rudolf couldn't be trusted. He was one of Liv's friends for a reason. But Sophia knew a lot about the Dragon Elite that couldn't be shared with others.

"Yes, of course," he admitted. "And I agree. I could go for a churro, too."

She relaxed, realizing he couldn't read her thoughts. "Once again, we're not in Spain."

He halted suddenly, sighing as he looked back and forth at a busy intersection. "I know that, my lady. We are currently lost. I'll go to Spain after I drop you off at daycare."

She narrowed her eyes. "First, off, stop calling me your lady unless you want me to rearrange your face."

He shook his head. "You make threats just like your sister. And if you don't want to be called 'my lady,' what would you prefer? Ms. Sophia? Lady Sophia? Señorita?"

With a heavy sigh, Sophia said, "Don't call me any of those. I don't need to be reminded that I'm a woman in a male dragonriders' world."

Rudolf shot her a confused expression. "You don't like being the only female in a male-dominated group?"

"It's not that. It's just that the guys all tease me for being younger, and I know they think I'm odd because I dress differently and do things differently. And yes, if I'm honest, I think they probably expect me not to be as successful as them because I'm a female."

Putting his hands on her shoulders, Rudolf looked straight at her, not caring that pedestrians had to swerve around them in the tight corridor. "You *are* different. You *should* dress differently. If I had those hips and that rac—"

"Don't finish that sentence," she interrupted.

Rudolf nodded. "That's probably a good idea. Anyway, my point is that you can either be a dragonrider who downplays her femininity, or you can be known as the best dragonrider, who is incidentally a female. If I were you, I'd be plastering my feminism all over my identity, broadcasting it proudly. I'd be Lady Rudolf, wearing skirts and talking about girl stuff while cleaning the blood off my sword's blade from the enemies I had slain."

Sophia thought about what he was saying. Lunis had said something similar. She'd listened but had to admit she'd regressed by wearing clothes that were more like the guys', mostly grays and browns.

Also, she'd been considering cutting her long blonde hair, and on several occasions, she'd caught herself before she started to talk about her fashion design interests or anything girly, really.

"Yeah, I guess you're right," Sophia said, her eyes distant in thought.

"And I bet you didn't like that little daycare quip," Rudolf continued, still holding her shoulders.

"I get teased for being young," she admitted. "I don't think they take me seriously because I'm young, inexperienced, and female."

"Good," he chirped.

"Look, *you* try assimilating into an ancient society of dragonriders who are stuck in their traditions and old ways of thinking."

"Girrrrl," he said, drawing out the word. "I get it. Who do you think pushed the world into the industrial revolution?"

"You?" she guessed.

He shook his head. "No, that's a serious question. I was wondering who pushed us into the industrial revolution. They'd be a good person to ask for advice about this."

Sophia tried to pull out of his grip, but he was adamant about her staying put. Rudolf lowered his chin and gave her a serious look.

"My point is, throw it in their faces," Rudolf lectured. "Remind them that you're a female and young and inexperienced, and do it while you're kicking ass. It sure is pretty amazing when a five-hundred-year-old dragonrider wins a battle, looking all courageous and rugged. But you know what?"

Sophia didn't answer.

"You know what gives me chills?" Rudolf pushed.

Again she didn't answer.

"A dragonrider who is just shy of two decades old standing victoriously on that battlefield, her blonde hair blowing in the wind and her beauty simply breathtaking while she wipes the grit of battle off her face." He looked at the sky as if picturing it. "She's got her sword in her hand and the blood of her enemies under her fingernails, and she's simply exceptional. She isn't successful despite being a woman and young. She's badass because of those things. This woman tackles problems with a fresh mind and a different perspective." He returned his gaze to Sophia, finally releasing her with a shrug. "I mean, whatever. If you want to keep those baggy clothes on and go by S. Beaufont. I'm cool with that. It's your call."

Sophia could hardly believe the inspiration Rudolf had filled her with. She found herself smiling broadly. "You know, Ru, that was exactly what I needed to hear. Thank you. And you're absolutely right."

"We should go for churros?" he asked, hope in his eyes.

She shook her head. "No, you should take me straight to the Great Library. I'm going to find it in record time and return, surprising them all."

"That's my girl!" he cheered.

"But first I'll change, so I show up with the news looking like myself." Sophia snapped her fingers, exchanging her baggy neutral clothes for sleek black pants that were braided on the side, showing a bit of skin. The snug pink and black armored top she wore was both practical and trendy.

Rudolf whistled. "That's what I'm talking about. If I get beheaded, I want you to do it, Lady Sophia."

"You're weird," she said, shaking her head. "Now, get me to the Great Library. I've got expectations to crush."

CHAPTER EIGHTY-SEVEN

"So, we're lost?" Sophia asked, continuing to follow Rudolf through the streets of Stone Town in Zanzibar, not having forgotten what he'd said about being turned around.

"Technically," he answered.

"Then the answer is yes," she stated dryly.

"No, I'm just trying to get my bearings." He stopped, sniffing the air. "What day is it?"

"Tuesday," she said.

Rudolf nodded. "And the time of day?"

Sophia used her magic to create a time orb. It floated in front of her face for a moment, showing the time. "Ten-thirty."

"In the morning?" he questioned.

She simply gave him a look that said, "What do you think, moron?"

"Here's the really hard question," he said, narrowing his eyes as he scanned the street.

Sophia braced herself, hoping she could answer the question.

"What year is it?" Rudolf asked.

"Are you serious?" she questioned.

He waved her off. "Yeah, I can't remember either. But I don't think it matters. My instincts tell me the Fierce is down this way."

"The Fierce?" Sophia hurried after him. "Who is that?"

"It's the guide who leads you to the Great Library," he explained. "You can only get there if he leads you to the place."

"So I have to find this guide? Why didn't someone just tell me that?" Sophia questioned.

"Well, most don't know his name, or that he's a guide," Rudolf replied. "They simply call it the light or the reflection. They spend eons looking for it because they don't know where it hides, depending on the day and time. But I know the Fierce better than anyone."

"Because?" she questioned, thinking the answer was important.

"I was him for a quarter of a century," he answered, embarrassment making his cheeks flush pink. "It wasn't one of my prouder moments. I lost a bet and had to pay a debt."

"So, you were the guide who led others to the Great Library? Why can't you take me there directly then?"

He shook his head, clicking his tongue. "That's not how it works. The path changes hourly, which is why those who seek the Great Library have to find the Fierce. He then directs the path, but finding him isn't the biggest issue. Still, that takes many at least a few weeks since they don't know what they are looking for and mistake him for reflections of light."

"What's the biggest issue?" she dared to ask.

"Oh, keeping up with the little bugger is tougher than cramming a whole donut into your mouth at once."

"You haven't really tried… Never mind." Sophia glanced around the street, noticing all the bright array of colors. "So, the Fierce is a light?"

"No, he appears to be one," Rudolf stated, pointing to crystals hanging in a shop window. "Notice the prism of colors they cast on the stone?"

Sophia smiled, enjoying at once the dance of lights that the crystals reflected. "Yes."

"The Fierce will look similar but different," Rudolf stated.

"How?" she questioned.

"It's hard to explain," he answered. "You sort of have to see it for yourself, which is why many follow the wrong twinkle of light until they've lost tons of time."

They turned a corner, and Sophia was overwhelmed with all the reflections on the pavement. She glanced up to find a garland of mirrored paper hanging overhead.

"Oh, is that to throw searchers off?" she asked.

Rudolf laughed. "It's to keep the birds away, but yes, it does the exact same thing."

He continued walking until they came to a square with beautifully mosaiced walls made from blue and green tiles as well as broken mirrors. The sunlight hitting the tiles created an array of lights around the area.

"Wow, I can see how this would be confusing," Sophia related.

"I bet you want that sangria now," he stated.

"No, but definitely later. How are we going to find the Fierce?"

Rudolf smiled victoriously. "I already have. Thanks to my years in his role, I know exactly where he hides at ten-thirty on Tuesdays."

"You do?" she wondered. "Where?"

He pointed up to a decapitated bell tower, the shingles crumbling on top and the building looking close to falling down. "On the roof of that building."

CHAPTER EIGHTY-EIGHT

"We don't have to go up there, do we?" Sophia said, staring up at the bell tower at the top of the building she feared might fall on her at any moment.

"Yep," Rudolf answered. "He won't move for at least an hour, and you said time was important."

"Is it safe to go up there?" she questioned.

"Absolutely not," he stated. "And as the kicker, when we get up there to where he is, that's when the race will start. Thankfully there are two of us to keep track of him, but the jerk will take off rapidly, flying through the air. We have to follow him if we want to be led to the Great Library."

"What if we lose him?" she asked, looking at all the sparkling lights she guessed could be confused with the Fierce.

"Then we start all over," he said. "It's part of the fun."

"Yeah, that sounds like a real riot," Sophia said, realizing why it had taken Wilder and Evan so long to find the Great Library.

Rudolf gestured to the narrow doorway that led to the stairs of the bell tower. "This is going to be a blast. I just hope not to chip another tooth this time."

Sophia grimaced with worry. "Me too. But since you're the expert, maybe you should go first."

He shook his head. "Oh, no. I insist that the lady goes first."

She sighed, taking off for the uneven stairs covered by a broken ceiling. "Thanks."

Sophia had never considered herself a claustrophobic person. However, inside the narrow stairwell that wound around and around, she felt short of breath.

"When we spot the Fierce," she said, trying not to open her mouth too much so as to not suck in ancient dust, "can I use a spell to trap it?"

"You can," Rudolf answered, hopping with both feet up the stairs behind her, unconcerned that the walls around them were cracked, the ceiling missing in places, and the stairs were slippery and uneven. "However, then he definitely won't lead us to the Great Library."

"Of course," Sophia remarked. "He wants us to chase him there."

"It is thrilling," Rudolf said, great fondness in his voice. "When I was the Fierce, I loved coming up with ways to outsmart my pursuers."

"Outsmart, you say?" Sophia said. "I'm sure that was painfully difficult."

"It was," Rudolf related. "I know you think of me as this genius king."

"It's like you really *can* read minds." Sophia had to duck to avoid hitting her head on a caved-in part of the ceiling.

"But I wasn't always the man you know now," Rudolf continued. "I used to be sort of dumb if you can believe it."

"It's hard to imagine, actually." The stairwell narrowed so severely that Sophia had to turn to the side to get through.

"Question," she began, holding her breath as she maneuvered.

"Twelve," Rudolf answered like he had already heard the question.

"Nope," she affirmed. "When we see the Fierce, we will have to race after him, but getting back through here fast will be difficult."

"Again, that's a part of the fun," Rudolf said. "And you can't use portal magic, or it starts the race over."

Relief filled Sophia's chest when she saw the sunlight spilling in from the top. They were nearly there, which meant the race was about to start.

CHAPTER EIGHTY-NINE

The sudden brightness made Sophia squint when she made it to the top of the bell tower. The stairwell emptied out onto a broad roof, and the bell tower stood on the far end facing the Indian Ocean, some twelve stories up.

Sophia narrowed her eyes at the bell, her enhanced vision catching sight of the Fierce immediately. He was sitting on the top of the bell, lounging as if he was enjoying a respite.

Sophia slapped Rudolf's arm when he came through the narrow doorway. "He's a fairy," she whispered, keeping her eyes on the tiny creature who was a man, just a really small one, covered in gold, with wings to match.

"Well, of course, he is," Rudolf said, rubbing his arm like she'd really hurt him. "How do you think I was the Fierce for all that time?"

"Why didn't you just say that he was a fairy?"

"Because he's the Fierce," he explained.

"But that makes it sound scary, and that guy doesn't appear menacing."

"First impressions can be deceiving."

"Fine," she said, keeping her eyes trained on the fairy, who she'd noticed had cracked an eyelid open. "How do we proceed? Do we sneak up on him? Speed over there? What do you suggest?"

"It won't really matter," Rudolf stated.

"What do you mean?" she asked.

"You can rush or sneak, but he's going to take off when you're five feet away regardless."

"How am I going to catch him, then?"

"You're not," he stated. "You're going to follow him. The Fierce can't be caught. Not really."

"All right." Sophia drew a breath, preparing herself for whatever came next.

Lunis? She reached out with her mind, hoping her dragon was close by.

Have you found the Great Library yet? he asked after less than a second.

Not even close, she answered. *Are you close by, though? I might need your help soon.*

How soon?

Within the next several seconds, possibly, she answered, taking careful steps toward the Fierce.

Thanks for the warning, he grumbled. *I just caught a fish the size of you, but I'll throw it back.*

I'll get you a different fish later.

You don't fish, he argued.

Just you wait, she said, carefully measuring the distance between her and the Fierce. The fairy's eyes were now wide, watching her with calculated interest. She smiled at the little guy, hoping that might earn his favor.

Just as Rudolf had said, when Sophia was five feet away, the fairy jumped to his feet and took off, his gold wings flapping as he sped through the air. He was a blur of golden light flying right toward them.

"Down!" Rudolf yelled, tackling Sophia from behind and pushing her to the surface of the roof.

She was so surprised that she didn't resist, allowing him to knock her down. Although she would have normally slugged him for such a thing, she wasn't given a chance. Rudolf sprang to his feet at once, turning and racing toward the edge of the rooftop.

"What did you do that for?" Sophia asked, sprinting after him while keeping her eyes on the Fierce.

"If he runs into you, it will result in a serious injury," Rudolf related as they ran.

"That little thing can hurt me?"

Rudolf gave her a sideways look. "He's called the Fierce. Remember that."

They both halted when they came to the edge of the roof. The Fierce sped across the alley, watching them from the opposite rooftop a few stories below with a challenging look in his eyes.

"Is he waiting for us?" Sophia asked.

"He's playing with us," Rudolf corrected.

The buildings were close together here, meaning that Sophia could probably jump it with her enhanced strength and speed.

"Are you sure?" Sophia questioned. "This is a different Fierce than you. He could operate differently. Maybe he's not tricky and simply wants us to follow him. He appears to be patiently waiting."

Rudolf pursed his lips, nodding. "Yeah, let's go with that. Why don't you pursue the little sucker and show me how he's just trying to be cooperative?"

"And what, you're just going to hang out here?"

He shrugged. "I'll keep an eye on him for you."

Sophia backed up. "Fine. Meanwhile, I'll follow the guide."

She burst into full speed at once, enjoying the power of the chi of the dragon. When she came to the edge of the building, Sophia leapt into the air, her arms and legs cycling as she passed over the narrow alley below her. With a soft thud, she landed in a crouched position on the rooftop only a few yards from the Fierce.

He hovered in the air in front of her, an unmistakably mischievous expression on his face. Then he flew straight at her again.

Sophia knew there was no time to swerve out of the way. She dropped to the rooftop as the fairy flew overhead. Rolling upright, she watched as the little jerk sped back across the alley, flying back up to the rooftop of the bell tower.

Rudolf ducked when the fairy flew in his direction. When he was safe once more, he straightened and looked down at her. "A trick. I told you."

Sophia grunted. The Fierce had put her at a disadvantage right off the bat, but unlike many, she wasn't out of options, even being on the shorter rooftop.

"And he's off," Rudolf exclaimed, running down the side of the roof, his maroon wings flapping. "You better follow if you want to get to the Great Library. I can't do it for you."

Sophia sprinted back the way she'd come. *Lunis, I need your help. I'm—*

I know where you are, he answered.

Okay, I'll meet you—

Just jump, Lunis replied as she neared the edge of the ten-story building.

Hesitation crowded her head, but she ignored it, launching herself off the side of the building with a blind faith she'd never known before. Under her were the crowded streets of Stone Town and the hard, unforgiving alley, which she was falling toward quickly.

Lunis wasn't anywhere around. Maybe he didn't know where she was, she worried, time slowing down as she plummeted to her death.

When she was about to close her eyes, Lunis smoothly glided under her, catching her with a soft thud.

Sophia was surprised to find herself securely in her saddle, her hands automatically finding the reins.

Lunis soared after the Fierce, easily catching up with Rudolf. "I told you I knew where you were. I will always be able to find you."

The fae turned to admire them as they passed. "Oh, look at you, catching a ride. However, the Fierce will find a way to get you off the dragon."

"Why?" Sophia growled, head down as she kept her eyes on the glowing dot up ahead.

"Because he's too much of an advantage," Rudolf said. "Remember that I was once a Fierce and think like him."

When he thinks, Lunis related.

He's right, though, Sophia said. *If we stay in the air, pursuing the Fierce on you will be easy.*

Which is why he's headed for the alleys, Lunis stated.

He was right, Sophia realized. The Fierce had dived and was headed for an alley that was easily half the width of Lunis.

I can make this, he encouraged as Sophia stiffened.

Are you sure?

She knew Lunis had been working on the condense spell, which allowed him to morph into a smaller size to fit through small spaces for brief periods of time while flying. However, she also knew he hadn't perfected it, which meant that serious injury could result if he didn't get it right.

However, the dragon didn't hesitate as he dove for the narrow alley, zooming after the Fierce. He dipped below the rooftops, zigzagging through various alleys.

Lunis copied the fairy's movements, turning to the side and gliding through the stone passages. Sophia thought it was an optical illusion until she realized Lunis had in fact shrunk under her, making him small enough to follow the Fierce.

Under him, something streaked. "Nice trick."

It was Rudolf, taking a position below and keeping pace.

"But do you think it will work on that?" Rudolf asked, pointing up ahead.

The little trickster had disappeared into the doorway of a shop at the end of the alley.

"No," Lunis growled. "This is where I'll have to leave you, Soph."

She petted him fondly. "Great job. You did it."

"Yes, but I can't maintain it for much longer," Lunis said.

Sophia knew she had to get off for several reasons. The Fierce was out of sight, and Lunis was growing back to his regular size.

"Go up," she ordered.

"But I need to get you down," he argued.

"Just do it!" she exclaimed. "I'll jump."

"But it's several stories down," he stated. "You won't make it."

"I'll make it," she said as his wings began to scrape the side of the buildings. It pained her as if they were her arms.

Sophia dove off her dragon, again free-falling through the air. However, she caught Rudolf's legs, holding on tight and making him straighten out vertically.

"What the he—"

They descended like Sophia was holding a parachute. "Just needed a lift. Thanks." She dropped to the ground when she was a safe distance away, sprinting straight into the shop with Rudolf on her heels.

CHAPTER NINETY

Sophia burst into the tiny shop, looking everywhere for the Fierce. Her eyes continued to swivel, her heart pounding faster with every second she didn't locate him.

She didn't want to have to start over. That would put her behind when she was hoping to get ahead.

Rudolf nearly knocked her over, halting behind her.

"Where is he?" Sophia muttered, mostly to herself.

"There," Rudolf said, pointing to a display case filled with hundreds of glittering, glass statues.

"Where?" she questioned, running her eyes over them but not finding one that stood out as the Fierce.

Rudolf held up his hands. "I'm not sure, and searching the figurines will take forever. However, I know one way to draw out the Fierce."

He held out his hand and summoned a baseball bat before briefly glancing at the shop owner, who was folding scarves in the back corner. "Sorry about this. I'll come back later and pay for everything."

The man shot them a worried expression.

"Rudolf, what are you going to do?" Sophia asked, her voice tense.

"Well, experience tells me that the Fierce might be tricky, but brute force will draw him out every time." Rudolf walked over to the shelves of glittering figurines.

"What are you do—"

Sophia's question was interrupted as Rudolf swung the bat through the first shelf of figurines, smashing them to bits and sending glass to the floor. Shards flew toward her, making Sophia shield her eyes.

The shopkeeper ran over, yelling.

Rudolf held up a hand, freezing the mortal in place. He shook his head. "I don't like having to do this, but I can't have this guy interrupting us now."

"You're destroying his shop," Sophia said, looking at all the debris on the floor.

"I'm going to replace it all and give him a very handsome reward for the inconvenience," Rudolf explained, looking at the other shelves. "So, you weren't there, Mr. Tricky-Ricky. Which means you could be *here*!" He swung the bat through the air as he spoke, demolishing another row of statues. They clanged to the floor, making a cacophony of music.

Rudolf shook his head. "That conniving joker is making this very costly for me."

"I thought you were rich," Sophia said.

"I am," Rudolf fussed. "But it's because I don't throw my money away by having to pay thousands of dollars in damages to a shop owner in Zanzibar. At least, I haven't in quite some time."

He sighed, drawing the bat back and aiming at the lowest shelf. Just before the bat connected with the first of the figurines, one of the statues lifted into the air and flew out the door.

"There he goes," Sophia cheered, racing after the Fierce.

CHAPTER NINETY-ONE

Sophia sped out of the shop full of busted figurines, nearly knocking into a cart of spices as she chased the Fierce. The streets were more crowded than before, hampering her progress as she tried to keep up with the speeding fairy.

"The king of the fae coming through!" Rudolf yelled from behind her, miraculously making the crowd part and giving Sophia a straight shot.

She picked up speed, closing the gap so that she was only a few feet from the Fierce, who was booking it through the narrow alleys.

For a second, she had the urge to reach out and grab the fairy but remembered what Rudolf had said about trapping the Fierce.

Her speed made it so that she nearly passed the flying fairy, who was also having to dart around figures. They ran through another square full of people and Sophia came to a halt, seeing her sister kneeling, cradling her stomach as if in pain.

Rudolf grabbed her by the shoulders and pushed her forward. "Don't stop! Continue on, no matter what."

Sophia pointed over her shoulder. "But that was Liv! Didn't you see that she's hurt?"

"Yes," he said, tugging on her hand and pulling her forward, making up the distance she had lost by stopping. "But what would Liv be doing here?"

"I don't know," Sophia reasoned. "But…"

That was when the truth dawned on her. "The Fierce. He creates illusions, doesn't he?"

"Yes, anything he can do to slow you down," Rudolf agreed. "Just keep your eye on the prize and your feet moving forward. We aren't far now."

"How do you know?" Sophia asked, continuing to run.

"Because I was once the—"

"The Fierce," she stated, finishing his sentence.

"Yeah," he agreed. "You have a horrible memory."

Sophia turned a corner, following the speeding fairy, smelling the ocean air once more. They passed another open area that was filled with exotic and yummy smells. She wouldn't have even noticed the cart of freshly baked pastries, but Rudolf slowed, saying, "Hello, Momma. Let's have a date."

It was Sophia's turn to retreat and grab his hand. "Stay focused. The Fierce is trying to distract you."

He allowed himself to be pulled forward until they ran out to the shore, where the white sands met the turquoise waters of the Indian ocean. The Fierce continued over the water toward the horizon.

"What are we supposed to do now?" Sophia asked.

"Get a boat," Rudolf remarked, running down to a dock and jumping into the nearest sailboat. "I'm commandeering this vessel!"

"But that's not ours," Sophia complained from the dock.

"I'll go into debt to replace this one after I crash it," he assured her.

"Wait, you're going to crash it?" she asked.

He shrugged, having magically readied the boat to sail. "Probably. Let's be realistic. But it will get us there."

Sophia threw caution to the wind and jumped into the boat. Even though she knew Lunis was an option, she decided to stay with Rudolf. As "special" as he was, he knew what he was doing in this regard, and she wanted him with her.

The boat took off, gliding over the waves and gaining on the Fierce, who was easy to lose in the sunlight. Sophia kept her eyes trained on the tiny fairy.

The raging waters of the ocean rocked the boat, nearly sending Sophia off her feet several times, but she quickly found her sea legs. She was going to help with the boat but was surprised to find that Rudolf had things covered. He appeared to be an expert sailor, and they were closing in on the Fierce.

"I think we're going to catch up with him," Sophia said.

He threw his hands up and sighed loudly. "Well, we were, but then you said *that*."

She scowled at him. "What's that mean?"

"We were going to sail up to the Great Library, but then you challenged the Fierce, and now—"

A giant creature covered in seaweed sprang out of the water, its mouth open wide as it hissed at them, displaying a large row of teeth and rocking the boat back.

"Oh, that…" Sophia said, thinking of a spell to defend against the creature.

Thankfully she didn't have to because from the clouds above, Lunis dove, spitting fire at the monster and making it sink back under the ocean. That allowed the boat to proceed once more over the choppy waters. The dragon continued to defend them from the sea monster, letting them follow the Fierce.

For what felt like hours, they followed the fairy. Sophia thought they might sail across the world, and worried about the sun and hunger overwhelming them. However, as she gazed at the horizon, she noticed a strange cloud on the water ahead.

Sophia blinked, thinking she was starting to see things. The cloud blew away, revealing a tiny island. Upon it was a rickety shack.

Rudolf put his hands on his hips as he slowed the sailboat, a proud smile on his face. "And here we are! We made it to the Great Library in record time."

"Yeah," Sophia said, giving the tiny, dilapidated structure a look of disbelief. "And...that's it?"

CHAPTER NINETY-TWO

"Isn't it incredible?" Rudolf asked, his chin high and pride in his eyes.

The Fierce was circling around the shack, which was built on rocks in the middle of the ocean. On the lowest rock was a rickety staircase that led up to the door, which looked ready to fall off and into the ocean with the rest of the building.

"It's something," Sophia offered.

"It looks better than the first time I saw it," Rudolf offered, steering the boat toward the stairs.

"Because it used to be a hut on a stone floating in the ocean?" Sophia asked.

He laughed. "No, it never changes. It's just so breathtaking."

"We're looking at the same thing, right?" Sophia asked as they steered up to the dock at the foot of the staircase, which looked close to falling into the ocean.

"I guess so," Rudolf said dreamily. "I see a tiny shack on a crumbling rock. What do you see?"

She shook her head at him. "A madman."

When Sophia disembarked from the sailboat, she found the Fierce casually sitting on the rail of the stairs that led to the Great Library. The fairy was staring at his nails as if they were of extreme interest to him.

"King Rudolf," the Fierce said, his voice surprisingly deep and loud. "I hope you won't be sharing my secrets with others. It would be a shame for the fae to lose their king to unfortunate circumstances."

Shaking his head at the fairy, Rudolf pushed the sailboat away, giving them no way off the tiny island when they were done. Sophia was hoping that meant they could portal out of there, but that seemed unlikely since secret magical places never allowed portal magic.

"Your threats won't work on me, Kyle," Rudolf said, turning around and looking at the Fierce directly. "Remember that I wrote the book about your job, and sharing secrets isn't forbidden."

The fairy crossed his arms over his chest. "My name is 'the Fierce!'"

"Yeah, whatever, Kyle," Rudolf said, grabbing Sophia's arm and hauling her up the dilapidated stairs to the shack at the top. "We have to go to the children's section first, Lady Sophia. There is a play area that makes Disney World look like a mortal theme park."

Sophia shot him a skeptical look. "That's exactly what Disney World is."

"I know," Rudolf said with a sigh, rolling his eyes. "It's a metaphor. That's how they work."

"Maybe you need to check out a book on metaphors," Sophia suggested.

He waved her off. "After I go for a swim with the sea monkeys in the Great Aquarium and hop into the world of Alice in Wonderland."

"I love that book," Sophia related, glad to finally find a common interest with the king of the fae. She hadn't known he could read until that point. But if he was reading *Alice in Wonderland*, he had excellent taste in books.

"Wait until you jump into the version they have here," Rudolf exclaimed.

She couldn't figure out why he kept using that verb for reading but decided it was just another Rudolf thing.

With an excited grin, he placed his hand on the door to the shack and faced her. "Are you ready to be amazed?"

"As ready as I'll ever be," Sophia stated.

Rudolf pushed open the door, welcoming her into the space.

Reluctantly, she stepped forward and nearly fainted. The Great Library wasn't at all what she expected.

It was a million times better.

CHAPTER NINETY-THREE

Like the ocean, the Great library went on for as far as Sophia's enhanced eyes could see. She stood at the front of a long aisle with an arched ceiling that was at least three stories tall.

The arches were mirrored by the rows of shelves that ran the length of the library. The place smelled of dust, wood, and knowledge. She'd never thought of the latter having a scent, but as Sophia drew a breath, she thought of history and science and other things she'd learned throughout her life.

Marble statues of various magical creatures stood at the front of each row. She brought her chin up, studying the two levels above her. The whole library felt open, although she sensed there were many nooks and crannies throughout.

"Pretty cool, huh?" Rudolf asked beside her.

Sophia choked on her response, momentarily speechless. "I've never seen anything like it. There have to be more books in here than in any other library in the world."

"Actually," someone said behind her, "almost all the books that have ever been written are in here."

She turned, surprised by the figure she found before her. It was a skeleton who seemed very much alive.

"H-h-hello," Sophia said, blinking at the creature. It was unusual when something took her by surprise since she'd grown up around the weirdest things on the planet.

"Trinity, how have you been, man?" Rudolf asked, offering the skeleton his outstretched hand.

Trinity took it, shaking the fae's hand. "Very well, my friend."

When Rudolf pulled his arm away, the skeleton's hand was still stuck to his, having popped off his arm.

Rudolf laughed. "Oh, I see you're still losing parts of yourself."

The skeleton laughed as he took his hand back. "Some things never change. Like, you, Rudolf, are still surrounded by pretty women."

Sophia blushed, deciding to curtsy rather than touching the skeleton's hand and risk taking it. "Hello. I'm Sophia Beaufont. A drag—"

"A rider for the Dragon Elite," Trinity interrupted.

"Yes, how did you know?" Sophia asked.

He snapped his bony fingers and a book appeared, one she recognized. "*The Incomplete History of Dragonriders* was recently updated." Trinity flipped through the pages. "Where is it again? Oh, yes, here it is." He read from the top of a page toward the back. "The newest addition to the Dragon Elite is Ms. Sophia Beaufont, the youngest rider ever, and also the first female."

He shut the book and smiled, although she wasn't sure how since he had no skin or lips.

"Who updated the book?" Sophia asked, leaning over to scan the text.

Trinity shrugged. "Beats me. Anyway, I'm Trinity Montgomery. It is nice to make your acquaintance. Congratulations on finding the place."

"Thank you," Sophia said, smiling. "Did you say that almost every book ever written is in this library?"

"Oh, yes," Trinity affirmed, holding his arms wide and proudly looking down the seemingly endless aisle. "The forgotten history of mortals is here."

"The *Forgotten Archives*?" Sophia asked, remembering that a lot of effort had gone into finding that book.

"Yes," Trinity stated. "It has been quite lonely here since mortals were prevented from seeing magic. The same villains who kept it hidden also kept the Great Library from being discovered, since the truth is held here. I believe you're my first visitors in quite some time. A dragonrider or two have visited, but that's about all."

"Oh," Sophia said. She wondered if that was why Trinity was a skeleton but decided not to ask about it.

"And besides the forgotten history, I have every book here that's ever been written, even if it was destroyed at some point," Trinity continued.

"Wow," Sophia said, looking around, marveling at the amazing place.

"Yes, I have every volume except for one," Trinity said, remorse marking his voice.

She looked at him suddenly. "Except for one? Which is it?"

The bones in his neck made a scraping sound when he tilted his head toward her. "Well, it's *The Complete History of Dragonriders*, obviously."

Rudolf scoffed, shaking his head at Sophia. "Obviously, Soph. Everyone knows that's the one book no one can find."

She scratched her head. "What? No one knows the complete history of the dragonriders?"

Sophia had guessed the title was simply to be accurate, but if there was a complete history somewhere, it made more sense.

Trinity nodded. "Yes, somewhere out there is *The Complete History of Dragonriders*, with information I can only dream of. Alas, I've been unable to acquire it."

"Do you mind me asking why that's the one book you don't have?" Sophia asked.

"Not at all," Trinity said, taking off down the long aisle, Rudolf and Sophia following. "There are powerful spells on that particular book that prevent it from being copied, which is how I gain my collection. As soon as something is written, it appears here. If it is updated, a new addition is added to the shelves. But *The Complete History of Dragonriders* was spelled before its completion to never be copied. As far as I know, there is only one in existence, and all my attempts to secure it have failed, for reasons I'm sure you'll understand."

"Why would I understand?" Sophia asked, striding beside the skeleton. She was trying to keep her eyes on him and not the incredible collection of books they were passing.

"Oh," he said with surprise, "because you know as well as anyone that outsiders aren't allowed in the Gullington."

"The Gullington!" Sophia clapped a hand to her mouth, realizing she'd just exclaimed in a library. "I'm sorry. I was just surprised," she said in a whisper.

Trinity waved her off. "There's no one here to disturb. It's just me."

She looked around, astonished that in this giant place full of millions of books, there was just this one skeleton.

"The Gullington, though?" she asked. "That's where *The Complete History of Dragonriders* is?"

He nodded. "Oh, yes." Trinity leaned in. "I don't suppose you could help me to locate it, could you?"

She pushed her lips to the side. "I don't think so. The Castle moved all the books to someplace we can't find and put them on a Kindle."

Trinity laughed. "That tricky Castle. Always up to no good. I suspect the book isn't on the Kindle."

"How has the digital age of books changed your job?" Rudolf asked, not sounding at all like himself.

"Well, indie authors have kept me quite busy." Trinity pointed.

"If you go sixteen blocks down, you'll find the beginning of their section."

"And the children's section?" Rudolf asked.

"It's just up ahead," Trinity answered. "I'll take you there."

"What about the other riders who have come here?" Sophia asked. "Did you ask them to help you find *The Complete History of Dragonriders*? The books only recently disappeared."

"Yes, I did," Trinity replied. "They weren't able to locate it, but I won't give up on adding it to the collection."

"Why do you think it's being hidden?" Sophia asked.

"That's exactly why I want to get my hands on it." Trinity held up his bony fingers, wiggling them. "The answer to that question no doubt lies on those pages."

"Yippee!" Rudolf exclaimed when they came to what had to be the children's section. He ran to the first aisle and pulled out a large book, opened it, and laid it on the floor. "I'll see you soon, Lady Sophia. For now, I'm going to go escape into a book."

She frowned, wondering why he'd put it on the floor and looked ready to jump. "Oooookay."

"Bye, Trinity," Rudolf said. "Come and get me if I'm not back in a week. I've got children on the way."

"You got it, my friend," the skeleton said.

Rudolf jumped into the air and landed on the book. He was sucked into the pages and disappeared as if he'd dived into a pool of water.

Sophia swung to face Trinity. "What happened? Where'd he go?"

Trinity chuckled. "He's in Wonderland. Specifically, he's in Alice's Wonderland."

"Like, for real?" she asked.

"For real," he replied. "That's a special volume which allows the reader to have an immersive experience. The last time, I had to go in and save King Rudolf from the Red Queen. Let's hope I don't have to do that again."

"Wow, this place is unreal," Sophia said, looking around, wanting a year or two to explore. She finally understood why it was so difficult to find.

"So, you're here to learn about the dragonriders," Trinity began. "As you already know, I can't offer *The Complete History*, but I can show you to a section which has quite a bit of information that will be of use to you."

"Actually," Sophia said, "I know that's why most new riders come here for, but Hiker wants me to look for something else."

"Oh?" Trinity appeared intrigued.

"Yes. I'm supposed to find the entrances to Mother Nature's temple. Can you help me with that?"

Trinity's mouth dropped open, allowing her to see his spine at the back. When he recovered, he said, "I hope you have a lot of time on your hands."

"Why is that?" she asked, stiffening.

"Because I can only point you to the books that mention Mother Nature," he explained. "That's how my cataloging system works. And here they are."

He waved his finger in the air, and all over the Great Library, thousands of books glowed brightly.

CHAPTER NINETY-FOUR

"All these books talk about Mother Nature?" Sophia asked, her brain cramping.

"Well, she is the most famous figure in all the...world," Trinity answered.

"Can't you narrow it down?" Sophia questioned. "Like, cross-reference with entrances to temples or something?"

"I'm afraid I can't," he stated reluctantly.

"Well, it sounds like you've read all the books. Do you know where to look, or maybe the answer?" she asked, hope laced into her tone.

"I'm afraid I don't remember," he said with disappointment. "It's been a long time since I've read much about Mother Nature. She was once a topic mentioned often, but in recent years, she's not as important."

"I thought you just said she's the most famous entity in history."

"Well, if we take all of history and combine the figures mentioned, then yes, she's at the top," he explained. "But in recent history, she doesn't get that many references."

Sophia slumped with defeat. "How am I going to read all these books to find what I need? I'm in a time crunch."

Trinity nodded. "They always are. I'm sorry I can't be of more help. Now, if you'll excuse me, it's time for my calisthenics. These calves aren't going to work themselves if you know what I mean."

It took great effort for Sophia to not glance at the skeleton's boney legs. "Thanks for your help."

"Holler if you need anything," Trinity said, striding down the long row toward the horizon of books.

Sophia took a seat on one of the benches, trying to not allow the overwhelming emotions in her chest to take over. *How am I going to find the right book,* she wondered.

Have you tried asking your dragon for help? Lunis said in her mind.

She jerked her head up. *Lunis! You're there. I need your help.*

I gathered as much, he replied dryly.

There are thousands, maybe hundreds of thousands of books that mention Mother Nature. I don't know how to find the one we need to locate the entrance to the temple.

Nor do I, he answered.

Sophia sighed. *Okay, well, that was less helpful than I would have thought.*

But, he said, making her pause, *I do know the premier source who wrote about Mother Nature.*

What? She stood and began pacing the rows. *Who was it?*

You know him as Papa Creola, but most know him as—

Father Time, Sophia said. *So I just have to find a book written by him, and I'll have the information?*

Ideally, Lunis answered.

"Trinity?" Sophia called.

A second later, the skeleton appeared, a headband around his skull. "Yes, Sophia Beaufont?"

"Can you narrow the selection of books mentioning Mother Nature down to one?"

He shook his head. "I'm sorry, but I can only search by one thing at a time. No cross-referencing. I'm not that fancy."

"Right," Sophia said. "Okay, well, forget searching by Mother Nature."

All the books that were glowing dimmed back to their normal appearance. "It has been forgotten," he stated.

"Will you please highlight all the books written by Papa Creola?" Sophia asked.

He nodded. "Yes, but there is only one."

Her eyes widened. "Really?"

In Trinity's hand, a large volume appeared. "Oh, yes. The Father of Time only provided us with one book, but it is quite a lovely read. Of course, he got rid of it when humans began using the information to break the laws of time, but I have it in my collection, regardless."

Sophia was anxious to get her hands on the book, nearly grabbing it from Trinity. She paused, her fingers inches from the volume. "I don't suppose I could check this out?"

Trinity pulled it back to his chest, thinking. "Usually, the answer would be no. However, what if we make a deal?"

A hesitant expression crossed her face. "What?"

"Well, you look for *The Complete History of Dragonriders,* and I'll allow you to borrow it," Trinity offered. "You don't even have to find it. I'll be happy if you simply search for it."

"That's all?" Sophia asked.

He held up a single finger. "But if you find it, I request you bring it to me straight away."

"After I read it, of course," Sophia added.

Trinity shook his head. "No. First bring it to me, then you can read it. That's the deal."

Sophia thought. The deal was actually pretty good for her. She got the book, and all she had to do was search for a tome she wanted anyway. She held out her hand. "You've got yourself a deal."

When the skeleton laid his cold, bony hand in hers, she grimaced but shook it regardless.

476

Lunis had taken Sophia back to Stone Town from the Great Library, where she was able to open a portal so they could return home. When Sophia got back to the Gullington, the guys were off on missions, as she expected. That *had* been how she'd gotten the Mother Nature case. She headed for Evan's room as she greeted Ainsley.

"I was thinking of cooking tonight, but since you're back," the housekeeper said with a coy expression on her face.

"I'll order UberEats, but you have to go and get it from the hilltop," Sophia said, sensing what she wanted. "I've got a lot of work to do tonight."

Ainsley shifted into the appearance of a small child with a freckled face. She clapped at once, looking delighted. "Thank you, S. Beaufont. You make a tired old elf's life so much easier."

Sophia laughed, pulling out her phone and handing it to Ainsley. "Order me something with lots of meat and cheese."

"From where?" Ainsley asked, scrolling through the options.

"You pick," Sophia suggested. "I'll be in Evan's room for a bit."

"Oh, because you fancy him?" Ainsley asked.

Sophia shot her a repulsed expression. "No, usually I want to murder him. But he did almost die, so I thought I'd check if he is still alive."

"He's alive and more unruly than ever after being confined," Ainsley said, striding down the hall with Sophia's phone.

She giggled as she turned in at Evan's door.

When she entered his room, he sat up, giving her a confused expression. "Oh, I thought you were Ainsley, coming to tell me I had to take that strange concoction again."

"Which one?" Sophia asked.

"I don't know," he said. He was looking more like himself, although his dreads had been shaved off and his hair was tight to his head. "It tastes like sewer and doesn't seem to have any effect."

Sophia shot him a cautious expression. "Are you sure it's medicine?"

He threw up his hands. "Of course, it's not. The weirdo is just taking advantage of my state. I should have known."

She couldn't help but laugh. "Speaking of which, how is your state? Are you feeling better?"

He ran his hands over his head. "I lost my hair, but I'm totally back to normal. Well, sort of. But I expect to be soon."

"That's good," she stated.

He coughed, shifting and looking suddenly nervous. "So…"

"So?"

His eyes slid to hers and then away. "I should say, 'Thank you for saving me.'"

"Well, don't do it if you feel obligated," she stated.

He sighed. "No, it's not that." Shame rose in his eyes, and Sophia understood immediately.

"You were saved by a girl," she guessed.

His nostrils flared when he breathed out. "Well, yeah. I was saved by an inexperienced one, too."

Sophia wanted to scream, but she remained calm. Rudolf's speech in Stone Town was actually helping. "Yeah, you were. But that doesn't reflect on you at all. I was here when everyone was gone. I saw the Elite globe and knew you were in trouble. But guess what?"

He cut his eyes at her, appearing annoyed by the leading question.

"If Wilder or Mahkah or even Hiker had gone after you, you'd be dead right now."

"Thanks, Soph," he chirped. "I feel so much better."

She laughed. "My point is, you might think it's offensive that you were saved by an inexperienced woman. However, I grew up around magical tech, which meant I was the right one of all of us to save you. I'm not as inexperienced as you might think, and my gender? Well, it shouldn't matter."

"It doesn't. It's just that I was raised to think that girls—"

"Weren't as good," she supplied. "But it looks like you've got as much education and retraining to do as Hiker. The world has changed. Women haven't, but now the world out there recognizes we're a force. You should acknowledge that. Or don't, and give me the advantage I need to body-slam you the next time we spar because you underestimate me."

He narrowed his eyes, but there was a smile brooding beneath the surface. "You know what? You're not so bad."

"I wish I could say the same about you," she said with a laugh, which he quickly joined in with.

He pointed to the book in her hands. "What do you have there?"

"A book," she answered.

Evan blinked at her dully. "Wow, thanks, Captain Obvious."

"Ms. Obvious," she corrected. "And somewhere in this volume is the location of at least one of the other entrances to Mother Nature's temple."

"Great," he said, rubbing his hands together, looking excited. "Hand it over, and I'll find it for you."

"Nope," she chirped. "Trinity entrusted it to me."

"He let you take a book from the Great Library?" Evan asked, sounding offended.

Sophia made for the door. "Yes. Also, Ainsley will be up soon with food from the modern world. I put in your order specially."

"Oh?" Evan looked suddenly excited. "What did you get me?"

"Haggis," she said, gliding out the door and toward her room.

CHAPTER NINETY-SIX

After hours of reading, Sophia's eyes were starting to blur. She feared she'd have to give up for the night, having been unable to find the location of the entrance to Mother Nature's temple.

She growled, looking up from Father Time's book.

The book was full of strange words and hard to follow. She hadn't learned anything about time travel or other ways to defy time. After the first hour of trying to decipher the complex text, she'd called her sister to see if she could get the information directly from Papa Creola.

Unfortunately, he was on his first vacation in a few centuries and wasn't to be disturbed for any reason.

Defeated, Sophia had returned to reading the book. However, she was considering taking a break again until the book made sense to her. The book was over a thousand pages, so she didn't think it would be easy to find even if she did understand the words.

Pushing up from her desk, she stretched. A thought suddenly occurred to her.

"Hey, Castle?" she said, looking at the walls. "Why are you hiding *The Complete History of Dragonriders?*"

Sophia didn't know what she expected, but the complete silence that followed wasn't it. She sighed. "Fine. It's just weird since you gave me the abridged version, but you're holding onto the original."

Again, there was no rebuttal from the Castle.

"If you ever want to share your secret with me… Well, don't, unless you want me to give it to Trinity," she stated. "I'm obligated to give the book to him first thing. But still, the whole thing is curious."

She laughed at her poor attempt at negotiation.

"Of course, if you want to help me with anything else, well, I'll accept it," she said out loud, realizing she must be crazy to talk to the Castle, just like Ainsley.

To her surprise, the pages of the book on her desk flipped rapidly, as if caught in a draft from an open window. Sophia waited until they stopped.

She then leaned forward and narrowed her eyes at the page. A gasp fell from her mouth at once. Looking up, she smiled at the walls. "I don't know how to thank you, but I guess I'll go do my job and hope that is gratitude enough for your help."

Sophia couldn't believe where one of the easiest to get to entrances to Mother Nature's temple was. It was incredibly ironic. Most wouldn't even know where this place was, but Sophia did. She was well acquainted with it, and Lunis even more so.

"What are you doing back here?" Hiker asked as Sophia sped down the grand staircase toward the entrance. He was just entering from the Expanse and had snow on his shoulders, although it wasn't snowing outside presently.

"I'm actually heading back out," she said, tying her traveling cloak around her shoulders.

"Still trying to find the Great Library?" he asked.

She shook her head. "No, I found it."

Hiker's eyes widened. "You what? Are you sure it was the real thing?"

"Well, it wasn't a Barnes and Noble that I mistook," she joked.

"A what?" he asked.

She shook her head. "Yes, I found the Great Library, and now I know where to go to search for the entrance to Mother Nature's temple."

"You *what?*" He looked at the grandfather clock in the entrance hall. "You haven't been gone a day yet."

"And you've already missed me, haven't you?"

Hiker grunted. "Are you sure you found the right—"

"Yes," she interrupted. "It was the Great Library, and I found the book that told me where to search for the temple. And now I'm off to do just that."

He held up his hand. "But you're not ready."

Sophia fisted her hands by her sides, trying to keep the insult in her mouth at bay. "But you said—"

"I know what I said," Hiker cut in. "If you're to actually go on this type of mission, which I think is out of your current expertise, you need to get clearance from Mahkah and Wilder."

Her eyes widened in frustration. "Thing is, they aren't here."

"The thing is," he countered, "they just returned. You can catch them before they refresh before leaving."

"If," she said, a great inflection on the word, "they clear me, will you let me go?"

He considered her for a moment. "Yes, of course. My word is good."

She was about to charge past him but stopped, noticing how weary he appeared. "How was your mission?"

He sighed. "It was more of the same; we're getting laughed at or dismissed. But I'm not giving up, as much as I want to. I guess I have you to thank for that."

"You're welcome," she said, reluctance in her voice.

He nodded. "And I'm looking into the facility north of here where you freed the slaves."

"Anything yet?" she asked.

He shook his head. "It's abandoned. Whatever was going on there, they've cleared out, probably due to your intervention. But after what you discovered at the Nocturne entrance, I think that something is going on right under our noses. Something that's close and also personal."

Sophia watched the Viking's eyes slide back and forth as he stared off in thought.

"We're going to figure it out, sir," she said in an encouraging voice.

He pressed his lips together. "I'm sure you're right. Mother Nature will be the supreme source to inform us, but you must find her first. If the men clear you, that is."

CHAPTER NINETY-SEVEN

Sophia found Wilder in the combat area on the Expanse, sharpening his sword.

"You're back?" he asked, looking up at her in surprise.

"Yes, and I found the Great Library, and yes, I'm sure it was the right place," she said, adding the last part as his brow scrunched with confusion.

He shook his head, continuing to sharpen his blade. "That has to be a record. What did it take you? A day?"

"A few hours," she corrected. "But who is counting?"

"I am," he said with a whistle. "That's a record."

"Well, I also found a location for Mother Nature's temple, but Hiker says you have to clear me before I can go."

He put his sword aside, a curious expression in his eyes. "You've found the entrance? After quickly finding the Great Library, which took me six weeks to locate?"

She sighed. "Look, I did something the Dragon Elite apparently never do."

"Tuck in our shirts?" he asked.

She laughed. "No."

"Chew with our mouths closed?"

Sophia shook her head. "Yeah, I'm totally sending you all to a finishing school."

"I don't know what that is, but I decline. What is it you did that shortened your search so dramatically?"

"I asked for help from someone who knows more and is a resource," she explained.

Wilder stroked his chin. "That *is* a unique strategy for a rider. We work alone. I mean, we riders help one another, but we don't ask for help from, say, the House of Fourteen or the giants or whoever else."

"Or from a fae," she added.

His eyes went wide. "You didn't?"

"I did," she admitted. "The king of the fae, actually."

"And he was able to help you locate the Fierce quickly?" Wilder asked.

"Yeah, because he apparently used to do that job. But that's my point. We as the Dragon Elite operate like we're an island. When everything was happening with the House of Fourteen and the war with those trying to control mortals, where were the Dragon Elite?"

He thought for a moment before shrugging. "'Not helping,' is the answer you're looking for, I think."

"And when you all were without missions because mortals couldn't see magic, why didn't you go to the House of Fourteen and explain the situation?" Sophia asked again.

"I guess because we are stubborn," he admitted.

"Right now, you're on this mission to try to get the world to see us as adjudicators, but I wonder if you're using resources, or just storming into government offices and demanding to be taken seriously?"

He combed his fingers through his chaotic hair, which immediately fell back in his face. "The answer is obviously the latter. Look, I'm simply following Hiker's leadership, and he's never trusted the other races. He says they don't understand us. That we're different."

She sighed. "We're all different. I'm different from you, and you're different from Evan, and he's different from the gnomes. And they are different from the giants. Which is exactly why we have to rely on each other or make our lives a lot more difficult."

"So you asked the king of the fae for help, and he got you to the Great Library in record time?" Wilder asked, trying to wrap his head around her situation.

"Well, he probably also slowed me down a bit with his antics, but yes, he helped me," Sophia admitted. "And the Castle helped me find the information in the book, and now, I'm ready to set off to find Mother Nature. All I need is for you to sign off that I'm combat-ready."

He crossed his arms over his chest, considering her. "Fine," he began, indicating his sword. "Get to my sword before me, and you can go."

"But it's closer to you," she argued, looking at the sword, which was some fifteen feet away, at his back. "All you have to do is reach out and get it."

"Which is why you'll have to rely on your—"

Sophia held out her hands. Wilder's sword was lying across her fingers; she'd summoned it directly to her.

"And while I was explaining, you used your advantage," he said with a smile, striding over and taking his sword back from her.

"Well, yes," she said with a shrug.

"Rely on your brains, and you won't need to worry about engaging in combat too much," he said, sheathing his sword. "You're not like any dragonrider I've ever met. We are taught to use brute strength. Most would have lunged forward and battled to the death to get to my weapon to win the challenge. None I've known or read about would have kept me talking while summoning it. Sneaky, but effective."

"So, did I fail because I didn't use combat?" she asked.

He shook his head. "No. If anything, you passed with bonus points. You didn't have to dirty your hands to win."

"So, I can go?" Sophia asked, afraid to get her hopes up.

"I give you my blessing, but remember something when you go wherever you go to find Mother Nature," Wilder said, his words cautious.

She waited for him to continue.

"We all lack advantages, based on our weaknesses," he stated. "You might outsmart us old riders because you rely on strategy over strength, but what if you don't have that? What if there is no strategic upper hand, and you have to win based on sheer strength, or something else completely? What will you do then, Sophia?"

She thought for a moment and then smiled. "I guess I'll call my dragon."

He shook his head. "Let's hope that's an option for you."

CHAPTER NINETY-EIGHT

Mahkah was sitting in the grass, his hands on his knees and eyes closed, when Sophia found him.

She didn't want to disturb him while he was meditating, but she needed his approval to leave. Uncertain of what to do, she stood awkwardly watching him.

"Would you like to join me?" he asked, eyes still closed.

Sophia swallowed. "Join you?"

"Yes," he answered. "Remember, I told you meditation was the best way to hone your senses, as well as many other things."

"Thank you," she replied. "I'd like to, but maybe another time. Right now, I need to set off on the mission to find Mother Nature, but I need you to sign off that I'm ready to go first."

Mahkah opened his eyes. "When I was younger, I kept thinking I didn't have enough time to meditate. I wanted to be out there doing things." He pointed to his head. "I didn't want to be in here when the world needed me."

She nodded. "Yeah, I can understand that."

"Ironically, when I started to meditate, I found that I had more time. The world's problems didn't go away when I meditated, but the way I viewed them did. The way I perceived them changed. The way I interacted with Tala changed. Everything I did to improve my skills outwardly paled in comparison to what I did internally. That was when things really changed for me."

"So, you think I should meditate?" Sophia said, frustration building in her.

"No," he answered. "I want you to do what you want. Being forced to meditate will do you no good."

"Well, it's just that I need to find Mother Nature and time is of the essence, and if I don't leave now, well, I'll lose my advantage. Hiker is impressed that I'm working so fast, and…"

"You want to get his approval," Mahkah stated.

"Actually, I kind of want to shove it to him, but yeah," she said with a laugh.

He smiled slightly. "Mediation is never about ego or what happens in the outside world. We meditate so we are at peace, and hopefully, when we open our eyes, we are more in control of the world around us."

She nodded rapidly. "Totally. I get that, and I really want to start when I get back. I was just hoping you could give me a task, and if I complete it, then I can leave."

"Absolutely," Mahkah stated calmly. He pointed to the Cave. "Tell me, what does Lunis see right now?"

Sophia looked at the Cave, where her dragon was lounging or doing whatever. She wasn't sure.

"And note that telepathically asking him isn't the way to pass this test," Mahkah cut in just as Sophia was about to reach out to her dragon.

She chewed her lip. "I haven't mastered scrying yet." Sophia was about to try to convince Mahkah that she'd work on that when she returned, but she read the look on his face and gave up.

"I'm guessing one of the most important skills Lunis and I can have in battle is scrying," she said, settling on the grass next to Mahkah.

"You and your dragon are supposed to be one," he stated. "For that to be true, you must bond."

Sophia nodded, knowing exactly what he meant. She closed her eyes, realizing that if they were going to be one, she had to see what he saw, and vice versa. She drew in a breath, forcing herself to meditate and bond with her dragon.

For what felt like hours, her mind wandered. She worried about the time she was wasting, sitting there meditating. The sounds around the Expanse were constant distractions. Just when she was about to give up, her mind blanked, and she thought of nothing. It was the most at peace she'd ever felt, and for the first time ever, she lost track of time and invited in the quiet.

The sun had set over the Expanse when Sophia saw her first vision of the Cave. It was as she had expected: dark, full of animal bones, and spacious enough for many dragons to lounge.

Her dragon raised his head, swiveling it until he was looking out the large opening of the Cave. Then, very clearly in her mind, Sophia saw herself sitting on the grass, her eyes closed, and a calm expression on her face. To her surprise, Mahkah wasn't beside her, although she hadn't heard him move away.

Her eyes popped open and she looked around, affirming that she was alone.

Good job, Lunis said in her mind.

She looked at the Cave. *Thank you,* she replied. *It seemed like an important thing to learn before we went to find Mother Nature.*

And also, Mahkah required it for you to leave, Lunis said.

Yeah, that too.

Sophia was surprised to find that her back wasn't stiff from the hours of sitting when she rose. She was also astonished to find that her stomach wasn't rumbling. Actually, she felt quite energized by the mediation session.

Before, she had felt the urge to bound off to the location of Mother Nature's temple. Now, however, she thought that resting for the night would be good. She didn't feel the fire burning within her. It was replaced by a calm knowingness that she was on the perfect path and would get there at the right time for her. It was so different than the rat race she felt like she'd been on recently.

Sophia smiled at the Cave, holding her hand to her mouth before angling it toward Lunis.

Tomorrow, he said, having read her thoughts.

Tomorrow, she agreed, turning toward the Castle. However, something occurred to her, and she turned back.

Liv told you before we left for the Gullington to do something every night. She said it was a Beaufont thing. Can you tell me what it is?

You don't know? he asked.

I don't, she stated.

Then I'll wait for you to figure it out, he stated.

It's something you do every night, even now? She asked.

Yes, and it is a part of your strength, Lunis answered. *Just as it was when you lived with your family.*

Sophia scratched her head, trying to figure out what it could be. *Maybe a spell?* she reasoned.

When Sophia entered the Castle, the men were all gathered around the table, most of them regarding their dinner with speculation.

"Why is it wrapped in paper?" Hiker asked, picking up the burger and eyeing it.

"It's fancy packaging," Ainsley explained.

He dropped the burger, shaking his head. "Will you just make us something to eat and stop ordering from Beyond Food?"

"It's Uber Eats," Ainsley corrected, glancing at Sophia. "I got you something too, S. Beaufont."

"That's okay," Sophia said. "Thank you, but I think I'm going to head up and get some rest. I'm not really hungry."

Her gaze connected with Mahkah, but she didn't feel like

singing her own praises and confessing she'd been successful. That was unusual, but there was such a sense of peace at her core that she didn't resist the feeling.

"Anyway, goodnight," she said, offering everyone a smile before heading up the stairs.

She was almost to the second landing when Mahkah called to her from below.

"I left you something in your room," he said.

"Oh?" Sophia asked, intrigued.

"Yes. I think it will make your mission tomorrow to find Mother Nature easier," he stated evenly.

"So you've approved me to go?" she asked, not feeling the giddy excitement she would have expected.

"Yes," he answered. "Best wishes."

"Thank you," she said, curious to find out what he'd left in her room.

Sophia reasoned that she was biased, but it was the most beautiful saddle she'd ever seen. She knew Mahkah had spent many hours working on the new saddle, and she had no doubt that it would fit Lunis perfectly and make their rides that much better.

She ran her hand over the fine craftmanship, suddenly disbelieving that she actually had a dragon who would wear this.

It was still awe-inspiring to Sophia that she was a rider for the Dragon Elite. Maybe one day, it would hit her and she'd really feel like she belonged here, instead of like an imposter. Maybe in a few hundred years, she thought as she curled up in her bed, ready to rest before the big adventure.

Sophia, Lunis said in her head, as he did every night.

Yes? she answered, a smile on her face and her eyes closed as the moon shone through her windows and across her bed.

With all my heart and all my soul, he began, as he always did.

I love you, they said in unison in each other's minds.

The dragonrider wondered why she hadn't figured it out before.

It was indeed the simplest things like love that brought the greatest strengths.

CHAPTER NINETY-NINE

Of all the places in the world that could house the entrance to the temple of Mother Nature, the one Sophia found in Papa Creola's book was ironic. It was the place Lunis had been born. It was in the backyard of the giant, Rory Laurens.

Lunis had been shielded when he and Sophia stepped through the portal and strode up to the giant's house on a quiet street in Los Angeles.

She hadn't called ahead, but she figured it would be okay to venture into the backyard. If it were anyone else, Sophia thought she might need to make special arrangements. But having friends, in this case and many others, proved helpful. The Dragon Elite just had to figure that out and stop making their jobs much harder.

"Are you going to fly into the backyard?" Sophia asked as they neared Rory's front door.

I'm already there, he responded. *Just waiting for you, slowpoke.*

Ha-ha, she said, leaning over to pet Rory's cat Junebug. He wasn't like Plato, but few were. Still, he had a fun personality, and he kept the rodents at bay.

Sophia rapped on Rory's door, deciding it would be best to ask permission. He might not know that his backyard had an entrance to Mother Nature's temple, and it would be nice to see the stoic giant.

The door swung open automatically, and she poked her head into the living room. "Hello?"

Rory was sitting on the couch, a laptop on his legs as he typed furiously. He looked up, his curly hair falling into this face. "Are you here to travel through the portal to Mother Nature's temple?" he asked.

She gaped at him. "How did you… Never mind. How are you, Rory?"

"I'm almost done," he said, nearly stabbing the laptop in his fervor. He then smiled triumphantly, a rare thing for the giant to do. "And there we have it!"

"You finished?" a blonde female giant called after poking her head out of the dining room.

"Yes," he affirmed. "I just finished my first novel."

"Great job!" Sophia said. She was quickly joined by Maddy, his girlfriend, who threw her arms around his shoulders and hugged him tightly.

"Great job, babe," Maddy said, pulling back and pecking him on the cheek.

He blushed. "It's nice to have it done, but we have more important matters." He pointed at Sophia, who felt like a child again, standing before the giants. "She needs to get into the portal."

"Oh," Maddy squealed with excitement. "We're going to open it tonight? I didn't think it would be so soon."

Sophia shot him a curious expression. "Firstly, you knew one of the entrances to Mother Nature's temple was in your backyard. Secondly, you knew I'd need access to it at some point?"

"Yes," he stated, walking toward the kitchen, where the backdoor was. "And I'm guessing Lunis is back here already."

"Yes, but I should warn you that—"

"Holy cow!" Rory said, opening the door and gaping at the large dragon in his pumpkin patch. He took up most of it.

"He's grown," Maddy exclaimed, clapping.

"Yes, I feed him his Wheaties," Sophia said.

Rory gave her a sideways look. "That was a Liv joke if I've ever heard one. Do you even know what Wheaties are?"

"I know," she said, although she didn't. "It's from an old commercial or something."

"And yes, Lunis has grown." Rory stepped off the porch and bowed his head to the dragon. "It is an honor to see you again in all your majestic glory."

"Said like a true writer," Lunis said to the giant. "And I thank you for giving me the home that kept me safe and healthy until I hatched."

"So the entrance," Sophia said, looking around. "Is it under a pumpkin?"

Rory shook his head, similar to the way he would when Liv made jokes. "No, it is the whole backyard."

"What do you mean?" Sophia asked.

"We will have to uproot the entire backyard to open the portal to the temple," Rory explained.

Sophia looked around at the beautiful backyard full of vegetable gardens and fruit trees. There was a large assortment of herbs along the back fence, and a stream Rory had installed when Lunis lived there in his egg. "I can't allow you to destroy your entire yard."

He gave her an impatient look. "So, what you're going to Mother Nature for isn't of any urgency or importance?"

She blushed. "I don't know why I'm going, actually, but I do know that trouble is brewing for the Dragon Elite. So much so that the House of Fourteen is aware of it."

"So it's crucial that you get to Mother Nature," Maddy said, snapping her fingers. The pumpkins and trees disappeared.

"Yes, but you don't have to ruin your yard!" Sophia exclaimed, panicking.

Rory turned to her, having been doing the same thing—clearing the yard. "Sophia, I can re-landscape my yard. Maddy and I can rebuild. But if there is something that requires Mother Nature's attention when she hasn't been unearthed in centuries, you have to go after her. And that means I need to destroy this yard to open the portal. If I don't, it won't matter if I keep my yard, because there won't be one. There won't be an Earth to call home."

Sophia'd had no idea it would come to this. Honestly, she didn't even know that things were this serious. She'd been charged with finding Mother Nature, but now, put into this context, she realized the severity of the situation. Mother Nature hadn't been "unearthed" in centuries. If she was being brought to the surface, it must be for something supremely important, and it was Sophia's and Lunis' job to get her.

She looked at her dragon, pure conviction bouncing between their eyes. "Okay," she said, looking back at Rory. "Let's open the portal."

CHAPTER ONE HUNDRED

Sophia didn't know how Rory had known she needed to get to Mother Nature's temple, and apparently, they didn't have time to discuss it. He mentioned as he and Maddie cleared the backyard that they had a small window to uncover the portal, which apparently lay just a few feet below the ground.

However, Sophia and Lunis had to enter quickly, and Rory would need to cover it back up within seconds, or it would suck in everything around it. That meant that she and Lunis would be trapped underground, and apparently, that wasn't the least of their problems. If they survived, getting out of the temple was a secondary concern.

She and Lunis watched quietly as the giants cleared the area. When there were no plants left, Rory turned to Maddie.

"Are you ready?" he asked.

She nodded, nervousness in her eyes.

Rory glanced at Sophia, sharing the look in the other giant's eyes. "Once we start, it's going to be fast."

"Okay," Sophia said, not knowing what to expect. The portals she'd used were all vertical, but she expected this would be more like an underground tunnel.

Rory and Maddie both stuck out their hands, palms up, as they started to chant words Sophia had never heard.

The ground began to crack under their feet, and Sophia noted that the giants didn't back up. She stayed at the edge of the yard, deciding this position was safe enough.

The dirt on the top layer of the yard blew off completely, flying in all directions. Sophia shielded her face but was impressed to see that the giants stayed stoically staring into the middle of the yard, chanting and focused even as they were blasted.

A glow shone through in the center of the yard, growing wider by the second.

"Get ready," Lunis advised from beside her.

She nodded, still covering her face from the flying debris as her hair whipped around her face.

A strange sound like a bell began to radiate from the center of the white glow, which was now five feet wide in diameter. It was such an enchanting noise that Sophia immediately found herself humming along like it was a song she'd always known.

"Now!" Rory yelled, pulling her from her distraction.

Sophia hurried forward and looked into the portal. All she could see was white. And she didn't know if she simply jumped into it or what?

"Climb down," Lunis ordered, sensing her confusion. "I'll go first."

Nimbly, the dragon gripped the edge of the portal and began to lower himself. He used his claws to anchor himself to the side as the wind whipped around them, growing stronger every second.

Sophia knew the powerful vortex that Rory had mentioned was forming. She had to get through fast so they could close the portal once more. Taking a position to the side of Lunis, she lowered herself, holding onto roots and stabbing her fingers into the ground for holds. Her boots found small holes in the dirt that allowed her to climb down into the brightness, which intensified as she descended.

"We have to close it!" Rory yelled, his voice barely audible over the howling wind.

Dirt began to fill in just above Sophia. It was piling in faster than she was climbing down. Suddenly she feared she'd drown in the soil.

We have to drop, Lunis said in her mind.

She knew he was right, but dropping into the unknown was easier said than done. But her hands and forearms were now covered in soil as it filled in from the top, closing the portal. Sophia had to yank her buried hands out as she continued to climb down. Another few seconds and it would be to her shoulders.

"Okay!" Sophia yelled. "On the count of three. One..."

She took a giant step downward, getting ahead of the dirt and hoping that maybe they wouldn't have to drop blindly.

"Two!" she yelled, taking another large step but not meeting the bottom, the swirling brightness the only thing she could see.

"Three!" she screamed, but before she could drop, one of Lunis' wings wrapped around her body, enfolding her as he pushed off the dirt wall, and they began to descend rapidly. It was like a rollercoaster ride, making Sophia's heart jump up into her throat. Lunis held her close as the bells got louder.

She was wondering how far they would plummet to an unknown bottom when they halted, floating in midair. Before she could stick out her head to see, they were flipped upside-down and accelerated. It all happened so fast that by the time Sophia knew what had happened, they were dropped onto a soft patch of ground, the world around them suddenly not as bright anymore.

"Are you okay?" Sophia said, feeling Lunis' heart pound close to her. It was the most comforting sound she had ever heard.

"Yes," he whispered, releasing her from his wing.

She stood, taking in the strange world they'd been dropped into. Strangely, she felt like they'd jumped into the *Alice in Wonderland* book in the Great Library and wound up in a brand new world full of extraordinary things.

"We dropped down into the Earth, right?" Sophia asked, looking around, mesmerized by the colors in this world, which also offered sounds.

"Yes," Lunis said again, his wing still protectively hovering over Sophia like he might enfold her again if any danger presented itself.

"Then why does it feel like we're on another planet?" Sophia mused, looking at the purplish night sky, which strangely had a sun in the middle, shining but not too brightly. Around it were eight moons. The first, she couldn't actually see, but it had to be the new moon. It followed by the waxing crescent, first quarter moon, waxing gibbous, full, waning gibbous, last quarter, and finally the waning crescent to complete the circle around the sun.

"We are inside the Earth," Lunis said, also mesmerized by the moons and sun and the many stars twinkling around them in the sky, which was both reminiscent of day and night.

"Yeah, it's like we fell into the Earth and were rotated upside-down," Sophia said, bringing her chin down to stare at the landscape surrounding them, which was more bizarre than the sky.

"It appears that what was below us is now above," Lunis stated wisely. "And what was underneath us before is in front of us."

They had been placed inside a magical forest. Mushrooms that were as big as houses towered in front of them, obstructing the horizon. Behind the mushrooms were trees, and behind those were mountains. She could simultaneously smell the salt of the ocean and feel the dryness of the desert. She was cold as if placed in the Arctic and sweating like she'd been in the humid rainforest. Somehow she felt like she was everywhere and nowhere at the same time.

"Where do we go first?" Sophia asked.

Lunis' eyes narrowed and he indicated the area in front of them, which was filled with large mushrooms. "The path is through there."

At first, Sophia didn't know what he meant, but when she focused on the ground, she saw a clear trail that snaked around the mushrooms, little white flowers littering its edges.

Sophia turned to take in the landscape behind her, which was full of erupting volcanos. She regarded them from a great distance, but that was close enough. "Yes, I also vote we go through the enchanted forest and not to the molten lava pits over there."

The pair started off, careful to stay on the path. When they passed under the giant mushrooms, they were cast into blackness momentarily since the sun and moons were blocked out completely.

A few times, Sophia noticed strange bugs and creatures that

scurried away as they progressed. Ahead were trees out of fairytales. They had faces and their branches swayed despite the lack of wind, but when Sophia studied them directly, they appeared to be ordinary trees.

When they'd progressed a mile or so, a bird Sophia had only seen in history books crossed their path. The animal was completely oblivious to them as they halted, not wanting to run into it.

"That's a dodo," Sophia said with a gasp.

"Which is extinct," Lunis added.

"How amazing," Sophia exclaimed, pulling out her phone. She wanted to take a picture of the animal. Liv and Clark wouldn't believe what she was seeing. However, she quickly realized her phone didn't work in Mother Nature's temple.

Sighing, she put her phone away as the bird waddled off the path to a copse of trees in the distance.

"If there are extinct animals here, you might want to consider the possibility of running into some that are a bit more dangerous than the dodo," Lunis stated.

Sophia stiffened. "Like dinosaurs?"

"Yes," he answered, angling his head toward a ridge in the distance, just outside the forest. "Or those."

Standing on the edge of a cliff and looking out majestically was a saber-toothed tiger.

"Do you think we're in any danger of being attacked by a woolly mammoth?" Sophia asked.

"I don't think so," Lunis answered tentatively. "But even if we are, I sense that we shouldn't attack anything here, even in self-defense. They are under Mother Nature's protection, and I fear it will bring a wrath we wouldn't survive."

Sophia gulped and nodded along as they came to a desert. It was strange to have so many different landscapes all connected. Her mouth was suddenly parched, and she longed for water.

"How do you think we'll find Mother Nature?" Sophia asked,

looking at the vast desert which seemed to go on for miles. Far in the distance, she spied the peaks of tree-covered mountains and longed for the lushness they provided.

As if anticipating her question, something invisible began to write in the sand they were suddenly trudging through.

Lunis and Sophia halted, reading the words as they materialized one by one.

"To find me, you must fight my greatest enemy and make it to the refuge of the forest in the mountains," Sophia read aloud, her mind suddenly reeling with possibilities.

"Who or what is Mother Nature's greatest enemy?" she asked Lunis, her eyes still on the sand.

"You know," he answered. "You just don't want to."

"Huh?" she asked as the sand in front of them cleared like a chalkboard being erased. Again, letters were drawn in the sand. Before the word was completed, Sophia knew what it was and that Lunis had been right.

The sand read Mankind.

"We have to fight mankind?" Sophia asked, looking around at the flat desert. "Doesn't that seem a little counterintuitive, considering they are my race?"

"It's a test," Lunis stated. "Remember that. Remember that they are our enemies, and we must slaughter them without mercy while also making progress to the other side."

Sophia looked at the sky. "We could just fly."

A bolt of lightning streaked through the air, illuminating the day/night sky.

"I'd prefer not to become roasted dragon today," Lunis stated.

She nodded. "Good call. Let's cross this desert, then. It appears pretty bare."

And on cue, like zombies rising from the grave, hands began to claw up through the sand. Soon heads popped up, and bodies pushed out from under the ground. Within a minute, a hundred men stood between Sophia and Lunis, staring at them with sand-encrusted faces.

Sophia yanked her sword from its sheath and put her back to

Lunis as he surveyed the desert full of enemies. "Shall we chop down some baddies?"

"After you, my dear," he said, bowing to her slightly.

Sophia charged forward, the fleet of soldiers ran toward them, and the battle commenced.

Although the men were unarmed, they proved to be a challenge, mostly due to their numbers.

Four at a time charged Sophia. She shot magic at the ones behind them to keep them at bay. Whirling with Inexorabilis, she sliced through men's chests, sending them back to the sand. Simultaneously, she shoved another with her foot and brought her elbows down on the back of a man who was diving for her waist, hoping to bring her down. He collapsed to the ground, and she stuck her sword into his back.

Those were her first kills, and they cut her from the inside even though these weren't real men. They were Mother Nature's constructs, brought to life for the purpose of this challenge. But it proved to Sophia that no kill went without consequences. Fighting was a responsibility one shouldn't take on lightly. The words of her sister came to her suddenly as she slew man after man.

"We fight to protect, but in doing so, we lose part of ourselves."

Daring to look over her shoulder, Sophia noticed Lunis scorching dozens of men as they ran at him. These fake men obviously weren't the brightest, running straight into the flames and dying.

Lunis picked up a man who escaped the fire in his mouth and slung him back and forth. The man's legs hung out of the dragon's mouth, kicking wildly before he chomped him in two. When he hit the ground, he continued to kick like a chicken with its head cut off.

Sophia progressed, stabbing man after man. Several grabbed her. Punched her in the face. Pulled her down. She yanked herself away, wielding Inexorabilis and defending herself as she backed toward the forest. It wasn't far now—only a hundred yards. And they'd slaughtered nearly half the soldiers meant to bring them down.

Sophia sent a blast of wind at a group that was closing in on her as she ran for the forest. They didn't have to kill all the men. Mother Nature had simply said they had to make it to the forest. They were nearly there.

"Come on!" she yelled to Lunis, realizing she was on the edge of the forest now. He was gobbling up man after man, seemingly enjoying the buffet. The dragon would scorch the ones farther away and then scoop a man up who was close, hardly chewing before swallowing.

She reasoned that he was probably hungry after their long journey, but still, they shouldn't stay there long. What if more rose from the desert?

"Lunis!" she yelled, waving him toward her. "Let's go!"

He ran, trampling a dozen more men. The dragon was almost to her when he halted, leaned over, and grabbed a man trying to battle him in his teeth. The man went into his mouth headfirst, his legs kicking awkwardly.

"Seriously?" Sophia asked, her hands on her hips now. "Spit that out! We have to go!"

"Spitth whath outh?" Lunis mumbled, chewing on the man as his legs continued to jerk.

Sophia shook her head. "You can eat later. We need to get into the forest. Our job is done here."

Lunis swallowed the rest of the man, looking over his shoulder at the scorched desert full of slaughtered men. The few stragglers didn't seem like they were going to charge the rider and dragon, who had already proved they didn't show mercy.

"Okay," Lunis said, licking his mouth as he followed Sophia into the forest that bordered the mountains.

They didn't know what they would find ahead, but it was certain it would be a challenge unlike any they'd ever faced.

CHAPTER ONE HUNDRED THREE

The hike quickly turned steep. Sophia found herself hunched over, having to dig her fingers into the ground as she climbed. Every step was harder than the last.

"We should fly," Lunis said, finding it difficult to negotiate through the close-knit trees.

"But the lightning?" Sophia argued.

"It's stopped," he stated. "I think it was mostly to keep us from avoiding those men in the desert."

"Okay," Sophia said, finding it hard to breathe. She dragged herself over to Lunis and pulled herself onto his back with his help. "Can you get to that clearing up ahead to take off?"

"Actually, I have a faster idea," he said, and kicked his front leg into a set of trees in front of him, knocking them down and creating a runway. Sophia grabbed on before falling back from the sudden movement.

"Ummm, …do you think that Mother Nature will be upset that you harmed her trees?" she asked. "You told me not to hurt the animals."

"I think if you spell them back to life as I fly off, we will be fine," he stated, starting to take off.

Sophia held the reins as she turned and spelled the trees to rise, repairing the parts of them that were broken. It wasn't an easy spell, but when it was done, the trees were back to how they had been. Hopefully, that meant Mother Nature wouldn't be taking her wrath out on them. Well, more so than sending a hundred soldiers after them, she thought as they flew up and over the mountains.

In the distance, she could make out the elegant stillness of the plains. Unlike the desert, which was also flat and went on without a hiccup, the plains were covered with grass that rippled in the wind like the waves on the ocean. Buffalos roamed, and Sophia was certain there were all sorts of creatures scurrying under the long grass, poking their heads up to watch the rider and dragon land.

She slid off of Lunis and looked around. "What do you think we're supposed to do now?"

"Probably head for the television and couch over there," he said, indicating a modern sofa and entertainment center.

"Was that there a minute ago?" Sophia asked.

He shook his head. "It just materialized."

She strode toward the furniture, indeed noticing many creatures scurrying around her feet, their curious brown eyes connecting with hers.

Since she wasn't sure what to do, she took a seat on the sofa, settling back. She found the sensation of relaxing more than enjoyable. "Oh, this is nice." Sophia closed her eyes and laid her head back, looking at the sky with its eight moons and one sun and a million twinkling stars.

"Well, I don't mean to interrupt, but…" Lunis said, his head hanging over the sofa.

She peeled an eye open and looked up, noticing that the television had lit up. Words began to scroll across the screen, which she read aloud.

"To find me, you must also play with that which seeks to replace me."

Sophia looked up at Lunis. "What? What wants to replace Mother Nature?"

"Well, I don't know," Lunis mused. "What do you want when the sunlight isn't sufficient to light your way, or the ocean breezes good enough to cool you? What do you seek for entertainment when nature bores you? What do you cook your food on when fire is too slow?"

"No," Sophia said, leaning forward. "We have to…"

She looked down, and to her astonishment, she held a video game controller. "We have to play a video game?"

That seemed too easy, and like it would be too much fun.

It didn't make any sense.

"It appears so," Lunis said, indicating the screen as it refreshed to show a video game starting.

"Okay," she said. "I'm pretty good at these. So leave this round to me."

"No problem," Lunis answered. "I'll just be right here."

She smiled up at him, but he was gone.

Sophia bolted to her feet, looking around but not seeing her dragon anywhere.

"Lunis!" she yelled, her heart thundering in her chest.

She expected to hear him in her head and to feel him, but he was truly gone. It didn't make any sense. Breathless, she looked around, not seeing anything but the ocean in the distance, which she hadn't noticed until then. It blended into the plains, but now she recognized the waves folding in on the shore. Still there was no Lunis.

Thoroughly confused, Sophia focused on the television in front of her, and there she found Lunis.

Standing squarely inside the television in a video game was her beloved dragon.

CHAPTER ONE HUNDRED FOUR

"Lunis!" Sophia screamed.

He turned his head, looking back at her from the screen.

"Get out of there!" she commanded.

I can't, he said in her head.

"How did you get in there?" she asked.

I'm not sure, he replied, *but I think you have to play me.*

"What?" she asked. "Like you're a video game?"

I am a video game at this point, he stated.

"But what's the objective?" she asked. "Can you go look around?"

He shook his head. *I only have control over my neck and head. I can't move.*

She glanced down at the controller she'd dropped. "Do you mean I have to control you? With a video-game controller?"

I think so, he replied.

Letting out a long breath, Sophia sat back down on the sofa, not finding it as comfortable as before. Carefully, she picked up the controller, not sure what buttons did what yet.

She pushed the joystick up and Lunis sped forward, his tail wagging.

"Oh, you're prancing," she said with a laugh of relief.

I don't prance, he said in her mind.

"Well, in this game, you do." She giggled.

Sophia tried another button, and Lunis opened his mouth and shot fire. "Okay, that's how you do that. And I'm guessing this makes you…"

Fly, he answered, launching into the air and flapping his wings. *I'm much more graceful when I fly.*

"Yeah, so you say," she said, still trying to get the hang of controlling him. "I still don't understand what the point is."

He turned his neck back and forth. "Do you hear that?"

"Hear what?" Sophia asked.

An arrow struck inches from her knee, landing in the sofa. Sophia's eyes widened.

She looked behind her, but there was nothing there.

"I don't get it," she said.

Get what? He asked.

"Who shot that arrow?" she questioned.

Arrow? he asked, then his eyes went wide. *I believe they did.*

"'They?'" Sophia said, not seeing anything different on the screen or behind her as three more arrows landed around her.

Change the point of view on the controller.

Sophia experimented, finally figuring out how to look out of Lunis' eyes rather than at him. That was when she saw them.

At the edge of the plains, with their bows and arrows ready and looking like they were about to charge, were a hundred Native Americans mounted on horses, menace in their eyes.

S ophia turned around again, not finding anyone at her back.

"What am I supposed to do, Lunis?" she asked.

I believe you're supposed to fight the tribe who's about to ambush me, Lunis said.

"Or w-w-what?" Sophia questioned. "Are they going to kill you?"

Multiple arrows landed around Sophia. She shrieked, leaping back.

No, Lunis answered, not having moved. *I think they will kill* you.

"Me?" she asked, still not seeing anything on the plains

Their attacks seem to land in your plane, he explained. *But you can only view them in mine.*

"So, I have to battle them as you?" she asked, looking at the screen. The horses were starting to get antsy.

I think so, he answered. *Think of it like the scrying we just practiced. You can see through my eyes if you look on the screen. Sit on the sofa and use the controller to move me. I can't do anything you don't initiate.*

Sophia let out a breath. "This is the weirdest thing I've ever done, but okay." She took a seat. "I'm not alone, right? You'll advise me?"

Yes. Start with putting me in the air, he nearly yelled in her head as the tribe thundered in his direction.

She directed Lunis into the air, making him circle in front of the warriors on horses. And then she saw it!

They were about to trample her as she sat on the couch. "Oh, hell!"

She slammed her finger on a button, sending fire from Lunis' mouth and making him blast the front line just before they hit Sophia.

Send me down there to cut them off, Lunis demanded.

"Okay," Sophia said, directing Lunis down. She nearly made him careen into the grass, but she pulled him up at the last moment. He swung his head to the side, and she made fire soar out of his mouth. The tribe wasn't deterred and shot a fusillade of arrows that landed inches from Sophia. She shot up from the couch and stood next to it.

"How do we get you out of the television?" she asked in desperation.

We have to win the level, he suggested.

She sighed. "For a dragon, you have way too much knowledge about technology."

Tell me about it, he said. *We won't survive using this approach for long.*

"So, what?" Sophia said, having Lunis charge a group of horses that was getting too close to Sophia's location.

We need a different strategy, he offered.

"Like?" she asked.

Like we need to use our advantages, he stated.

Sophia stared at the television screen. The mounted warriors reconvened, rounding into a circle. "We have you, and that's it."

No, we have fire, wind, and stuff that can catch fire, he corrected.

"I get the fire part," she said, narrowing her eyes at the screen.

"But what else are you talking about?"

Look, we just have to make them retreat, he offered. *Killing them all will put you in mortal danger. Instead, let's make them retreat. Set fire to the brush and use wind to make it spread.*

"Genius," Sophia cheered, turning her full attention to the screen. She sat down on the couch, hunching to present less of a target.

Expertly, she sent Lunis over the long grass that hadn't been trampled and therefore caught fire easily. It caught immediately, sending up flames. Then Sophia steered Lunis around to the other side, where she was located. She brought her dragon, using the game controller, in front of the small line of fire.

They had the tribe's attention now. They looked around, bows and arrows at the ready, about to shoot. Before they did, Lunis, with Sophia controlling him, angled his body into the air and flapped his wings. Not fast, but to fan the flames.

And it worked, sending the line of fire surging toward the horses and Native Americans, the dry grass catching and spreading fast.

The horses whinnied. Many arrows were shot.

Many yells of protests were made. Lunis halted in midair and dropped to the ground with a thud. It didn't matter since the enemy was retreating as the fire followed them, the one beast they couldn't beat.

Lunis, finding himself once more in reality, swished his tail, making sure he was in the right plane. Then he proudly turned to Sophia, triumph on his face.

"We did it," he stated, heading toward the sofa. "Great job."

It wasn't until he rounded the sofa that he found his rider sprawled on the grass, blood seeping from her leg.

Sophia had been shot.

CHAPTER ONE HUNDRED SIX

With pain she'd never felt before, Sophia pushed herself back up. Sucking in small breaths, she braced herself to pull the arrow from her leg.

"Are you okay?" Lunis asked, worry in his eyes.

"Yeah," she said despite not feeling okay right then. "We won, didn't we?"

"We leveled up, but I'm thinking that means we have more to face," he answered.

She wailed long and loud as she yanked. The arrow came out, pulling flesh with it, but the leg felt better after she was done. Still, she threw herself back on the grass, thinking she might vomit.

With the bloody arrow still in her hands, she tried to pull in a breath, but each made her chest convulse with unease.

"I'll carry you," Lunis offered. "But you have to wrap that."

Sophia nodded and pushed herself off the ground. She ripped fabric from her traveling cloak, and with great effort, wrapped it around her wound, which was already feeling better. "That's strange," she said, grateful but still curious.

"It's the chi of the dragon," he stated. "It heals you, but it wasn't going to work until you made the brave move to get the arrow out."

She shook her head as she tied a knot. "That was one of the grossest things I've ever had to do. I nearly passed out."

"Me too," he agreed.

Sophia used the sofa to help her up. When she tested her balance, she was surprised to find it fairly steady.

The pair set their sights on the ocean.

"I think we have to cross it," Sophia stated.

Lunis knelt beside her, offering a wing. "I think I have to. With you in tow, of course."

Sophia smiled affectionately. "Of course. And thank you," she said, mounting her dragon.

The ocean soon ended at another shore, which quickly turned into mountains once more. The wind was suddenly full of chill, and the icy turbulence made it hard for Lunis to negotiate.

"I think I'll have to land," he said after being blown off-course three times.

"There," Sophia said, pointing to a flat patch of snow in front of the mountains, which were thickly covered.

He landed, kicking up snow. He enjoyed the sensation on his feet. It was a first in this lifetime.

Sophia slid off, enjoying the opportunity to walk and the fact that her leg was well enough to do so.

It was a winter wonderland all around them. The snow-covered mountains stretched to the sky, and at their backs, the vast ocean reflected the moons and the sun. Sophia had never seen anything so beautiful.

Turning back to Lunis, Sophia smiled. "Well, are you ready for the next challenge?"

"Yes," he answered.

"What do you think?" she asked. "Will we have to face a hundred wolves or a hundred Santa's elves?"

He shook his head. "I'm afraid it will be much more daunting than that."

"What?" she asked, confused.

"You seemed to be enjoying the beauty around you," he stated. "I didn't want to interrupt that, but the next challenge has already been stated." He indicated a patch of snow in the distance, illuminated by the moon and sunlight.

It read:

To find me, you must face mankind's greatest adversary.

Sophia read it several times. "Who is that?"

Lunis' head lowered, nearly resting on her shoulder. "Dear one, I know the answer, and I'm sorry you don't. It's common knowledge among dragons."

She glanced at him. "I don't understand. Who is mankind's biggest enemy?"

Lunis looked at something behind her. "If it makes you feel any better, the answer is the same for dragons."

Sophia's mouth fell open, and she turned to find two black figures. One was a shadow of Sophia. The other, a shadow of Lunis.

"What?" she hissed.

"Our greatest enemies are ourselves," Lunis replied. "Dragons kill more dragons than anyone else and the same for mankind. Humans are what will make the human race extinct, and nothing else. We are a danger to ourselves."

"So we have to battle our shadow selves?" Sophia asked.

"No," Lunis said, melancholy in his voice. "It's worse than that. We have to *kill* our shadow selves, which I fear will feel like cutting out a piece of our own hearts."

CHAPTER ONE HUNDRED SEVEN

Sophia stepped forward, grateful her leg was feeling better. "What's the tip here?" she whispered to Lunis, who stood beside her.

"I'm sorry, but there isn't one," he explained. "That Dark Sophia knows everything you do. She's as strong and brilliant as you, and so is that dragon."

She watched as the dark figures prepared to face them, Dark Sophia pulling out a sword identical to Inexorabilis and Dark Lunis swishing his tail and extending his wings.

"Then how do we win?" Sophia asked, finding it hard to breathe due to the cold.

Lunis let out a long breath, smoke billowing from his nostrils. "We figure out how to be better than ourselves."

Never before had Sophia been so daunted by a task. She was expected to level up right then and there or die by her own blade, wielded by her own hands. It was a cruel joke.

"Okay," she said, turning her full attention to her dragon and running her hand over the side of his face. "I know we're going to get through this because we have many more battles to face. And, well, we can't stop here."

"We can, and few have made it this far," he said, bursting her bubble.

Sophia shook her head. "No. We aren't dying here. You're going to face that awful version of yourself, and I'm going to kill that Sophia. Whatever they do to us, we will heal. Together. But the bigger point is, you have to return to me. Do you understand, Lunis?"

The dragon didn't answer in words, but a language as old as souls passed between them when he laid his head close to hers, pressing into her with a gentle warmth.

Sophia swallowed. Tried to smile. Instead, she simply pressed a kiss to the side of his head before taking a step back and turning to face her greatest nemesis—herself.

"Are you ready, Lunis?" she asked, her sword in her hand.

"I am," he said nobly, his chin held high.

"I'll see you when you're done," she said, a promise in her voice as she sped toward the enemy.

CHAPTER ONE HUNDRED EIGHT

The twin figure of Sophia wasn't what she expected. It had her shape, and when she threw her sword up, Dark Sophia met it in exactly the same way she would have reacted. However, the figure was all black. There were no eyes or features, just darkness, like it was truly a shadow.

Sophia pushed back the dark one's sword, staggering in the snow. She was finding it hard to maintain her balance in the thick stuff.

She took a moment to glance up at Lunis, who had launched into the air, flying after his dark self. They sped toward each other, meeting with claws and teeth and rolling in the air like a ball.

Her breath caught in her throat from worry for her dragon, but that was interrupted by a familiar scream as Dark Sophia charged her. That was a common approach she used, so Sophia easily rolled to the side, avoiding the brunt of the attack.

The two sparred for what seemed like hours, neither gaining the advantage. It was hard to get the upper hand on yourself. The shadow self always seemed to know what was coming. Thankfully for Sophia, she did too, defending herself in time.

She was certain that they'd all die from exhaustion before they actually killed the other. And then no one would win.

When she was granted a moment, Sophia caught sight of Lunis fighting in mid-air with the black version of himself. She'd been sad to see Dark Lunis get a few good hits on hers, and she had to admit Dark Sophia had gotten her a few times. But they were both still standing, although the snow around them was marked with both their blood.

Breathless, Sophia stalked in an arc, looking at herself as she dragged her sword beside her, finding the weight of it taxing by that point. If she was honest, killing herself felt wrong. Maybe she wasn't really pushing herself to win, but that wasn't the crux of the problem.

Something that Wilder had said when testing her before she left came back to her.

"We all lack advantages, based on our weaknesses," he stated. "You might outsmart us old riders because you rely on strategy over strength, but what if you don't have that? What if there is no strategic upper hand, and you have to win based on sheer strength, or something else completely? What will you do then, Sophia?"

She gulped, feeling the icy air drop into her lungs quickly as the shock hit her. What if that was it? Sophia approached everything strategically. What if she fought this Sophia in a way she had never faced anyone? What if she used a totally different weapon—one of deception?

Lunis, do something you'd never do, she said quickly, fearing that time was of the essence.

What? he asked, changing direction in the air.

To defeat ourselves, we have to act in an incongruent way, she explained. *So do something you would never do.*

Of course, he said, sailing away from the pursuing dark figure.

What are you doing? she asked.

I'm retreating, he stated.

Lunis would never do that.

She found herself snickering, which was typical behavior for her. Looking up, she found the Dark Sophia regarding her with concentration. She was trying to figure out how to out-strategize her, and that was fine. That was what Sophia would have done. But it wouldn't work here.

Instead, she decided to do the one thing Sophia would never do.

"You know what?" Sophia said out loud to her dark self. "I give up. I lose. You win. Mother Nature wins. I'll take the punishment, whatever it is, but I can't keep battling myself. It's just not going to work. There's no way I can harm myself."

The shadow nodded, sheathing her sword.

Sophia smiled, offering a hand. "But what an honor. Thank you. That was the best fight of my life."

Dark Sophia seemed confused for a moment, but finally took a step in the blood-flecked snow. She extended a hand as if she was honored as well to have had this meeting. In a rash movement that definitely would scar Sophia's heart, she drew her sword and plunged it through Dark Sophia's heart.

The gurgling breath she pulled in after she fell to the snow cut Sophia on the inside. Still, she didn't let up. Instead, she kept her hand on her dark self as she shoved the sword through until it hit the earth. When Dark Sophia let out her last breath, Sophia felt lighter, but not in a good way. It was like she'd lost a piece of herself. Still, she pulled the sword from the body and looked up to find Lunis removing his mouth from the neck of his enemy, having killed him in the same way.

They'd had to deceive themselves to win, and there would be no remorse. There had been no other way.

CHAPTER ONE HUNDRED NINE

Sophia and Lunis didn't say anything for a long time as they flew over the snowcapped mountains. He wasn't one to flee. She wasn't one to deceive. But that was what they'd had to do in order to defeat themselves. It was trickery and it was wrong, and they both knew it, but it had worked. That was the worst part.

Both worried that they would be defeated by something similar in the future. If they stood by their morals in battle, they would be slain by those who didn't. When others didn't fight fair, they would be in danger.

"There's flat land there," Sophia said, pointing to a river surrounded by lush grass. "Let's take a break."

She could feel Lunis' energy waning. She couldn't blame him. She was hungry and tired, and the glistening river was the best thing she'd seen in years, or so it seemed.

Lunis landed ungracefully, probably due to Sophia's exhaustion. She apologized at once, laying her head on his neck and hugging him. They'd been through so much—slaughtering men, having to use each other in simulations, and fighting themselves.

She needed a moment to relax before the next challenge presented itself.

"I bet you're hungry for something delicious," a woman said in a thick Southern accent.

Sophia pushed herself off Lunis, blinking at the figure standing next to the river. The woman was short, plump, and wearing a green jumpsuit. Her hair was shoulder-length and huge like the women in the South wore theirs, bangs making a large arc over her forehead. The woman's face was caked with makeup, and her eyelashes were impossibly long.

Not quite ready for the next challenge, Sophia slumped back down on her dragon. She felt the same thing within her dragon; he was tired and emotionally spent. "Tell Mother Nature to hold on a minute. We need a time out before she runs us through another challenge."

"Okay, hun," the lady said. "Ring, ring."

Sophia jerked her head up. The woman was holding her hand next to her head like it was a phone.

"Yeah, Mother Nature?" the woman said to her hand-phone. "Your guests are all tuckered out. They don't want any more challenges."

She pretended to listen and then nodded. "Oh," she said with surprise. "Yes, I'll let them know."

The woman pulled her hand away, looking straight at Lunis and Sophia, who was sitting up now. "It appears that Mother Nature doesn't have any more challenges for you. It must be your lucky day."

"Really?" Sophia said, squeezing Lunis in relief. "That's wonderful. Can you tell us where to find her?"

Sophia glanced at the mountains in the distance, wondering which wonderful place would be the site of the great temple. It was more than she could fathom right then. Simply overwhelming. She pictured herself bowing at the feet of a giant goddess, a majestic figure who took her breath away.

"I sure will, darling," the woman said. "If you look straight ahead, you'll find her."

Nearly stumbling, Sophia got off Lunis and looked around. "Straight ahead, like where? I'm sorry, I've lost my bearings. Which way is north or straight or whatever?"

"Straight ahead, like I said," the woman stated, pointing her manicured finger at herself. "I'm Mother Nature, and it is quite the pleasure to make your acquaintance, Sophia and Lunis."

"Y-y-you're Mother Nature?" Sophia asked.

The woman who appeared to be a southern bumpkin smiled. "You were expecting a goddess covered in vines and moss, weren't you?" She laughed. "I gave that up years ago. It's nice for appearances, but this suits me better. There are some things that are great about the modern world, and this is one I've adopted." She rubbed her hands over the sleeves of her jumpsuit. "Have you worn velour? It's dreamy."

Sophia shook her head. "I'm sorry. I'm confused, but it's an honor to meet you, Mother Nature." She dropped into a low bow. Lunis did the same beside her.

"Oh, you two," Mother Nature said, shaking her head of big hair at them. "Get up, already. You're going to get your boots dirty. And don't call me Mother Nature. It makes me sound so unapproachable."

"Well, you *did* just have us slaughter our shadow selves to get here," Sophia admitted.

Mother Nature covered her mouth as she giggled. "A cute little game, wasn't it?"

"Like, if we lost, it was no big deal?" Sophia asked.

"Oh, no," Mother Nature said. "You'd die, most assuredly. But that's the way the challenge goes." She held up a hand, ticking off three fingers. "You have to battle mankind, technology, and yourself to get to me. I can't change the rules." A shrill laugh spilled from her mouth. "Well, of course I can. I'm in charge, but why would I change things? They've kept the unworthy from finding me for ages. But you two passed, and I must say, I'm so happy to see another. It's been…well, a very long time."

"We're the first to find you in how long?" Lunis asked.

"Oh…" Mother Nature thought for a moment. "The years all roll together. I guess it's been several centuries. I've been hiding."

"Well, that's why we're here, Mother Nature," Sophia began.

"Oh, no. Like I said, don't call me that," the old woman urged. "Call me 'Mama Jamba.'"

"'Mama Jamba?'" Sophia asked, disbelief in her voice.

"Oh, yes, and before we get down to business, I suspect you two are exhausted. I made you something to eat. How does that sound?"

Like he was a dog, Lunis' tongue fell out of his mouth. "That would be great."

"Well, ladies first," Mama Jamba said, suddenly holding a tray of steaming cornbread. "I made Sophia a pan of cornbread, and there's a whole pitcher of sweet tea to go with it if you're so inclined."

"I'm inclined," Sophia said, rushing forward and taking the offered tray from the woman. She looked around, ready to sit on the grass, but suddenly there was a dining room table, complete with place settings and a vase of flowers. She took a seat, and magically, a pitcher of tea and a glass appeared. "Thank you. This smells great."

"You're very welcome, my dear," Mama Jamba said, turning her attention to Lunis. "And for you, how about this?"

She whirled her finger, putting a pile of hay in front of Lunis.

He regarded it with disgust. "Hay? Yeah, that's a pass."

She clicked her tongue. "Well, I don't offer meat to my visitors. You understand that we must be strictly vegetarian. What if I put salad dressing on the hay? Some ranch? It's my favorite."

"Hard pass," Lunis said.

Sophia, enjoying the high of having the food, laughed. "Lunis, you ate like three of those men back there. You can't be all that hungry."

"I ate four," he stated. "What do the saber-toothed tigers eat?"

"Well, they don't," Mama Jamba stated. "They are magic, now aren't they?" She drew in a breath, looking fondly around at her world. "Everything you see here is magic. It's the world as it once was, full and complete. This is where I live now since the world outside no longer needs me."

"Mama Jamba," Sophia said, pushing the cornbread away. She was unwilling to eat if Lunis couldn't. "That's why we're here. You've been gone for a while, apparently, and so have the Dragon Elite. Apparently, there is a new evil, and only you know about it or how to defeat it. Is that right?"

Mama Jamba pursed her lips. "It's absolutely right, but most would put their heads in the sand and ignore it. Hasn't that been the way of the Dragon Elite for centuries?"

"Yes, but Hiker is trying," Sophia stated.

Mama Jamba sniffed. "I'm sure, but most around the world don't care about the Earth anymore. They won't even notice if little by little, evil takes over." She laughed, but there was no joy in it. "I think they'd sign over their planet if they were offered a good deal, so what is the point of me helping anymore? My children have sold me out to technology and power, but that's not the worst of it. Greed was what sent me here, and why I stay."

"Mama Jamba," Sophia said, rising from the chair. "You can't abandon us. The Dragon Elite are back. We're your fighters, and we will do as you direct. We will wake up those who have forgotten your importance, but more importantly, we will fight those who damage your home. *Our* home."

The woman pulled a handkerchief from her pocket and tapped it on the end of her nose. "Oh, Sophia Beaufont. You've always been one of my favorites. I should have known you'd be the one to come and find me."

"Does that mean you'll help us?" Sophia asked with hope.

Mama Jamba drew in a breath. "I really don't know about that. You have to excuse an old woman with a broken heart. Kick me once, you know?"

Sophia nodded.

"How about I take you home and meet with Mr. Hiker Wallace?"

Sophia nearly clapped with relief. "Really?"

"Well," Mama Jamba said good-naturedly, "you can't get home from here on your own, and you did come all this way to find me, passing the challenges that have slain too many to count. The least I can do is return you to your beds. And yes, I'll meet with Hiker. It is overdue. I'll tell him a thing a two, but what he does about it? Well, that's out of my hands."

"But Mama Jamba," Sophia began, rushing forward. "You can't abandon us after that. We're back, and we're the adjudicators for this planet. We're going to protect it, and we'll make companies and governments and whoever else take care of this place forevermore. You'll see."

The smile that spread across Mama Jamba's face was the most beautiful thing Sophia had ever seen. "Oh, bless your heart. Darling, I admire your passion, but you haven't been around long enough to realize that in the end, even I'm not strong enough to save this place. It would take a very concerted effort, and I just don't see that happening in your lifetime or mine."

Sophia narrowed her eyes, clenching her fist and gritting her teeth. "Well, no offense, Mama Jamba, but don't discount our inexperience. That's exactly why we will succeed. No one told me I couldn't learn magic at age four or that children didn't magnetize to dragon eggs or that females weren't riders, so guess what? That was exactly what I did. I didn't know any better, and it's been to my advantage ever since."

"But saving this world," Mama Jamba said quietly. "Are you sure that's something you're up for?"

Sophia glanced at Lunis. "What do you think?" she asked him.

He stood, his head held high. "It's not about what we're up for. It's about fulfilling our duty. Mama Jamba, the dragons and their riders have always served you. Give us a chance, and we will turn this world around. Mortals have awoken, and it's time for us to take back our role and oversee the peace of this place we call home."

The Castle was deserted when Sophia entered with Mama Jamba. She suddenly deflated, afraid Hiker was gone and all her efforts would be for nothing. She was worried that at any moment, Mama Jamba would retreat once again, abandoning them.

Sophia looked around in the dark entryway. It was late, but she expected to find Ainsley talking to the display case or Quiet moping around the dining room.

"If Hiker isn't here, will you please—"

"He's here," Mama Jamba said plainly.

"Can you sense him?" Sophia asked.

The old woman snickered. "No, he's standing right there." She pointed to the top of the stairs.

"Mama," Hiker said in a hushed voice, his voice disbelieving as he ran his eyes over the woman before him. He nearly fell down the stairs as he hurried toward them. When he was in front of the woman, he dropped to his knees and rested his forehead at her feet.

"Oh, would you stop?" she fussed, seeming tickled by the whole thing. "You know how to make an old woman blush, don't you? Now get to your feet, Hiker, and let me feast my eyes on you."

He nearly stumbled as he rose. "You're really here. It's been so long, and you look so different."

"Well," she said, drawing out the word. "I didn't see any reason to stick around this hellhole you all call home."

Hiker shook his head. "The one you created. Planet Earth."

"The one you've all allowed to go to poo-poo," she replied.

"It isn't really that bad," he stated.

"Oh, and you'd know?" she questioned. "Tell me, what's the world like outside the Gullington?"

"Well, I hadn't gotten out much before, but I'm trying now," he argued.

She harrumphed. "That's just the thing. Papa and I came up with a deal. We were tired. So tired. I agreed he could retire, and I could too."

"He's back, though," Sophia said and realized that the other two had forgotten that she was there. "Hey!" She waved. "Anyway, Papa Creola is back and managing time once more."

"Good for him," Mama Jamba said with a smile. "He never could relax for too long. Such a workaholic, and his processes need more micromanagement than mine. I just set the seasons on autopilot and everything goes fine. Well, except for those glaciers melting and that ozone problem, and the host of other problems. But it's not like I'm counting."

Sophia stepped up beside Mama Jamba, looking at Hiker meaningfully. "I told her that if—"

"You found her," Hiker said with disbelief.

"Well, yes, but what I was saying was—"

Hiker interrupted again. "I didn't think you'd—"

"He sent you to your death," Mama Jamba cut in.

"That's not what I did," Hiker argued. "I simply didn't think she'd weather the challenges. No one has, in my lifetime. Not since you went into hiding when I was young."

"Oh, that *was* a simpler time, wasn't it?" Mama Jamba said.

"You sent me to my death?" Sophia asked.

"You asked to go," Hiker replied. "I thought you'd figure out you were in over your head and return."

"Well, I did return," Sophia said defiantly.

Mama Jamba cackled. "Oh, this one will have you pulling out your hair in no time."

"She already has," he said.

"I think you owe her a little something," Mama Jamba stated.

Hiker backed up, looking overwhelmed. "I just can't wrap my brain around all this. You're here, Mama. And Sophia, you brought her here."

"Yes, and I'd love a cookie bouquet as a reward, but right now, you have to listen to what Mama Jamba has to say," Sophia said. "There's something out there, and we have to stop it. Then we have to convince her to not leave again."

Mother Nature had pulled a compact from her purse and was checking her makeup when she looked up suddenly. "Are you talking about me? Oh, I'm here for now, but I really don't think coming out of retirement works well for my complexion. The smog in this air clogs my pores."

"Then we will fix it," Sophia stated with passion. "Hiker, listen to her. We have to do whatever—"

"Whatever it takes," Hiker said, finishing her sentence and looking at Mama Jamba with conviction. "We are the adjudicators for this world. You once gave us that holy role. Circumstance sent us away, the same way it did you. But, Mama Jamba, I'm not backing down from this fight. I'm here for good." His eyes cut to Sophia, pride marking them. "And although our numbers are small, I think we will have the best team in history soon. Please tell us what we must do to make things right for this planet and maintain peace."

Mama Jamba considered him for a moment. "Oh, Hiker. I always loved you, but I have to admit, I haven't liked you."

This seemed to be a blow to the Viking, but he blanked his face, not allowing the hurt to overwhelm him.

"You hid," she stated, then sniffed like she might cry. "But I did too. I guess we thought it was over because mortals were seemingly asleep, and in your absence, your greatest enemy rose to power. Now he's taken over, little by little. He runs the biggest corporations, and they pollute and ruin this Earth. He's behind every government, ensuring their legislation keeps the laws from harming his businesses. It's always been one man who put this world's health in jeopardy, but never before has he been so powerful."

"No," Hiker said, shaking his head with disbelief.

"Oh, yes," she stated.

"I killed him," Hiker argued.

"You think you killed him," Mama Jamba replied.

"But if he's back, then…"

"Then the Dragon Elite have much worse problems than trying to take back their role as adjudicators," Mama Jamba stated. "And saving this planet? Well, that's a longshot at best. Its time is ticking down, I'm sorry to say."

Hiker covered his face, looking overwhelmed once more. "He'll come for all of us. He is probably already working on it."

"Who?" Sophia asked, looking back and forth between the two.

"Thad Reinhart," Mama Jamba said simply.

"Who is that?" Sophia questioned, looking at Hiker.

He lowered his hand from his face. "He's the reason there are so few Dragon Elite."

"What?" Sophia asked.

"Thad," Mama Jamba began, "didn't like that the Dragon Elite did my bidding, keeping peace and maintaining justice. He decided the best way to circumvent that was to destroy my adjudicators."

"He murdered most of my friends," Hiker said, looking at a painting on the wall that Sophia had passed a hundred times. It showed dozens of dragonriders.

"I know you thought you killed him," Mama Jamba said. "But you didn't, sweet man, and while you had to sleep, waiting for mortals to see dragons again, he grew powerful. He took over the modern world, and he owns it now. Finding him will be difficult. Ending him might be nearly impossible." She sighed, tears in her eyes. "I love this planet more than anything, but I'm not sure there's a way to save it. It has less than a century left. Maybe more, but not much."

"I know there is a way to save it," Sophia said, pushing her chest out.

Hiker stared at her. At first, she thought he'd cave with defeat again, but something shifted in him. "I agree."

"You do?" Mama Jamba asked.

"Yeah. We've been asking to take back our roles as adjudicators," he began, "but that will stop now. Tomorrow we start intervening in world matters big and small. We stop asking for permission and start saving the world little by little."

"Oh, that sounds all good and well, but Thad will come after you and your riders once he gets wind of this," Mama Jamba cautioned.

Hiker's jaw flexed. "Good. Draw him out. I want to know everything there is to know about this man and the magical tech I suspect he's been using to try to kill us. That killed Adam."

Sophia let out a gasp. "It was him?"

Hiker nodded. "Yes, he must have been the one behind Adam's death. And the one who laid the traps at the Nocturne entrance Evan found."

"But why would he have his facility so close to the Gullington?" Sophia asked.

"Because," Hiker said, shaking his head like it was dawning on him as he spoke, "he was pulling from the energy of this place. Something he used to do. I thought we ruined him. Took him out. But if we didn't, then he's laid low and leeched off our powers."

"And he didn't want us finding Mother Nature," Sophia guessed.

"Because I'd tell you what I've just told you," Mama Jamba said. "I do appreciate your gumption on this, Hiker, but you're at a serious disadvantage. You've lost most of your riders. The world has changed, and I'm sorry to say it, but it's going to shit. What if we all just tuck in here for another century and call it good? I've always liked the Gullington. I'll hang out here with y'all."

"No!" Hiker said adamantly. "We are fighting this even if it kills us all. I'm not letting Thad win. I'm not letting him take this planet. I'm not letting him steal a single fight. We will restore peace little by little, and then we're going after him. When we're done, you, Mother Nature, will be proud to call this place your home once more."

CHAPTER ONE HUNDRED TWELVE

Things always got worse before they got better, Sophia told herself as she climbed the stairs to her room.

Very assertively, Mama Jamba had dismissed her, telling Sophia it was well past her bedtime.

"I'll see you in the morning," Mother Nature had said from the entryway, standing next to Hiker with a promise in her eyes.

Maybe the look on Sophia's face said she didn't believe it, but for whatever reason, Mamba Jamba quickly added, "I'm not going anywhere. Not yet. If Hiker is going to try, then I will too. And if you and Lunis are part of the efforts, well, I daresay our chances have improved."

Sophia nodded, feeling a flawless love for the woman at the base of the stairs. She felt connected to her in every way possible. When she breathed, Sophia could feel Mother Nature in her soul. Now that she'd brought her out of hiding, she never wanted her to leave. It was like spring had bloomed for the first time in her life, and every day was full of promises she'd never known before. Potentials that couldn't have become realities were possible all of a sudden.

However, Sophia didn't allow herself to celebrate, since Mama Jamba's reappearance had brought new problems to light. Before, Sophia had known that taking back their roles as adjudicators would be difficult, but now, with the full reality made clear, that was actually the least of their challenges.

Thad Reinhart. He was the evil in the world they had to face. The one responsible for killing most of the Dragon Elite. The one behind Adam's death. And worst of all, a greedy villain who would rather destroy the Earth for his own gain than allow it to be a home for all it belonged to.

It made Sophia furious. No one owned this planet, and she would die rather than allow someone to abuse it.

Thad Reinhart had apparently gone unchecked for too long. She desperately wanted to believe that he could be stopped. Hiker had a fire lit in his belly again. There was a spark in his eyes that she'd not seen since she met him. Mother Nature was sticking around.

It couldn't be too late to save everything. It might take time, but Sophia had to believe with all her soul that the Dragon Elite could take back this world, preserving it for another millennium and more.

Sophia was lost in thought when she got to her room, nearly running into Ainsley, who was pacing, frantic worry on her face.

"What's wrong?" Sophia asked the housekeeper. She grabbed her hands, which were shaking violently.

"I-I-I need your help," she said in a tense whisper.

"Of course, Ains," Sophia stated, suddenly wide awake. "What can I do?"

She clutched at the loose red strands hanging by her face. "You have to help me fix my hair."

"What?" Sophia asked in total disbelief.

The elf pulled at her loose brown dress. "And my clothes. You have to help me find something else to wear."

Running her hands over her eyes, Sophia tried to determine if she was already sleeping and had forgotten the trek to bed. Maybe the exhaustion had caught up with her and she was actually already in bed, and this was one of those strange dreams, like when she'd dreamt the other day that Lunis wanted a pedicure.

"I don't understand," Sophia said, thinking she might need to pinch herself to see if this was real.

Ainsley grabbed the sides of her head and started to pace. "Mother Nature is here. In my Castle. The one I take care of. And she's going to see me soon. I need you to give me a makeover."

Sophia let out a breath, realizing this was real. The ones with Ainsley always felt like strange dreams. "You're nervous about meeting Mama Jamba?"

"Oh," Ainsley said, her eyes wide. "That's her real name? You know it. You've met her. Did she touch your hand? Can I hold it?"

Sophia laughed. "She's lovely. The best...well, ever. And she's going to absolutely love you. She already does. I'm certain of it. Mama Jamba knows us, even if we don't know her. And she's a riot. Like a Southern debutante with a modern flair."

"I know," Ainsley said, in a whisper. "I heard. That's why you have to help me with my appearance. Give me big hair and a jumpsuit."

"Ains," Sophia said. "You're a shapeshifter. Why don't you do it?"

The elf shook her head. "She'll see through the illusion. You have to fix the real me."

Sophia gently touched Ainsley's arm. "There's nothing to fix. You're perfect just the way you are."

Her friend blinked at her as if she'd just spoken a different language. "A shapeshifter never believes such things."

"Because you're always changing for one reason or another, like there's something wrong with you?" Sophia guessed.

The rawness in Ainsley's eyes was palpable when she nodded.

"Well, I think you're perfect as is," she affirmed. "And no one will love you more than Mama Jamba. She'll appreciate the way you take care of the Castle. I daresay she'll relate since she takes care of Castle Earth."

"But she's back," Ainsley said urgently. "And she'll be here at the Castle. *My* Castle. And what does this mean for the Earth?"

Sophia smiled. "I don't know. I think it's been running on autopilot for a while. But she's back now, and that means the Dragon Elite is too."

Ainsley crossed her arms, rubbing them like she was suddenly cold. "I've heard about Thad Reinhart. S. Beaufont, there isn't a worse person in all history, I promise you that. If he's alive still, I fear for us all. But more than anything, I fear for you."

"Why me?" Sophia asked.

Her mouth twitched. "He won't like what you represent. He loathes the riders. He tried to get rid of them, as you now know. But you? You mark the birth of the new generation. I suspect that when he finds out about you, you'll be the first target."

Sophia nodded. "Okay, well, we'll have to deal with that. I want to talk to you more about this. I want to learn everything you know about this man—"

"He isn't that…a man," Ainsley cut in. "Not anymore anyway, I suspect."

"I understand," Sophia continued. "Whatever you can tell me, I want to know, and I'll need your help finding something here in the Castle." She looked around, feeling a deep appreciation for this place she now called home. It was weird, and oh, so right. "But right now, Ains, I need to sleep. Will you please wake me up in the morning? Otherwise, I fear I'll sleep the whole day away?"

"Of course, S. Beaufont," Ainsley agreed, forcing a smile. "You, of all of us, deserve to sleep for a year if you like."

Sophia shook her head. "No, just a full night, please. We have too many things to do, and they start tomorrow."

Without warning, Ainsley rushed forward and hugged her, a full embrace that Sophia didn't realize until that moment she sorely needed. She hugged the elf back before pulling away.

"If I haven't said it lately," Ainsley told her fondly, "I'm glad you're here. The Castle is, too."

Sophia smiled. "Thank you. I've felt out of place all my life, but not anymore. I belong here. With you. And the others."

Ainsley backed away, tears in her green eyes. "Goodnight, dear one. I'll see you tomorrow."

"Goodnight," Sophia said, opening the door to her room and breathing in the smell of home. It felt good to be back. And more than anything, she couldn't wait to curl up in her bed.

Striding to the windows, she manually pulled the curtains closed, her magic reserves too depleted to do it. Before they were all the way shut, she caught sight of the gnome standing in front of the Castle, looking into the starry sky.

There was something about knowing Quiet was always out there and watching over things in the way he did that comforted her. He, like Ainsley, was integral to the Gullington. There was something more than magical about this place, but this wasn't the right time to ponder such things. There would be opportunities for that tomorrow when she awoke, fresh and ready to tackle the new challenges.

Sophia crawled into bed, her heart full and her mind overwhelmed.

For a moment, she felt wide awake and worried she wouldn't be able to sleep, too consumed by her thoughts regarding the new events. However, a voice echoed in her mind, and she was instantly at peace.

Goodnight, Sophia, Lunis said, a smile in his voice.

Goodnight, Lunis, she replied.

And always and forever, I love you, my rider. My soulmate.

I love you, she said, and with that, she closed her eyes and fell asleep, resting for the adventures that would surely come and change everything.

Thank you so much for reading. This book went on preorder and I sort of freaked. It wasn't just about this crazy deadline to get a huge first volume done in record time. It was also the pressure to deliver a book you all loved. I hope I did. The better the preorders did, the more I freaked. Michael was like, "The preorders are going well." And I'm all like, "Oh, hell, the preorders are doing well!" It's all about tone of voice with those two lines.

I never thought I'd write a dragon series. It's not that I don't love dragons. Who doesn't? Well, that one guy, but we don't mention him around here.

It's just that I've never been one of those readers who devoured dragon books. Of course, I did read the entire Eragon series. Those giant doorstopper books take some time to get through. And that ending… I can say no more. But other than that, I tend to like more science in my reading than fantasy. Think Phillip Pullman. So that's why dragons are a new beast for me in writing. Oh, yes, see what I did there?

I was really worried about writing this series because of my lack of dragon experience. I mean, it wasn't like I could run out to the local dragon conservatory in Malibu and ask to spend a day observing the animals. And reading a bunch of books on the subject, like the infamous Dragonriders of Pern, seemed like a bad idea. I've apparently missed out by not reading those and I will, but doing it right before starting my own dragonrider series seemed like a bad idea.

I wanted to create my own dragon world, not steal or borrow from others. And I hope that's exactly what I did. I have to admit, the world inside the Gullington with the Dragon Elite is unlike any other world I've created. Hopefully my lack of dragon knowledge made this tale unique in that way. I didn't want to do epic dragons with rugged riders who died in a Braveheart kind of way. I wanted to do an urban fantasy take, with unique riders who made jokes and teased their dragons while finishing off a bag of Doritos.

Mmmm Doritos. I would cut a dragon for one of those salty treats right now. Okay, I regress, per usual.

As I write these notes, we are exactly one week away from release day. I have to wait until then to know if my take on dragons was successful or not. Yeah, no pressure. Just please pass the wine…and the Doritos. Real classy, I know.

So far, the JIT team has been very positive about part one. I just sent over part two, so now we wait.

Drinks

But in all seriousness, the most wonderful feedback that I've gotten is how readers who know me, hear my little girl, Lydia when Sophia speaks. They know that I modeled the character after her starting in the Liv series. And they tell me they can hear my fondness for her in the character. Okay, I'm sort of crying a bit.

One reader told me, *You must be a good mom if you care about your daughter the way you care about your characters.* I'm paraphrasing, but oh-mi-gosh that meant the world to me. I don't really have boundaries between the people in my life and the ones in my head. They are the same, in a way. And getting a compliment on being a mother, well that's the best compliment ever. If I do nothing else in this life, I hope to raise a child who loves herself, loves life and hopefully loves me. That's really my greatest hope.

Oh, hell. The tears. I'm not even drinking yet. It's early morning on Halloween. But I am a bit sensitive. Last year, I was at the 20Books conference, enjoying myself immensely when I got the call that my city was burning to the ground. I'm not exaggerating.

I rushed back, got my child and cat and we evacuated for about five days. We returned to a home full of smoke damage, a city that was still smoldering and a loss like I've hardly experienced before. 100,000 acres burned. Homes were lost. We all were a bit traumatized.

My reason for telling you this is that at almost the one-year mark, we are braced for evacuations today. Lydia has been out of school for days and today it was cancelled again. It's hard to tell her she can't go trick-or-treating because the winds could knock us out, but it's also not hard, but she's understanding like that.

My point is, that I'm sensitive. I didn't think I would be, but I guess the experience of last year lives in my bones. I lost my childhood home to fire and it's tough to process. Different from death. It's like losing a part of yourself that you never realized was so important to you. But, as I do with most things, I'm channeling. So the fires that rage around me right now will go into a story about dragons scorching the earth and burning down factories. That brings me to my final point about this series.

Magitech!

I got a review on the Liv Beaufont series that said, *I love that this involves magic and tech. Why don't more authors do that?* I was thrilled. Sci-fi is my passion but I'm not as hardcore about it as the Martelle's of the world. I wish, but I need to have that fantasy angle. So I loved the idea of sneaking magical technology into my books. That way I got that sci-if aspect while also avoiding the whole science part.

"It's magic, people."

"Oh, but how do you explain—"

"MAGIC! It's freaking magic! I don't have to explain how the rocket defied gravity because no one knows how magic works! So there."

I don't think Phillip Pullman has these same internal conversations with himself. If he's reading this, call me, Phil! I need to know about the internal dialogue you have with yourself. Oh, and let's have coffee…everyday…for the rest of our lives.

And just like that, I proposed to someone I don't know…in my author notes. Real classy.

Okay, that about wraps it up for me. But I should say a special thank you to Michael for well, just about everything. I really enjoy collaborating with you. At first when you threw out the idea of dragonriders as adjudicators, I was hesitant. Mostly because I didn't know what that word meant. But slyly, while you weren't looking on the video conference call, I went and looked it up. This doesn't really need to be said, but MA has a great instinct for things that will do well in a story. I've learned to trust it. I've also learned to allow him to push the story to new levels. So far, I say, it's working.

Anyway, thanks Bird Killer! You're the best.

What Sarah Giveth, Sarah Taketh Away!

First, thank you for reading this book! It has been interesting for me to watch Sarah go through all of the emotions (I did not realize she would) putting this book out.

Since last time, she has finished her first hugely successful massive storyline with Liv Beaufont, had the first Liv book translated to German (Thanks Jens and Jeugen!), worked hard to finish these two books (yes, there are two books in this release, not one) and has gone through a large stress filled series of time as the books were beta read.

Will they like the stories, will they not? She asked, biting her nails.

They do, replied the JIT team on Facebook (LMBPN for Ladies group.) Not only liked it, LOVED it.

Off Sarah went to (drink?) celebrate. I was not doubting or worried this whole time. Sarah didn't share her concerns with me, and I have the utmost confidence in her storytelling ability. She OWNS these characters – they talk to her as if they were her daughter, her cat, her best friend…

And now we are down to just 4 days before YOU get the story

and find out if you liked it, as well. Perhaps less than Liv, perhaps more than Liv, perhaps you haven't even read Liv but love the Dragon on the cover and picked it up… Awesome!

We just hope you like this crazy world we have built and want to thank you for joining us in it.

So, in Sarah's notes she said some very sweet words at the end about me… And then she called me bird-killer.

Those nice feelings squashed like a bug, the ichor now running slowly down the curved surfaces in my brain.

Well played Sarah, well played ;-)

I'll never tell you about <redacted> as you might use THAT against me, too.

Ad Aeternitatem,

Michael

ACKNOWLEDGMENTS
SARAH NOFFKE

I feel like I'm on the stage at the Oscars, accepting an award when I write my acknowledgments. I stand there, holding this award, my hands shaking and my words racing around in my mind. I'm not an actress for a reason. I'm a writer and talking to people in "real life" is hard. Not to mention a ton of people all at once.

I picture looking out at the audience and being blinded by spotlights and forgetting every word of the speech I memorized just in case I won. The speech would go like this and it's meant for all of you, not the guild. For the fans. The supporters. The people who are the reason I would ever stand on any stage, ever.

Okay, here we go. I clear my throat and smile, looking up at the camera, holding the little golden man. And then I begin:

This was never supposed to happen. I was never meant to publish a book and then another one. And then another. I was supposed to write in private and live a life that Henry David Thoreau called a life of "quiet desperation." I would always hope to share my books, but never bring myself to do it. And you would never read my words. But then, in a crazed moment of brashness, I did share my books and you all liked them. And because of that,

I've never been the same. And here I am feeling grateful all just because…

That's why I'm here. Because of you. Thank you to my first readers. The ones who picked up those books that I didn't even outline and you still liked them. You messaged me and maybe you thought it was no big deal, but when your ego is new to the publishing world, it's a big deal.

I can't thank you readers enough. I've found that reading your reviews helps me to start a chapter when I'm stuck or lazy.

I really need to thank someone who has made this all possible and that's my father. I was going to quit. I can't tell you how many times I quit. But when I wasn't making it, he was the one who told me to not throw in the towel. "Give yourself a timeline," he suggested. If I didn't get to my goal by then, I'd quit. And apparently there was magic in that advice, because I'm still doing this. Dad, you're the pragmatic one, but when you believed in me enough to tell me to not quit, I knew I had to follow your advice.

And I thank all my friends who are constantly supporting me with thoughts of love and encouragement. Most don't read my books. I'm sort of self-deprecating, although I'm working on it and will be the first to tell my friends, "My books probably aren't for you." However, every now and then a friend surprises me and says, "I was up all night reading your books." It's always a total shock. But my point is, that even if they didn't read, I still have the best friends ever. Diane, you're my rock. And I love you, even though you will probably not read this.

Thank you to everyone at LMBPN. Those people are like family to me, although I'm not sure if they'll let me sleep on their couch. Well, who am I kidding? They totally will. Big thanks to Steve, Lynne, Mihaela, Kelly, Jen and the entire team. The JIT members are the best.

Huge thank you to the LMBPN Ladies group on Facebook. Micky, you're the best. And that group keeps me sane.

And a giant thank you to the betas for this series. Juergen you are my first reader and friend. Thanks for all the help. And thanks to Martin and Crystal for being some of the best people I know. What would I do without you? A huge thanks to the ARC team. Seriously, if it weren't for you all I might pass out before release day, wondering if anyone will like the book.

And with all my books, my final thank you goes to my lovely muse, Lydia. Oh sweet darling, I write these books for you, but ironically, I couldn't write them without you. You are my inspiration. My sounding board. And the reason that I want to succeed. I love you.

Thank you all! I'm sorry if I forgot anyone. Blame Michael. For no other reason than just because.

Sarah Noffke writes YA and NA science fiction, fantasy, paranormal and urban fantasy. In addition to being an author, she is a mother, podcaster and professor. Noffke holds a Masters of Management and teaches college business/writing courses. Most of her students have no idea that she toils away her hours crafting fictional characters. www.sarahnoffke.com

Check out other work by Sarah author here.

Ghost Squadron:

Formation #1:
Kill the bad guys. Save the Galaxy. All in a hard day's work.
After ten years of wandering the outer rim of the galaxy, Eddie Teach is a man without a purpose. He was one of the toughest pilots in the Federation, but now he's just a regular guy, getting into bar fights and making a difference wherever he can. It's not the same as flying a ship and saving colonies, but it'll have to do.

That is, until General Lance Reynolds tracks Eddie down and offers him a job. There are bad people out there, plotting terrible things, killing innocent people, and destroying entire colonies. **Someone has to stop them.**

Eddie, along with the genetically-enhanced combat pilot Julianna Fregin and her trusty E.I. named Pip, must recruit a diverse team of specialists, both human and alien. They'll need to master their new Q-Ship, one of the most powerful strike ships ever constructed. And finally, they'll have to stop a faceless enemy so powerful, it threatens to destroy the entire Federation.

All in a day's work, right?

Experience this exciting military sci-fi saga and the latest addition to the expanded Kurtherian Gambit Universe. If you're a fan of Mass Effect, Firefly, or Star Wars, you'll love this riveting new space opera.

NOTE: If cursing is a problem, then this might not be for you.

Check out the entire series <u>here</u>.

The Precious Galaxy Series:

Corruption #1

A new evil lurks in the darkness.

After an explosion, the crew of a battlecruiser mysteriously disappears.

Bailey and Lewis, complete strangers, find themselves suddenly onboard the damaged ship. Lewis hasn't worked a case in years, not since the final one broke his spirit and his bank account. The last thing Bailey remembers is preparing to take down a fugitive on Onyx Station.

Mysteries are harder to solve when there's no evidence left behind.

Bailey and Lewis don't know how they got onboard *Ricky Bobby* or why. However, they quickly learn that whatever was responsible for the explosion and disappearance of the crew is still on the ship.

Monsters are real and what this one can do changes everything.

The new team bands together to discover what happened and how to fight the monster lurking in the bottom of the battlecruiser.

Will they find the missing crew? Or will the monster end them all?

The Soul Stone Mage Series:

House of Enchanted #1:

The Kingdom of Virgo has lived in peace for thousands of years...until now.

The humans from Terran have always been real assholes to the witches of Virgo. Now a silent war is brewing, and the timing couldn't be worse. Princess Azure will soon be crowned queen of the Kingdom of Virgo.

In the Dark Forest a powerful potion-maker has been murdered.

Charmsgood was the only wizard who could stop a deadly virus plaguing Virgo. He also knew about the devastation the people from Terran had done to the forest.

Azure must protect her people. Mend the Dark Forest. Create alliances with savage beasts. No biggie, right?

But on coronation day everything changes. Princess Azure isn't who she thought she was and that's a big freaking problem.

Welcome to The Revelations of Oriceran. Check out the entire series here.

The Lucidites Series:

Awoken, #1:

Around the world humans are hallucinating after sleepless nights.

In a sterile, underground institute the forecasters keep reporting the same events.

And in the backwoods of Texas, a sixteen-year-old girl is about to be caught up in a fierce, ethereal battle.

Meet Roya Stark. She drowns every night in her dreams, spends her hours reading classic literature to avoid her family's ridicule, and is prone to premonitions—which are becoming more frequent. And now her dreams are filled with strangers offering to reveal what she has always wanted to know: Who is she? That's the question that haunts her, and she's about to find out. But will Roya live to regret learning the truth?

Stunned, #2

Revived, #3

The Reverians Series:

Defects, #1:

In the happy, clean community of Austin Valley, everything appears to be perfect. Seventeen-year-old Em Fuller, however, fears something is askew. Em is one of the new generation of Dream Travelers. For some reason, the gods have not seen fit to gift all of them with their expected special abilities. Em is a Defect —one of the unfortunate Dream Travelers not gifted with a psychic power. Desperate to do whatever it takes to earn her gift, she endures painful daily injections along with commands from her overbearing, loveless father. One of the few bright spots in her life is the return of a friend she had thought dead—but with his return comes the knowledge of a shocking, unforgivable truth. The society Em thought was protecting her has actually been betraying her, but she has no idea how to break away from its authority without hurting everyone she loves.

Rebels, #2

Warriors, #3

Vagabond Circus Series:

Suspended, #1:
When a stranger joins the cast of Vagabond Circus—a circus that is run by Dream Travelers and features real magic—mysterious events start happening. The once orderly grounds of the circus become riddled with hidden threats. And the ringmaster realizes not only are his circus and its magic at risk, but also his very life.

Vagabond Circus caters to the skeptics. Without skeptics, it would close its doors. This is because Vagabond Circus runs for two reasons and only two reasons: first and foremost to provide the lost and lonely Dream Travelers a place to be illustrious. And secondly, to show the nonbelievers that there's still magic in the world. If they believe, then they care, and if they care, then they don't destroy. They stop the small abuse that day-by-day breaks down humanity's spirit. If Vagabond Circus makes one skeptic believe in magic, then they halt the cycle, just a little bit. They allow a little more love into this world. That's Dr. Dave Raydon's mission. And that's why this ringmaster recruits. That's why he directs. That's why he puts on a show that makes people question their beliefs. He wants the world to believe in magic once again.

Paralyzed, #2
Released, #3

Ren Series:

Ren: The Man Behind the Monster, #1:
Born with the power to control minds, hypnotize others, and read thoughts, Ren Lewis, is certain of one thing: God made a mistake. No one should be born with so much power. A monster awoke in him the same year he received his gifts. At ten years old.

A prepubescent boy with the ability to control others might merely abuse his powers, but Ren allowed it to corrupt him. And since he can have and do anything he wants, Ren should be happy. However, his journey teaches him that harboring so much power doesn't bring happiness, it steals it. Once this realization sets in, Ren makes up his mind to do the one thing that can bring his tortured soul some peace. He must kill the monster.

Note This book is NA and has strong language, violence and sexual references.

Ren: God's Little Monster, #2
Ren: The Monster Inside the Monster, #3
Ren: The Monster's Adventure, #3.5
Ren: The Monster's Death

Olento Research Series:

Alpha Wolf, #1:
Twelve men went missing.

Six months later they awake from drug-induced stupors to find themselves locked in a lab.

And on the night of a new moon, eleven of those men, possessed by new—and inhuman—powers, break out of their prison and race through the streets of Los Angeles until they disappear one by one into the night.

Olento Research wants its experiments back. Its CEO, Mika Lenna, will tear every city apart until he has his werewolves imprisoned once again. He didn't undertake a huge risk just to lose his would-be assassins.

However, the Lucidite Institute's main mission is to save the world from injustices. Now, it's Adelaide's job to find these mutated men and protect them and society, and fast. Already around the nation, wolflike men are being spotted. Attacks on innocent women are happening. And then, Adelaide realizes what her next step must be: She has to find the alpha wolf first. Only once she's located him can she stop whoever is behind this experiment to create wild beasts out of human beings.

<u>Lone Wolf, #2</u>
<u>Rabid Wolf, #3</u>
<u>Bad Wolf, #4</u>

BOOKS BY MICHAEL ANDERLE

For a complete list of books by Michael Anderle, please visit:

www.lmbpn.com/ma-books/

All LMBPN Audiobooks are Available at Audible.com and iTunes

To see all LMBPN audiobooks, including those written by Michael Anderle please visit:

www.lmbpn.com/audible